DARKEST BEFORE
DAWN

I0563636

AVA VIXION

The author acknowledges the trademarked status and trademark owners of various products referenced in this work of fiction, which have been used without permission. The publication/use of these trademarks is not authorized, associated with, or sponsored by the trademark owners.

Copyright © 2015 by Ava Vixion

Published by

LFP

Lucid Fyre Publishing

First Paperback Edition: August 2015
Cover design by Stephanie White of Steph's Cover Design
Interior design and formatting by JT Formatting

All rights reserved.
Without limiting the rights under copyright reserved above, no part of this publication may be reproduced, stored in or introduced into a retrieval system, or transmitted, in any form, or by any means (electronic, mechanical, photocopying, recording, or otherwise) without the prior written permission of the above copyright owner of this book.

Library of Congress Cataloging-in-Publication Data

Vixion, Ava
Darkest Before Dawn (a novel) — 1st edition
ISBN-13: 978-0692490488 | ISBN-10: 0692490485

DEDICATION

For my children, you are the source of my strength, love and inspiration. Without you, I am nothing more than a stubborn fool.

To my dearest Angels...Joseph Chase thank you for moments of encouragement and love, Charlotte Parker for always believing in me, Anne Nelson, Brianne Chouinard, Jennifer Pizzi, Dwayne Dee, Tony "Squishy" Harper, Katie Frisby, Laura Poole, Sarah Babineau (Tapeworms burn down HELL!), Jonathan "SD" Diozzi, and to my personal guardian angel Ken Towle, I can never thank you enough. Thank you all with every beat of my heart for keeping my spirits going, causing my outbursts of laughter, listening to my ramblings when life has taken another toll and just truly being such an amazing, wonderful and supportive part of my life and my creations. I am a very lucky and blessed woman indeed!

To my dear passed Leo, I love you with each passing day Fathead...Always in my heart. Tyson, my freaky furbaby, thank you for all the love you shared with us. Luna ....babygirl furface Luna, please stop sleeping on my laptop kitty.

LEAGUE of GUARDIANS

GLOSSARY
OF TERMS

Darkling: A pre-transcended dark angel. A human/angel hybrid thought to be extinct since the Great War.

Dark angel: A fully transcended Darkling, who fights for the side of Heaven.

Daemon: A Darkling who's transcended into evil. Serving Hell as an earthbound hunter, seeking other Darklings to serve in Hell or destroy, causing worldwide chaos.

Hellistic demons: Demon minions; a product of Baphomet the Underworld God of Hellas.

Barghest: Hound of Hell. Triple the size of a standard American grey wolf.

Cillé: Heaven's version of Hell's dungeon. Holding cell for upper level Demons.

Desmoterion/Desmons: Hell's dungeon.

Djinn: Vampire/demonic genie hybrid.

Dhampyr: Vampire/angel or demon hybrid.

Fallens: Fallen angels exiled from Heaven for their sins.

Watchers: Fallen angels serving Heaven and Hell equally.

Mo Aingeal: My angel; mo milis aingeal: my sweet angel.

Амитиел: Serbian translation for Amitiel.

Кадолон: Serbian translation for Kadolon.

Braća: Croatian translation for Brethren.

Brimrag: The Underworld's version of heroin and ecstasy mixed with brimstone ash.

Dreistil: An insult meaning a demon's standing is lower than a minion; traitor.

Screamers: Starving prisoners held in the Desmoterion.

Siltchins: Underworld body-wrappers.

Shivical saliva: Saliva from the Shivical demon: poisonous and burns on contact. Also known to cause paralysis and death if ingested or injected.

PROLOGUE

"She's just a baby!" The choked cries of a mother's panic echoed off the stark walls. Fear for her baby enveloped her, and she held the babe close to her heart. Tears trailed down her flushed cheeks as she ran the length of the long hallway.

How was she going to protect her child? *The bathroom.* She could feel the heat of her husband's fury nipping at her heels. Every question one would think when in dire situations raced across her mind, but only two circled her thoughts now. Why hadn't she left sooner, and was she going to be able protect her child from the monster coming after them? She ran to close them in a room with a lock, keeping them safe from his rage, and prayed it would be enough.

Her feet bit into the crushed carpet, and nearly tripped over a heap of clothes left on the hallway floor. "She's your daughter! How can you do this?" Her pleas fell on deaf ears as she pushed through the bedroom door, throwing the lock into place, and gunned it for her bathroom, to hide behind another locked door.

"She's a perversion to nature!" he snarled, and quickly she realized the man she had known since childhood was gone. This man, who had replaced him, was nothing short of malevolence wrapped with a violent nature that had grown since the car accident. "She needs to die!" As he pounded his fists and thrashed against the door, the hinges groaned from the pressure. "Give her to me, goddamn you! She will be the death of us all. You have no idea what she's capable of!"

Elsa knew two things for certain. Someone was going to die, and it wasn't going to be her daughter. Her sobs were thick with fear as she crouched down in the tub. Her precious, beautiful baby girl remained tucked against her chest where she would stay until the police arrived. Surely one of her busybody neighbors would call the boys in blue after hearing all of the screaming, as they had done in the past. While a fresh wave of tears streaked down her cheeks, soaking the black curls of her baby's hair, she prayed for their swift arrival. Sure, his temper had exploded multiple times in the past. His rages had nearly killed her many times before, when she tried to take their daughter and leave. Scars and bruises riddled her body from all of the fights from the past months, yet she stayed. Too afraid to leave. Too afraid to stay.

Clutching her daughter tighter, she saw the world in her baby's eyes. No, he wouldn't kill their daughter. She'd give her life to save Aingeal.

He thrashed against the second door, the wood bowing a little bit more with each thrust of his body. "Give her to me!" he cursed.

"I love you, Aingeal." Her soft, Irish accent was blurred in her cries as she kissed the soft black curls atop her baby girl's head. Her daughter's little hand cupped her face, and her tiny fingers stopped the tears from falling farther down her cheeks. The emerald green light in her eyes shone like beacons welcoming her home. Gazing into the babe's eyes, she saw something unsettling. Glorious dark wings surrounded this child as a silver glow emanated from her body. Her gentle smile and warm embrace calmed her.

The penetration of the knife stung her back into reality, causing the breath to escape her lungs. Her arms wrapped fiercely around her reason for living, for dying.

"Give her to me," the acidic voice of her husband growled once again.

"Never!" Elsa embraced her child tightly against her chest, as she turned away from him, resolving herself to pay for her daughter's safety with her own life. Her defiance enraged him more, and his face distorted into something unrecognizable as he pulled free the .38 caliber from his waistband. He stumbled back, and leveled the gun at her baby's head. Her eyes grew wide when the next words trembled through his lips.

"If I don't kill her, she'll kill us all."

The loud shrieking of metal against metal skewered the air as the gun went off. The bullet missed his intended target, but only by inches. Cries wailed from the child as she pushed herself up. Her green eyes stung with crystal tears as Aingeal called to her. Aingeal's little hands curled around her cheeks while crimson streaks trickled down her face. The rivulets cut across the matching stare of emerald green eyes. Beautiful eyes grew colder with each passing second as her soul left her lifeless body. Invisible to the world, Elsa hovered over her body, gasping as she watched her baby.

"Mama." Tiny hands clamored to her, leaving little blood-soaked handprints behind while Aingeal's wails littered the air. Elsa reached out to cup her child's face and soothe her fears away but she couldn't. She was just an apparition, gazing down upon the soft face of her Aingeal and the corpse still embracing her child.

Gunshots rang out again, and Mark's growls and thrashing came to a sudden end. "He's down. Check his vitals," the gruff voice called out. "I'm gonna check on the woman." The voice had spoken coldly, and a pair of heavy footsteps crossed the linoleum floor. "Oh dear Lord," he gasped, frozen in place, seeing the same thing Elsa saw. Black curls matted to her porcelain skin, blood staining both Aingeal and herself. Her long black hair clung to her skin as she vacantly stared off into space.

"Mama," the babe cried as the male reached down to pull her free, clinging to Elsa's neck with all of her might.

"Shh, it's all right. You're safe, little one, I'll protect you," he whispered gently to her, pulling her close to his chest. "You're safe now." Elsa watched the male gently cup her daughter's soft cheek, as she once had. "Your mother was right to protect you, little one, you're meant for something greater." The male's eyes lifted, catching Elsa's. She had never seen eyes so deep blue, but he saw her. "It's time for you to go. I'll watch over her now."

She tried to argue, and wondered if he would actually hear. Before she opened her mouth to try, he simply gave her a nod as magnificent wings unfurled behind. "Thank you for protecting her, Elsa."

CHAPTER ONE

In the distance, the familiar sounds of car alarms wailing and breaking glass filtered in with golden beams of sunlight, through the cracks in the windows. Ferrian had become accustomed to the daily ritual of vandals leaving their marks across the Chicago's West End streets. She didn't live in the best part of the city, but it was safe. At least by her standards.

She rolled over again in an effort to get comfortable, but it had become a fruitless search. Her body wouldn't give her a moment of peace. The odd lumps protruding alongside her shoulder blades had once appeared like any normal deformity, and yet, Ferrian never imagined they would start to grow again as an adult. Twisting back and forth, she winced again. The aching in her back paled in comparison to the screaming pain ripping through her head.

Scrubbing her face nearly raw, her hand passed the jagged scar from the corner of her brow to her chin, which was one of her constant reminders she was a monster to the world outside of her door. She traced the thick band of flesh with the pad of her index finger as the memories of the night she'd received it rushed back with a renewed urgency. *Shit!* It was a road leading to nowhere, and she didn't want to travel down it … again. Blowing out another ripe curse, Ferrian reined in her thoughts and pushed herself off the stiff mattress and on to her feet. A whole new world of what-the-fucks struck her as she reached down to get her beat to shit black cargo pants off the floor. "Okay, the tilt-a-whirl ride can stop now, thanks." Shoving her slender legs into the pants, she worked on shaking off the dizzy feelings as she tugged on her baggy black hoodie.

Coffee … nectar of the gods. Dragging her body sluggishly from the tiny bedroom toward the breadbox-sized kitchen, she realized the bane of restlessness was taking its toll. There wasn't much to rifle through for food, so she found and pulled out the large blue container of Maxwell House coffee. To her dismay, all she had left were a few protein bars and some expired milk. "Damn," she muttered, slamming the refrigerator door close. The soft gurgle of her stomach, which demanded something to eat with a pathetic whine, was going to have to wait until she made it to the docks.

Like each night before, it would be nothing more than another endless night to pass her time with work. Lately it was all Ferrian seemed to do. Running twelve-hour shifts six days a week wasn't enough to keep her mental muscle busy. In truth, the loading docks hardly entertained her mind at all, but there she could remain safely anonymous.

No one knew her name, much less could guess she was female. *Hell, I highly doubt anyone even knows what color my hair or eyes are.* The truth was, it was fine with her. The less anyone knew about her the better. Ferrian's appearance had driven the few people she knew away. It had hurt at first, being alone and on her own without as much as a friend to talk to, but gradually she became at ease, to the point she didn't need anyone. She prided herself on being resilient instead of the classic girly girl, who wanted to shop and get weekly pedicures. She barely brushed her waist-length black hair, much less curled and styled it. Instead, she preferred to keep it tied back, and safely hidden inside of her hoodie.

Beholding her tiny place, she noticed it wasn't much to see, let alone admire. It was quiet, aside from the neighbors' nightly screaming match in the apartment next to Ferrian's. As the nightly ritual of yelling commenced, she threw on her Docs and went for the door. Times like these, she relished the fact she chose to work third shift. The quiet of night, when the world should be sleeping, was when she found a small semblance of peace.

The bus stop down the street was her only connection to the world, and she rode the bus night after night with the other ghosts of the city. Staring out of the bus' smudged windows as it passed broken streetlamps that flickered with waning electricity, she gazed down each dirty alleyway, housing the lost souls left to wander the city in search of a warm building to find temporary shelter. The fading memories of when she was one of those ghosts flashed across her mind each time she saw another lost teen fighting for survival, and she wished she could reach out and help them. Sinking back into the hard plastic seat, she wanted to forget where she came from, and what she'd had to do to survive those first few years on the streets until she was old enough to rent an apartment.

Ferrian's heart sank deeper as she spotted a mother

with her two small children, huddling against the chilly October wind in the old mill building's alcove entrance-way, trying in vain to fight off the cold. A prick of jealousy stung her as she watched the unfortunates clamor together. Then it hit her. Even though they were freezing, the family of three still had something she did not. Love. It was written all over them as the mother leaned down to hug her children close and kiss the tops of their grungy heads.

Her past had more than dictated her present, and Ferrian feared for the future … what little she expected of it. Scanning the roads as she rode by the city, it seemed like a fitting analogy for her life. Devoid of warmth or compassion. Getting lost in the sounds of the city's soundtrack, the echoing cries between the vacant buildings in the commercial shipping district, played its sullen melodies. Buildings, which once boasted of a prosperous era, now were indistinct, desolate and deemed unlivable.

Peering over the sparse streets of Chicago's edges, Ferrian understood why anyone would run on broken shards of glass to get away from here. The eerie vacant buildings housed more than rats. And the gritty, dirty streets—seeded with thugs and street walkers roaming the night for their next victim—made her guts want to revolt as the steel beast she rode rolled by them. Everyone was trying to make a buck, whether it was to steal a buck, fuck for a buck, or beg for a buck.

No one in their right mind would live on this side of the city. During the day, it was a veritable ghost town, with an odd assortment of religious do-gooders pleading with the sinners to repent and come back to Jesus. Nighttime was a different story all together. The leftover newspaper sitting beside her heralded more stories of the rise of crime in the safe front of the city. "Well no shit. The poor get poorer." She rolled her eyes and tossed it back down as the bus came to a stop.

The chill of the October night bit at her cheeks as Ferrian stepped off the city bus. She huddled into her hoodie, the only real warmth coming from a lukewarm cup of coffee wedged between her palms. Ferrian's normal route to the loading docks took her past one of Chicago's last real orphanages. The barred-up windows shone dimly with the soft glow of pale yellow lights, and children peeked outside for one last glance before sleep. It was a sight all too familiar to Ferrian. Raised in a world of state services, Ferrian—like so many—dreamt of a world where rich, loving parents came and saved them from the cold, stark rooms of Chicago's state-run group homes. But they never came. Curling her fingers around the cup of coffee, Ferrian had to wonder if the wealthy had ever traveled down the cracked roads, leading to these yards she called work.

Her thoughts scattered around images of the past, of the childhood Ferrian wanted desperately to forget. It didn't surprise her when they shifted to her father. Darkness surrounded those thoughts as she recalled the night he had killed her mother. "Morbid. Get over yourself," she whispered upon the cold night's air. What if her father had succeeded in killing Ferrian? "Maybe he had been right after all." Maybe she was what he'd said she was. To him, Ferrian was a freak of nature, from her acute stare and the odd lumps on her back, down to the strange marking on her wrists. It had been too much too bear, and sent her father over the edge. More importantly, Ferrian wouldn't have caused the deaths of two beautiful souls. Cutting off her thoughts, she forced herself to walk faster to the loading docks.

Night after night, she worked as one of the faceless masses and left as the sun began to break across Lake Michigan. By tugging her black hoodie down, Ferrian's goal of staying invisible was easily done. Glancing behind her, she saw the nameless grunts who sat at the worn out Formica tables, thronged together over their coffees, like she was, talking amongst themselves. No one sat with her, no one offered her meaningless chitchat, but it didn't bother her. No one cared if you sat with him or her at lunch, or if your cat had a bad case of tapeworm.

CHAPTER TWO

The day was waning, slowly shifting to night as a painting of pinks and purples splashed across the horizon, gradually giving way to encroaching darkness. Remi had been assigned to be Ferrian's guardian since the day she'd been born, a job he didn't take lightly. How could he? She was the first Darkling born in nearly a thousand years. She was the key to finding the others. Still, he found a strange comfort in watching Ferrian for hours at a time. To say he was fascinated by his charge was a complete understatement. Although he was invisible to mortals, he carefully stalked her from the shadows as she meandered down the littered street, and waited until the bus she climbed out of pulled away. He couldn't understand why anyone, human or not, would willingly live in a rundown ghost town. More to the heart of it, he hated the fact his charge was constantly surrounded by human scum who thrived off the misery of others. His keen eyes watched Ferrian with laser-like precision, as she walked past the alleyway opening across the street from where he hid.

The glare of another zeroed in on Ferrian's small

frame, too, and sent Remi's internal warning system on high alert. She didn't see it coming, but he sensed Ferrian knew something was about to go down, given the way she shoved her fists into her pockets. The pronounced bones from her delicate knuckles ribbed the black cotton cloth as Ferrian lowered her head and lumbered forward. It wasn't the first time he'd seen a knowing look cross her face while she had quickened her pace. His heart clenched, waiting for the inevitable. It was her curse, her cross to bear, and he hated what was about to go down. Remi had no choice but to step aside and allow nature to takes it course. Such bullshit.

Ferrian's attacker came out the alley, rusted knife in one hand and broken bottle in the other. She tried to run, but the male nailed her in the back of skull. The male was a blur, coming at Ferrian faster than any human could. With one blow, he knocked her to the ground. The hard thud of Ferrian's body bouncing off the broken concrete from the hit had startled her, and her hood fell away from her face.

The acrid stench of the indigent's breath wafted through the air, making Remi's stomach want to revolt. Clutching his fists into tight balls, he considered how bad things could get for him with the council if he stepped in and destroyed the male attacking her. His heart tripped, and he silently urged her to make a run for it. "That's my girl. Get out of there." Her Docs bit into the crumbled concrete, but Ferrian had barely made it two steps before her attacker knocked her back down.

Remiel sank back against the wall, and his fingers dug into the brick-face as he bit back the angst brewing deep in his chest. He knew he should leave it alone—he was only there to watch over her—but what good would Ferrian be to the future of humanity if she were dead?

His instincts were screaming to help her as Ferrian kicked furiously at her assailant. Finding ground beneath her feet, she launched off the concrete again, throwing punch after punch anywhere she could land a hit. Landing her pocketknife in the male's thigh, she sliced a sickly gash wide open, tearing her blade from his leg. She was gaining ground … until he came at her with another beer bottle. With a heavy swing, he smashed it against Ferrian's head, shattering the dark brown glass in a chaotic halo upon impact.

Clenching his teeth tightly, Remi's stomach balled into a knot the size of a cantaloupe while he clung to the grey brick corner piece. Like a bad movie playing out before his eyes, he continued watching as blood wept from her brow and trickled down into her eyes. Shards of glass stuck into her skin, glittering against the harsh streetlight as she landed another kick to his gut. A part of him wanted to cheer her on. She wasn't taking any shit, and damn if he wasn't turned on by her holding her own in this impromptu street fight.

He couldn't break his gaze away when Ferrian steeled herself, turning to run. He heard the distant sound of Ferrian's heart thundering as loudly as a freight train when she lunged forward. The male gave chase with a wooden board in hand. She had made it only a handful of steps away before the hard crack of a two-by-four against her skull sent her hurtling to the ground once more.

A sickening smile crinkled her assailant's face, reaching up to a set of black eyes. It was then Remi realized this was not a 'by chance' meeting. She was in deep shit. A

Hellistic demon stood over her listless body. It held the bloodied two-by-four in one hand, and broken bottleneck in the other.

"Shit!" The pounding of Remi's heart was deafening in his ears. He couldn't stand aside anymore, all Heaven and Hell be damned.

His body dissolved into thin air, materializing before the demon male half his size. Crushing its scrawny throat, Remi squeezed until the sickly crack of vertebrae breaking echoed through the air. The demon's black eyes rolled back in its skull as his last breath shuddered from his lungs. This one reeked, the stench of booze coating the air as Remiel dropped it to the ground. "Figures."

He gazed down on Ferrian, shaking off the momentary knock out as she turned her face over her shoulder. Her eyes tried to focus on him when Remi lowered himself closer to her. His heart dropped to his stomach at the sight of her battered body and terrified stare.

"Don't hurt me," she meekly pleaded, twisting into a tiny ball. Her hands shook as she tried to cover her head.

"I won't. I would never hurt you, Ferrian." His soft-spoken words were coated in a solemn vow. Slipping his arms around her, Ferrian stared into his eyes. Trepidation glared back at him between wary blinks. The exhaustion from the attack seemed to overwhelm her, and her body sagged in his arms. Remi cupped Ferrian's head gently to rest against his warm chest.

"Sleep, m'aingeal, sleep." His warm breath whispered against her cheek. As her body became lax, Remi curled Ferrian into his embrace. Lifting her from the ground, he shook his head in disgust. Remi had watched her for years, and had seen too many scenes like this. This time was different. This time the attacker was a Hellistic demon who was on a mission. Biting back a curse, Remi wished there had been more time to treat her assailant to a more fitting demise.

He sucked in a ragged breath, noticing the way Ferrian's soft ivory skin had become a duller grey as of late. And her back twisted in Remi's hold as if she were in pain. Glancing down to her face, the deep 'v' setting between her brows confirmed his suspicions. It was a sign of things to come, and things were only going to get worse for her from here on out. Stretching out his wings, he lifted them up into the velvety night sky. The wind fanning through his feathers was a welcomed relief as he soared over buildings heading toward Ferrian's apartment.

Landing soundlessly on the fire escape outside of Ferrian's bedroom window, he popped the locks with a simple mind command and carried her into the small room. In a few strides he reached her bed, laid Ferrian down gently on the crumpled blankets, and summoned his healing gift. The golden aura pulsating through his body exited out of his hands, coating Ferrian with warm, healing light, mending her cuts and bruises. Each shard of glass dissolved away and the swollen contusions subsided within moments. However, the one thing he couldn't heal was the damage left behind in Ferrian's mind. Although he desperately wanted to, Remi was incapable of it. Ferrian had proven immune to it from the first time he'd tried it on her as a small child. He had pushed himself hard, trying in vain to erase the memories of her mother's death. In all of his existence, Ferrian alone had shown to be the only mortal his gift wouldn't work on.

As gently as he could manage, he pulled off her black

Doc Martin boots and matching hoodie. And waited for her to jolt awake and try to fight him off. Seconds dashed by and not a flicker of movement or hope that she would rouse came. His eyes danced over Ferrian's healing skin.

Her soft murmur caught his attention as Remi pushed away his plans for destroying whatever demon had caused all this. Stroking her delicate skin with his fingers, he studied her brows as they knitted together more tightly. Ferrian's supple lips pulled back into a soundless scream and she thrashed about. Closing his eyes, Remi invaded her mind and saw into her dreams. Her cortex was flooded with the scenes from earlier, replaying them with perfect clarity. He laid his warm hand against her brow.

Her body turned fiercely, rolling away from him, which he assumed was an instinct she subconsciously had. As she twisted away, her shirt slid up her ribs and back, exposing a few thick silvery scars running in jagged arcs in what seemed to be an endless map of pain. He carefully tugged the shirt back down because he didn't dare expose anymore skin. What he'd seen had been enough to set off his primal instincts to destroy every single person who'd had a hand in destroying this beautiful angel.

Crushing his fists into tight balls, fury seared through his veins, warring with his need to comfort her. The thick silver marks and twisting scars ravaging her skin were a constant reminder of her past. Was she strong enough to push past the wrongs, which had been done to her, or would her future be corrupted because of it? Only time would tell. He prayed to God Ferrian chose the right path. She alone held the power to save humanity, and locate the other Darklings. Right then and there, while gazing down at the agonizing torment splashed across her face, he vowed she would never again know pain like this. Even, if it meant his wings.

CHAPTER THREE

errian's eyes popped wide open and her body jolted up. Cold sweat poured off her as she cleared away the scream stuck deep in her throat. Scanning the room while her eyes and mind adjusted, a new fear bubbled up in her gut. She had no idea how she'd gotten home. Her memory was a blur. The faint recollection of a brilliant warm glow coming toward her, cradling her, had her wondering if it all had been a dream. A familiar scent of rich dark spices assailed her again, and Ferrian warily turned her head to find the source of the smell.

Jumping back against the tattered wallpapered wall, she tried to scream again, but her voice was lost. The male was massive, with an air of peace glowing around him as he sat on the edge of her bed. In the dim light, his huge frame threw off a shadow of a giant, blackening most of the room.

His penetrating ice-blue eyes stared straight through her with an intensity that could crack a glacier with one blink. She haggardly sucked in a deep breath, praying the male wasn't here to kill her … or worse, she worried as those eyes followed her every movement like he was stalking prey. His long black hair was tied back, swaying softly as he eased back. His broad chest was thick with corded muscle, and even through his grey cashmere sweater Ferrian could make out the striations across his muscled torso. His expression was unreadable as she curled deeper into a ball. *Dear God, what does he want from me? Who the hell is he, and why does he have to look like a walking GQ model?*

"Please," she begged while peeking up at him from under wet lashes. Her voice shook. "Don't hurt me. Please."

"I said I would never hurt you, m'aingeal. Please, you can trust me." His deep voice was thick with sincerity, causing Ferrian to slowly uncurl herself. "You were attacked. I brought you back here."

"I-I … God, it's all a blur. Who are you? Why did you bring me back here?" Ferrian's voice grew accusatory, but he didn't budge, didn't even move a muscle. "How did you know where I lived?" The sickening feeling that her mysterious guest knew more about her than she was comfortable with skittered down her spine, and she shifted her body farther away from him.

"My name is Remi, and I saw the indigent go after you with a two-by-four. I found your address in your backpack. I thought it best to bring you back here." She listened to the disdain seeping from his lips as he spoke. Her pulse kicked up the longer he sat there. The way Remi stared at her, as though she were exposed, left her feeling a little too vulnerable. She didn't frigging like it, not one little bit. Although, there *was* something oddly familiar about his eyes, and the way they penetrated her. *I swear I've seen those eyes before, in a dream maybe.*

He didn't make a move. It still didn't change the fact that she was on the verge of losing it completely. And this male, this perfectly composed ode to creation—not only gorgeous to gaze at, but also sent a rush of moist heat blooming between her thighs—was a danger to her resolve to remain alone. "Please leave. I don't know you. I-I need to … need you to leave."

Rushing off the bed, she realized her body had other ideas. She tried to run off, but her head began to spin at the same time as her legs gave out. *Oh shit*! Before she hit the floor, a pair of thick muscled arms surrounded her, scooping her up and stopping her body from colliding with the hardwood. His embrace was warm and comforting and it scared the shit out of her … more than getting cracked over the skull with a damn two-by-four.

"No, Aingeal. I think bed is the best place for you. I believe you might have a concussion. Please," he urged her, but his kindness was a language foreign to Ferrian. Why would anyone care enough to help her? It didn't make sense. "For me." His bass voice rumbling through his chest, vibrated against her skin and resonated throughout her whole body. She opened her mouth to speak, to argue with him, but words were lost to her. Remi slowly lowered her back onto the bed. "Are you hungry? I could order some food. What do you prefer, Chinese or Italian?" Behind the sultry curves of his dusky lips, Remi exposed a set of pristine white teeth when a smile spread across his chiseled face.

A smile of her own hinted at the edges of her lips. Why was he being so nice to her—what was his game? It was setting her on edge, because no one ever did anything nice or out of the kindness of their heart without expecting something in return. "No, I'm not hungry." *Lie*. "Honestly, I'm fine. You should go." *Bigger lie*. Trying to steady herself, she subtly pulled away from Remi, hoping her worst fears weren't about to come true.

Remi saw the fear radiating from Ferrian's beautiful green eyes. Those eyes alone spoke volumes he would love to read. Watching her throughout her life wasn't the same as being with her in her private space. His body ate up much of the room in the tiny apartment. He didn't miss the subtle way Ferrian shifted from him, as the tick in her jaw strained. The distress in those eyes made him realize too much damage had been done to her in the past. Kicking himself, Remi deserved every ounce of guilt. He wished to Heaven and Hell he could turn back the clock and take Ferrian away from it all, and protect her from everything. But he couldn't and never would be able to. His heart ached for her, seeing her recoil from him, even in her sleep.

Clutching his fist tightly into ball at his side to keep from scaring her, Remi risked a gentle brush across Ferrian's flushed cheek with his other hand. "It's all right, I promise I won't hurt you." Sincerity leaked from each word. "Let me order something for you. You look half-starved." The grumbling and gurgling coming from her stomach confirmed his suspicious.

Ferrian's expression said she didn't believe him, but how was he going to get through her barriers enough to gain her trust? "Please," he gently begged, and a flicker of hope pricked his gut when she nodded.

His wings tingled with a stinging sense where they had absorbed into his shoulder blades, sending a familiar shockwave to his nervous system as Amitiel sent her usual summoning. Like all pure angels, he had the ability to hide his wings by calling them into his ethereal body until he needed to use them. Amitiel's call grew more intense, and he gritted his teeth against the irritating sensation. Shaking it off, Remi reached into the pocket of his black leather pants and pulled out his cell. "So what do you like, Chinese or Italian?" *Please say Italian.*

"Doesn't matter, food is food." Her voice was eerily flat. She sat curled up in a ball, with her arms wrapped around her legs. The distinct impression she had never enjoyed one of the greatest pleasures—food—greatly bothered him for some reason. Sure, food was a source of nourishment, but that didn't mean it couldn't also rock your taste buds' socks off. Glancing at Ferrian, with her sallow chin propped up on her knees; a sudden pang of sadness struck him. How long had it been since she had eaten anything of substance anyway? "I take it you're not a foodie?"

"No." Her expression was as stoic as her voice. Shit, how was he going to get her to open up when she was fighting him with silence?

"Okay, would you mind if I chose then? I've been craving Capellini di Mare, what would you like?" Smiling his best impish grin, he tried desperately to ease her, and assure her he wasn't evil. It was proving harder to do than he wanted it to be.

Cocking her thin brow at him, he could see Ferrian almost wanted to smile, but it quickly faded. "It doesn't matter."

Think dammit, there's got to be something she's willing to talk about. "Haven't you had Italian before?" He may live in the Angel-Realm, but he came down to Earth whenever he got the chance to try new foods. His mouth watered thinking about fresh marinara sauce and soft, hot garlic bread.

"Sure, if you count mac-n-cheese and spaghetti."

Observing her carefully, he noticed she'd slowly let her physical guard down. Her knuckles weren't bone white anymore, and Ferrian's breathing slowed into a relaxed, even pace. Forcing her to like him wasn't going to work; he'd tried to send her calming vibes, which did nothing. She was the first charge to resist him, and how it was even possible was going to keep him up late at night wondering. He wasn't about to let her go another day without filling her stomach with something more satisfying than store brand craparoni and cheese, so he shrugged it off for the time being.

"Listen, I know you mean well ..." she began to say while pulling the blanket over her shoulders. He didn't miss the subtle shaking, but why was she trembling? It wasn't cold in the little apartment. "I'm fine. You should go." Her eyes hesitated on his face, yet Ferrian curled into a protective ball once again. Pushing her any further wasn't going to win her trust. He had made some progress, but Remi wasn't going to give up on his pursuit.

Nodding, he allowed Ferrian this one, but it wasn't going to be the last time he tried to crack her self-protective barriers. Slowly he rose from the edge of Ferrian's bed, and her gasp as she took in his immense size sent a shiver of fear down his spine. "Okay. I'm going to leave you my number. If you need anything, please don't hesitate to call me." Whipping out a business card he went to hand it to her, but realized Ferrian wasn't letting go of the circle she'd formed with her arms around her legs. He laid the card on the nightstand. "Remember, Aingeal, don't hesitate to call me anytime, for any reason." His eyes lingered longer than he had expected to, on the dark shadows around Ferrian's haunted gaze.

Turning to leave, his reluctance to walk away jarred him. His insides were clawing at him to turn around and encase Ferrian in his arms. Hold her close in his embrace, and whisper in her ear that he would stay by her side as long as she needed him to.

The heat of her gaze remained on his back as he walked through her door. He silently kicked himself while making his way down the narrow hallway. She was safe now, and the best thing he could do for her, and would have to do, was to give her time. Build her trust up. Starting first with ordering food for Ferrian the second he closed her inside of the apartment.

Invisible to normal humans, Remi would be Ferrian's true guardian angel. It was only she who mattered to him now. She was a fire in his veins. A fire, which had ignited the moment he had stared deeply into her hypnotic eyes. "Why didn't I step in sooner? Oh right, because I'm a moron who obeys rules."

His wings tingled again with frustrating vigor. The timing of Am's summoning sucked as usual. Pulling out his cell, Remi punched in the digits, still amazed the reception was as clear as it was, reaching the Angel-Realm. "Where the hell are you? Get your ass back up here, Remi, and I mean now!"

Not at all surprised by her snarling demand, he rolled his eyes.

He was half tempted to bring back a case of Midol, or maybe hire an incubus to do her a solid, if it meant she would get off his back for ten minutes. "No can do. My charge was attacked, she has a concussion. I can't leave her yet."

"Well heal her, dammit. We have a shit-storm to deal with."

Always the eloquent charmer. Sure, Remi had a duty to the League of Guardians and checking in with his brethren was a part of the protocol, but it was starting to irk the crap out of him that Am was throwing her seniority around as if he actually gave a damn.

"She's resistant to my gifts." The audible huff of Am's annoyance was also getting old fast. "Outwardly sure, I can heal her body, but not her mind. If I didn't know better, I would swear she's immune to it." Remi's jaw clenched as he worked the thought over in his mind again. Of all of the Darklings in the world, he had to be the guardian of the one being he couldn't fully heal with his gift. That was just fanfreakintastic!

"What do you mean she's resistant? Break through the barriers."

Did Amitiel think so little of him, for all of the millennia he had served, that she honestly believed he hadn't tried to do it? "Geez, mom, why didn't I think of that? Oh right, I did. I've already tried and guess what … it didn't work. I'll be back in a few hours. I want to make sure she's all right for now."

"Fine," Am snapped, clicking off the phone before Remi had the chance to ask what was going on Realmside.

"Damn, she has an attitude lately." Shoving it off, his next call was to Piccola's, his favorite Italian shop. Smiling, he realized Ferrian would probably freak-out, but he wasn't about to let her starve. Leaning against the building, Remi wished it could be him cooking Ferrian a nice meal and conversing over good food and a nice bottle of wine. Suspecting it probably wasn't going to happen, ever, he stored the thought away in his vault full of what-ifs.

CHAPTER
FOUR

Ferrian sagged back against the wall, resting her head on her shoulder. Glancing around the sparse room, her world seemed almost safe again, alone in the quiet space. Raking through the tangles of her hair, she hated the idea she was a target of life's inside joke.

She was still slightly dazed and confused by the turn of events, but Remi had left a strange sense of ease with her. Then again, he hadn't seen what she truly looked like underneath the layers of clothing, either. As much as she wanted to cringe at what he must have been thinking, she had to admit it to easier to stomach knowing he would never see her completely naked. Sinking into her world of wishful-thinking, she couldn't get the heat in Remi's ice-blue eyes, or the way she swore electricity licked across his irises when he held her close, out of her mind.

Her mind travelled down the fairy-tale road into the realm of delusions, where she was a perfect beauty. Where no one regarded her like a monster from the depths of Hell, sporting horns, and split tongue and tails. In a world where a man like Remi would actually look at her in awe, instead of taking pity on some pathetic chick who took beer bottles and two-by-fours to the head like a drop-out pro. Her thoughts drifted off in a dangerous daydream, imagining what it would be like to curl up next to him and stare into his beautiful eyes without fear of Remi wincing at the sight of her ravaged face. To feel the warmth of his skin as his fingertips swept over her lips.

Shaking the ideas from her head, she reminded herself she knew better. She was what she was. Yet Remi had taken pity on her to save her. He put his life at risk to make sure she survived. *Damn, he is a saint, isn't he?* "Either he's a seriously good Samaritan or an angel. Why did he save me? He could've walked away like any other person would have, but he didn't." Dropping her head into her hands, she crushed her palms against her closed eyes. The question of why he'd done it plagued her like a bad case of acid reflux.

The growl of her stomach echoed around the quiet room as she idly patted her abdomen. Anxiety bubbled up when she glanced down to find she wasn't wearing her black hoodie. "What the hell?" She remembered wearing it when she climbed off the bus, burying her fists deep in the pockets and palming her trusty old pocketknife. Searching the room, she saw it folded neatly, sitting on the chair adjacent to her bed.

A skitter of fear washed over her. She wondered what a man like Remi must have thought seeing her scars. *Why does it matter what he thought? I'm never going to see him again.* What she couldn't figure out was why a small stab of concern, wondering if Remi recoiled when he first saw them, pricked at her now. She had gotten over what others thought of her long ago. She had grown a tougher skin than most, and yet the idea of him seeing her weaknesses in full view paralyzed her to the core.

The scent of dark spices wafted from her clothes when she pulled her hoodie over her head. The smell tickled her nose as she breathed it in deeply. It was warm and inviting, and she could only assume he was wearing ridiculously expensive cologne.

Flashes of her attacker shot across her mind. She bit back a gasp, remembering a pair of pure-evil filled black eyes staring down at her, and teeth gleaming with the intent to tear flesh from bone with one bite. The longing to kill her glinted in his face as he lifted his broken bottle-filled hand higher. With her head pounding and her heart racing she tried to scramble away. The swift crack against the back of her skull was all it took to knock her senses offline. It was long enough for her to miss out on the why's and how's of ending up in her bedroom with a stranger watching over her.

The appearance of menace quickly dissolved into comfort as her eyes fluttered against her will. Remi perplexed her when he curled her tiny body into his broad, warm chest. His skin radiated with fiery heat, licking her cold body down to her marrow. At the time, Remi's touch seemed to comfort her in an odd way, as though he was caring for a sickly loved one. Slowly, her body relaxed in his powerful arms and the darkness consumed her. Waking up to see him sitting on her bed, watching her sleep, sent a rush of liquid heat searing down her body, pooling between her thighs. Her skin tingled like a live wire, pulsing to life for the first time, and was still flushed from the idea of being so close to him, even if it was while she was out cold.

Shoving her body off the bed once again, she made

her way to the bathroom—stumbling as she went—and put on the shower. She stood in front of the mirror while billowy clouds of steam filled the tiny space, and suddenly the hairs on the back of her neck stood straight. Searching to find the source of her uneasiness, she sensed a pair of eyes watching her, intently. When she scanned the room, she found nothing, yet the feeling lingered. Walking slowly over to the window, Ferrian's hands tightened to small balls at her sides as she peered out into the dark veil of night.

Making quick work of her footsteps, she stepped back inside the tiny bathroom and locked herself in. Thick plumes of steam engulfed her as she peeled away layers of clothes. When she tried to toe her boots off, she was momentarily shocked to find them missing as well. How had she not noticed they were gone? Then again her head had had other ideas, and taking inventory of what she was, or rather wasn't wearing hadn't been on the agenda. Opening the door, she hid behind it as she checked around the room for them. They sat tucked under the same chair where her black hoodie sat. All she could do was smile, and closed the door again. *Either he's some OCD serial killer, or the catch of the century.*

Staring at her blurry reflection, she realized she preferred this view. In this altered reality, she appeared normal. The silvery scars, which ravaged her body, disappeared. There was no sign of her odd lumps pulsating painfully and protruding from her back. She appeared ... normal. Stripping off the rest of her clothes, Ferrian stared into the fogged over mirror as her body faded out, hiding what she hated to see. A few yellowish bruises still clung to her shoulders and thighs from the attack. Having seen worse, she shrugged it off. Popping off the last of her body's coverings, she laid her leather wrist-cuffs on the counter, which exposed her constant red scars. She couldn't quite figure out why after nearly five years they persisted appearing angry as ever. They were the only marks Ferrian had caused and carved into her flesh. They were fatal wounds and she knew it, but somehow she awoke the next morning, wounds closed and aching. The question as to why she hadn't died at the time troubled her often.

Stepping under the powerful spray, she soaked up the hot water as her body sagged from another bout of exhaustion. Crimson drops slipped down to the floor when she loosened her tattered braid to scrub her head free of the dried blood matted in her hair. "Sssssss ... damn, Ferrian." She winced from the pain, her head was throbbing from the light scrubbing. Her body welcomed the hot water as it sluiced down the curves of her body, yet it didn't compare to the heat that had radiated from his body when he'd held her in his thick, muscular arms. *What is wrong with you? Stop thinking about him!*

Reaching for the sponge, she gingerly soaped up her skin, and imagined it was him doing the work for her. Rolling her head back on to her shoulders until the hot spray ravaged her face; Ferrian envisioned his huge hands caressing her body, leaving the soapy suds to trail down her skin after him.

In her dreams, the thick bands of scars twining around her flesh dissolved away as though they were nothing more than dirt needing to be washed down the drain. Sparks of those ice-blue eyes flashed through her mind, his sun-kissed skin and rich scent saturated her thoughts, provoking a foreign desire. Her skin flushed a deeper shade of crimson imagining Remi's lips on hers, as she licked along the seam of his perfect plush mouth.

Who are you kidding? So not happening. She scolded herself for even thinking it; she hated this pastime. Day-dreaming of a Greek god look-alike, filled with empty promises, could do more damage than good. Nope, she needed to forget him, and had to clear her head quickly before another round of *'please seduce me, sir'* kicked in.

Shutting off the delicious hot spray, she quickly toweled dry and wrapped herself up. The last thing she wanted to see was her bare skin exposed when the fog cleared from her bathroom mirror. The rapid knocking at her door startled her, sending her heart into panic mode. Throwing on a pair of black yoga pants and matching tank top, she finished it off with her black hoodie and quickly made her way to door. As she edged along the wall she clutched the baseball bat that she kept next to the entrance. "Who's there?" Holding her breath, Ferrian waited for a reply, tightening her grip on the bat.

"Piccola's delivery."

Peering through the tiny porthole, she saw a young male doing his best impression of a mafia wannabe hit man holding a brown paper bag. She rolled her eyes at the cliché standing outside of her door. There wasn't a chance in hell she was going to open the door to him. "I didn't order anything."

"Someone did. Look, lady, I was told to bring this here and not leave until you accepted it. I ain't getting any younger here. So whats you say, yous open up already."

Slowly she unbolted the locks, eying them suspiciously. She didn't remember getting up to lock them when

Remi left, but locked they were. Shaking it off as a rattled memory issue, she figured the day had taken its toll on her already and her brain wasn't in the mood to decipher anymore mysteries. She slid the chain into position before pulling the door ajar, leaving enough space to see out into the hallway. The deliver guy was anxiously fidgeting with his collar button as he waited for her to open the door. "See, lady, it's only food, no severed horse heads or nothing." The mouth-watering scent of warm bread sticks and pasta sauce wafted through the small opening, punching the growing hunger in her empty stomach into consume and devour mode.

"What is it?"

"Capellini di Mare, some chicken and gnocchi soup, breadsticks, and chocolate velvet cake."

Her stomach growled at the idea of food and her lips grew slick with want. Gulping down her food desires, she pondered the situation. She hadn't ordered anything, but she remembered Remi suggesting the same fare. So what were the odds the food happened to show up a half hour after he left? "Who ordered this?" Eyeing the male suspiciously, Ferrian fingered her hair to shield her face, as she slid her hoodie into place.

"Don't know. Look, are yous gonna open up and take this or am I gonna have to leave it at the damn door? Yous know it's disrespectful to waste food."

Rearing back, she grasped the bat tighter, considering him. After a long moment, she decided wasting it wasn't worth it. She was starved, and her stomach was grumbling vehemently at her. Setting the bat against the wall, Ferrian shut the door and slid the chain lock free.

"See, wasn't so hard, was it?"

Don't push it, asshole. My bat would look great shoved so far up your ass that you'd end up tasting it for days.

"How much is it?"

"It's been paid for, but if yous wanna slip a tip my way, I'm okay with it." The disgusting way he visually undressed her with his wandering eyes set her on edge.

"I don't have any cash, sorry."

The smell of his cheap cologne swamped her as he leaned against the doorjamb. Garlic reeked from his breath, nearly choking her. "It's okay. I think we might be able to work something out." He licked his greasy lips, pouting them out to her, and grinned, as if his bad impression of one of the Jersey Shore boys was going to win her over. Ferrian slipped her hand around the bat, closing her fist tightly. This was heading downhill fast, and she didn't like where it was going. As hideous as she knew she appeared, males seemed to be drawn to her, and not in a good way.

"Never mind. I'm all set." Waving him off, she slammed the door in his face.

"Wait, come on, baby, we could have some serious fun." Stepping his foot in the small space between the door and jamb to keep the door open, he leaned in closer. "Come on, how about yous play nice? I'll be a good boy, I promise."

Her heart froze, until the sound a feral roar made her head snap back, searching for the source as white-hot anger boiled her veins. Lifting her best friend behind her back, she slowly pulled the door open. The male's expression went completely blank, like a mask had been placed over his carnivorous glare.

Erring on the side of caution, Ferrian held her bat close. Her eyes stayed trained on his expressionless face. He nodded his oily-haired head and apologized, then walked down the common hall. Exhaling in shuddering breaths, she slowly slid the chain free and opened the door to retrieve the food. Making quick work to shut herself back inside, she sagged against the door and dropped the bat back to its resting place. She was careful, locking the dead bolts and checking them twice. "Too freaking weird."

CHAPTER
FIVE

His eyes stayed fixated on Ferrian. He couldn't break away from her; afraid he would miss the slightest detail of her delicate features as she searched the room for something. The deep furrow of her dainty brows knitting together left him wondering what more she had to say, and why she hadn't allowed herself to say what she'd wanted to. Sinking deeper into the shadows, Remi trained his sights on Ferrian as she leapt from the bed.

Shaking his head, he saw the same thing she did ... the pathetic living arrangements. Her resolve to live there, almost accepting this as her life, sent a wave of emotions he shouldn't be feeling crashing down on him. He longed to set Ferrian free, to show her who she truly was. His heart nearly stopped when her eyes flashed to his, hoping she didn't see him watching her.

To human eyes, he could walk amongst them without the fear of being seen. Humans couldn't see angels, but Ferrian was different. Angel blood coursed within her veins, tethering her senses in magnetic ways. Ferrian had no idea who she was, or was meant to become. Not yet anyway, but that was about to change … and he hoped with every fiber of his soul she'd come out on the right side of things.

Raking a hand through his thick black hair, he studied her every move, His breath caught like a lump of rock in his throat when her finger passed over his card. The simple action made a small smile start to spread across his mouth. She continued fingering over the embossed lettering, glancing down at his name. Her dusky lips twisted up into a sweet, innocent smile, sparking a primal urge to taste them, as he lashed his tongue over his lower lip. Unfortunately, her smile fell faster than a stone dropping from the sky, and he followed her eyes tracing over the hand touching the small card. He knew what she was seeing. The burn marks in between the web of her thumb and forefinger, and the spider-webbed bands of scars across the top of her hand and knuckles. He bit back a curse; it was one of many memories Remi wished he could erase for her. Better yet, wished he could have spared her from it happening in the first place.

He followed her as she padded to the bathroom. The lovely length of her braid swishing from side to side with the sway of her sinful hips had his body stirring in ways it hadn't in centuries. Underneath all of the black garb of unisex clothing hid the body of a beautiful woman, and now he wished—more than anything—he could caress the small of her back while pressing her body against his.

Sinking deeper into the darkness, his hands clutched the rotting iron railing of the fire escape as he leaned his butt on it. She turned around to peer out the window. He swore she was staring directly at him; sitting perched like a voyeuristic deviant. Her tiny hands balled into fists as she walked to the window. For one brief moment, they shared a connection, which defied rational thought. It was clear to him she knew someone was watching her. She came right to him without knowing he was on the opposite side of the glass. *Not possible.*

Holding his breath, he knew he couldn't move. She was staring directly at him. However, she didn't see him in the dark. Letting out a soft curse, Ferrian stepped away from the window. The hairs on the back of his neck electrified, standing on end. "M'aingeal," he murmured, reaching out to touch the one woman in the world he knew would shy away from his touch. Turning back to the bathroom, Ferrian stepped into the steam-filled room, and stood before the mirror. He didn't have to be a mind reader to figure what she was seeing before she shut the door.

Remi was temporarily relieved and irritated at the same time. He couldn't see the beauty standing behind the door, shielding herself from the world. The simple idea she was undressing a few feet from him had his blood pumping and heading down to the one place that would be more unwelcomed than the rest. "Out of all the charges, why her? Why now?"

Ferrian hadn't been his first charge, or even the seven hundredth, but the pain she held inside cut him deeper than all of the rest combined. She didn't blame anyone for it. For whatever reason, she took it all within herself. She accepted it, and he needed to know why. He had so many questions he wanted to ask her, but more than anything, he wanted to climb inside of her head and figure her out from the inside. For all he knew about her, it seemed as though he barely knew her at all. What made her tick, what made her smile? She was a mystery he had been following since the day she was born, and yet, Ferrian was so much more than he could imagine.

Lost in his thoughts, the scent of fresh baked bread sticks and the sweet, acidic sauce wafting through the air brought him back as the sound of the shower water cut off. *Perfect timing.* His heart jacked up a little more, wondering if she would come out of the bathroom sans towel, damp, with droplets trailing down her soft ivory skin. *Doubtful. Nope, just as I thought. Why can't you see how truly mesmerizing you are?*

The hard knock on the door visibly startled her, and she jerked open the door, spilling dissipating clouds of steam out. He couldn't take his gaze off her sinuous body as she hurried to get dressed. Ferrian was half hidden from view, but it was enough for him to see her slip her well-defined legs into tight fitting yoga pants. His cock twitched as his eyes trained on the curve of her breasts while she tugged roughly at her black fitted tank top. Both pieces hugged the curves of her slender frame perfectly, only to be covered by with the oversized black hoodie she lived in.

There was no mistaking the alarm in her eyes as she edged closer to the door, or the apprehension in her voice, asking who was there. Remi gripped the railing tight enough to leave indents, forcing his body to stay where he was.

The huff in the male's tone set a new tick in Remi's jaw, and it caused Ferrian to set the chain lock in place. *Good girl.* Her trembling hand held the bat in a white knuckled grip.

I'm right here, m'aingeal, I won't let anything happen to you. Damn right, he wouldn't. One wrong move on the delivery boy's behalf, and Remi would be on him like flies on shit.

God, he wished he could tuck her behind him safely, and answer the door for her. His muscles coiled as the male's harsh voice sliced through the air.

"Who ordered this?" Her voice was stoic even as she tried to steady her shaking hand.

Her spine went rigid and she leaned back slightly. He heard her stomach growl loudly once again, as she set the chain in place, and slowly opened the door.

Steeling himself against the iron cage of the fire escape, Remi's fury grew with each syllable the male uttered. He didn't like the way the male mentally undressed Ferrian, from head to toe, licking his lips like she was his next meal. *In your dreams, dickwad, and not even then.* He fought back the urge to materialize right in front of her and simultaneously punch the scumbag for even considering what was on his greedy mind.

Her voice sounded eerily detached, as she recoiled from the male. *Shit.* He knew this tone; Ferrian was expecting the worst to happen, and seeing her hand gripping the bat until it appeared as though she would snap the thing in half, was all the conformation he needed.

Slam the door in his face. He was close to losing it. Keeping his veil of invisibility on, he materialized next to the male with his hand firmly gripping the guido's throat. Punching a strong mental command into the male's brain, Remi held his desire to slam the guy's brainpan off the brick wall. *Back away from her and apologize now!*

"What did you say?" Her eyes darted up, confusion riddled in them. *No way. Not possible.* He shook the thought from his head the moment the male stepped away.

His heart was thundering as he focused all his energy on the pathetic menace. *Do it now!*

"I'm sorry, miss. Here's your food. I meant no disrespect." The male's voice was detached and his eyes were glazed over in a zombiefied state.

Now put the bag down and walk away. Hastily dropping the food by her door and stepping backward, the male left without another word said. *Forget you ever saw her and never come back.* The venom in his command suffocated the air as the male ran from the invisible intruder. He partially hoped the guy left pissing in his panties.

The shock in her eyes at the male's quick exit had her cautiously slipping the door open far enough to reach for the food and slip back inside as fast as she could. Shutting the door, Ferrian slid the three dead bolts back into place while Remi materialized back to the fire escape to watch her. Glancing down at the bag, the mien of questions on her delicate face sparked a small smile. *Eat up, m'aingeal. Next time, I'll be the one cooking for you.*

His eyes lingered on her as Ferrian carefully removed each plastic carton from the bag. Her small smile slowly grew, and the tip of her pink tongue licked over her lips with each new container she opened and inhaled with childlike happiness. Her hunter green eyes warmed up to emerald green pools, gleaming as though it were Christmas morning and she had been given the world's best gift. His heart swelled. To him, it wasn't much—just food—but to her it was clearly a kindness she hadn't known. "Thank you, Remi, wherever you are. You must be some kind of saint."

A saint, no. Hardly an angel most days. For you, I'll be whatever you need me to be.

Sliding off her black hoodie, she set it down on the same chair Remi had placed it on earlier. Catching glimpses of her silvery scars glinting in the dim light, running in sporadic arcs and slices down her shoulders and arms, regret punched him square in the gut for not stepping in sooner. All of the torment she had endured had left their marks on not only her skin, but also her soul. With time running short, he knew Ferrian was on the edge of slipping, but which way he wasn't sure. *God, I hope you choose the right way. I know you have it in you.*

CHAPTER SIX

The cool wind blowing off Lake Michigan sent another round of shivers down Ferrian's back, as she buried her fists deeper into her pockets. She couldn't shake the feeling she was being watched. Somewhere deep within her mind, she sensed the same pair of ice-blue eyes had been following her since the night of her attack, two weeks earlier. Electricity skated over her skin as she slid her sights from side to side, taking notice of everyone around her. Paranoia had become her own personal warning system as she palmed her trusted friend. The cold steel of her pocketknife gave her a small measure of reassurance that she wasn't completely defenseless.

Resting her forearms on the cold steel railing, she gazed off into the distance. The serene splashing of water against the concrete walls seemed finite as she noticed the small crests of white water crashing against the barrier. The tiny amount of relief, which usually came from staring out in the water wasn't there this time. Observing the sad life of the lake, and the limitations of its flow, made her own reality much more obvious. The water was trapped, unable to break past the walls, and she found a similar proverbial wall closing in around her as well. The waning of her life had been like a blessing, accepting the fact any day could be her last.

All of the times she had begged to be free from this life, as though she actually deserved it, only made the inevitable fire in her stomach swell with rage at her own weakness. "If there's a God, he frigging hates me," she mused over the sound of the breaking water.

"No, he doesn't." Spinning around to face the deep, raspy voice, her eyes grew wide, taking in the sheer size of the male standing a few feet behind her. The cold steel in her palm bit back as she clutched it tight, expecting to use it. Warm blood pooled around the grip, and she bit her lip, wincing from the slice.

Locking eyes with the male, her heart lodged in her throat as she tried to force air into her lungs. "You." She reached out for the railing right before her knees buckled. Her head swam as those twin ice-blue eyes gazed back at her, glowing like beacons in the night.

"Me." His smile gleamed as the last of the sun's ray kissed his skin in a wash, making him appear more a demigod than a GQ model. Her eyes traveled up and down the length of his immense body. Taking in his six foot four frame, she guessed he weighed closer to two thirty, given the thick muscles flexed in all of the right places leading down to a tight abdomen. The night she had awoken to him sitting on the edge of her bed, concern in his eyes as he cared for her, Ferrian had sensed something *odd* about him. When he'd caught her before she nearly hit the floor, Remi's movements had been blindingly fast, but she couldn't mistake the heat that rolled off him in droves, and licked like lightning through his eyes as he cradled her closely.

Why would somebody as drop dead sexy as you come strolling around here? What's your game, buddy? His grin was devilishly sexy, knocking another one-two punch to her baby-maker. He didn't make a move toward her. "Why are you here? How did you find me?" The hairs on her neck stood straight up as she edged closer to the wall, praying she didn't have to use the pocket knife she kept open and ready.

His small laugh littered the air, and he was smiling impishly when he spoke to her. "I come down here from time to time."

Sure you do. And I happened to be America's next Top Model! Considering him for a long moment, Ferrian reminded herself that a man who looked like him would not have gone unnoticed. Least of all by her, and she wasn't buying his bullshit. "Right … I haven't seen you here before."

"Normally, I like to come down late at night and watch the fish jump out of the water. It's sort of soothing down here." There was no edge to his voice, only cool calmness. She loosened her grip on the blade, unsure of what it was, but something about Remi eased her. "I'm surprised you didn't call."

Oh-kay then. So this is why you came. To give me shit about not calling you. Awesome. She didn't want any connection to the outside world. His expression seemed to ask the question of why she didn't, almost feigning the border of hurt. *Are you kidding me? You actually expected me to call? I don't think I'm not the only who has hit their head recently there, buddy.* Before she could tamp down the desire to turn and walk away, she answered his silent question, "I don't have a phone." Okay, why had she been compelled to explain herself? She didn't care anyway, did she?

"Oh." His smile turned down right sinful as he cocked his head, mulling it over.

Gulping against the spike in her pulse, she glanced up. His eyes caught hers in an intimate hold, causing her to crawl out of skin, and wish she could hide in a cave somewhere in the Rocky Mountains.

"So what brings you down here? Don't tell me you like to watch the fish jumping, too?" His throaty laugh vibrated through the air, sending a rush of heat licking down her body. Her lips pulled in a tight smile as she tried to break her eyes away from him.

"I, uh, I have to go." *Um, yes I do. Otherwise I might do something I'll regret, like actually smile and warm up to someone. Can't have that now, can we?* Ferrian quickly turned, breaking the connection from him. The sting of turning away was like a cable snapping, and the backlash smacked her with the force of a gale wind. Dashing past Remi, she hoped she could hide from him. It was bad enough he had seen a few of her scars, and she assumed he only stayed to talk to her out of pity. She had been so weak in those moments. In fact, so much so that a complete stranger had had to take care of her.

She barely made it two steps before Remi caught her by the arm to stop her. "You're bleeding." When he turned her to face him, the alarm in his voice shocked her.

Furrowing her brows, she stared up at him through the thick fringe of her black lashes, wondering how he could have known she had cut herself. She hadn't taken her hands out of her hoodie. Although the warm liquid wept from the wound, there wasn't any way it had bled enough to wet the front her sweatshirt. *Doesn't matter*, she told herself, but who was she kidding? *Either he has the nose of a bloodhound, or I'm losing my damn mind.*

He clasped her bicep, and a swell of heat from his touch radiated through her body as he closed the distance. Her breath shuddered, and she tried to imagine what his arms would feel like circling around her body, holding her close as his breath skated across her face. The image quickly faded as she envisioned his fingers tracing over the length of scars covering her back and arms. The idea of anyone seeing her naked skin revolted her, causing a quiver in her belly.

"I'm fine," she grumbled, tucking her hands in deeper. "It's nothing."

"Please." His fingers slid down to encircle her wrist, cautiously pulling her hand free. "Let me have a look." Trembling against his touch, she flinched when the coppery tang of fresh blood assaulted her nostrils.

"What are you, a doctor or something?" Sure, it sounded snarky, almost cutting and cynical. Yet, in her mind there was no way that a man as handsome as Remi, her saint and savior, could work in some dismal excuse of an emergency room, wearing a set of blue scrubs and stethoscope … unless he was playing Dr. McSexy on a sitcom. Braving a glance up to see his expression, she saw that a gentle smile laced his lips.

"Maybe." Slowly he coaxed her hand free, revealing crimson rivulets pooling into Rorschach inkblot test, leaving a sliver of flesh uncovered. "Why did you do this? Were you trying to hurt yourself?"

The fuck! Are you freaking kidding me? Oh yes, I look

that desperate, so I must be a cutter. The concern in his eyes settled over her like a lead blanket as she swallowed against the rising lump in her throat. "No. It was an accident."

Arching a single black brow, he stared hard at her. "An accident, huh? Sure." Yep, he wasn't buying it, and his voice didn't hide the fact.

"It was!" She ripped her hand free of his, unable to stand another pair of eyes staring at her so incredulously. It was an expression she had seen too many times, and each time it stung a little more. Shoving her fist inside her pocket again, she took off running. Her boots bit into the crumbled pavement as she hauled ass away from him, and his hypnotic gaze which read too deeply into her.

"Ferrian! Please, stop. Let me help you," his voice called after her, pleading almost, as she rounded the corner. Her chest pounded, nearly knocked the breath out of her lungs with each huff. She was a handful of steps away from rounding another corner and being clear of him when she spared a quick glance behind her to see if he was following. If only she had been focusing on what was in front her. The hard crash of something solid knocked her back to the ground. "Shit!" she screamed, purchasing a piece of the pavement with her backside. "Watch where you're going."

Shaking off the hit, her head cleared and she focused on the hard mountain of flesh standing before her. Her breath caught, fear iced over her veins as Ferrian stared into the same pair of ice-blue eyes she had just run from. "Impossible." Who the hell was this guy? Hercules, Superman? In the deep recesses of her mind, one word pinged with the force of an electric shock. *Angel.*

"Damn it!" He had been trying hard not to scare her, however, Ferrian's levels of trust had obviously been set to 'trust no one … ever'. Although the wound first appeared bad, Remi saw through the red stain to see the slice was clean and superficial. A few seconds of his healing ability and she'd be right as rain, but gaining Ferrian's trust was like climbing Mount Everest. He held no illusions it would be easy. It was going to be a long and arduous journey he had to take. Cursing himself in every known angelic swear word he could think of, he decided he needed to come up with a better game plan than randomly showing up at the docks like some psycho-stalker.

It was there in her eyes, the hurt and anger pouring out when he'd assumed what she had done was on purpose. The accusation seemed to be a cut deeper than the one she held in her hand. *Nice going, dipshit. Nothing like accusing her of hurting herself, when you don't know all of the facts.* He shouldn't have been surprised when she stepped back from him, but the reason she did still sucked.

Her warm blood contradicted the cool flesh of her soft, trembling hand. "It was!" There was no mistaking the acid in her verbal bite as she pulled her hand from his. The defiant anger he adored about her kicked up on display for him.

His deep voice echoed off the water and vacant buildings, calling out to her. Dematerializing to find her, he landed in front of the old paper mill building soundlessly, just in time. She turned the corner, and slammed into his hard chest, knocking her to the ground. *Great! She's probably got another concussion.* Rubbing his chest, he bent down to her. He had to hand it to Ferrian, she hit him harder than he thought possible.

It only took a moment of recognition for Ferrian to realize he was crouching down beside her; arms folded loosely over his knees, and a gentle smile spread across his face. Her eyes screamed of shock as she shrank back from him. She was studying him, waiting to see what his next move would be. "I'm sorry, I didn't mean to scare you, or assume things. Forgive me for being …" What? An ass, a brick wall, possibly the dumbest male she had ever laid eyes on? Maybe all three. Extending his hand, he hoped she would accept his offer and allow him to help her. It was doubtful given her past experiences. "Please."

His eyes were soft on hers as Ferrian hesitantly slid her hand into his. Remi's body sizzled with a frenzy of elation as her cool fingers brushed over his palm. "How did you get here so fast?" She stared at him incredulously, trying to process things. Her brows knitted together in a deep furrow as he helped her up from the cold hard ground.

"I have my ways." He smiled smugly, hoping she'd chalk it up to being dazed long enough not to notice things. "Are you okay?"

Separated by only inches, the heat of her breath skated across his skin as her body slightly trembled the longer he held Ferrian's gaze. "Hi," he said hesitantly. Seeing deep into her soul, his breath caught. A war was dancing around inside of her, where good versus bad tangoed on even footing. A single act of kindness or devastation would write her future and thus her true path.

His fingers closed around hers as Remi absently placed their hands over his thrumming heart. He took the moment to inhale Ferrian's sweet jasmine scent down into his lungs. His eyes caressed the curves of her face, sweeping up and down as though he was seeing her for the first time. "I'm uh, fine." Her eyes sparked with a new awareness as Ferrian sucked in a shuddering breath. Drawing in a sharp breath himself, Remi could've sworn he had seen his future, *their future*. A future where Ferrian, adorned with her majestic black wings, like all of the earthbound angels before her, and her matching raven hair streaming out behind her, jovially dancing in the wind. As quickly as he'd seen it, it disappeared when she withdrew her hand.

"Please, let me walk you home and clean up your cut."

"No, I'm fine. It's no big deal." Pulling away farther, he wondered how long he had this time before she bolted again. *Shit! Keep her talking, anything.* Fisting his hands to his sides, Remi watched idly as a tendril of her black hair covered her cheek. Inside he longed to feel the silkiness of it as he tucked it behind her ear.

"I won't hurt you," he murmured to her, hoping she would relax a little, but his eyes locked firmly on hers. "Please, let me help you." His heart paused as Ferrian considered it. Throwing a quick prayer skyward, he hoped there was a chance in Heaven or Hell she would agree to it. *Please say yes, please give me a chance, you'll see I'm not such a bad guy.*

"I have to go." Her voice was eerily detached as she walked past him.

"Can I at least walk you home?" Damn, he sounded pathetic. What did he have to lose by asking? Regardless

47

of what her answer was, he was going to see to it that Ferrian made it home safely; whether he walked with her, or flew above her.

"No worries. I'll manage," she called over her shoulder. "Been fine my whole life without a babysitter. Don't need one now."

"Sure," he snorted sourly, "and what about what happened a couple of weeks ago? You know, when some crazy-ass psycho hit you over the head with a two-by-four. Are you telling me you had it handled then, too?" It was a low blow, but he wasn't going down without a fight. Even it if meant stalking Ferrian from the shadows like some peeping tom creep. *Yeah, because everyone loves a voyeuristic angel following them home and peeking in their windows while they shit, shower, and shave.*

She wheeled around to face him. A spark of fury coiled behind her Darkling eyes, and screamed he'd stepped over the proverbially line and now she was livid. *That's not normal.* Her hunter green eyes sparked with silver and gold flecks, lashing at the irises like lightning strikes. In the twenty-four years he had been assigned to watch over Ferrian, this was the first time he had seen this kind of reaction. Was she closer to transitioning than he originally thought? Her twenty-fifth birthday was months away, and as far as he could remember, Remi had never known a Darkling to change early.

"So what! Like I said, I had it under control. I don't need a knight in shining armor bullshit. What do you want? My gratitude, like I owe you for scraping my sorry ass off the ground?" The more she snarled at him, the more the lightning storm kicked up in her eyes. "Say what you want so we can go on with our lives. You want money? Sorry, man, no can do. I'm broke. You want a date? Not happening. So please, don't waste my time." He didn't miss the acid in her words as she snapped at him. He wanted to feel sorry for instigating this, yet instead he found it surprisingly ... sexy. Even when she was vulnerable beneath the surface, afraid of his intentions, Ferrian still stood her ground like a true warrior. *Damn, that's hot.*

"No, Jesus!" *Well, a date, maybe, definitely.* "I only want to see you make it home safely. You owe me nothing." Scrubbing his hand through his black hair, he stepped closer, hoping he wasn't in for an ass-kicking.

"You're saying you only want to walk with me to my building, no ulterior motives?" Slowly her gaze softened, and she pulled her shoulders back. The way her eyes swallowed him whole, even as she coyly licked her lips, made his cock jump with desire. *Well if you let me, I would snake my arms around you, tackle you to the bed, and kiss you long and slow until you were breathless.* Shaking the thought from his head, he focused his efforts to keep his libido intact.

"Pretty much, yeah." He smiled with a genuine softness. What was happening to him? Was he actually desiring his charge? *Down, boy, we have a duty to do!* Reluctantly she nodded her head, accepting his request. "Thank you." The deep bass of his voice vibrated with the small elation of the moment. It was only a walk, yet it was so much more.

CHAPTER
SEVEN

Since the night Remi had walked her home, Ferrian had seen him pop up with regularity over the last couple of months. Still, the surprise of seeing him rattled her to the core. It had been three days since she had last seen him standing at the docks. Idly, she wondered if he was waiting there for her, or was it she was noticing him more now? *Get a grip. Why on God's green earth would he do that?*

The thought tickled her brain as she tossed and turned in bed. Glaring at the small alarm clock, she groaned, realizing it was only four in the afternoon. She still had a few hours to kill before she needed to get up for work. Hell, she had killed most of the day already thinking about Remi. What were a few hours more?

The odd lumps in her back were throbbing more with each day; yet, she never noticed them or the pain when Remi was around. For now she was chalking it up to 'being in the moment' with him. For whatever reason, Remi had taken an odd fascination in her. *Why? What is so special about me?* she found herself asking a lot in the recent weeks.

She couldn't figure it out, but his presence had a peculiar calming effect on her. And he had been true to his word, so far. By some miracle, Remi hadn't hurt her, nor had he laid a hand on her since the day she'd sliced her hand. A strangely wonderful tingling had skittered down her body when he'd held her hand to his heart. The feeling of his strong heart, beating beneath her palm, had sent ripples of fiery need coursing through her blood. At the same time, a swarm of butterflies had kicked up a category five hurricane in her stomach.

The way his eyes stared into hers, regarding her so carefully, made her want to fall head first into the beautiful pools. She couldn't remember the last time someone had actually looked upon her, if ever, the way Remi did. The thought alone sent a shudder down to her core. Her fingers ached to caress the hard cut of his jaw, and brush across the light blush of his cheek. In one single moment, Remi had ignited a fire deep in her sex, and warmed the chill perpetually lingering over her.

She hadn't expected to feel her heart falter when the shallow breaths she was trying to force from her lungs had stopped completely the second their eyes met. And yet, she couldn't see any malice or anger hidden behind a façade of deceit. *Don't get too close, freak. He wants something from you. You need to figure out what it is.* Did he though?

Rolling over again, the comfy spot she searched in vain for alluded her once more. As much as she wanted answers to her questions, a part of her—a deep, hidden part—wanted to know more. Were his lush lips strong and domineering, or tender? Flames licked up her spine as she imagined those lips, lavishing kisses down her throat to the junction of her shoulder. Would he be as gentle as he had led her to believe he was, or would he take the opportunity to break out an aggressive side, that all together didn't exactly scare the ever-living shit out of her?

The feeling of longing was unfamiliar and unsettling as she shook the thought from her head. She had never wanted anyone before. Ferrian couldn't deny there was something about Remi which intrigued her as no one had before, and it made her want him more. A trickle of panic washed down her. "Nope, not going to do it! I can't see him again." She may have thought it before, even lightly resolved herself to the notion, but when she said it out loud her voice betrayed her, dripping with want.

Scrubbing her hands through the tangles of her hair, Ferrian couldn't shake the niggling feeling he was near. She couldn't deny she liked finding Remi waiting, with a wistful smile to greet her. It still stunned her to know Remi actually wanted to talk to her, and listened to her talk, although she hardly said anything. She dreaded to open to him, fearing the ugliness deep inside of her would swallow him completely. When he'd asked her about her childhood, she had clamped her jaw tight as a stubborn child, shaking her head in refusal to speak. "It's nothing worth discussing." *I don't want you to run away screaming if you found out the truth.*

When he pressed her on it, Ferrian turned away and fell silent. Her past wasn't worth the effort in retelling it. Each time she saw him, he tried to coax a little more information from her. Each time, she shot him down with more silence. The truth had cost too many their lives, and she wasn't willing to risk his. Not for the sake of knowing.

The longing to see him warred heavily with her need to protect him from her. He had already come too close for comfort, and allowing him any closer wasn't worth the repercussions. Setting her resolve firmly in place, she vowed to walk away this time. But *this time* never seemed to happen. "Shit." Raking her fingers through her hair again, she hated herself for where this train of thought was going.

There was no fighting it, sleep wouldn't visit her. She was too agitated thinking about the reasons she chickened out of sending Remi away. Her nerves ignited with electricity as she swung her legs off the bed. "You can't do this to him." It wasn't a suggestion, she demanded it of herself. "Jesus, need to get out of here." The suffocating silence of the room was jacking up her anxiety levels the longer she stayed there, dwelling on every damn detail of the things she should, or rather shouldn't do. Yanking on the black hoodie, black camo pants and boots, she sensed the rush of panic setting in again. It had become too familiar over the years. The heavy feeling of foreboding tingled down her spine, and abraded her skin.

With a few hours before the sun was due to sink down into the horizon, and she was to begin her shift at work, Ferrian had no doubt where she would end up. Stuffing her hair into the hood, she palmed the small pocketknife and left.

CHAPTER EIGHT

Amitiel paced anxiously around the study, focusing on the floor to ceiling bookcases, housing all of the information throughout history. "Do we have any idea who sent the Hellistic after Remi's charge yet?"

"Nothing concrete. Word is, it may have been a Hellistic assassin." Cassiel scrolled through his emails, recalling the intel he'd received. "It seems to me … as though someone's changing the rules of the game."

"And who sent you this information? How do you know it can be trusted?" Amitiel pegged him with a harsh glare, awaiting his answer.

"I've got my sources. You might call them 'Watchers'. One in particular is working on getting back in our good graces."

"Fuuuuuuuck … you don't mean Focalor? Dude! Boy jumped ship ages ago. He's seriously not right in the head," Nisroc barked. "What makes you think he can be trusted now?"

"He's never lied to me. And because *you* don't know him. You don't know what he's been through, or the reasons behind why he fell." Cocking his brow at Roc, the disbelief on his brethren's face grated his nerves. "What makes you think he isn't worthy of trusting? Have you ever met him?"

"Hell no, he was banished before my time. He can't be trusted, he's a Fallen!"

"He's a Watcher now, appointed by God. Until you know a person, don't judge them." Slamming the lid of his laptop down, the cells in his body vibrated, seething in frustration as he pushed off from the desk.

"All right, girls, can we kiss and make up now? Roc, cut the shit. If Cassiel believes him, then I say we see where this leads us. What else can we do?" Am's voice sliced through the tension, bleeding Cassiel's anger, but he refused to budge on the topic. "Girls, I said kiss and make up."

"Dude, I'm only busting your nuts. Seriously, relax before your perfect complexion starts to wrinkle." Scrubbing back his mohawk, the shining green tips made a stark contrast to his electric blue eyes, which flashed with lightning strikes. He exuded a look of menace, and he relished each second of it.

Turning back to Amitiel, Cassiel's voice dropped low and warned, "I think we need to bring Focalor up here for a little first-hand intel."

"I agree. Send for him ASAP. If there's something else working against us here, we need to be prepared, to expect any and all threats to be directed toward Remi's charge. Ezekiel, I want you to go down there and get him. Drag him back up here by force if need be," she barked out her orders, and the weight of what was coming suffocated the air around them.

"What if he refuses?" Ezekiel stared down at her

through the furrow of his brows. His cold, calculating stare penetrated the room like ice as the edge of his words cracked the air with the whip of his tongue.

"I don't care what you have to do, get him back up pronto. There's more at stake here than an accident-prone Darkling. Got it?"

"Yes." Pulling himself from the leather wingback chair, Ezekiel nodded to her command.

"Remember," he paused, barely glancing over his rigid shoulder at Amitiel, "whatever it takes to get him back up here."

Nodding in reply to her request, he let her know he would follow through like the soldier he was. "Yes, Amitiel. I understand." A cold rush of wind followed behind him, swallowing the room with its icy caress, breaking only when the ornately carved door shut behind him.

"Life of the party, isn't he?" Blowing out a ripe curse, Roc's harsh laugh barked out like nails on a chalkboard as he sidled over to the couch, and plopped down into the supple leather cushions. The possibility of a new threat had him keyed up and ready to go into search and destroy mode. Tapping his fingers along the long line of his thighs, the coiling of his muscles visibly bounced in anticipation. "So what do we do now, boss lady?"

"Nothing, Roc. We wait and do more research. Find out how reliable Focalor's information is and go from there. However, I will say this ... if there is a threat against Remi's charge, then we can assume whatever is trying to get to her may find their way to the other Darklings. I think we need to be prepared for all possibilities at this point."

"How can you be so sure there are other Darklings

out there? I mean, Remi's charge is the first one we've known about in nearly what … a thousand years?"

Kakabel swung her silver locks over her shoulder as she idly flipped the pages of the last edition of Vanity Fair. "Well, we can't assume anything. Nevertheless, I think it's safe to presume where there's one Darkling there will be more. It's history repeating itself."

"They don't happen randomly, Roc. If she's the first, Bels is right, there will be more, but we won't know anything for sure until she transitions. The big boss knew about her, but hasn't said anything about more." Concern etched across Amitiel's face. Cassiel had served alongside Am during the last uprising of Darklings. They were tumultuous times, when the war between good and evil was on the brink of tipping. "I think we're only seeing the beginning of this. I want everyone to get prepared for the rise of the Darklings. Cass, get Focalor up here now. I think we need to find out what he knows.

CHAPTER NINE

T he morning sunrays shot through Ferrian's head and a dull ache began to grow as she kept walking toward her neighborhood. Rounding the corner, the lingering feeling of being watched crawled up her spine. Her back twitched and mildly burned where the lumps resided alongside her shoulder blades. Squinting her eyes against the rising sun, she scanned the road all around her. It wasn't the comfortable eyes she had grown accustom to watching her. No, these held an air of menace. The tingling sensation that she needed to book it out of there sang down her spine. She walked faster, glancing behind every dozen paces. Her mind flinted over images of a black metal beast screaming after her, as glass shattered all around her.

"Shit!" She hated seeing these visions. The stronger they were, the more probable it was to happen. Palming her pocketknife, she convinced herself that whatever was coming, she would face it head on. She may have been a victim to life's circumstances, but she was not a victim.

Holding her breath as she passed the alleyway her last attacker had stormed from, the stare Ferrian shot down the darkened path only showed a few overstuffed dumpsters teeming with city rats. She was a couple of blocks away from her apartment, and the pounding in her head increased with each step. She sucked in a sharp breath, as her vision began the wavy vertigo dance. Her silent warning in her nervous system kicked up higher, the farther she lumbered on.

Each person she passed was a potential threat, life had taught her as much. Clutching her pocketknife tighter, and curling into herself, Ferrian tried not to draw attention as she sped up. Her heart raced at the unseen threat and anxiety rippled through her body. If she could only make it the last two blocks, then she could shield herself from the world and sink into the abyss of her physical pain.

"What's the matter, Aingeal?" Remi's gaze followed her every step, watching her coil inside of her hoodie. His hair stood up on end, sensing something wasn't right. He had been trying to keep his distance; only popping in at random times to check in on Ferrian. It had been almost a week since he had spoken to her last … more like she knew he was talking to her. She had no knowledge of his silent intervals of watching Ferrian sleep, whispering words of comfort that fell on slumbering ears. Remi never left her alone. He couldn't. The strange tingle pulling him back for more was unexplainable. He couldn't remember ever feeling the need to protect a mortal, the way he did over Ferrian. He didn't want to care about her, and tried to break his fascination with her. She was his charge and this was his job. Yet, he couldn't help but feel the overwhelming need to curl up beside her each time she coiled into a tight fetal position, wrapping her arm over her head. It was the same thing each time he watched her sleep. One arm covering her, the other gripping a small pocketknife for dear life.

Shaking his head, remorse washed over him like a tidal wave. And seeing her on edge now was another punch to the face. He'd kept his distance and it had cost her so much over the years, and yielding to the commands of others instead of doing what was in his nature to do was boiling his blood. "Damn it, why can't I take her away until she transitions?"

"Because you were sent here to watch over her. Nothing more," Ezekiel snapped at him, like he was disciplining a disobedient child. The chill of his presence made the cool morning air feel as if winter had decided to show earlier than normal. "You need to detach yourself from your charge."

Yeah, that's not happening anytime soon.

"Easy for you to say, you haven't seen what I have. I've kept my distance for far too long, and look what's happened to her!" He spun around to face Z, matching heated stares. This was something he wasn't going to back down on, and no amount of convincing was going to change it. "Don't you see what she's become? She isolates herself from the world, and refuses to trust anyone. I can't honestly say I blame her. She screams from nightmares nearly every time she sleeps, when she actually sleeps that is. So excuse the hell out of me for being a little overprotective of my charge. She's been through more than any one being I've ever known yet she's still standing." A ripple of anger prick at his gut.

"Exactly! She's still standing, Remiel. You know as well as I do you can't interfere."

Tilting his chin over his shoulder, Remi arched his inky brow at the steely gaze of sea green eyes staring back at him. "How can you be so callous? And why are you here anyway … to bust my balls?"

"No," Z said crisply, sending out another wave of arctic wind. "Amitiel is requesting you Realmside. There's a matter which requires *all of us*."

He knew Amitiel could be a bitch at the best of times, but this sounded heavy. Especially with the weight of it coming from Ezekiel's mouth. "What do you mean?" he asked, spinning around.

"Am will explain at the meeting. I was sent to bring you back."

"Man, don't you have a lighter side to your demeanor? What could be so damn important?"

Z fixated a deadly glare on Remi. "Like I said, she'll explain."

Huffing out a curse, Remi turned back around to see Ferrian one more time. His breath caught the second he found her and watched as a black Dodge Charger drove straight into her, launching her over the hood.

"Shit!" His eyes grew wide with panic and he hurled himself over to her, catching Ferrian before her slender body slammed against the pavement. He didn't have a chance to glance down at her bloodied face and assess the damage before the Charger slammed on the brakes and the driver cranked it in reverse, aiming straight for her once again.

Pulling Ferrian against his chest, his heart raced as Remi shot straight up into the air, missing the tail end by a few feet. "Z!" he roared, landing on the iron fire escape outside of the apartment building.

"Got it!"

Storming over to the car, Ezekiel slammed his fists down hard on the hood, kicking the rear end off the ground, and grunted a bitter laugh when the car flipped right up and over his head. A pair of black, soulless eyes stared back at him, as a jagged set of teeth snarled and cursed. "Shit. It's a Hellistic demon!" It wasn't the first time he had seen one, but it had been centuries since he'd tangled with one. "Get her out of here, Remi!"

Tossing the car on its side, Ezekiel ripped the door free from it dented hinges and fisted the demon, ripping it out of the mangled car. "Who sent you?" When no answer came, Z gripped its throat. "I asked you a question, demon."

"Screw you."

Ezekiel stared down at the demon through lowered brows. His hands pulsated, glowing from a surge of energy running down to his fingertips, itching to destroy what was in front of him. "Guess your master didn't tell you about me. I'm the one angel you shouldn't mess with."

"Why don't you go flutter away and mind your own business, bitch."

"How about you play nice, before I—" Talk was cheap. Z smiled and decided he'd let his gift speak for itself. "Never mind." Slamming both hands around the demon's throat, the male's eyes bulged out as he twisted his mangled limbs to pry Z's hands away.

Firing up his gift, Ezekiel transformed the demon,

draining him of his subservience to his master. It would only be temporary, but it would be enough time to find out who was behind the attack. An ominous yellow glow surrounded the demon as he writhed and screamed like a banshee. "Go on, boy, sing for me."

CHAPTER TEN

"**W**ake up, Aingeal, come on, wake up for me!" She hung lifeless in his arms as Remi dematerialized from the fire escape overlooking the destroyed Dodge. It would only take seconds to reach her apartment, but each passing moment seemed like an eternity as precious life drained from her cooling body. His heart was thundering like a train speeding out of control as they materialized in Ferrian's bedroom. He mentally commanded the shower to turn on, and plugged the tub. She wouldn't have the energy to stand, let alone lift her head. The idea he had to take care of her like this—so intimately—should've warmed him, but it didn't.

His eyes scoured the curves of her battered body, examining the damage thoroughly. *Chrissake, how can I protect her when I keep getting called back up Realmside?* The rhythm of her pulse weakened with each passing minute. "Come on, babygirl, wake up for me."

The shallow hints of breathing barely escaped her blood-rimmed lips. Carefully, he laid her down on her bed and began to peel off her hoodie and boots. His hands shook, surveying the damage. There wasn't an inch of her absent of injury. Forcing himself to concentrate, Remi tried to steady his hands enough to fire up his healing ability.

Ferrian didn't move, nor flutter in response to his voice. Her delicate ivory skin was paling rapidly as more blood leaked from gashes. Smoothing back her blood-soaked hair, anger coiled deep inside of him, right beside the fear of losing Ferrian rooting itself in his gut.

"M'aingeal, please, wake for me." There was no hiding the edge of desperation in his voice as he placed one hand on her forehead and the other on her shin. Envisioning each broken bone and torn muscle in Ferrian's rumpled body; he ignited his healing ability, letting it flow fiercely through his hands. The swell of heat and light exploding from his palms shook the bed from the force. The radiance of his gift encapsulated her, casting a silvery glow around the small room.

The more he poured his healing inside of her body, the faster the gnashes knitted back together and bones mended as muscles stitched themselves up. The longer he tried to infiltrate her mind, and wake her, the more irritation rode him. He had tried multiple ways to gain access to help her, but he couldn't reach her inner sanctum. Ferrian was lost to the abyss of her nightmares, and he sensed she was reliving the accident in a hellish, ongoing movie reel. The best he could hope for was entering her dream-state and convincing her to wake up. It was a long shot, but he was running out of options.

Biting back a few dozen curses with the passing minutes, his stomach twisted into a pretzel, praying she would open her eyes. Her breathing would slowly return to normal, only to spike up with shuddering silent screams.

"Ferrian! Ferrian, can you hear me? It's Remi, please ... wake up, Aingeal." Hope tied a fierce knot in his gut as he contemplated what he wanted to do and what he should do. "You're stronger than this. I know you are. Wake for me," his quivering lips whispered against the curve of her ear, but she didn't respond. "God, I'm so sorry. I should've protected you better."

Resting back on his haunches, he laid his palm over her forehead. The chill of her sallow skin conflicted with his warmth. Still, she didn't move. Closing his eyes, he forced his mind to calm before entering hers. Sucking in a deep breath, Remi let his mind reach out to hers. Slowly the familiar scene opened up for him; the moment she flipped over the top of the black metal beast vying for her. He tried to run for her, but he couldn't. Remi was a figment in her dream. The crushing scene wasn't any easier to see the second time around, or the third. It was one thing to watch a mortal's dreams as a third party, but he needed to get inside the abyss of her mind, to see and feel everything she did.

Delving deeper into her subconscious, Remi slipped past her barriers and entered a deeper hole of her mind. The scene became more gruesome as he observed and studied each and every second. The hammering hit of the car nearly knocked the breath from his lips as the world spun out of control, and he glanced back involuntarily to see what she was seeing. *Oh my god!* Ferrian had seen him running toward her. Anger and fear stained his face as he pulled her into his arms carefully, calling to her to stay with him. Seeing through her eyes in her hazy vision, the dark-haired man barely registered, but she curled subtly into his warmth before the darkness consumed her. Remi's heart was fluttering wildly behind his sternum. *Wait, it's not my heart, it's hers.* His chest grew tight as he watched her mind flip back to the start of the nightmare reel.

"Ferrian ..." he murmured as the memory replayed again. Remi could only hope she'd snap out of it soon and return to him. A fresh wave of ire rolled through him as he tried to pick apart every detail of the scene. This time he saw the way her muscles twitched as she slightly turned her head back, as if she somehow knew the car was gunning for her.

No way. This isn't possible. She sensed it! Holy shit, she knew it was coming after her. Sure, some mortals were blessed with gifts of clairvoyance, or high functioning intuition. Remi wasn't convinced it was either of those things. The buzzing sensation in her body was reacting like an internal warning system.

There was no mistaking it was a Hellistic demon going after her. The rancid scent of brimstone and sulfur wafted through the air. Why hadn't he noticed it before, when this was happening? The hollow black eyes staring back at her, raged with hatred. The throttle of the engine revving lifted the front end up, screamed of its intentions.

The hit was direct and meant to kill as her body torque and twisted, flipping over the hood and roof of the car. The muscles in his body coiled to lunge for her again, catching Ferrian before her body came close to slamming down onto the unforgiving pavement. Then again, he already was there. Even in her obscure memory, she remembered someone catching her, holding her close.

Her eyes glanced back to him, and a glimmer sparked in her face. The fluttering of her eyes as she tried to focus on to him stopped his heart and stole his breath. "Impossible." Had she seen him, was it possible she knew he was there? If only he could break through and help her to wake up, then maybe she could fill in the answers to his questions. "Ferrian! Ferrian, wake up. Wake up now," he screamed, pounding his fist against the invisible wall.

But he was too late. The scene began over again as she hit the roof, and then the dream strangely morphed into somewhere else. The dark place where life died and hell trapped her with a crushing vice, dragging her down into the cold, black recesses of her mind. "Oh shit. No, no, no! Ferrian, wake up! You need to wake up right now. Please, Ferrian, open your eyes!"

He knew where this was going, and it sent a strike of terror down his spine. The air around him changed. Mildew scented the cold air. Concrete walls surrounded them from corner to corner around the circumference of the room. He was standing close enough to smell her fear mixing with fresh tears and blood. Remi knew this place well. It was the last place Ferrian had been confined and nearly beaten to death. Her small body was rumpled, curled into a ball, shivering. Her only source of water was a dirty dog bowl she could barely reach. A length of chain tied her ankle to the far wall, but she didn't try to move.

Swallowing against the rising bile in his throat, Remi reached out to her, and grabbed her hand to wrench her from this tortured memory. "Ferrian," he murmured softly, hoping she would glance up to him, "it's Remi." He tried to hide the tears threatening to spill. "Please, you need to let me help you. You're trapped in here. It's another bad dream. I need you to wake up, beautiful."

"Re-mi?" Her voice broke his name in two as she peeled one swollen eye open. "How … did you?"

"You need to wake up. This isn't real." Sucking in a sharp breath, he finally broke past the barrier of her mind's wall and gently brushed his fingers over her bloodied brow. "It's only a dream. You're home, in bed. I need you to wake up."

"I'm trapped." Was the only thing she could utter before she slipped back into the abyss of her subconscious.

"Shit!" There was no reaching her now. Fighting back the urge to yank her into his arms and break her free of this nightmare, Remi reluctantly pulled back. He couldn't free her from her mind no matter how much he wanted to. Biting back a bitter curse, he opened his eyes to the same bloodied beauty lying before him. She resembled the girl in the dream, but the edge of life had cut profoundly into the delicate features of Ferrian's face.

Mentally shutting off the water, he slowly undressed her and carefully peeled back the layers, hoping she would awaken to the unwanted attention and fight him off. Nothing. Her listless body laid there, striking his heart with more worry. Cautiously he pulled her camos down, careful to keep from exposing what she wouldn't want seen. Remi wanted to gaze at her in awe, and admire the natural beauty she was, but there was no hiding the guilt welling up for wishing it.

Guarding her privacy, he left her boy-short panties on, and then he gently lifted her back and shoulders to peel off her bloodstained black tank top, leaving her black bra in place. He hesitated as he reached for her leather cuffs, knowing she only took them off when she went into the shower, hiding the ugly secret hidden under them. His fingers trembled as he popped each metal button from its groove. The stark reminder of how she ended up with them hit him like a wrecking ball.

Although covered in blood, the raised welts pierced through as the jagged marks ran up and down the length of her body. Twisting in odd slices as bitter stains of her up-bringing, but he didn't see them. His eyes saw past them and to the magnificence of who she was. The woman she hid beneath the layers. How she could consider herself a monster, he would never understand.

Slipping his thick arms under her limp body, he care-fully drew Ferrian to his chest, climbing to his feet. Her innocence covered her like a shroud, although life had seemed fit to torture her. Ferrian was who she was, even if she didn't understand who she truly was … yet.

She is going to hate me, hate everyone when she finds out. His stomach twisted at the thought of explaining not only what her existence meant to humankind, but also the purpose she still had to fulfill. The thought of telling her she had angel blood running through her veins and she was constantly being tested, and put through the worst atroci-ties to see if she chose the right path, made his insides coil, wanting to revolt. Yep, she was going to hate him when she found out that God needed her to go through all this to show humanity that anyone can choose the right path.

If she chose the right path, she would become more powerful and invincible than she could imagine. Even though her slender frame draped limply in his arms, she was every bit the street warrior she portrayed. Glorious and fierce, her true nature was hidden behind the flesh of a being who understood the human condition. A niggling worry gnawed at the back of his mind. What if she chose the wrong path and failed the final test? Shoving the thought aside, he refused to entertain the notion. *There's no way she's turning evil. Not on my watch dammit.*

Slowly he lowered her body into the hot water, watching her face for any twitches or signs of awakening. The clear water quickly turned pink as the blood saturated it. Remi kept one hand firmly behind her neck to keep her from slipping under the water. Cupping handfuls of water in his other palm, he doused her hair and watched as the bloody drips of liquid trickled down her skin. It was only when he reached for the shampoo that he caught the glimpse of her eyes briefly opening, gazing at him. "Ferrian, are you okay?"

"Remi, I … I saw you there," she murmured as her eyes slid closed again.

Dammit!

"Come on, babygirl, don't do this. Open your eyes for me." His desperate pleas fell on deaf ears; his heart kick-started again. Brushing his knuckles over her cheek, he urged her awake again, but she didn't move. She laid there in the tainted liquid like a living statue. "Come on, Ferrian! Come back to me. Fight this! I know you can. You're so much stronger than you realize."

She had seen him. The thought raced around his mind as he poured a small dollop of shampoo atop her head. Her words sank in as he gently scrubbed her hair. *Could it have been a fluke?* It gnawed at him like a packed of hungry wolves. *She couldn't have seen me. She's trapped inside and probably a bit delusional right now. Come on, man, snap out of it.* A huff of breath blew from his lungs as he focused on stripping the last remnants of blood from her hair. Gently lowering her to the water to scrub the last of the suds out, his eyes traced the visible scars on her face, neck, and arms. He wondered how much more Ferrian could take before she finally snapped and tried to kill herself again. It had been the only time he was ever allowed to intervene. But it wasn't the first time he disobeyed the rules and stepped in, in the aftermath.

He sank into the shadows, and trained his sights on her as she paced the docks for hours. Pain masked her face. Her trembling hands balled into iron-tight fists with each new lap, when a sudden resolve blanketed her. In a blink of an eye, she turned around to walk back to her apartment. He hoped she'd found some relief from her restless state. Then again, after surviving another attack, he wouldn't have been surprised if she lashed out violently and sought retribution from the scum who had trapped her in the basement. Chained to the wall, using her for their pleasure any way they saw fit.

Two years had passed since he was forced to sit idle, and watched what they did to her, until they finally tossed her battered and violently sexually assaulted body into a dumpster, leaving her to die. Remi had pulled her from the dumpster, damning humanity for allowing such things to happen. It had been the turning point in her psyche when death seemed like a better option.

He followed closely behind her that night as she made her way back to the apartment; her face grew more stoic by the minute, and fear tickled his gut. Something was off, way off. If only he could've told Ferrian he had dealt with those terrible creatures and they would never again see

the light of day. He might not have been allowed to interfere with what was happening to her before, but it didn't
stop him from taking revenge for her.

The problem wasn't merely he had destroyed the
males. Rather, he had enjoyed doing it. He could admit to
himself, and eventually to Roc, how he relished tearing all
three of the males' limbs from bloody limb apart, and leaving them screaming as the hungry mouths of Colorado's
finest wildlife crept up on their freshly spilt blood.

The sight of her standing over the bathroom sink—
slicing her wrists, as hatred wept from her eyes—was an
image which nearly broke him completely, and would forever be stained into his memory. She was willing to end
her life to save herself. Even as she cringed at her weakness for taking the easy way out, Remi watched horrified
as she methodically sliced down her other wrist. A small
hiss slipped past her lips as she closed her eyes, and her
blood flowed freely down to the tiled floor.

He couldn't blame her for wanting to get out of life,
but dammit, he couldn't let her leave it like this. She was
too important, and he wasn't the only one who knew this
as a buzzing text came through, demanding him to step in
and save her. The gashes were flowing quickly as pools of
red liquid covered the floor around her. Her eyes rolled
back into her skull and finally fluttered closed, as her skin
grew paler. Remi listened to her heart slowing as he materialized next to her in the tiny bathroom.

"Hang on, Aingeal, I can't let you die. You're meant
to do great things." Firing up his healing ability, he sealed
her wounds, knitting back together muscles, tendons, and
skin. She had fallen unconscious, and he figured it was for
the best. The dark shadows around her eyes were far too

deep set. She needed sleep, and he feared it would consume her for hours in mentally torturous cycles.

Pulling her into his arms, surprised by her natural fragrance, the sweet scent of her blood hit him. There wasn't a hint of the metallic coppery tones to it. He cursed himself when he glanced back down at the wounds, which though healed, glowed red like a newly healed scar. He couldn't understand why they didn't disappear completely. "What the hell?" Sure, he had healed her, he could clearly see it, but they were another set of scars she would have to bear for the rest of her life.

CHAPTER ELEVEN

The memory didn't only scar her, but burned a hole in his heart each time he saw her finger trace over the red marks left behind. His hands shook as he reached for the washcloth and soap. Ferrian had never lost the shadows from under her eyes, and even in her sleep, the stark contrast to her ivory skin made the point all the more obvious.

Lifting her back from the water, he admired the way the water sluiced down her skin. Gently holding her in his other arm, he scrubbed the soap over the cloth, ready to wash away the dirt and bloodstains from her skin. Gingerly he stroked the length of her back with the soapy cloth. Slowly and surely, his large palms covered most of her skin with each pass. His eyes danced over the anchors of her shoulder blades, the subtle bumps of her future trembled against his touch as a small mew spilled from her lips. His chest tightened as he listened for another sound, hoping she was finally coming around. Nothing.

"Ferrian." Was he hearing things, or was his mind playing tricks on him? He couldn't be sure.

The moment passed, and he made another long, slow

stroke down the length of her back. Coming back up with more warm water, he softly caressed the other bump and another mew littered the air. *What the?* Unknowing of what had caused the reaction he brushed the knuckles down her shoulders, then over the anchor spot. An erotic purr bubbled up from her chest, making his cock jump excitedly.

She still didn't move. *What the hell is going on? Did I really hear her purr from touching her?* He lowered her back, hoping this time Ferrian had awoken to validate what he'd heard. Her eyes remained shut, locked in her nightmares and unmoving as if she were practicing for her coffin. His lungs burned for oxygen as he waited to hear another sign she was coming around.

What the hell is going on? I know what I heard. She moaned when I touched her. But was she moaning because I touched her, or was she crying out from her dream? That was definitely not a scream, but it sounded sexy as hell though. Nothing made sense.

Blowing out a heavy exhale, Remi resumed washing away the rest of the blood. Ferrian's honey-jasmine scent assaulted his nostrils. Patting the cloth lightly across her face, wiping away the last remnants of blood from her head wound, he wondered what it would be like to wake up beside her, her face glowing with satiated bliss after a night of making love. *Dangerous thinking, man. Cut it out.*

Resting her head back on his arm, Remi cautiously slid down to her chest and abdomen. Taking painstaking care not to endanger her covered privacy, he wiped away the streaks of dried blood. "I'm so sorry, Aingeal, for not … God, for all you've had to endure." Fury and sorrow soaked into his mind as his eyes stroked the delicate curves of her face. "I wish I could go back in time and change it all. I don't expect you to, but I hope someday you'll be able to forgive me." Standing on the edge of sanity, he wanted to rip apart each person who had hurt her; shred every moment that had caused Ferrian to turn into the silent warrior she had become.

He had always done his duty. Whatever God wanted done, he did without question. But now, as he held Ferrian's limp body in his arms, he couldn't understand why someone as pure and innocent as she should have to fight her way through life, attack after vicious attack. Maybe it would've been more merciful to let her die. Yet he had listened to the powers above. He was forced to save her, only to have her suffer more violence, and all because God needed her to. *Fucking great! Sorry, boss, but you suck sometimes.*

Neither thought held any weight anymore; he'd saved her, even if Ferrian hadn't wanted to be saved. How she hadn't turned yet was a mystery to him. He had witnessed firsthand how easily the soul of man can change for less reasons and become an unbearable evil unto mankind.

She was altogether different. There was no denying it. How could he? From birth she had fought for her life, each day became a struggle to survive. From the first time he'd held her as an innocent baby in his arms, taking her away from the violence left behind thanks to her father, he had known she was going to change the world. Elsa had given her life to protect Ferrian, and she was right to. He would make sure to tell Ferrian of her mother's sacrifice. *If only she knew how much she resembled her mother.*

The water began to cool as he reached for the drain plug. Gently resting her against the tub wall, he reached over for the towel and waited as the water disappeared down the drain, before covering her with the towel. *Let's get you dried off and into bed.* He could only hope she wouldn't remember him undressing her and bathing her. Though he wished she would open her eyes and smile, welcome his touch as he thumbed over her cheek, he knew better. None of this would be welcomed. He slowly pulled her to his chest and inhaled the scent of her shampoo wafting from her hair. Staring down at her face, he briefly envisioned a life where they were free to be together. Where Ferrian had no fear of his touch, let alone his presence. It was a thought he would have to stuff back into the 'never gonna happen' drawer and lock it away. Fitting her perfectly pressed against his chest, Remi carried her to the bed as though she were weightless in his arms and eased her down.

He could only imagine what she would feel like naked with her arms wrapped around him, as he carried her across his immense bedroom and laid her down on his heavenly soft mattress. The idea of her raven hair splayed out like a dark halo around her head as she sprawled out on his silver sheets, and the golden rays of sunlight dancing over her sinuous body as she urged him down on her, had his blood coursing straight for his shaft. Imagining her coaxing him between her thighs split wide for him, ready to cradle the weight of his hips, was too much to handle. His breath shuddered harder the longer he fed into his fantasy.

Tamping down his growing desire, he slid to the floor and tried to bring his erection to heel. It was a useless effort as he stroked the soft sinews of her neck. She was an electric shock bringing him back to life. Blotting her skin with the towel, his couldn't help but trace each scar with his eyes, surprised to see an intricate pattern, and what appeared to be the word *'Darkling'*. Gasping, he reared back and shoved his hand in his pocket to pull free his phone and capture a picture of what he was seeing. *Fuck no!* It couldn't be purely coincidental he decided, studying her arm closely. His fingers grazed over the pattern only to confirm to himself that he wasn't crazy. She had been marked! All this time and each cut she sustained, it had been to alert others of what she was. "I can't believe this!" His chest tightened. He didn't want to believe it, but it was as if someone had covered her in a bright red tape, alerting all demons to find her as she made her way through life.

Scrolling through his phone he pulled up Am's number and sent the picture with a message of what he saw. Next call he had to make was to Ezekiel. Shaking his head, Remi prayed he wouldn't be the only one seeing things. "Z, I need you to get over here, stat! Shit turned critical."

Easing over the demon corpse, Ezekiel swallowed the Hellistic soul before it had the chance to return to its master. It hadn't taken much to convince the demon to talk, once he'd pulled the veil of subservience out of him. "JesusHChirst!" Scrubbing his hand through his long blond hair, he could feel the evil from the dead demon swimming in his gut like battery acid. Making a meal out of dead demon souls wasn't his favorite part of the job, but it gave him an advantage no other angel possessed … the ability to travel through the Underworld without being seen if he so chose.

He palmed his phone when it vibrated. *What now?* "Yeah?" he barked, waiting impatiently for Remi to start talking. "I don't got all day. What do you want?"

"I need you to come validate something for me."

"Like what? You're skipping out on your other responsibilities lately. You're not a one man army, Remiel."

"Z, this is serious. It's Ferrian … she has these markings on her, I need you to tell me if you see what I do."

The rushed request bored him to tears, but given the new information the demon had unwillingly offered, he nodded his head and agreed. "Yeah, man, I'll be right over. Found out some interesting news you're going to want to hear."

"What is it?"

"I'll explain it when I get there."

"Sure, whatever. Just get your ass over here, I need a second set of eyes."

Clicking the phone off, Ezekiel let his magnificent iridescent wings unfurl, spreading wide as he stretched his shoulders and back. Z bounded to the sky, the feel of the wind through his wings was the only gentle feeling he welcomed in his life, and he relished it as he flew faster than the speed of light to Ferrian's apartment.

CHAPTER TWELVE

"They've marked her. Those sons of bitches marked her! How in the hell did anyone know what she was?" Remi paced the length of the roof, considering what Ezekiel had said to him. The more he thought about it, the harder it was to keep his feelings in check. Anger boiled deep inside as he turned for another lap.

"What about the Darkling? Does she have any idea about any of this?" Stepping in the path of Remi's course, arms folded tightly over his chest, Ezekiel stopped him abruptly in his tracks. "Does she know what she is yet?"

He shook his head in reply; she had no knowledge of it, let alone believed in angels. "No. As far as she's concerned, Ferrian believes she's cursed. I don't know how much more she'll survive though. I can't reach her mind to wake her. She's shut down from the inside out."

"Did you try healing her?"

Cocking a sardonic brow at Ezekiel, he allowed the 'are you kidding me' look to pour out his frustration. "What the hell do you think? Come on, you know better. I pumped everything I had into her and nothing. She didn't even flinch. Although …." Turning away, he realized he wasn't sure how much information he should divulge to his brethren. Considering him with a wary eye, Remi steeled himself to ask about Ferrian's reaction to her soft anchors being touched. "Did you ever come across a Darkling who reacted to their …" Blowing out a ripe curse, he tightened his lips and decided it sounded too crazy to keep going with his question. "Never mind. It's nothing."

"Are you asking me if any of my charges purred when their wings were touched, before they popped out?"

Yes! That's exactly what I wanted to know. His eyes grew wide as he stared back at Ezekiel. "Yeah, I guess I am."

"Only one … and I recommend you keep your distance. Remember its business, don't make it personal." Shooting him an arctic glare, his disapproval covered Remi with a silent warning. "I'll give you five minutes to check on your charge, then we head back Realmside. Got it? Am and the others need to know what's going on. Maybe with the information Cassiel has, we can figure this out."

Nodding reluctantly, he slipped back into the apartment to check on Ferrian. She hadn't moved a muscle, remaining more like a statue frozen in time; her breath was barely raising her chest. Lifting her slender hand to his lips, he brushed them over, kissing each one of her fingers before smoothing her hand along his cheek. *'Business, not personal.'* Ezekiel's words cut him like a rusty knife, leaving the residual sting long after he left. How could she not be personal? He knew he shouldn't care for her as much as he did, but how couldn't he? He had seen her at her worst, beat down and bloodied, from things, which would've destroyed any normal person. She lived when others would've died, and still she showed compassion to the beings no one else saw.

In the silent moments of daybreak, when Ferrian walked to the bus stop, he watched as the same raggedy skinny orange cat followed her, callously curling around her leg, begging for attention. And each time she reached down to pet him, offering him love when no one else would bother. After a few days of the same routine, he observed in amazement as she reached in her pocket and pulled out a can of cat food. Since then, she had made a friend for life with a simple gesture for a famishing soul. She was half-starved herself, but the cat must have given her something no else could. After that day, he imbued the little beast with immortality; making him Ferrian's other guardian. Animals' souls are pure; charging them with guardian-ships had become a common occurrence for angels.

Stroking her hair lightly, laughing to himself, Remi thought about all of the little details he had overlooked about Ferrian before. *M'aingeal, please know I will always be with you. It doesn't matter which way you turn.*

A sharp buzzing in his pocket broke his moment of peace, and he quickly palmed his phone. "I'm coming," he snapped, and cut off the call. He hated to leave her alone and vulnerable, but so much needed to be said to Am and the brethren.

Kissing her forehead, he whispered his promise to return soon, then mentally commanded all locks to shift into place and left his own alarm there to warn him if any intruders came within walking distance of her building. He had no idea how long she would stay in her coma, but leaving her without any protection scared the hell out of him. She was utterly defenseless in her current state, and spending any longer than necessary Realmside was out of the question.

"Are you friggin' kidding me? You expect us to sit idle while those pricks are out there? Oh hell no!" Roc's voice bellowed loudly as Remi stalked into the library.

"Roc, it's not the brightest idea to walk into the Underworld and start spraying DMT juiced bullets everywhere, when we don't have the full intel on what's going on. Get your gun out of your ass before you blow your head off." Shaking his head, Ezekiel shot Remi an annoyed stare through lowered brows. "About time."

And there it was, his famous ice cold welcome. Sinking down into the leather couch, he scanned the room, eyeing each one of the brethren, waiting for someone to fill him in. "So, what's the deal?" His teeth were on edge as the silence continued for a moment longer. "Jesus, spit it out already!"

Kakabel sank down on her hunches, as the look of resolve to catch him up to speed weighed heavily on her shoulders. "Remi, there's a problem."

"What? What's going on? Does this have anything to do with the picture I sent?"

Her silver eyes were soft, but Remi saw the apprehension she was trying to hide. *Oh shit ... whatever it is, it's fucking bad.* "We think it does, yes. But we're waiting to hear back from a Watcher. Ezekiel informed us your charge has fallen into a coma."

"Yeah. She took a helluva hit tonight."

Z stepped up, his arms crossed over his broad chest,

and his head dipped low. "We think the Hellistic demon was sent to kill her. Seems Lucifer might be behind the attack." His sharp voice cut like a knife.

Jumping out of his seat, the hot sting of Remi's blood pulsing with fury again sang through his veins. His muscles twitched to hurl bodies into brick walls and acid leaked into every word with ravenous venom. "I'm going to track down that asshole and make sure he gets a true taste of Hell before I kill him!"

"There's more," Cassiel interjected as Remi's pacing set an electric charge through the air. Tension wrapped around the brethren in thick ropes, setting everyone on edge. Eyes flashed from one to the other as they waited to see Remiel explode from Cassiel's news.

"What? Don't hold out on me, Cass, what is it?" His sole concern was Ferrian and keeping her alive. Marching right up to Cass, Remi leveled him with a challenging glare.

"Well, for starters, you were right. The markings on your charge, it's an old code for Hellistic demons to track down their prey."

Holy Mary mother of frigging Christ! Deep down, he already knew the truth, but hearing it confirmed spiked his blood pressure to stroking out levels.

"Wait a sec … so what you're saying is Rem-dog's Darkling is like a walking target? Dude, talk about a shitty deal!" Scrubbing his mohawk back, Roc lost all rebellious façade as Cassiel continued.

"Yes, well from the research I've done, it's something Lucifer began back in the Dark Ages. Kind of like a beacon for the lowlifes to find their mark. And that's not the half of it."

"Wait, there's more? You're joking, right?" *Please tell me you're joking, because I'm about to tear down Heaven and Hell at this point if it means saving Ferrian.* His hands curled into bone-white fists, itching to strike anything in range.

Cassiel leaned against the desk, his sandy blond hair hanging in his face, hiding the concern Remi knew was in his eyes. "Sorry to say, but yes. The word I got is they use Daemons to replace humans to do this, and have been for quite some time. My guess is, since the day your charge was born they've been placed in the way to keep watch, so to speak, over her, just as you have been her guardian. And since they are half-humans, they are harder to track down. It would seem Satan has Lucifer running interference."

He wasn't sure if the universe had been struck with an earthquake hitting one hundred on the Richter scale, or if he was about to have a heart attack. *How could I have not known? All this time, it was right in front of me, and I never frigging knew!*

"Think about it. If you wanted to mark a Darkling, but you couldn't do it yourself, how would you go about marking your target?" The room fell deadly silent as each member stared at the other in dark realization of this news.

"Do you think there are more Darklings out there?" Kakabel slipped past Remi and Roc to search Cassiel's sullen stare. "Cass, do you think there are others out there?" Cupping his cheeks, she forced Cassiel to look into her eyes. A small gasp burst from her mouth. "You do, don't you?"

"Yes. I think she is in fact the key to unlocking the rest of them. This is only the beginning and," turning his gaze back to Remi, the weight of his words rested heavily on everyone's shoulders, "she will be Satan's downfall, unless he kills her first. Remi, given light to this new information, she is more important than we originally thought. Until we get things figured out, Am, I think Remi should be on charge duty twenty-four-seven."

His heart fell into his stomach when the news struck him harder than a wrecking-ball.

"Remi, there's more."

"You've got to be kidding me? Cassiel, how many more bombs are you planning on dropping here, because I have to tell you, I'm about to hit the damn wall right about now."

"I know. I'm sorry, brother. I'm letting you know, Focalor is a Watcher now. He's been busy keeping an eye on the dark side for me ... well us, and emailed recently stating there's been a lot of activity. Lucifer has been keeping the demons busy and there's been some talk about building an army. He hasn't heard much in the way of Darklings, but given how secretive Xaphan has been, and Naaman has gone into hiding, Focalor thinks we have an uprising to worry about. He'll be here later to explain more."

"Good. Find out every fucking thing you can. I'll be damned if she turns to a goddamned Daemon!" Crushing his fists down on the mahogany desk, Remi bit out each word with careful deliberation. "Get Focalor up here stat! Saddle up, boys, seems like we have some demon hunting to discuss." He had no idea how he would protect Ferrian should war break out, but one thing was for sure, he'd die trying.

CHAPTER THIRTEEN

Kakabel couldn't bear the rabid strain Focalor's arrival had brought. From the moment he walked in, Roc and Z had made like bookends, surrounding the Watcher as he stalked into the library. Tensions ran high as each Guardian took turns grilling him for more details. The only new information they had ascertained was Ferrian's death would bring about the rising of the Army of the Undead. One master would control Darklings, who are neither Daemons, nor earthbound angels who are dead to the world. Ferrian was the key to crippling destruction or a revelation for good. Yet she was still a mere human, fragile and trapped by her own mind. A living, breathing prisoner of her past, and Kakabel had no idea if this human would be strong enough to choose the right path.

Her silver eyes trailed down the length of Ferrian's arms, as she laid motionless on the bed. The jagged marks cutting into her ivory skin left encoded brands human eyes couldn't see. Her fingers idly traced the odd pattern. "You poor thing, I wish you hadn't lived this life. I wish you could have known some happiness."

"What are you doing?" The harsh voice startled her, and she snapped her head toward Remi's rigid stare. "Don't touch her! She doesn't like to be touched."

Throwing her hands up, she slowly moved away. "Sorry, I-I didn't know. I needed to feel the markings, is all."

"Why?" He considered her with a wary eye. "Why was it necessary for you to touch the markings? Did you learn anything new?"

Shaking her head, a long tendril of silver hair fell from her messy bun. "Cassiel was right. It was Daemons who caused them. It's like they were cut into her purposely to …"

"To what, Bels?" he pressed. "Damn it, Bels, what is it?"

"Nothing, never mind. Although, you should probably know there will be more unless Lucifer gets his hands on her."

"It'll never happen. I won't let it."

"Oh God, Remi, do you know what this means? Do you have any idea what will happen if all seven Darklings are found?"

"Yes, I know the prophecies." It was obvious he didn't care about the other six. To him they weren't Ferrian. "If all seven Darklings turn to the side of good, then Hell will fall into perpetual darkness. All Daemons and demons under Lucifer's rule will forfeit their existence, and Lucifer and the rest of the shitheads will fall under Satan's boot heel. They'll be trapped in Hell forever."

"Exactly! Satan can't step in, neither can God. However, he can use his second in command how he sees fit. Shit, what the hell are we going to do?" Kakabel's gentle silver stare considered Remi with a childlike innocence. The last thing she wanted was to see the world fall to ruin. As daughter of the moon and God, she feared for what was coming.

"We defeated them before. We'll do it again," he said flatly through gritted teeth.

"Remi, can I ask you something?" She arched a thin brow, knowing what she was about to ask wasn't going to sit well, let alone be easy to answer. "Did you know from the beginning what she was? I mean, did the boss man tell you?"

He stepped around her, closing the distance between him and Ferrian. Dropping down on his haunches, Bels couldn't avert her eyes. The care and compassion shining through her brethren both warmed her heart and sank it at the same time. The way his eyes locked upon Ferrian's furrowed brow, as his fingers thumbed over her skin, was a tenderness she had never seen from him before. "Remi?"

"Yes. I knew." An audible gasp popped from her lips, but it didn't seem to faze him as he settled next to Ferrian. "You should go back Realmside. I've got this."

She stood over him as he told her the news. Although there had been much speculation about the purpose of Remi's charge, no one had known with certainty. Flashes of each one of her charges rolled through her mind as she tried to figure out if any had been keep in secret. She had had thousands of charges since the dawn of time, but she couldn't remember even once God asking her to keep a charge a secret. And here was Remi, all in the know, protecting the one human who could change the face of humanity ... forever.

She didn't bother to say a word when Remi told her

to leave. Glimpsing Ferrian once more, she saw the fate of humankind in the twisted expression of his Darkling. Bels dematerialized to the roof of Ferrian's apartment building. Realmside could handle things without her for a few hours. Remi had his hands full watching over his charge. Stalking around the edges of the rooftop, she watched and waited for any unwanted guests. Remi might not have wanted any help, but she didn't give a shit anymore. She was going to help him, even if he didn't know about it.

CHAPTER
FOURTEEN

The battle of her mind had finally ended when Ferrian forced her eyes to open. The golden streaks of sunlight sprayed across her room as she squinted from the brightness. A sudden flash of being hit by a ferocious black metal beast smacked the reality back into her, as she jolted from her bed. "No!" she screamed as breath caught tight in her chest.

Springing to her feet, she ran for the bathroom. *Whoa! Um, wait a minute ... something isn't right here. Why am I not in agony? I must still be dreaming. Or maybe I'm dead!* She was amazed at how easily her body reacted without the aches in her muscles and bones. The rush of the moment was short lived when she stopped short at the bathroom mirror. There were no bruises! Was it all a dream? It had to be, because she couldn't remember the last time she wore the color purple. *Oh shit, I really am dead.*

"Glad to see you're finally awake." Remi's deep voice vibrated through every muscle in her body. Her heart flipped over at the sound of his voice, plunging into the pit of her empty stomach. Spinning around to face him, her arms instinctively covered her exposed skin.

"How did you get in here?" Her words came out in a harsh, frantic demand. "Well?"

His eyes sparkled a brilliant blue, scanning her from head to toe as a soft smile spread across his face. "You were hit by a car. I found you lying on the pavement. So I brought you home." His long, angular frame leaned against the doorway between the kitchen and living space.

"Why didn't you bring me to the E.R.? Why bring me here? Thought you'd get lucky or something?" She knew it sounded bitter and nasty. A part of her wanted to rip out her tongue for sounding like such a bitch, considering he had been nothing but nice to her since the day they'd met. Regret skittered down her spine, but the tick in his jaw showed she had hit a nerve with him.

"No, I didn't think I'd get lucky. And I can heal you better than any doctor in a hospital can."

What the hell, was he mental? "What do you mean you can heal me?"

"I'm a healer. Natural medicine you'd call it." His words showed no inflection of lies as he followed her with pinpoint accuracy. This was twice now Remi had been at the right place at the right time.

"Why are you following me?"

"I think a little gratitude would be appropriate considering things," he shot back, crossing his massive arms over his chest defensively.

Yeah, he definitely wants something from me. The longer she stared at Remi, the more his picture perfect smile fell into a tight line.

"I could've let you die in the street, you know."

"Why didn't you?" Her eyes stayed locked on his.

Unflinching.

"You long for death?"

"What do you care what I long for?"

"Obviously I care. I stayed with you for over a week while you were unconscious."

"Holy shit—a week?" Shifting only slightly, Ferrian secured her arms more tightly around herself.

"Yes, more like nine days. You were in a coma." Her jaw nearly dropped to the floor when he answered her silent question. He quirked a small smile, as she tried to think back to the last thing she remembered. "Your mind has been running a marathon, why not give it a break and get something to eat?"

It was as if he knew what her body was thinking, when a loud growl erupted from her stomach agreeing with his suggestion. "I'm not hungry."

"Yes you are. Now sit, please. I was about to make some spaghetti." He turned to leave for the kitchen as she lowered her protective imaginary armor. The swath of soft fabric was odd to her as she looked down and noticed the lilac purple cotton shirt. She hadn't owned anything of color since she was a teenager.

"Why did you change me? And what is with the color?" The sound of boiling water and steam filtered through the small apartment.

"I didn't change you. My sister did."

Shit! He has a sister, and she's seen me naked, with all the scars? Oh. My. God. No one had seen her naked since the last attack, and even then, and they weren't beholden to her. "You brought your sister here?" She stared at him through incredulous eyes, her fear ratcheting up tighter. "How many others have seen my naked ass? Great.

Friggin' wonderful. Get out, pervert!"

"No one else saw you. I promise. As for my sister, she followed me here. She is also a healer of sorts. I promise you, she used discretion caring for you.

He didn't have to be a complete imbecile to sense Ferrian's panic attack kicking into high gear. The pitch of her voice rising higher has she spoke confirmed what he already knew. Stirring in the noodles, he casually peered over his shoulder at her once again. "Do you want alfredo or marinara sauce? I wasn't sure if and when you would wake up, so I stockpiled your kitchen." The blush on her cheeks deepened as she forced her jaw to close.

"Didn't I tell you to get out?" she asked, cocking a brow at him.

He couldn't stop the small smirk from lifting at the corner of his lips. He had found it quite endearing she was ordering him away, but damn him if he didn't love how much of her fiery spirit lit the fuse inside him.

"Yes. You did, but what kind of healer would I be if I didn't see you fed? Besides, I don't have anything better to do. Food will be ready in ten minutes."

"I'm not getting rid of you, am I?"

"Nope. Hope you like breadsticks."

"Oh shit!" She ran for her boots and hoodie, frantic energy rolling off her droves.

"What's wrong?"

"My job! If I've been out of it for as long as you say,

then I've probably been fired. I need to go talk to my boss. Explain what happened." Remi closed the distance between them in a couple of well-placed steps, as Ferrian fumbled around the room.

"It's all right. I already spoke to your boss. He says get some rest." Her mouth hung agape, staring back at him. "Please, don't get yourself all worked up. I don't need you freaking out and ass planting yourself."

"He knows? You spoke to him?" Considering this, she dropped her boots and glanced around the apartment. His eyes followed her, realizing what she was seeing. "You cleaned this shit hole? Why?"

"Because you couldn't … remember?" Tapping the side of his head, the obvious came to the forefront. "Ferrian, what do you remember about the accident?"

She sank down into the chair beside her bed, and the edges of her brows seemed to slam together when she tried to think back on it.

"Sorry, I guess I should give you some time, instead of hounding you with the details. My apologies, m'aingeal." He turned to head back into the kitchen; at least it's what he told his body to do. Yet, he couldn't dislodge his eyes from her face, as he watched her carefully move from one emotion to another.

"I could've sworn the maniac was aiming for me," she murmured. Her body slumped back into the chair as she inhaled another sharp breath. "I would swear he saw me there and purposely tried to run me over. Jesus, I sound like a frickin' looneytoon. Guess being accident prone has made me kind of paranoid."

Lowering down onto his haunches, Remi caught her eyes, locking her in. "What do you mean? You saw him aiming for you?" He had seen the apprehensiveness in Ferrian, in her dream, glancing back over her shoulder. He needed more information to go off of, and if she was willing to spill, then he would take it for what it was worth.

"Well, kind of. I don't remember the details too well, but I would swear he saw me. I mean, he had to have seen me, right? But why would someone purposely try to run over someone?"

"Don't doubt yourself." How much should he tell her? His insides itched to explain it all to her, but it would go against the rules. The same rules he was ready to wipe his ass with and flush down the damn toilet. "There are things out there we can't explain." Ferrian's heat radiated through his entire body as her breath caught. Like a magnet attracted to its mate, his hand caressed hers gently before he could realize what he was doing. The simple touch made her body flush, and inside his heart flipped over her reaction. It didn't last long. She jerked her hand away, tucking it between her arm and ribcage as she put up her guard once again. Except this time, she didn't turn away or run for the door, which was a good sign.

CHAPTER FIFTEEN

Winter had been fairly mild as far as snow was concerned, but the fierce wind bit into Ferrian's bones, as she huddled deeper into her black hoodie. The sun was at war with the moon, demanding to make an entrance as grey haze covered the dawn sky. "Guess it's too late to move to California, huh?" she scoffed, blowing a lungful of warm air into her cupped palms, surrounding her mouth.

"Here, this'll warm you up." Shoving a caramel hot chocolate into her hands, Remi shielded her from the next wind gust. "Damn, woman—" he smiled, and rubbed her arms briskly to ward off the cold. She returned a sheepish smile, as a swell of heat flooded her cheeks—"don't you have a warmer coat? No wonder you're freezing your ass off."

"Thanks for this." Since the hit and run a couple of months back, she found it easier to be with Remi the more he was around … and he always seemed to be around. She dared herself to admit he could be trusted as if he was a friend. *Almost.*

Though she knew little about him, and still hadn't met

this Good Samaritan sister of his, she was comforted to have him near. It had been years since she had spoken to anyone. His patience surprised her, especially when she refused to say anything. His kind words didn't falter even when she could see the frustration in his eyes.

The slow and cautious cloud of self-protection gradually lifted the more Remi was around. Relief washed over her knowing he hadn't tried to touch her deliberately, even when it appeared as though he was straining to keep himself in check. Although, there were times when their hands would brush against each other's without thought. And the heat rolling off him would warm her from the inside out. In those fleeting moments, she swore she sensed his heartbeat kicking up a notch. In truth, she couldn't be positive it wasn't her own. He incited a slow burn, which grew more intense by the day, and it scared the hell out of her.

A warm pool of wanting settled between her thighs at the idea of his skin touching hers. God, she wanted to know if his skin was as supple as it appeared to be. Did the rich, dark scent she loved to inhale until it burned her lungs come from him, or some expensive cologne? How badly she wanted to reach out and touch him; graze the delicious curve of his lips with her fingertips. Beating the thoughts back, she reminded herself it would remain her private fantasy.

"Are you ready to return home?" His angelic voice wrapped around her head, luring her like the ocean calling a sailor home. Her teeth chattering was answer enough, yet she bobbed her head and curled deeper into her hoodie.

"Either you let me buy you a new coat or I'm going to tuck you into me. If you haven't figured it out by now, I'm like a furnace." The sinister way he rolled his brows as his impish grin grew wide with the latter idea, had the swell of want swimming in tides in her belly. Without an argument, she tucked herself willingly into his body. She was too cold to feel how carefully Remi placed his arm around her back to pull her in closer. All she cared about was the magnificent heat radiating off him. He hadn't been kidding when he'd said he was a radiator, and she reveled in it on the long walk to the bus stop.

As they climbed aboard the city bus, he resumed warming her, cautiously rewrapping her in his arms and caressing her gently to warm her. Maybe it was a mistake, maybe he'd take it the wrong way, but she couldn't help but to sink deeper into him. *If I told you I could stay like this forever, would you think I'm a freak? Sinful and heavenly can't describe you.*

She inhaled his dark, spicy scent until the aroma nearly knocked her out from intoxication. It wasn't until she braved a glance up to see a pair of sparking blue eyes fringed in lush dark lashes staring back down at her, she saw something different about him. His gentle smile carried a promise of protection and kindness, things Ferrian had known little about, and longed to feel.

"Are you warm enough yet?" he whispered into her hair.

Was she warm enough? Well, yes, but strangely she didn't want to admit to it, least of all to him. She shook her head no and sagged into his arms. His welcoming embrace circled her tighter, and his big hands stroked her arms with the kind tenderness she had read about in romance novels. *This is not happening. I must be dreaming, but if I am, please God, don't wake me.* As her muscles de-thawed, all of her aches began to reappear. All except one … perhaps two. Pressing her shoulder blades harder against him, she realized she couldn't feel the familiar pain. There was no trace of the increasing discomfort, which surprised her, and at the same time she couldn't feel more grateful for the break.

"Are you okay?" The innocent concern pouring out of him milked her of her defensive energy. Staring back up at him, her half-lidded eyes grew wide. She didn't know what to say. *You bet your ass I am! This is the best I've felt since, oh I don't know when ...birth maybe. Keep doing what you're doing, and I won't be forced to tie your arms around me, k?*

"Um, yeah. I'm okay." She settled back into his warmth. The idea of the bus ride ending too soon, before she'd had her fill of Remi holding her, stung her the longer she dwelled on it. The city passed them by in waking life of morning traffic as she stared aimlessly out of the window until blackness surrounded her.

"Wake up, m'aingeal," a kind voice whispered in her ear, "we need to get off now. Unless you want to ride longer?"

"What? Where are we? Damn, did I fall asleep?" Stretching out all her achy limbs, she gazed outside the bus window and realized she had slept most of the way home. "Shit."

"Ummhmm, and here I thought a hot chocolate had enough caffeine to keep you up all day." He laughed, and damn if the sound of his voice wasn't sexier than Enigma's Mea Culpa.

"Funny." Climbing to her feet, a wave of panic shot through her skull like a warning siren, screaming to take cover. Her muscles froze in place as she caught sight of a city waste management truck, veering straight for them. "Remi!" she tried to yell, but her strangled voice barely carried as the shattering sounds of exploding glass and metal shrieking sang all around them.

A hard hit took her down, but she didn't land on metal. Bouncing off Remi's steely chest, he held her tightly, coiled in his thick arms, and shielded her from the splintering glass raining down. Her head swam as she glanced around, seeing the bus she was on split-in two, and the garbage truck smashed all to hell. Shaking her head to clear it out, the metallic scent of blood punching up her nostrils confirmed what she thought was pooling red puddles in the streets. The cries of the injured passengers, and pedestrians alike wailing for help rang in her ears, as she surveyed the area. Smoke oozed from the engines and the scent of fuel licked the wintry wind.

How did we end up out here? She caught her breath as she glanced down, and saw that his eyes were glued to her face, as if he was scanning her for injuries. "Remi! Are you hurt? Answer me, please!"

Snap out of it! Oh my god, he must be in shock. Think, Ferrian, think! Crushing her lips over his, Ferrian convinced herself Remi wouldn't want to feel her this close. Man was she wrong. She tested her welcome, sliding her tongue along the seam of his mouth, only to find he met her with an urgent kiss of his own. Her heart nearly exploded, as his hot tongue ravaged her mouth, then shirked away.

His panting breath swept across her face, but she couldn't tell if it was shock or disgust. "Are you okay?" he blurted out, his eyes unflinching from her eyes.

Damn, maybe I freaked him the out by kissing him.

The thought stung, but it was better to have a coherent Remi, than a comatose one.

"Yeah, but how the hell did we end up out here?" She heard the strangled alarm in her voice and involuntarily let her fingers do the walking. The cold tips of her fingers brushed across the chiseled crest of his cheek, before he snapped back.

"Oh thank God. I'll explain later. Come on, let's get you somewhere safe." Hauling her up with him, she thought about how effortlessly Remi lifted her up as they went vertical. He cradled her gently, yet snug against him, regarding her with care. He was graceful to a fault. The way he spoke, and moved. "Are you hurt?" He didn't give her a chance to answer. Draping his arm around her, Remi ushered her down an alleyway and out of sight.

She didn't know exactly what was going on, but she sensed the life she knew was fleeting. With each new accident, it occurred to her they were more like warning signs, telling her time was running short. Now Remi was caught in the midst of her *accidental nature*. Nearly getting killed, along with countless others, was too much to bear. She wouldn't let her fate become his. Pulling herself from his grasp, Ferrian knew the only way to keep him safe was to walk away. As much as it pained her, it was the right thing to do.

"Stop!" Her hands shook as she pooled all of her courage to do what she didn't want to. *Dammit! Why does this have to be so hard?* Clutching her chest, she felt her heart pounding harder than she had ever thought possible, and the idea it could pop out of her body didn't seem so farfetched anymore.

"Ferrian, we need to get you out of here. It's not safe.

Come on." He reached for her, but grasped only air as she backed away from him, shaking her head in defiance. She knew she would be the cause of his death if Remi stayed with her. She couldn't let it happen. She wouldn't let it happen.

"I can't. No, you need to walk away from me, before you get hurt, too! I won't let my curse kill you like it has done the others." She turned to run, but he moved much faster. Grabbing her by the arm he whipped her around to face him. Fury rimmed his eyes and the overwhelming feeling of his stare froze her in place.

"You're not leaving my sight. Understand? You are *not* cursed." He didn't mean it to come out curtly, but it was what it was. The cold resignation in her face as she turned to run said if he didn't stop her now, he'd lose her for good. She had come so far in a couple of months and now it was as if none of it mattered.

In a flash, he was in front of her, cupping her arm tightly as his hackles rose in alarm. The acidic stench of Hellistic demon blood wafted down the alleyway, stinging his nostrils like a punch to the face. There was no time to investigate the scent, although he knew it all too well. *It's getting closer, shit.* "Ferrian, there's no time. We have to go!" He didn't wait for her answer. Scooping Ferrian up in his arms, he ran down the grimy, litter-ridden street.

"Put me down dammit! I'm not some indolent, fragile girl." She beat her fists against his chest, struggling to fight him off. Any other day, he would've respected her courage if he weren't already busy trying to hide her from the real danger.

"I know you're not fragile, but I feel like it's my job to protect you. Now stop yelling and let me get you out of here before real trouble comes looking for you!" He didn't want to snap, and he didn't have to look at her to feel the angry stare she was burning into him. His heart plummeted to his feet when he realized how close she came to dying … *again.*

It didn't take long for him to run the distance from the alleyway and back to her apartment. She hadn't spoken a word to him and it was probably for the best. He knew Ferrian had questions. Questions he couldn't answer yet. Pacing anxiously across the small apartment, he had a bitch of an itch to unleash his rage on the demons. His muscles bounced and coiled, ready for a fight, and he wasn't overly convinced they hadn't been followed either.

He scanned the window for any signs of Lucifer's minions, if they had been nearby. A fuel ready to explode welled up deep in his gut as he paced from window to window. His agitation rose the longer Ferrian remained silent, watching him with wary eyes. What the hell was she thinking? Out of all the times she'd gone silent on him, this was one of those times he wished he could persuade her to speak.

Stopping long enough to peer out the kitchen window, the only sign of life he saw nearby were the yellow and brown leaves whipping by in a flurry of wind.

"Remi," her sweet voice called from the doorway. Ferrian stood there watching him, rigidly holding herself. "I realize we almost died, but I think you need to walk away from me." The words slapped him hard, and he whipped his head around to face her. The eerily cool tone to her voice scared him to his core. "I'll bring you nothing but death if you stay around me any longer. Please … go. Leave. I'm curs—"

"Don't say it," he ground out bitterly, cutting her off. Hearing how cursed she was, was only going to ratchet up his frustration all the more. "Don't you dare say it! You are not cursed," he bit out sourly, and then gave himself a proverbial kick in the ass for it. The way she held the idea so close to heart made him want to wrap his arms around her, and spirit her away to an uninhabited island so she could see how *not* cursed she was. He watched as her spine become ramrod straight as his strides ate up the distance between them.

As if lightning had struck him right in the balls, he grasped the reason behind her reaction. She was waiting for him to lash out, as others in her life had; strike her down and take what they wanted. She didn't see him as a friend. No, her eyes screamed of fear. Sucking in a sharp breath, Remi stared deeply into her forest green eyes, and forced himself to accept what reality was, what it had always been for her.

"Ferrian, I know you think you're cursed, but you're not. Trust me, you're not." His fingers brushed back her hair, revealing the scar she tried to hide from him. "Unlucky maybe, but you're not cursed." No she wasn't cursed, she was something else entirely. "What you are is beautiful."

Ferrian held her breath as his fingers lingered on her cheek. He didn't know what made him do it, hold her gaze longer than any time before, or what drove him to touch her face in the first place, but it was too late. He was falling in love with her. Hard.

CHAPTER SIXTEEN

*I*f *only you knew how truly beautiful you are.* He couldn't deny it to himself any longer. Her eyes burned like fiery coals and ragged breaths sawed in and out. The urge to pull her close and brush his lips over hers made his chest seize. Cupping her cheek, he did the unthinkable. His heart hammered against his chest as he descended on her lips. The supple flesh welcomed him without a fight, and it was then he realized his heart was no longer his. It belonged to her. His lips urged her to open, gently coaxing her to let him in. Slowly, carefully, he lavished her lips with hungry kisses. "M'aingeal, please …" he said breathlessly, caressing her lips. Her hands slid up his chest, holding onto his shoulders, as her body gradually eased into him. "Let me in … please."

Desire seared through his veins, burning him straight through to his primal core. Ferrian slowly unfurled for him, her firm body pressed softly against him. All hesitation gave way as she curled her fingers around the nape of his neck, enticing him more. The sweet taste of her was intoxicatingly exquisite the deeper she allowed him to sink into their kiss. Nothing had ever tasted so divine and he prayed to God he would never forget how sinful this moment was. *Screw the rules, she's mine!* As blood coursed through his veins like liquid fire, it swelled the one thing he wished he could control.

He slipped his hand around the curve of her hip, only to feel her recoil and break her lips from his as she backed away from him. *Shit!* He had done exactly what he had sworn he wouldn't do. *Dammit, way to go, asshole.*

"I—can't do this." Turning from him, she walked into the bathroom and shut him out, without a second thought.

"Ferrian. Please, I'm sorry. I don't know what I was thinking. Please come out, talk to me." He had crossed the line. The line no angel was allowed to cross. Falling in love with their charge was a dangerous situation. But it was the line he'd promised to Ferrian he wouldn't cross that pitched a wave of regret in his gut.

"Leave me alone." It was hard to tell what was going through her mind; her voice sounded shaky although she made her demands clear.

"M'aingeal, please, come out and talk to me."

"Stop calling me that. I don't even know what it means, but stop! Get out of here, Remi. Now!"

It was no use, she wasn't going to come out. She had made it clear, and as much as he loved her strength, her stubbornness was gnawing at his heart. "Fine," he conceded. "Call me if you need me."

He left his cell on the counter and headed for the door.

"I can't, remember? No phone," her muffled voice grumbled through the barrier. The scent of her tears wafted from under the door, kicking him in the balls with more guilt.

109

"I'm leaving one here for you. Hit send. My number is the only one programmed."

"Don't bother. Get as far away from me as possible. I don't want to see you again."

What the hell was he thinking? Any chance of building her trust was gone, wiped out in one fleeting moment. Scrubbing his face, he scanned the small apartment once more, and hoped she would crack the door before he walked out. *Good going. You scared the shit out of her, and for what? Because you can't keep yourself in check.*

"Talking to yourself again, I see." Remi spun around to find Ezekiel leaning against the wall. His eyes were covered by jet black Ray-Bans, and his classic disapproving scowl stretched across his face. "Some would think you'd lost your mind."

"This coming from Mr. Personality himself?" Remi glared at him; he wasn't up for another pissing contest, let alone bullshit from one of his brethren. "Back off, man." The door had barely clicked shut before he heard the muffled sounds of Ferrian's sobs. Regret stabbed him with each step he walked farther away from her and out of the building. "Is there something you want, Z?"

"Well, since you mentioned it, what the hell happened on the bus?" It was irritating how Ezekiel could speak about demons skewering humans and sucking their marrow out with the same coolness as if he were discussing the weather. "Well?"

Grinding his teeth, he stopped short, figuring if he didn't explain it now then Z would be all over his ass like an STD. "Hellistic demon in a garbage truck decided to turn the bus we were on into an accordion."

Letting out a low breath, Ezekiel clapped him on the

back. It wasn't the first time Remi had seen demons this ravenous to get to a Darkling. It didn't make it any easier to swallow, either.

"You know things are going to get worse from here on out, don't you?" Ezekiel pointed out with a brief shrug, as if it were nothing. To the Angel of Death, all this was just another day at the office. Nothing new. To Remi, it meant everything. The ability to keep Ferrian safe warred with his own selfish desires to sink down into her body for days, and protect from the comforts of his king-sized bed.

"Ya think? Thank you, first mate of the 'captain obvious' league of know-it-alls. Any other observations you'd like to make? By all means … write them down and shove them up your ass." He knew all too well what was coming for them. Luckily, he didn't need to be up Realmside daily to get the latest intel. His brethren made damn sure he stayed informed and up to speed with relentless text messages and hounding calls. It had been three weeks since he reported in. Staying with Ferrian was his top priority; at least that's what he told himself. Anyone of his brethren would come down for a few hours and stand guard for him. The problem wasn't that he didn't trust any of them, it was so much more. She meant too much to him to let Ferrian out of his sight for any length of time.

He wanted to deny the truth—it did him no good to feel the way he did because it was impossible for so many reasons—but it didn't stop his heart from feeling for her. The sinful idea of claiming her as his own revved him up and sent blood coursing straight for the one place demanding so much more. But she wasn't his, and never would be, or more to the point, could be. Ferrian was a Darkling on the brink of turning. Her path still was unclear.

"Damn, Remiel, are you done wrestling with your conscious, or should I run to the 7-Eleven and grab you some Midol?"

Jokes weren't Ezekiel's strong point, and right now it grated on his nerves. "Piss off, Z. Why are you here anyway?"

"You might want to tone down your attitude, my young brother." Z slowly folded his black leather clad arms over his chest, deliberately flexing and creaking the thick fabric. He knew the stare-down he was getting, as well as the condescending tone and use of 'young brother' all too well. He was either in for a lecture or some news ... and not the good kind. It wasn't often Ezekiel brought the good kind of news in any case.

"Why are you here, Ezekiel?" he repeated, and the long moment of silence seemed to stretch out for an eternity before his question was finally answered.

"Seems like you're spending an awful lot of time with the Darkling, am I wrong?"

"It's my job! Or did it escape your mind, since you obviously don't remember what it's like to watch over a charge?"

"Easy, brother. I think it's time for you to step away and clear your head. I believe this Darkling has become something more to you, and it's impairing your ability to see things clearly. Remiel, you know the rules."

"Whatever. Don't talk to me about the rules. I know what the damn rules say! I'm not some newbie who earned my wings yesterday. She's my charge, I watch over her well-being. Got it?" he ground out through clenched teeth. Remi was on edge and needed something ... no not something, more like someone to relieve him. Someone to sink down into, lavishing sensual kisses upon the luscious mounds of flesh until those small pink beads hardened from his touch. *Cut it out, man. Not helping right now.*

Slamming his lids close, he tried to shut out the world, but all he saw was her. Ferrian's long, black hair splayed out around her in an ebony halo, her soft, milky skin contrasting against the navy blankets, reminding him of how perfect she looked in her sleep. Innocent and pure. Those long days while she was in a coma, he'd sat by her side. Holding her soft hand, and focusing on the rhythmic beat of her pulse. Too many thoughts surrounded her. "Call Kakabel. Tell her to watch over Ferrian."

"Smart choice. By the way, Am's looking for you."

"Yeah, okay. I'll be up in a few." After he exercised out some of this anger on some demons of course, and didn't matter which kind. He had no doubt a few Hellistic demons would be lurking around the neighborhood, acting as spies for the Underworld. If he couldn't get his relief one way, he sure as shit would another way. His tightly coiled muscles bunched under his shirt, anxious to crush something, and destroy anyone who attempted to hurt his angel. *She's not your angel. Get it through your thick head. She doesn't even want to be around you, thanks to your screw up.*

"Yup, you keep wrestling with your conscious. Let me know how it turns out." Z unfurled his immense wings and shot straight up into the early morning sky.

"One good punch to the brainpan would knock the jerk right off his friggin' pedestal," he muttered to Ezekiel's quickly departing back.

Sucking in a ragged breath, Remi conceded. He knew Z was right. If he didn't clear his head, he'd be no good to anyone. Even if Ferrian refused to see him in person again, Remi still had a duty to watch over her, protect her. Stalking down the back alleyway, he cursed himself for giving in to his desire. But what if she wanted him? What if for even the briefest of moments, she felt the same way? The memory of her lips pressing against his, hesitantly at first then slowly melting into his kiss seemed more real, more intense than anything he had ever known. "No way. You're fooling yourself. Did you see the look in her eyes? You scared her. She didn't want it. Why did she hold on to me the way she did, then?"

His hands were balled into bone crunching fists by the time he picked-up on the first scent of a Hellistic demon. Grinding his teeth, his feet bit into the pavement as he hauled ass down and around the corner. The vile, acidic stench of a demon filtered through the air the closer he got. His body coiled for the attack, ready for any outcome as he stalked toward the odor. Knowing it would take a few seconds to find his unknowing victim, he scanned the doorways and side-street vendors.

"Bingo." The deathly stare of sunken black eyes and smoke-stained skin clung to lanky frame leaning against a black Camaro. The demon was watching Ferrian's apartment from a safe distance down by the corner store. A slow smile spread wide across his face as he hurled himself into the demon, crashing them both against hard metal and shattering glass. The alarm screamed into the void as Remi slammed his fist into the demon's face, knocking his skull back. He had found his prey, and unleashing on it was pure ecstasy times ten.

"Shit! What's wrong with me?" Panic crept up in her throat, bubbling out in hysterics. "He'll die! I can't let him die. Why did I let him kiss me, why?" Sinking down to the floor, her mind raced with a ton of questions. She couldn't help scolding herself for the careless act. Her fingertips idly brushed across her lips, feeling for the warmth of his kiss still there. Ready to shatter into a million pieces, she hadn't been able to stop herself from kissing him back …and she hated herself even more for it. Most of all, she hated admitting how much she truly wanted him. It was wrong, and she knew it, but more than anything, she wished it were right.

Remi's voice was sincere if not concerned, but she wasn't going to risk his life. Sending him away was the only option she had. The sound of his footsteps thundering across the floor as he'd stormed out had sent waves of relief that he would be safe washing over her. She tried in vain to force back the tears welling in her eyes. As little droplets of moisture trickled down her cheeks, she swiped angrily at the salty wet trails.

Ferrian had spent weeks imagining Remi's body pressing against hers, his lips hovering above hers, while soft, tantalizing caresses of his breath warmed her. However, in the moment, her body gave way to shivers running down her spine from the first touch of his fingers, grazing her skin. The fire in her belly ignited into an inferno from a single touch, and she gave in without a fight. It'd pained her to push Remi away, but he would die if he stayed close to her.

The bus accident was proof enough. He refused to walk away from her, and if she was being honest with herself, she wasn't sure why she couldn't walk away easily either. "No, damn it! Walk away from him. You've already killed two people. Do you want a third death on your hands?" The weight of her guilt crushed her as a fresh batch of tears poured from her eyes. "Walk away." Raking her hands through her hair, she wanted to rip it out by the handful, and had to stop herself from pulling at it.

How could she have let this happen? What happened to being sort of friends? Her head was a mess. Her heart wasn't looking much better. Twisted-up with barbed wire, she feared each glimmer of hope she gave in to would cut another little slice from her. She'd tried to stay clear of allowing this to happen, and failed miserably. Her lungs burned for air as the memory of his immense body covering hers, and the gentleness of his hands feathering down her skin, made her flesh heat with need all over again. There had been no telling where she ended and he began once she'd finally opened for him.

For the first time in her life, Ferrian came alive as though a free-flowing electrical current set on high voltage had been infused with her DNA. Her nerves lit up, and sang like lightning strikes when his hand had slid around her hip, heading to the small of her back. She wanted him and couldn't deny the obvious fact. In a breathless rush, she had pushed him away. Was it to save him, or herself? The same questions ran around her head in circles, driving her crazy.

Remi was the first person she'd allowed herself to care about since Margaret. She didn't know how it happened, but there was no turning back from it now.

"Damn it to hell!" Pushing herself off the floor, she ripped the door free from the jamb and ran for the apartment door. She had to find him. But what would she say to him, what could she say? It didn't matter. She had to make Remi understand she could never see him again. Pausing, her hand shook while holding the doorknob. "No! I-I, he'll try and talk me out of it! No … I have to leave here."

Scavenging up the few things she had, Ferrian tossed her clothes and cash into her backpack and gunned it for the door once more. There was no turning back now.

CHAPTER SEVENTEEN

"Feel better, man?" Roc's voice echoed across the training room as Remi stacked another set of fifties on the bar. The clanking of metal against metal screamed through the silence. "Z said you were a little pissy earlier. Gotcher rag or something?"

Casting a sardonic glare toward Roc, he slipped underneath the bar and lowered his sweat-soaked back against the bench. The acidic stench from the demon had taken up residence in his nostrils, and every breath he inhaled made him cringe at the reminder of the blackened puddle of minion soup he'd left behind on the street. Hefting the weighted bar off the arms of the bench, he slowly lowered and pushed it back up. Sweat beaded across his furrowed brow as he repeated the process. It didn't take long for him to forget about Nisroc standing off to the side, staring him down like a rattlesnake ready to bite.

"Don't bust your O-ring, my man. You actually do need to breathe, contrary to popular belief."

Grunting, he pushed the weight off his chest; exhaling a winded, "Piss off," through gritted teeth.

"Fine, but don't come crying to me when you crack

your ribs!" Throwing his hands in the air in surrender, Roc turned around and made for the showers. "All this over a human chick? Dude, all human chicks are good for is a little carnal action. Don't get your panties in a wad over her," he muttered under his breath as the door closed behind him.

"A chick," Remi grounded out, throwing the weights back onto the support arms. Ferrian wasn't some chick, a passing fling, or an amusement. Clutching his fists tight to his sides, Remi planted his feet to keep from storming after Roc and slamming his knuckles into the male's face. The echo of the door hung in the air, leaving him once again alone with his thoughts. His feet dragged heavily as he hauled himself over to the pull-up rack. What good was thinking about her doing him anyway?

Pulling himself into a curl-up, his felt the burn in his arms. His legs ached, and his head was exhausted from running mental Olympics and replaying his last encounter with Ferrian. His heart was pounding behind the bone cage in his chest as he strained his muscles to exertion. The phone on the counter rang every two minutes; he ignored it for the twentieth time. He had spoken as much as he wanted to, to anyone. All of the burning in his muscles could not compare to the sight of Ferrian pulling away from him in surprise, hearing her cries as she tried to muffle the sound in the bathroom. "What the fuck have I done?" He shook his head, more pissed at himself than anything Roc could goad him into.

The ringing of his cell had become more than a distraction when it didn't stop. Gnashing his teeth, he stalked over to the granite counter, and snatched up the small device with the intention on throwing it against the concrete walls. His eyes caught the name on the glowing screen and he sucked in a quick breath. "Where is she?" he bit out, before the voice on the other end could get a syllable out.

"Remi, I don't know. I've checked all around her apartment and the neighborhood. I can't find her anywhere."

"Check out where she works, down by the pier, everywhere, Kakabel! How could you lose her like this, dammit? I trusted you to watch over her. Shit, no never mind, I'm coming down there."

"Chill the hell out! She was gone before I got there. What the hell happened to make her leave, Remi? She's missing some clothes and her backpack, too."

The blood drained from his head as he realized she was on the run. It wasn't the first time she'd done this, but the reasoning behind it this time was painfully obvious. He was the reason she ran. "Stay where you are, I'll be there in five minutes."

"Remi, something feels off. Better get here like right now."

"Why did he kiss me? Why did I let him kiss me?" Ferrian's sobs poured out in waves as she curled into herself. The stench of yesterday's trash covered the alleyway as she sank down into a pathetic ball. Pulling her knees close to her face and burying her eyes from the world, she prayed no one would witness her break down like this.

With each shallow breath she inhaled, his rich, spicy

scent lingered, wafting from her clothes and in her hair. His warmth had covered her like the summer sun long after he'd left. His kiss, a delicious mixture of sweet and salty, left her yearning for more as she thumbed over the same spot, and her heart hammered against her chest as she envisioned him holding her so close. *Walk away, Ferrian. This is for the best.* What she wanted to do was turn around and race back to her apartment in hopes of finding Remi waiting there for her. All she had ever done was run away from the pain in hopes of sparing anyone she cared about from meeting an untimely fate. She already had too much blood stained on her soul.

Night was approaching fast. The cold sting of fear shot down her spine as she pushed herself off the ground and forced her feet to walk again. Numb from the mental thrashing, she had no idea where she was going, nor did she honestly care. Anywhere was better than the grimy alleyway where she had spent the last hour crying.

With the bus station in view, she wasn't surprised when her feet lead the way while her brain shut down to self-preservation mode. Pulling her black hoodie tight to her face, her eyes lowered the closer she stepped to the ticketing agent.

"Where are you heading?" a gruff voice behind bulletproof glass chuffed out through the slotted holes. The stinging scent of stale cigarette smoke and grimy sweat filtered out, gagging her.

"Umm …" Where was she going? "Shit."

"Excuse me?" The male appeared to be about a hundred years old. A cigarette hung out of his wrinkled mouth with a halo of smoke loaming over his greasy head. "Come on, honey, where you heading to?"

Cringing in her skin, a feral growl screamed through her head, and blood pulsed to life in electric waves as she considered smashing her fists through the glass.

CHAPTER EIGHTEEN

"Ferrian! Ferrian, where are you?" Remi raced around her apartment, searching for her. Panic riddled him. He knew she wasn't there, but hoped with everything inside of him she would return.

"Remi, she's gone. Can't you sense her?" The calm urging in Kakabel's voice barely registered as he marched past her, leaving the apartment. "You're not leaving me here."

"Fine, then go home." Ice covered each word he snapped at her. He pushed passed her and shot down the stairs, heading for the street below.

"I'm not leaving you, dammit. Wait up! You might need back up."

"I'm fine. Go home, Kakabel." He planted his feet on the cracked concrete, not up for the sorrowful sibling routine. "I can find her myself."

She jumped out in front of him and didn't make a move to leave. Folding her arms over her chest, Kakabel stared him down. The air of annoyance shrouded her delicate features in a fierce scowl. "Let's go, Remiel. Now," she commanded, and led the way.

Throwing his hands up, he realized it was an argument he wasn't going to win. She was right, he might only get one shot to find Ferrian if demons were involved. He needed the backup, in case she was hurt and in need of healing. "Fine!"

He needed the distraction of another person there. Otherwise, nothing would stop him from tracking down Ferrian, tucking her to his chest, and locking her there with his arms wrapped around her. There was no doubt in his mind she would fight him, or try to fight him off, but it wouldn't do her any good. He would take every hit and kick Ferrian had to offer, if it meant keeping her safe.

Her sweet, natural perfume barely clung to the wind as he inhaled trace scents of her. It was fading fast as he scanned each alleyway in hopes she would pop out of thin air. His strides ate up the pavement as Kakabel walked soundlessly beside him. *I swear to all that's holy, if something has happened to her, I'm gonna end up going apocalyptic on someone and then myself for being the dumbass who left her.* Fear raked down his spine as he followed her aroma down the same grimy alleyway. Her small imprint of heat, invisible to the naked eye, glimmered against the grime. She was so close to finding out the truth of who she was. Each passing day was one more day she was in danger. It didn't matter about the prophecy; Satan wasn't exactly known for sticking to the strict guidelines. He had his number one, right hand demon, Lucifer, to do his bidding. Then there was the speculation Lucifer was using his underling, Xaphan, to handle the dirty work for him. Thanks to Focalor's intel, the League of Guardians had more demons to contend with, and time was of the essence.

The hair on the back of his neck electrified as his

heart seized. Something was off; someone was too close to her, he could sense it as the familiar flicker of alarm shot straight threw his body. "Damn it!" The soles of his shitkickers bit into the pavement, leaving potholes behind. He didn't care who saw him. "M'aingeal."

"Hey, buddy, where ya going?" the nasally voice chirped out, grating Ferrian's nerves. The way he stared at her like she was another piece of worthless trash roaming the bus station for a free ride boiled her blood. Distorted images of her running her knife through his guts tantalized her as she gripped her pocketknife tighter.

"Go for it, you know you want to." She had no idea if the voice in her head was her imagination or something else. "No, it's not your imagination, Darkling." A tinge of menace edged the voice. Fear skimmed down her body with each syllable he spoke. "Go on, you know what he's thinking. He wants to rip the fabric off your body, like your foster father did, and shred your skin to nothing."

Her blood froze. The eerily familiar voice assaulted her memories. "It can't be." There was no hiding the snarl burning from her lips. Her eyes grew wide as she watched the male behind the glass take another pull between his greasy lips with nicotine-stained fingers.

The stinging, sickening sense of danger walking right up to her, made the hair on her body stand straight up—as it had so many times before. Spinning around, Ferrian came face-to-face with the source of the same nightmare she had had since childhood. A pair of black, soulless eyes deep as an abyss stared into hers. Icy fingers clawed up her throat as she struggled for breath. *Oh God, not you!*

The sounds of the diesel thrummed bus engines disappeared, as did the flurry of scattered voices around the bus depot. Anger and fear trembled through her body as he leaned against the brick-faced wall. A satirical smile stretched ear to ear.

"No way. No friggin' way!" It couldn't be happening, this wasn't real. Her mind raced back to the last time those eyes had pinned her with sickening depravity. The rancid stench of his breath skated around her head.

"Ah, so you do remember me, splendid." Her skin turned to ice as she balled up all of the fury and despair from her past. Her pulse sprinted like a freight train while she scanned around him, searching for a way out of this. "Don't bother trying to get away, Ferrian. There's no point, you belong to me, child."

He held a casual stance against the wall, with his arms folded arrogantly across his chest. He was much taller than her five foot eight frame. There was no disguising his well-muscled, lean body. His clothes accentuated his muscles in sheer perfection. His bronzed skin perfectly offset his gleaming white teeth and straight black hair. And was more out of place on this side of town in his black on black pinstriped suit than a bag lady would be in a runway fashion show.

Her head spun and vision grew blurry as her body went numb. Sucking in a deep breath, she willed herself to focus and run away. Springing forward, desperation launched her into gear. Shallow breaths hitched with the few strides she managed before running into a solid wall of meat. "Oh shit!" she shuddered out. The arctic grasp of steely fingers wrapping around her throat stole her next words.

"Oh no, no, no, my pet. It's not polite to run from me. At least, not until we get better acquainted." The male made no effort to hide the malice in his voice as his grip tightened around her throat. "I don't know how you've survived this long, but I promise you, you will be mine.

CHAPTER NINETEEN

The buzzing in his skull vibrated down to his toes. Ferrian was in danger, and he feared if he didn't find her soon, there would be nothing left to find of her. The ripping sound from his silver wings unfurling cried through the air as Remi launched skyward. He flew too fast for humans to see, but he couldn't have cared less even if they did. Terror pulsed through his body as he scanned the street corners and door-stoops in search of her.

"Where are you, Aingeal?" His gut was shrieking bloody murder. Whoever had her, had no intentions on letting her go. The thrumming of her heartbeat rattled in his chest as a fresh wave of panic catapulted his need to find her higher.

The hellish scent of sulfur brutalized his nostrils as he circled around to the front of the bus depot. His eyes locked on Ferrian's thin body, lifted inches off the ground as she clawed and struggled to free herself. She was nothing more than a ragdoll in the hands of the male who gripped her throat. Fire licked his veins as he dove down to ground level, knocking the male to the ground in a graceless tumble.

His knuckles connected to flesh in a crushing punch, one after another with his bodyweight atop of the male. Anger blurred his vision as his fists repeated the beating until a hard kick to the chest threw him off the bloodied male. Knocking the wind out him, he realized glaring up at the face of his opponent exactly who he was facing off with. "Xaphan."

"Remiel," he clucked. "I would say it's nice to see you again, but then I'd be lying." His howling laughter ricocheted off the steel beams and concrete walls. It rumbled through the air like a fast approaching storm. Remi's lips peeled back into a sneer as he squared off, ready to take aim once again. "You know it's only a matter of time before she comes looking for me, don't you?" Cocking a dark slash of his brow, Remi's blood turned to pure acid as he imagined Ferrian laid out before Xaphan, her black hair fisted in his hand as her black wings curled around her body.

He slipped a glance around, needing to find her, to see she was okay before he tore Xaphan limb from bloodied limb.

"Looking for your little Darkling? Well, she won't be a Darkling for long, I'm sure." He flashed an arrogant grin at Remi's attempt at subtlety. "She's over there, moron." Motioning his hand backward, Remi followed with his eyes until his breath caught in his throat. "You should be more careful with your toys, Remiel."

Her body laid crumpled against the wall, unmoving. He wanted to make a move, run up to her and pull her into his arms where she would be safe and secure. Xaphan knew all too well if he succeeded in bringing Ferrian to the Underworld, even in her Darkling form, she would be trapped and more than likely forced to become a Daemon.

A silver beam of light caught his eye as he ease back on to his heels. Kakabel had followed him after all. Barely sparing a glance up to her, standing on the rooftop of the bus depot, he knew why she was here. No words needed to be exchanged; it was a classic distract and go deal.

Xaphan's eyes were locked onto Remi's, waiting for his next move. "Why are you here? Doesn't the Underworld scum usually send minions up to fetch fresh meat for you? Or is Lucifer pissed off at you for sucking Mephistopheles's dick instead?"

"If you think provoking me into a fight is going to work then you're sadly mistaken. You know she's going to turn. And when she does, I'll be there to guide her in the right direction." The abyss of Xaphan's black eyes lit up with a thousand images of Hell's hospitality.

"You're sick." Remi's muscles coiled tightly as his hands curled into rock hard balls, ready to launch at the right moment. "You won't get close enough to touch her, you hear me? Never!"

Considering him with an arrogant stare, Xaphan brushed off Remi's words with a curt sneer. "I won't have to, she'll come to me. And when she does, the Dark Lord will sing my praise."

Fury ripped through his chest as he barreled toward Xaphan, Lucifer's second in command. The fact he was topside with Ferrian in his grasp was all the warning Remi needed, indicating shit had hit the critical stage. They knew she was the key and they were pulling out all the stops to seduce her into darkness or kill her for denying them.

Words were fleeting as his primitive instincts welcomed a good old fashion ass-whooping. His fist bit in to flesh before Xaphan had a chance to move. There was nothing stopping him from ripping the demon apart.

"R-Re-mi," Ferrian's weak voice called out, barely able to focus on what was going on. Pushing her body from the wet pavement, a venomous roar scraped up her throat. Remi flipped his head around in time to see the twisted glint in her eyes as she spotted Xaphan. Her eyes radiated revenge, and if it were up to him, he'd gladly let her take it out on Xaphan. But it wasn't up to him. Ferrian's skin grew paler as a sneer curled up her lips. Reaching around to the back of her waistband, she freed the pocketknife she kept hidden beneath her black hoodie.

His blood ran cold. "Bels, get her out of here now!" he ordered through clenched teeth. Ferrian was now witnessing him in the most primal of moments, and called out for him as the darkness she held inside demanded to come out. He was thankful for a fleeting second when Kakabel did as he'd commanded without argument, and caged Ferrian in her arms before she launched skyward.

All it took was a second to land Remi on his ass, with Xaphan on top of him, thrashing punches into the side of Remi's skull. *This isn't going to end pretty.* Launching another crushing punch to Xaphan's sternum, a whoosh of air exploded from demon's mouth as the sound of bones cracking knocked the wind out of Xaphan's lungs.

Gritting his teeth, Remi kicked him off hard, sending Xaphan sailing across the slick pavement. "You stay away from her!" The demon peeled back his lips, revealing his true form hidden behind the meat-sack of skin he wore to disguise himself. "You can't have her!" Remi made damn sure his words sank in as he hammered another crushing blow to the demon's chest. Black blood, reeking of sulfur and burning oil, choked out of Xaphan's mouth as the demon tried to squirm away.

"She has to decide … remember?"

Xaphan's words echoed loudly in Remi's ears. It was the truth, but these demons weren't playing fair. The stakes were high. Dread assailed him as he thought about the look in Ferrian's eyes. The twisted vengeance pouring out of her tightened the knot deeper in his stomach.

"She won't become one of you! I'll die before it happens."

"Then die you shall, and I will relish stripping your flesh from bone—maybe using those precious wings of yours as fans."

The sickening stink of blood assaulted his nostrils as Remi pushed himself from the ground, and threw a punch to Xaphan's face.

The closer Ferrian was to changing, the more he feared he'd lose her. He didn't need to hear the words to know what would happen if she turned into a Daemon. All of the other Darklings would be lost, as their connection would be severed forever. Ferrian was the key to finding the others.

A chill from the possibilities ran down his spine when he thought back to the way her darkness peeked out moments earlier.

"You will lose," Xaphan uttered before dematerializing from view. The rush of bus engines and patter of rain and human voices echoed in a resonating symphony as life returned undisturbed, and unknowing of the fate hanging in the balance.

CHAPTER
TWENTY

"**L**et me go, dammit!" Ferrian snarled, struggling against the powerful arms circling around her body. She couldn't see the face of her captor, as the curvy yet strong body held Ferrian's back to the woman's chest. The smell of water lilies rose from soft skin as a small recognition hit her upside the head. "You, I know you! Let me go dammit."

"Yes, Ferrian, I sat with you while you were in a coma." The soft voice reminded Ferrian of harps as the lithe tone spoke next to her ear.

"Where are you taking me?" she demanded.

"I'm taking you home. Now please stop squirming."

"How did you find me? You should've left me there! I had him. That sonofabitch deserves to die." Her heart raced as she fought against the death-grip hold the woman Ferrian only knew as Remi's sister had on her … but what was her name again?

"You need to stay away from him. He's dangerous, Ferrian. Too dangerous for you to meddle with."

"I had it under control." Her blood was still boiling and her voice was filled with vengeance as she kicked harder against the female holding her captive. "He deserves what's coming to him." It should have sounded more menacing than it had, but still she meant it with every ounce of hatred in her body and soul.

"Don't let the past eat you alive. If you don't let go of it, you will be consumed by it."

"What do you know about it? You don't know me. You don't know what my life has been like. Dammit, let me go. Now!" A fresh wave of anger seared through her body before the female's arms encircling her eased up.

About friggin' time! Damn she's strong.

"Listen, whatever your name is, leave me alone. I don't need a babysitter, got it?" Spinning around on her heels, Ferrian came face-to-face with the most stunning woman she had ever seen. She towered over Ferrian, standing at least six feet tall, with a thick silver braid hanging over her shoulder, falling down to the her waist. The sight of Remi's sister, standing casually with one hand propped on her hip as she glanced down at her nails, wasn't what Ferrian had expected. Hell, she looked like she belonged on the Swedish Bikini Team, not dressed in all black leather and knee-high lace-up shitkickers. *How did I end up on the shit end of the gene pool? Geesh, who were their parents, Aphrodite and Adonis?*

"Remi asked me to watch over you, keep you safe, but I won't hold you hostage. You're welcome, by the way."

"Who are you?"

"My name is Kakabel, but you may call me Bels, and yes, I am Remi's sister. Well, sort of."

"Wait what? What do you mean ... *sort of*? Never mind, I don't give a shit, I'm out of here."

Thrusting her hands in her pockets, Ferrian realized she still clutched the knife in her hand. The cover of dark skies and broken city lights flickering down the alleyway increased the feeling of uneasiness as she stalked toward her apartment. How they had covered so much ground so quickly was beyond her, but she didn't care either. Her head and body were throbbing, and she had a big aspirin with her name written all over it waiting for her.

The slapping sounds of thick soles against wet pavement catching up to her irritated Ferrian, and she stomped harder to make her point known. "You can't out run me, Ferrian. Besides, you need to see a doctor. You took a pretty hard hit back at the bus station," the singsong voice called after her. What was with these people and the constant Good Samaritan bullshit? "Listen … hey, wait up! Remi would be pissed if I let you out of my sight."

Considering it for a moment, Ferrian stopped short, glancing sideways at her unwanted companion. "I don't give a rat's ass. And another thing, what the hell happened back there?"

"What do you mean?"

"You know exactly what I mean. Whoever he was, he was not the same Remi I know. What the hell is he?" Cocking a slash of her brow toward Bels, she hoped for some understanding of where she was going with this. She might have been a little disoriented, but Ferrian knew what she had seen. Bared teeth and animalistic growls ripped free from his lips. If she wanted to be honest with herself, the bulge of something coming out of his back had caught her off-guard completely. He had appeared to be almost inhuman, pummeling the hell out of the devil himself.

Remi had thwarted her shot of taking down the evil

bastard she had feared since childhood. Pissed off didn't begin to cover what she was feeling. Seething with white-hot rage was more like it. She deserved her vengeance, and no one was going to rob her of it again.

"Come on, we need to get out of sight. It's not safe out here." Kakabel reached for Ferrian's arm, only to come away empty handed.

"Don't touch me." Her hands plunged deeper into her pockets.

Throwing her hands up, Kakabel stepped aside and motioned her on. "Geesh, not like I was going to throw you down to the ground and kiss you or anything. Lighten up, young one. You'll give yourself grey hairs."

Shaking her head, Ferrian stalked back to her apartment. She was half a block away from locking the world out and settling in for a nice little planning session to find her living nightmare and kill him. She didn't care if she died in the process. If it was the only contribution she would make to the crappy human race, then it would be one worth dying for. This wasn't over, and she wasn't ready for it to end. Not tonight … not now, and not by a long shot. The urge to go after him grew stronger. Waiting wasn't going to work. Getting away from her self-appointed babysitter would be the tricky part. *No! It needs to be now, dammit!* The soles of her boots bit into the slick pavement. Racing around the corner, she knew she wasn't going to be denied.

"Ferrian!" the musical voice called after her, but it was too late. Her mind was made-up and nothing or no one would change what was to come. Dismissing Kakabel, her heart thrummed in her chest as she raced down the street after her prey. She hid her face from the world with her head hung low as she turned down West Harrison Street. Pumping her arms and thighs in unison, she rounded another corner, getting closer. Her senses were lit up like a live wire … until she hit the hard wall in her way.

The collision knocked the breath out of her burning lungs, and her head spun. What the hell had she run into? Her vision was blurry, filling with black spots, giving her the distinct impression she had knocked her brain offline for a few seconds.

"Damn it, Bels, I told you to get her back to her place!" The deep voice dancing around her fading consciousness hinted it was Remi's, but her mind decided to let her play the guessing game.

"Sorry, Remi, she flipped out and took off on me."

"Ferrian," the voice she tried to place spoke frantically, pulling her heavy limbs into a pair of thick muscled arms. Why was she having déjà vu? Her head rung like church bells as she tried to make sense of it all. "Ferrian, can you hear me? Blink if you can hear me."

Blink, sure I can do that. Come on eyes, blink.

"Shit, what do you want me to do?"

"Get her bag and go unlock her place. We'll be there in a minute. I think she has a concussion."

"Damn. You'd figure she would be used to getting knocked out by now."

"Not funny, Bels. Now go."

"Geesh, fine. What happened to Xaphan?"

"I'll tell you later. When you get back to her place, unlock the door, then head back Realmside and update them. I'll be up as soon as I can. Tell Cass I need to talk to him stat. Have him meet me at Ferrian's place, but not to enter. He can text me when he gets there. Got it?"

"Yes, sir. God, Remi, this isn't my first day on the job you know. Oh, and make sure to get rid of the knife on her waistband. Don't need her going all vigilante on you."

CHAPTER
TWENTY-ONE

Rolling onto her side, pain shot throughout her body. Fuzzy details flashed before her weary eyes as she dug her knuckles in to rub away the sleep. Her eyes hurt and still found it hard to focus as she blinked back the slivers of golden sunlight peeking through the thin curtains.

The throbbing sting had scarcely subsided as she reached around for her bottle of aspirin she kept on the nightstand. Her muscles pounded with a renewed sense of bodily hatred as she moved over to pull the drawer free. The lumps on her back were more tender than usual, and reminded her of the feeling of cracking a turkey's wish-bone. The bite of them as she pulled herself to the side unleashed a ripe curse meshed with a loud hiss.

She was in a no-win situation; between the pain in her head, the deep aches in her body, and the dire need to pee, it was a no-brainer. With a heavy push, she struggled to get off the bed and stand up straight. Being vertical made the room spin like an amusement park ride and she had no desire in riding it for long. Balance decided it didn't want to play nice either as she stepped forward only to crash into the wall. "Oooowwww. Damn it." Stumbling as subtly as a drunk, she slid across the wall until she found the bathroom door. The idea she couldn't handle the basics like walking gave her the distinct impression she had, in fact, ran into a brick wall at full speed without wearing a titanium helmet. This was going to be an interesting day if she couldn't get her head straight.

Ferrian heard a pair of muffled voices when she woke, which sounded too close to come from the sidewalk, since she lived on the third floor of a one-hundred-year-old apartment building. The voices, which brought about another strange thought, as she stared confused at the beat-to-shit brown door. "How did I get home?" Her brain ached at the idea of trying to figure things out, but her bladder refused to be dismissed. Shaking off the question for a moment, the porcelain throne called her name. "God, I must have hit my head harder than I thought."

She twisted the knob in the tub, and plugged the drain. Then turned back and stared blankly into the mirror. There she saw grey tinting her already pale skin; dark circles swallowed up her forest green eyes. The flickering light bulbs buzzed wildly above her head, as she splashed cool water on her skin. There was no hiding the hell written across her sunken face as she slumped over the chipped counter. Her head was fuzzy with the night's events, but a few sporadic memories flinted before her eyes. The stinging glare of sixty-watt bulbs burned with the same intensity of the sun. *Jesus, I feel like shit stomped over!* There was no grace to it as she slapped the light switch off, and reached under the sink to pull out a few candles.

Pushing off from the counter, the rushing sounds of

water filling up her bathtub and steam filling the air, begged for attention. The solace of a long, quiet hot bath was her only medicine. Plugging her IPod into the portable speakers, she hit the play button and played Evanescence. Unclipping her wrist cuffs, she clumsily dumped them on the floor next to her clothes, ignoring the fiery red scars. She was too tired to give a shit, and too sore to care.

She wanted nothing more than to forget about the world outside of her door. However, the nagging feeling of foreboding was riding her back like a lead monkey harder than before. Sinking down into the hot water, her memory fought against the barriers to remember what was lost. It was there on the edges, an image haunting her, a pair of black eyes staring back to her, gleaming with lust and death. Raking her hands through her raven hair, she hated not knowing what was gnawing at her; each bite mimicked a hundred hungry sewer rats all vying for the same morsel.

Time lost all meaning as she leaned back against the cool porcelain. Something about those eyes stirred her blood, burning through the vessels with revenge, and knotting her stomach in a bow. "Give it up, lady. It's useless." Everything before it was a blur, and anything after was all black. Her head squealed in agony when she came close to remembering some small detail. Giving up, she closed her eyes, feeling the heavy pull of exhaustion ride her hard as she sank deeper into the tub.

The hot water was too inviting, too soothing as she traipsed her fingers down the scars covering her body. Each one done deliberately with nothing shy of malice and cruelty. Each one she remembered with care. For too many nights, Ferrian laid awake wondering what would drive another human being to do such a thing. Finally, when no reasonable answers came, she settled on the notion of humanity was one big fat failure.

A flash of porcelain skin, splashed with crimson and green eyes fading into darkness, filled up her mind. But who was she? It wasn't the first time she had seen the female's face, but the scent of this woman—her sweet, flowery smell mixed with sulfur—clouded the calmness of her bath. A niggling feeling there was something familiar about her, like her heartbeat matched Ferrian's, made her brain itch. Nothing made sense anymore. Was she losing her mind?

The hot water may have been soothing to her aching body, but the solitude was eating away at her sanity. Making her wish for once she wasn't alone, or for someone to distract her from going insane. But who was she kidding? Being alone was all she knew.

"Remi." The name broke from her lips before she even thought about it. The startling vision of his eyes bearing down into hers, intensely heated and locking her in an invisible hold to keep her from falling over the edge, shot a surge of liquid lust between her thighs. Her muscles tensed as his deep voice vibrated wildly through her body. The sound of his guttural growl triggered a response, a very carnal, primal reaction that had her breath hitching as she held onto the moment longer. *Where are you, Remi? You kissed me once, get back here, and do it again.* Biting down hard on her lip to keep from saying his name again, she knew it so wasn't happening.

"What does she think happened? You're going to either have to tell her what the deal is or walk away. If she reacted the way you say she did last night, then she's close to changing. You know the rules. You know what you have to do."

"Yes, I know the rules." Frustration poured out of him with the constant reminder. Remi knew all this. After seeing Ferrian's feral reaction to Xaphan, he knew the side of darkness in her was clawing to come out. All he could be thankful for was it was anger turned toward the enemy verses a civilian. "To tell you the truth, I have no idea what to do here."

Leaning back against the chipped brick wall, the silence circling them was deafening. He loved and hated the city in the early morning hours. Being at ease with the possibility of things finally settling down wasn't top on his list. Cassiel stared him down with a knowing look, the same one which called anyone's bluff as bullshit.

"Remi, let me ask you something." Cassiel mimicked Remi's stance, leaning against the pitted grey brick face, folding his arms over his chest. His gut twisted, suspecting what Cass was going to ask. "Listen, I get it. You want to save her. She's your charge and all, but are you sure this hasn't become more of a personal thing than a job?"

"Look, man, I didn't ask for you to come all the way down here to break my balls." Cracking each knuckle with diligent care, he didn't bother to hide the fact Cassiel had touched a nerve.

"Like I said, I get it." Cassiel shrugged, but it was clear he wasn't about to let it go. "What if there weren't any rules? What if it wasn't forbidden to be with your charge, would you do it? Would you be with her?"

A lump lodged in Remi's throat as he adjusted himself once again, leaving a long conversation hanging in the air. Words weren't necessary. Ferrian had touched a part of him and left a permanent scar, visible to those who knew him well. Cassiel's uncomfortable stare made him twitch. He knew what Cass was reading … the markings of his soul, and he had no doubt what it was showing. Closing his eyes, he rested his head back against the brick and left his thoughts and truth hanging in the air. What could he say? He couldn't deny it, not to Cassiel.

"Shit. Maybe it would be in your best interest if you stepped away from her for a while. Get your head on straight."

Shaking his head, he admitted to himself that there wasn't any right course of action to take. It wouldn't matter whether he left Ferrian for a few hours, months, or even years. He couldn't lie to himself; no amount of time would quench his need to be near her. Not only had his desire to be close to her overruled his rational thinking, but the need to stay close after Xaphan's appearance set his priorities to another level completely.

"Listen, Remi, why don't you take a few days off? I'll watch over her for you," Cassiel tried again.

There was no way Cassiel was going to sell him on the idea. Even if it was for the right reasons, and they both knew it was, the idea of leaving her made his stomach recoil.

"No."

"I know you think you've got this under control, but believe me, Am and the rest of the group are going to need all of the information you can give them."

Considering him through knitted brows, Remi sucked

his balls back up, and let out a long sigh before he silently agreed with a simple nod. He hated it when his brethren was all leveled headed and right.

"How long has she been out?" Was he going to do this—step aside and let his team pick up the pieces, all because his boxers were in a bunch? "Come on, man, I need some details here."

"A few hours. She ran into me. Knocked herself out." *Second time actually. Because what you don't know is, I've been busting my ass at trying to gain her fragile trust, and stupidly scared the shit out of her a few months back.*

"Well, damn. I know you're built like a stone house, but did you have to give her a concussion?" Clapping Remi on the shoulder, his failed attempt to lighten the mood did little to change the effect.

His scowl burned into Cassiel. Swallowing a curse, Remi bit back what he wanted to say and pushed on. "I'm not sure how much she'll remember, but I'm sure there will be something. She sees things like no other, Cass. Her mind is her worst enemy and best ally."

"So she's still out cold then?"

"No, she's in the bathroom. Cassiel, don't go in unless it's absolutely necessary. I don't need her feeling anymore exposed than she has already been. I thought I could hide Bels from her, but Ferrian sees us. All of us. Tell her you're my brother if she asks."

"Shiiiiiiiiit. This puts a different spins on things." Sinking back against the wall, Cassiel snorted. "You are kidding me, right? I can't recall the last time a Darkling could see angels or demons so freely."

"Nope, not kidding. It surprised me, too. I'll be back as soon as I fill Amitiel and the rest in. Keep me updated.

If she leaves, I wanna know when, and I want you to follow her. Don't let her out of your sight, got it?"

"You should try and get some rest, too, Remiel. You look like something Roc would bring home."

If he resembled anything Roc would bring home, then it was safe to say it was time for a few minutes of sleep. His body sagged with the idea alone. Remi had been running on all twelve cylinders for months, protecting Ferrian twenty-four-seven. "Geez, thanks, pop. Next time I want a pep talk, I'll go stand in front of a bullet train," he countered. "All right, I'm out. Remember, anything happens you call me stat. Understand?"

The seriousness in his tone warned Cassiel one wrong move and his ass would be handed to him on a silver platter with his balls served on the side.

"Yeah, man. I got it. Oh, hey, if you see Focalor, tell him I need to speak with him."

He knew Focalor had been in contact with Cassiel over the past six months, but he still had his reservations about the Watcher. "Um, yeah, okay. You two are getting pretty chummy there. You're not thinking about changing teams are you?"

Cocking his brow, Cassiel shook his head. "Get the hell out of here, go get some rest."

Smirking at his brethren's disapproving glare, Remi unfurled his silver wings and launched into the darkness. The night had worn him down, and he had to admit he was damn tired.

CHAPTER
TWENTY-TWO

"**S**o good of you to join us, I was beginning to think you changed your address," Amitiel snapped the moment Remi stepped into the library. Her cutting glare fueled the room with white-edged tension. In no mood for her bullshit, he rolled his eyes and stalking pass the desk.

"My charge was hurt."

"Your charge is always hurt."

"Well, no shit! It's what she was meant for, right? What all Darklings are made for? To swallow pain, and for what … to prove free will still exists? Seriously, how much do you expect one being can take before they break?" Raking his hands through his hair, vengeance skated over his skin with red-hot steel nails. "That's what she's for, isn't it? To prove a mortal being like Ferrian can take anything thrown at her and she'll still choose to be a …" Using his cynical version of air quotes, he stopped dead in front of Amitiel to make is point loud and crystal clear. His eyes bore straight into hers as he readied himself for a good old fashion throw-down. "… *good angel* for all of mankind. I mean, it's not like she doesn't have every reason to despise humanity, God, Satan, even us!"

"Calm the fuck down. You know there's more to this besides the Darkling. The existence of the entire fucking planet is in jeopardy."

No shit, Sherlock! Someone please give the overbearing, sexually frustrated one a frickin' medal. "So you're saying we serve her up as bait, then? I think you're forgetting one important fact here. Xaphan has been tracking her down, and make no mistake; he will continue to hunt her down, until he claims her. Am, you have no damn idea what went down tonight. You didn't see the look in her eyes. Something inside of her snapped. I would swear she's closer to changing then I originally thought." Ferrian's face, twisted in bloodlust, splashed across his mind. She was out for retribution, but it was the darkness trying to come out he feared would consume her.

"Was she out to kill innocents? From what Kakabel told us, your charge was going after that prick Xaphan. Truth be told, if she had killed him, it would be one more sick bastard knocked off our top ten hit list. Why would you stop her anyway?"

He stared at Amitiel in complete disbelief as she sank down into the leather wingback. His mind rushed to understand what she was saying to him. Ferrian killing Xaphan was a good thing? No, she must have been screwing with him. What was she actually playing at? "So, you expect me to believe, if my charge actually killed Xaphan," stopping a few yards from her, his arms laced over his chest and he leveled her with contempt, "it would be acceptable? Riiiiiiight. I'm not willing to risk her becoming a Daemon. Not for some off chance it would be all right with the powers above."

Am sat up pin straight, challenging his stare with a harsh returning glare. "Are you forgetting something called freewill? This is not your decision. You would be wise to remember it."

"And what would become of her if she did kill the sack-of-shit? She would damn herself to the service of Satan. For eternity mind you! All we worked for, all we have protected since the dawn of time would be wasted, and all because you have some idiotic thought that maybe it would be okay for *my charge* to go after Xaphan. Listen to me, Amitiel, and listen closely. I'll spell it out for you if I have to. It won't happen. Understand?" He knew the anger in his voice showed his true nature, but he didn't care anymore. Remi wasn't about to risk losing her, so she could potentially be forced into servitude in the Underworld. If he was certain of anything, it was her soul was pure. The purest he had ever seen, including his own.

"Then I suggest you and the brethren find Xaphan and eliminate the source of her potential downfall. You can't decide for her."

It was a punch to the balls, but she was right. His fists clenched tighter as his knuckles fought against the strain. A heavy hand landed on his shoulder. It was all of the warning he was going to get to calm down. He didn't have to turn to see who it was; as a wave of serenity threatened his mood. Charoum, the Angel of Silence, had his bullshit gift of calming one's mind. And didn't it piss him right off, or tried to. The bastard couldn't say a verbal word, but he could put thoughts into anyone's head, and right now, he was challenging Remi to a battle of wills. Shrugging off the hand, Remi turned to the door.

"Where are you going?"

"None of your business. Can't a guy take a piss around here without you being up in their ass? And thanks for backing me up in there, Bels ... real freaking awesome of you," he snapped, cutting her a bitter glare. "Oh, and tell Focalor Cass needs him stat."

"Whatever. Go ahead and act like a bitch because you can't handle playing like a big boy!" Bels' acidic tone barely rose above a whisper, but it hit him hard, sure as a right hook to the face.

"Being a bitch, am I? All right then ... Wait, you'll see what I mean when it's your charge in this position! We'll see how you handle things then." There was no more reason to stand around and listen to the same shit he had heard a dozen times before. Biting back a curse, he turned from Kakabel, stalking off down the hallway. The training center would be empty given he knew everyone's location. Going a few rounds with the heavy bag had a more appealing ring to it as he envisioned the one face he wanted to see crushed under his knuckles.

"He's a ticking time-bomb, boss lady. Want me to shadow him?" Roc leaned forward, resting his elbows on his knees, fist curled around fist. He was on edge, itching to drop kick some sack of demon shit into the bottomless pit of purgatory. Observing the room, where rows upon rows of pristine books with their glistening gold and silver leather bindings were housed, and the prissy Victorian-style sofas decorating the room gave the impression it should be tea time, he knew this wasn't him. The sight of English tea roses stitched into canvas under his ass was enough to make him want to spray paint the damn thing black. All he wanted to do was drop down Earthside and sink into the background of his favorite bar, The Dirty Dozen. Where the delicious scent of frothy brews and the cheap perfume of dozens of seductively dressed women danced around the room.

"No, Roc. Let him blow off some steam. Seems Remi has some demons of his own to deal with."

"Come on, Am. Ferrian has been his charge since she was a baby. It's only natural he would care for her like he does," Kakabel cut in the verbal tango before Roc could to add his own special flavor of insult to injury comment.

Rising slowly from her chair, Amitiel's wings expanded out, as she pegged each one of the remaining angels with a hard glare. "Well, kids, I think it's time to start preparing."

"Fuck yeah! Those Underworld bastards want a war, they've got one. I'll gladly shove my size thirteen's straight up their asses and knock them into ash and shit."

"Roc!" Amitiel cast him a harsh glare as she walked within an arm's length of him.

"Yo."

"Cut the shit, shut your mouth, and realize you aren't a one man League of Guardians. I meant prepare. Looks like we might be welcoming a Darkling soon enough."

"Fuuuuuuck." The last thing Roc wanted to deal with was more drama and female sensitivities. "Great, should we stock up on Pamprin and Tampax then? Maybe I could run down to the video store and buy out their section of chick flicks. And while I'm down there, I'll swing by the

Assassin's Den and pick up a fresh set of throwing knives to stab my eyes out with when I'm forced to watch the crap playing on the big screen."

"Cut the shit, asshole. Just because we have breasts doesn't mean we all watch *The Notebook*." Kakabel ghosted up behind him, her hand making an audible crack as it smacked against the flesh on the back of his head. "Don't judge a book by its cover." Her smile quirked at the corner of her lips as she glanced back and winked at Amitiel. "And for the record, I'm a *Die Hard* girl, or *Batman*. So you can kiss my budunkadunk, okay, cupcake?"

"Bend over, baby. I've been meaning to tap that ass anyway." Rubbing his hands together, Roc edged closer to Kakabel as she not so subtly slinked back.

"Um, ewww. Not in a million years."

"Then you shouldn't have offered. Jesus, you're such a tease." Man, if there's one thing he liked, it was egging on the females of the realm, and Bels was an easy target.

"Bite me."

"See, there you go again. Making offers. Now, Bels, seriously, I'm starting to get a little offended here."

CHAPTER
TWENTY-THREE

The smacking sound of his knuckles hitting the leather-bag opponent littered the cool air as Remi hammered another uppercut followed by a cross jab. Sweat beads trailed down his brow and trickled over his torso. His head was pounding from the all of the mental gymnastics as he leveled another crushing blow square on the bag. Biting back another grunt, he swung hard, nearly breaking the chain holding the bag on its tethers.

It didn't matter if he tried to focus on new ways to kill Xaphan, or if the brethren needed him to buckle down and stop wasting time trying to save Ferrian from herself. Each thought he tried to concentrate on circled back around to her. From the taste of her soft, sweet lips, to the way she had tugged his body closer, wanting his touch. In the deep burn of her forest green eyes, he saw the real her, for the first time. He saw what she was capable of becoming. Even when she thought her innocence was stolen, she retained a purity and strength he had never witnessed in another mortal in all of his long years.

Why did she have to be so damned hard to resist? He fought against the reasons why he should stay away, twisting the knot tighter in his gut. The images he had of her tore at his senses; eating away at the façade he tried to hold in place like a flesh-eating virus. It was useless. It took only one kiss to intoxicate him, creating a feverish addiction he thirsted for more of.

He was slowly beginning to realize that nothing he could do would change her outcome. Nearly breaking his teeth from biting back a curse, Remi tried in vain to forget about how close she'd come to becoming Xaphan's plaything. His heart cringed thinking about the look in her eyes. Instinctively he knew it wasn't going to be the last time he would see her frenzied gaze, bordering on pure hatred. Hell, she deserved to feel the way she did. Giving in to it though, was a whole other box of what-the-hell, which had the potential to cause a monumental shitstorm.

She had come incredibly close to death so many times. Worn the scars like armor, and yet she only fought back against the one thing she feared above all. Love. What did he know about love? Sure, he was an angel with wings and all, but what did he know about love? Angels loved everyone. It was in the job description. Except for Nisroc; it had been rumored he had been dropped on his head a baby and the love leaked out before the wound had properly healed.

Pacing around the bag, he wished he could knock himself out from slamming his head against a concrete wall. It would've been a godsend to be relieved of thinking for five bloody minutes. His heavy footsteps thumped into the concrete floor as he stalked over to the treadmill. "This can't be happening. Seriously, why can't I shut it off? Stop thinking about her dammit!" He had tried to lock the images of Ferrian away, only to feel the sting as each one hit his frontal lobe with vengeance. Punching the buttons he went for a full out run, praying his mind would burn out before his legs did.

Her raven hair splayed out around her while she stayed locked away in a coma. The way her soft skin paled where it wasn't covered in blood as he settled her bruised body in the tub, and he washed away the residue. He couldn't turn it off; another image of her green eyes burning into his before he sank into the luscious warmth of her mouth grabbed ahold of him for dear life. His body remembered the moment perfectly. What he wouldn't give to go back and feel the soft, supple curves of her warm lips as they quivered against his. Ferrian's shallow, ragged breathing ignited a part of him, which he should've beaten to the ground, but instead became a spiraling ball of lust in his nuts.

The more he pushed himself to forget her, the more he slipped into the fantasy of her small body wrapped around his. Where the warm, summer sunlight filtered in through ivory gauze curtains covering the oversized bedroom windows, and the soft, golden light shimmered across her milky white skin. Ferrian's body lay across his, naked and warm … chest to chest. For a second, the mere thought she could ever be more to him, warmed him from within. Sure, maybe they could set up house, white picket fence and all. Right, it was definitely not happening. It was nothing more than false hope. She could barely stand to be in the same room as him, and now he was supposed to let her run off to face Xaphan on her own. All the while, Amitiel and the white feather crew stood back and took bets on whether she'd succeed or die trying … *Oh hell no!*

"Fuuuuuuuuuuuuuuuuck!" His heart jackhammered

against his ribcage as one single thought ran rampant around his mind: the moment when revenge snaked deep in her eyes, glinting with fury and lust for blood. She'd appeared to enjoy the taste for retribution. God knew she deserved it more than any being on the face of the planet. He hoped, for everyone's sake that she wouldn't take her newfound passion for destroying evil incarnates as a potential new career.

What was the point in thinking about it? If she survived to earn her place as a true Dark Angel, then she would face the Underworld's merry band of psychopaths anyway. *Awesome*. Over his dead body would he ever let it happen. Punching the speed button, a surge of anger stinging like liquid fire coursed through his veins as he pushed his body harder, pumping his massive thighs with the force of boulders cracking. Gritting his teeth, he bit into the speed on a dead run. Taxing his body on the damn machine wasn't going to solve his dilemma, but right now it took all of his will to stay on the mechanical sidewalk, instead of exploding out of the training center, out of the manse, and down town to see her. Sweat dripped into his blue eyes, and the stinging, salty droplets blurred his vision.

"Hey, fathead, you're not running for the gold. Whatta say you climb off the treadmill and we go grab a beer?" Roc's cool voice echoed off the walls as he leaned against the doorjamb. "Hey, asshole, did you hear me?"

Shooting Roc a sharp glare, he reluctantly punched the stop button and slowed to a walk before stepping down. His legs were grateful for the reprieve almost as much as his lungs. Fresh oxygen sawed in and out of his chest as he reached for a towel to wipe off his face. "What

… do you … want, Roc?" His lips were numb as he panted out each word, but the idea of a beer didn't sound half bad.

"Thought maybe a couple of cold brews and a round of pool would chill you the fuck out. Damn, man, how can one chick wrap your nuts up so tightly? Have you even banged her yet?"

Remi leveled him with a 'don't-you-dare-say-another -word' glare as Roc grinned and threw his hands up in mock surrender.

"Piss off, and keep Ferrian out of your thoughts, dickwad."

"Whoa, whoa, whoa … so now you're referring to your charge by her name?" Cutting him a knowing glare, Roc slumped against the wall, his thick arms crossed loosely across his chest. "Doesn't it, oh I don't know, go against the rules or some such bullshit?"

"Did your mother feed you paint chips as a baby?"

"Ya, and I'm pretty partial to Behr brand, number six-ty-nine, pretty in pink." Waggling his pierced brows, Roc failed at subtly. "Come on, man, get dressed. There's a bar on Sixty-Seventh I wanna take you to, it has a killer mi-crobrew."

Exhaling a deep breath, Remi tossed his towel at Roc's head, and strode off to the showers. He hated to ad-mit it, but a beer and some mind-numbing time of listening to the ranting and bullshit of an ass like Roc to take his mind off Ferrian might work. The break from the mental gymnastics he was working overtime on was more than welcomed at this point. "Fine, give me twenty minutes."

"Yep." His grin reached from ear to ear as he pushed through the doors. "And seriously, dude, don't get all ma-chismo styling your hair and shit. It's a hole in the wall bar."

Launching a basketball at his head, hoping for a good shot square in the guy's face, he didn't care if Roc returned fire or not.

"Missed, bitch."

"Piss off." Even though Nisroc was a complete chauvinistic dick, the guy had a way to make you laugh when he busted out his fairy rendition of the word 'Bitch'.

CHAPTER TWENTY-FOUR

Inching around the tiny bathroom, Ferrian gripped the counter for dear life as she stumbled to the toilet. Try as she might—until a migraine was firmly rooted inside of her brain—she still couldn't recall events since she woke up days earlier with a faint recollection of black eyes staring down at her. What was her brain trying to protect her from? What was she actually doing at night? For all she knew, maybe she was a secret assassin hired by the IRA deep undercover. So deep, she couldn't even remember herself. *As if! Sure, keep smoking those crazy pills.* Snorting at the absurdity of the idea, she leaned over and flipped on the shower. Her body hated the concept of moving, but the chill that was settling in her bones needed to disappear.

It was her night off from work, and the idea of staying in bed all night lost its appeal. *Huh ... I wonder where Remi's been for the past few days. I thought he would've been down at the docks.* She was too restless to try to sleep, but ached too much to do anything more. Walking was a dodgy notion at best.

As quickly as a lightning strike, she shot up when a

threatening sense impaled her. A current of vibrational energy buzzing over her body was calling her somewhere, and glimpses of a building downtown flickered before her eyes. "What the hell?" The thick grey mortar of surrounding aged bricks and grimy windows of an abandoned building lit up like a neon sign summoning her. She blinked a few times, pivoting her head for another viewpoint, trying to gain her bearings. Excruciating white-hot pain shot through her, making her body double over. She fell against the wall for support as she forced her lungs to work. Her breath shuddered with weak inhales. The wave of burning pain slowly subsided, enough for her to stand up straight once again. Whatever was there was calling her, demanding her immediate attention. Cries of agony rang loudly and nearly deafened her in the tiny bathroom. Steam wafted around her, like thick ropes of fog chaining her in place.

As swiftly as the feeling came over her, it disappeared. There was no making sense or reason of it. She struggled to focus on an image in the fogged over mirror, seeing only a faint outline of her body, morphing into something else. Dropping her shirt to the floor, the person in front of her no longer resembled the woman she saw daily. Darkness closed in around her. She didn't need the lights on to see what the reflection in the mirror was showing her; silky black and silver wings stretched out behind her. Slashing a hand streak over the mirror did no good. The steam filled in the gap as quickly as she wiped away the moist residue away. "Not possible! God, I must've slammed my head harder than I thought." Turning away from the image, she climbed into the shower and let the water do its soothing magic.

Where are you, Remi? Ferrian longed to see him, hoping he'd randomly show up with his charming smile, and gentle presence. The days had rolled on since she'd last seen him, when he had laid a kiss sweeter and sexier than anything she had ever imagined on her.

Soaking up the delicious feel of the shower, her mind wandered freely, letting go of what she couldn't remember anyway, as rivulets of hot water trailed down each curve with care. Visions of vibrant green grass crushed beneath her feet as she stepped toward the unknown, where billowy white clouds clinging to the azure sky coaxed her further into fantasy. In the distance, she heard birds chirping summer songs, and a rushing waterfall. A sound unlike anything she'd heard before lured her as if a steel cable tied to her gut, forcing her to follow. At first, the noise was tempered, until it gave way to an ear-splitting shriek. Moments of sun-filled day and serenity slipped into the shadowy darkness of a twisted forest the farther she walked.

A familiar sense of terror began to fill her gut. The sudden urgency to turn and run plagued her as she searched for a way out. Gnarly limbs of ancient trees blocked the way she'd come from, oozing with black tar, and reeking of rotting death. Dropping to her knees, she tried to focus on finding a way out as panic crept into her bones. The Alice in Wonderland vibe was freaking her the hell out.

"Wake up, dammit, wake up!" Slapping her face, her skin began to crawl as footfalls crowded around her. Slinking back against a thick oak tree, she prayed her presence would go unnoticed.

"Hello, Ferrian," a deep raspy voice spoke, thick with malice. *Xaphan.* She had no idea how she knew his name, but it was etched in her frontal lobe along with the hatred that burned through her veins. Her heart raced the moment she caught sight of his black Prada shoes, and trailed them up to the soulless eyes of the ghost from her past. Wrath spiked up her, the raw abhorrence searing through her blood.

Gnashing her teeth, Ferrian's desire to rip him apart with her bare hands ignited the horrific scenarios she had dreamt up. Shooting to her feet, her hands curled into claws as her muscles tensed, ready to lunge after the one person who'd tormented all of the hellish nightmares she'd ever had. He wasn't a person, though, not to her. He was a pure monster. "You!"

"So you do remember me? Lovely! And here I thought after the other night you would have forgotten all about me," he smirked, reaching out to touch her hair.

Rearing back, she hurled a wad of spit in his face, readying to throw a punch. "You're dead." Eyeing Xaphan cautiously, she spoke with absolute resolve to kill him or die trying.

Xaphan held himself with regard, standing firmly with an ebony cane topped with a silver wolf head underneath his palms.

"Tsk, tsk. Now why would you want to kill me? Do you not realize the gift I've given you?"

"Gift!" she snarled, ready to tear his eyes from their sockets and shove them straight up his ass. If it showed him how big of an asshole he was, she was game. "You stole my childhood and replaced it with a nightmare existence! A gift would imply I actually liked it." She focused solely on one thing: vengeance. "How did you manage to drag me into this dream, Xaphan? What's the matter, are you afraid to face me in the real world?"

"Oh you silly girl!" He laughed, but no amusement leaked from it. "I'm not going to destroy you here. No, no, my pet. I'm grooming you for your destiny. Don't you see? Everything we've done to you was for a reason."

"You sick bastard! Destroying me was nothing more than a ... what? A game, a job?" Fury balled up in the center of her chest, and the longer she stood there staring in disbelief at his casualness it built with the intensity of a hurricane.

"Now, now, my pet."

His tone and use of the word 'pet' grated on her nerves. She swallowed down the bile rising in her throat at the idea of being his pet.

"You're being summoned. I suggest you wake up and get out of the shower. You don't want to keep our guest waiting."

"What are you talking about? You know what, I don't want to know and screw you!" Her knuckles cracked as white bone surfaced. Before she even willed it, her fist flew out in front of her, nailing Xaphan square in the jaw. Adrenaline jolted her into motion as she launched another punch at his face. The cracking sound of bone connecting to bone excited her, stoking the fire of hatred in the pit of her stomach. He wasn't responding, barely even flinching, which set her rage into full-on apocalyptic proportions. Releasing a wrathful howl, she vowed to rip off his head with her bare hands and shove it so far up his ass he would taste his ash-filled heart.

The more she focused on him, the less she noticed anything around her. "Look around you, my dear." Waving his hand at the scene he had created in the first place, she watched as the forest melted away like a bad acid trip, dripping down black canvas into muddled pools of wet paint around their feet. "Do you think you can hurt me here?"

Her breath caught as she realized what he meant. This was all in her head. Slowly the sprays of the hot water consumed her senses as thick clouds of steam choked the air she breathed.

"Wake up, Ferrian. You have work to do. Follow your mind, and you shall find what you've been longing to know all along. The truth of who you are." She lost sight of Xaphan as the darkness crept in and reality scoured her senses. Anger and confusion rippled through her mind as the thunderous crack split her subconscious wide open.

"Fuuuuuck!" Everything Ferrian thought she knew, thought she had any grasp on, was breaking in her hands and melting. Memories, which had been locked away of the night she encountered Xaphan at the bus station, flooded her with the impact of an atomic bomb going off and she fell to her knees. Her eyes flitted over the scenes playing out like a movie. She saw herself run for Xaphan, the murderous intent masking her face as her lips peeled back in a snarl and teeth bared. Ready for the fight of her life.

The stench of death and brimstone littered the air, and the black pavement glistened with remnants of rain. Her heart thundered loudly in her ears as breath sawed in and out of her burning lungs. She wanted to kill him in the cruelest and most sinister way possible. The deepest instincts inside of her screamed she needed to do this, but it wasn't she who stopped herself. No, it was him. Remi's startled blue eyes grew wide as he stepped in front of her.

Crashing into him with the force of a freight train hitting the ice-covered valley floor is what had caused her body to still ache in all of the wrong places. The impact of colliding with the hardened muscles in his body had knocked her senses offline completely. She could feel the bruises beneath the skin, and wondered why she didn't resemble a cheetah with all of the spots from the night's events.

Steadying herself, she slowly lifted her body up from the shower floor. The echoes of screams pulsated in her ears, as a pain she could've sworn was a hot poker speared her gut. Gripping her stomach for dear life, she prayed it would stop, but the agonizing torture carried on, crippling her to the floor once again.

The screams she had always stifled broke free, absent of her control. She knew pain, had become best friends since childhood, but this wasn't *her* pain. She couldn't contain her cries, as a fresh wave of fear and crying broke from her trembling lips.

Ferrian's piercing shrieks splintered his concentration, and Cassiel bolted from the ledge. "What the hell?" Hitting the end button on his cell, he flashed down to her fire escape in a blink of an eye. His heart raced picturing the worst-case scenario. Could Xaphan have slipped past him? His hands grew slick with sweat as he willed the window open and stepped through. His eyes were intent on finding the source of her terror. Palming his Sig Sauer P220, he hoped the DMT infused bullets were going to be enough to stop Lucifer's right-hand man.

He remembered the last time he had faced-off with the demon, when he had used swords made from a rare material found beyond the realms of the tiny universe they watched over now. It had been nearly three centuries since he had fought Xaphan and modern technology had come a long way. One shot to the brainpan, and a chemical reaction similar to the Hiroshima explosion happened within sixty seconds as the DMT invaded and destroyed the cells within their body. The Dimethyltryptamine infused bullets, when shot into the body of demons or Daemons, reacted like a carcinogen. It destroyed the evil within, using the pure spirit of God's Light. As Cassiel's hand gripped his pistol firmly, he was more than tempted to fire a warning shot to draw out the perp.

Another ear-piercing scream broke from Ferrian. Cassiel knew if Remi found out, he would hand him his ass on a silver platter if he didn't charge in there and destroy whomever was attacking her. Slowly he stepped forward, sensing for anyone else inside her apartment. Questioning his instincts, he wondered why he didn't detect anyone else around them.

"Ferrian ... Ferrian," he called slowly and softly. Her muffled sobs in between screams came from the bathroom, and he prayed he wasn't about to walk into something short of a bloodbath. Her small frame was twisted and contorted in unnatural ways, retracting back to a curled up ball. Agony stretched across her face as her naked flesh bruised right before his eyes. "Holy shit!"

"I need to find her," Ferrian cried out, as she curled tighter into herself.

"Who?"

"The one he's torturing! I can feel her!" Pushing off the floor, she winced as she rose and hurried past him to pull on her clothes. "Who are you?"

"I'm Remi's brother, he asked me to watch over you." Cassiel never took his eyes off her as she scrambled to yank on her black jeans and black tank. He knew Remi would probably hammer his nuts to a wall for seeing her like this, but what Remi didn't know, wasn't going to hurt his beloved jewels.

Ferrian reached for her hoodie as another scream exploded from her lips and her body contorted. "No!"

He reached out to catch her as her body snapped backward. Ferrian's eyes rolled back as her body took a beating by unseen forces. "What the hell?" Catching her lightning quick, Cassiel slowly lowered her to the floor as her body twisted into another tormenting contortion, bellowing out more cries of pain. Palming his cell, he glanced down at the one number he had no choice but to dial. Blowing out a low curse, he punched the send button.

CHAPTER TWENTY-FIVE

"Come on, man! What kind of shot was that? Jeee-sus, when's the last time you kicked it down here and dropped a few pockets?"

It was a loaded question for sure, and Remi had multiple reasons why he wasn't up on the latest bar scene. However, it all boiled down to one undeniable truth, and it was clear as day. Ferrian. "Some of us take our jobs seriously," he countered as he struck the cue ball. "You should try it sometime."

"Annnnnnnd, some of us need to learn to lighten up. Otherwise your nuts are going to shrivel up, and singing soprano won't be much of an issue anymore." Taking a long pull from his IPA beer, Roc considered his brethren for a half of a second. If he didn't know any better, he would assume Remi was about it snap his jaw in half with the intensity he held deep in his face. It was there, Roc recognized the signs. "Oh for chrissake, you're really into this chick aren't you? Seriously … are you screwing with me right now? Dude, she's your charge. Someday, I'm assuming real soon, she's going to grow her wings and fly away. What then, Einstein? What are you going to do, follow her around like her angelic stalker?"

Remi pulled himself up, leveling Roc with a vicious stare. His knuckles cracked as he gripped the pool cue between both hands. "Roc, if you know what's good for you, you'll shut the hell up right now. Last warning."

"Calling it like I see it, bro, and for the record, you can stuff your warnings up your ass. Try to keep your head in the game before you start going soft on us, because all you're going to do is put not only your precious little Darkling in jeopardy, but the rest of humanity. You don't see the bigger picture right now. All you see is *her* and not what needs to be done. Feel me?" Rolling his shoulders back, Roc caught sight of two scantily clad women. A brunette with her breasts pushed up high in her low-cut shirt and tight jeans, and her overly processed blonde friend wearing more make-up than Lancome sold. Licking his lips, he knew dessert was but a wink away given the way their eyes trailed up and down his body. The scent of their arousal wafted off them, blaring they were ready for him.

First thing was first. He needed to convince Remi to quit acting like some lovesick bitch and pull up his big boy pants. Winking at his prey, Roc set the game in motion and returned his attention back to his brethren.

Remi considered him for a moment, easing his grip off the pool cue, and reached for his beer. His eyes never left Roc's as he pressed the cool brown glass bottle to his lips and drank down the rest of his lager in a few swallows. The longer he stood there, the more visibly irritated he grew. "Are you serious? Those two? I don't get it." Remi knew Roc's game; he didn't care much who the players were, as long as they had the right qualifications.

As long as the players were female and had ample assets it was game on.

"Hey, at least they aren't off limits. You should try it sometime. It's quite liberating," Roc smirked, glancing over at his ladies of the night. "Might help you put things into perspective, if you catch my drift." Leaning down over the table, he puckered an air kiss to the women and took a blind shot, nailing the eight ball in the corner pocket. "Pay up, bitch."

"Where the hell did the boss find you anyway?" All of the brethren knew there was no hope of turning the angel into anything resembling a 'good' being. Between the tattoos covering up his back, neck, and hips, plus both his of arms, and the piercings on his nipples, and scattered around his head, it was known Roc took great pride in his appearance. "I don't get what they see in you, man."

"It's the tongue piercing, gets 'em every time." Waggling his tongue to disgust Remi, Roc barked out a laugh as he tossed Remi the rack. "Rack 'em up, bitch. Double or nothing."

"Anyone ever tell you, you have about as much class as a sack of dog shit sitting on the side of a road in the desert heat?" Reaching for the balls, Remi slammed them down with more force than needed.

"Easy, kid. Don't go busting my balls now."

Yeah, that earned him a curt glare. Stifling a laugh, Roc guzzled down the rest of his beer before reaching out for another IPA.

Suddenly, Remi's face fell. *Oh crap, here we go again!* "Ferrian." Thundering past him, Remi's boots couldn't carry him out into the waiting night fast enough.

"Dude, what the fuck? Hey, you can't bail out like

this! You owe me fifty bucks."

He didn't say a word, didn't bother to shoot Roc back a 'piss-off' glance either. Punching through the door, Remi took to the sky without a second thought.

"Shit." Palming his cell, Roc scrolled down to Cassiel's digits and hit the send button. "He's on his way."

Letting out a reluctant breath, Cassiel quickly explained he'd been dialing Remi's number when Roc had broken through. "How in the hell did he know?"

"I don't know, but our boy nearly took down the front door on the way out." Looking back at the two women he had been visually undressing for the past hour, Roc hit the end button, slid the tiny cell in his coat pocket, and winked as an invitation to his new playmates for the evening.

"So, ladies, either of you wanna come handle my set of balls?" Waggling his pierced brows, he coaxed them closer with a subtle promise of a downright sexy time. "Come over here." He wiggled his finger to the blonde-haired woman with fake breasts spilling out of her low-cut top.

"I'm not good at shooting pool. Do you have any tips, you know, to give me an edge?"

"I might have some good hard advice to give. Now, stand right here … yeah, good. Now hold the cue like this—that's it, you've got it." Her giggle was a mix between a drunken Fran Dresher and nails on a chalkboard. Didn't matter. He pressed his hard body against her backside and lowered her body down, sliding one hand down her thigh and guiding the other over the cue. "Go ahead, sweetheart, take your shot."

CHAPTER TWENTY-SIX

"N ooooooooo!" Ferrian cried out, trapped by chains as another lashing cut across her raw skin. How had she ended up here? She'd been in the shower, but now she was struggling to open her eyes as pain scoured across her body. She inhaled sharply, noting the throbbing of her internal organs. The distinct feeling someone had pulverized them with meat-mallets made it hard to take the next breath. She attempted taking shallower breaths, and gnashed her teeth at the stinging sensation it caused. Peeling one eye open, she searched for a way out of the disgustingly dingy room. Broken concrete gave way to dirt-packed floors. Flickering lights seared with the horrid buzz of electricity, casting ghoulish shadows around the room. Concrete walls closed in around her like a tomb. "Where the hell am I?"

Something wasn't right about this. She couldn't re-member anything after scrambling to pull her clothes on. So how did she end up in some modern day dungeon? Staring down at her beaten body, the lacy top she thought possibly could've been pink at one time was now soaked with fresh blood. Long fingernails were shredded and broken, and pale hair clung to her skin.

Holyshitballs! Shock shot through her, when she realized it wasn't her body. Glancing once again around the room, she discovered an ominous shadow watched in horror as she sustained another kick to the gut. A whoosh of air burst from her bloodied lips, and she curled into herself. Hit after hit, she took every single kick and punch, as the apparition in the corner shouted for help. How was it possible she could have jumped into another's body without leaving her own? She racked her brain, but it didn't make sense why it was happening.

The heavy clanking of chains as they slid through the round, iron loops hanging from the grey, concrete-blocked walls sounded when they yanked her unmercifully up. Lifting her battered face, a pair of red burning eyes stared at her with nothing short of delight-filled malice. It's twisted grin and black claws grasped the blood-covered aluminum bat, giving her no hope she was going to survive this. Yet it wasn't her body, was it?

Glancing back at the fear stricken shadow, the female mouthed words of apology, as glistening tears streaked her cheeks, but never left evidence of their wetness on the floor.

"Ferrian." The deep voice vibrated through her skull like a sledgehammer. Scanning around the room, she sought out where it could have come from. Other than the two distorted goons beating the shit out of the body she invaded, and the spirit hanging out in the corner, no one else was there. "You need to heed what I am about to tell you. Understand this; you were made to take this. You will protect this soul from purgatory by freeing her spirit from this pain. I need you to take this, to protect her."

That was so not happening. She must've lost her dammed mind if she was listening to a voice tell her to take this beating to save another's soul! Hadn't she sustained enough hell in her lifetime? Now, she was being told to accept what was happening to her, in order to protect someone she couldn't give two shits about! What sick game was she in?

"Listen to me, my child," the voice grew firm and she snapped her head back, startled, "you were created to save the innocent from these atrocities. It's why you've been able to overcome and handle the events you've been through to this point in your life. She needs to be free of pain and torment. Only you can do this."

Sucking in another shallow breath, all she could manage was a meek, "Fuck you," before the crack of the metal bat knocked her out.

Remi's heart was racing as he landed on her fire escape with a soft thud. He caught the sound of scuffling on the floor. His muscles coiled as he launched himself through the window. "Ferrian!" He stopped short when he saw her small body crumpled next to the bed. Long moments passed as he watched in dread while Ferrian thrashed and contorted on the floor in abnormal ways. His stomach dropped to the ground at the sound of the excruciating screams breaking from her lips.

A dark growl rumbled through his chest as he gripped Cassiel's throat and lifted him off the floor, slamming him against the wall. "What happened here, Cassiel?" His teeth gnashed as his eyes pegged his brethren with an infuriated stare.

Glancing back, his heart skittered to a stop when her body finally fell listless, lying helpless on the floor. She reminded him of a rag doll carelessly tossed aside, setting off his fury into atomic mode.

"Reeee—mmmiiiiii." Cassiel tried to explain what had happened, but Remi's iron grip closed in tighter, cutting off his air supply. Grabbing Remi's arms, Cassiel tried to pry away his hands to no avail. "Shhhhheeeee co—llapsssssed." He slowly loosened his grip. "Please, brother, listen to me."

His blood had barely began to cool, but he finally set Cassiel down.

Catching his breath, Cassiel rubbed at his neck, grunting back to clear his throat. "I heard her screaming, it scared the shit out of me. So I came in through the window and found her curled up in a ball on the floor, writhing like this." Sucking in another breath, Cassiel continued. "I thought maybe Xaphan or one of his minions had come to pay her a visit, but when I searched around, I found nothing. Then, like someone had flipped on a switch, she jumped up off the floor and threw on clothes, as if she was in this huge hurry to go somewhere. She barely noticed me. Then it happened again. Her body twisted unnaturally, as she let loose this horrific cry. I swear to you, I've never seen anything like it. She was awake, I tell you, wide-awake, but her eyes were vacant! Next thing I knew, it was like her body was being beaten-to-shit by some invisible force. I caught her before she hit the floor. Then I called you."

Remi scanned over her body, from head to toe as he lifted Ferrian off the floor and placed her on the bed. "How long did this go on for, Cass?"

"I don't know. Minutes … maybe. She's been unresponsive since she dropped, until you got here." Clapping Remi on the shoulder, Cassiel spoke volumes with his silence. "I'm not sure what happened, but I swear to you, no one was in here. I would've sensed another being. It's like she was …"

Letting out a heavy sigh, he knew where Cass was going with it, and didn't like it one bit. "Locked in a living nightmare. Yeah, I know." Covering Ferrian up with her comforter, he glanced back over his shoulder. He had overreacted to the one person who had stood by his side for eons. "Hey, I'm sorry." His temper was running high and his tolerance levels low, but Cassiel didn't deserve to be thrown into his emotional bullshit.

"No, man, I get it. Thought you were going to rip my head off for sure, but I get it."

Cocking his head to hear better, the sound of water spraying out of a faucet grabbed his attention. "What's that sound?"

"What sound?" Glancing around, Cassiel heard the water from the shower still spraying. "I got it."

Slanting his head back, he considered Cass for a moment. "Wait, you meant she jumped out of the shower and curled up in a ball on the floor? What the fu—" Before Cassiel reached the bathroom, Remi shut the water off with his thoughts. "Cass, don't you find it odd she left the water on? Or the fact she got dressed in front of you?" He wanted to be pissed about the idea of anyone seeing Ferrian naked and soaking wet, but now wasn't time. An odd feeling niggled in the back of his mind, warning him something far worse was coming for her.

"Well, yes … I do. She seems pretty shy about exposing herself from what you've told me. Look, man, I swear I turned away." Sinking down into the roughed-up chair across from Ferrian's bed, Cassiel raked his hand through his sandy blond hair and watched the wheels turn in Remi's head. "I mean, the screaming I heard … well," Cassiel considered his words carefully as he let out a heavy sigh, "it seemed unnatural. I didn't think she was the type to yell. Hell, I honestly didn't know what to think. She has been pretty quiet since I've been standing guard."

"Exactly!" Creasing worry lines edged his eyes as he studied her facial expressions. "I've seen her at her worst; she shuts down and she doesn't scream out in pain. Ever!"

"So the question remains then, why now? For her to jump out of the shower, it's almost like she was in a trance or something."

"If what you've told me is correct, then we need her to wake up, and soon." This wasn't going to be easy to figure out, especially when his star witness was out cold. Pacing the room, he watched Ferrian with pinpoint intent. The way her breathing slowed to nothing and her heart raced then faded into a normal rhythm, filled him with constant dread. What was going on inside of her head? Panic flooded his mind, imagining the worst. *Why didn't I follow my instincts and return to keep an eye on her? God, I'm so stupid!*

"I don't know what you want to do about this. Do you want me to go back to Am and give her a heads up, or stay here? You know, in case whatever is messing with her manifests into something real. Tell me what you want me to do here." Cassiel saw the pain and frustration in Remi's eyes. "I'm sorry, man."

Waving off his apology, he let him know there was nothing for his brethren to be sorry for. "No, I'm sorry. I overreacted. Listen, I've got this. Why don't you hang out for a while? Once she wakes up, we'll figure this out and find out if there's something we need to fill in the rest of the crew about."

Nodding at his request, Cassiel sank back into the worn cushions and exhaled a curse. Whatever was going on with her wasn't going to be pretty.

CHAPTER TWENTY-SEVEN

The scent of death welcomed Xaphan when he entered the Great Hall to speak with Lucifer. Ebony painted bone sculptures lined the edges of the room as he crossed over the black marble floor riddled with blood red veins. The clacking of his shiny black wingtip Prada shoes echoed loudly as he approached Lucifer confidently. His shoulders pulled back; leveling his master with a devious stare and a smile to balance it.

"Xaphan," his master's voice cracked the sultry air like a steel cable whipping it, "what news do you bring me?"

Stopping twenty feet from Lucifer, his master's four sentries lined up in front of him. "May I approach?" His voice remained poised as he waited for an answer. If he could say anything negative about his boss, it was the fact the guy was paranoid as shit, and slow as a frigging turtle trying to mount its mate, when it came to answering anything.

Staring at the second level throne where Lucifer sat, he realized it had been ages since Satan or Lilith had occupied the Great Hall. Come to think of it, he hadn't seen much of Mammon, Satan's little shit of a son, either.

Snapping his fingers, Lucifer's sentries split apart, allowing Xaphan a closer audience. He managed to climb up two steps when Lucifer held up his hand to stop him from coming any closer. "Has the Darkling turned yet?"

"No, but she's so close. She has the taste for murder now. I saw it in her eyes. The bitch was nearly frothing at the mouth to get her hands on me." Shaking his head, his chortled laugh hung in the air. His master considered it for what seemed nothing short of an eternity. "I asked Vepar to help me infiltrate her mind. I thought it was time to step it up a notch, and had him tie her subconscious to one of our prey. She won't be able to stay away for long. She'll keep feeling the effects of what the Hellistics do to the human rats. Either she'll run to the victim," licking his teeth, Xaphan relished the idea of watching her break as the seductive lure of murder and torture consumed her mind, "and feel the need to help them, where therein my minions will take her down, or Vepar will infiltrate her mind on a deeper subconscious level and convince her the innocent rats are other demons. Either way, we win. She'll either turn or die."

Lucifer stared down at him, as he reached for one of his favorite delicacies, the charred hearts of virgin souls. His stomach churned a little more watching Lucifer shove another piece into his mouth, masticating it as his spoke. "Well played. I'm rather impressed with your inventiveness."

Swallowing back the bile rising in his throat, Xaphan glanced past his boss to the vacant thrones as his master continued on chewing and talking at the same time. "So, please explain it to me in detail how entering her mind and tying her to other's pain works. I can't say I'm familiar with this technique."

Xaphan refocused on Lucifer, his smile spreading wide as he stepped back down to the base floor. "We both know humans have weak minds. However, she's a Darkling, so her subconscious is a bit trickier to maneuver. Upon entering her dreams, I realized, if I could open up her mind to unlimited nightmarish situations, and make her feel the pain of others, not only physically but emotionally, it would be but a matter of time before she cracked. I can't imagine she'll last long before either seeking out my calling card or slicing her own throat. Every time one of my Hellistics demons tortures an innocent, she'll feel it. Every cut, every hit ... even death itself."

Sinking back against the velvet cushions lining his throne made of human and Darklings' bones, Lucifer's fingers feathered over the armrests as his blue eyes lit up. "Brilliant. Clearly you've put a great deal of thought into this. Kill this Darkling and the line of Darklings dies. Turn her into a Daemon and see this empire rise like never before. Fail, and consider yourself ... well, I think you understand what will happen should it occur. Are we clear?"

"Trust me, she won't last long. Either way she goes, the Darkling's soul will belong to the Dark Lord."

Lucifer leaned forward, glowering at him. "Do not fail me, Xaphan."

"I don't plan to, my liege."

CHAPTER TWENTY-EIGHT

R emi sat on the edge of the bed as the hours rolled by. Ferrian continued to twist and scream in agony, randomly launching out of bed with her eyes wide open, only to fall back into a deep slumber. The longer she lingered in the dreamscape world, the more he feared her mind was carving out another notch, leading to madness. "When the hell is she going to wake up?" With one hand, he gently massaged her calf, and the other raked through his thick black hair once again. At the rate he was going, it wouldn't surprise him if he ended up with a bald spot from worrying.

"Hey, I'm going to head back Realmside. I know asking you to leave and come back with me it pointless. Be careful, man, okay?"

"Yeah, all right. You should probably let Amitiel know what's going on, too, while you're up there. Something tells me whatever is going on inside Ferrian's head was planted there purposely. You know I can't leave her here like this."

"You're right. You can't, and don't do anything stupid. Got it?"

He glanced around the small apartment, and the sudden feeling of claustrophobia overwhelmed him. Why was she still living here, in this piece of shit ghetto penthouse? His mind circled back around to the last dream he'd had. Ferrian's soft body lying across white satin sheets. Her raven hair fanned out around her as slivers of sunlight danced across her milky skin. This was no place for her. And whoever had inserted the mental wormhole she was currently trapped in, obviously knew how easy it was to get to her. "Xaphan!" he grumbled, mulling over the idea.

His stomach tensed the more he labored over the notion of her staying in this apartment. Scooping up Ferrian's listless body into his arms, he lifted her off the bed and rose with the intent of getting her somewhere safe. She appeared so fragile, and yet he knew the truth. He had to steady himself the more he thought about who she truly was. She was more than the hope for humanity; she's the woman he had fallen hard for, and no amount of denying it was going to change the fact.

"What are you doing?"

"You're right, I can't leave her here. It's not safe for her, and I won't risk her again."

"Where in the hell do you think she'll be safe then?" The glint in Remi's eyes said it all. "Oh, no you don't! Am will be apocalyptically pissed off if you bring her Realmside, especially before she transitions. No. No ... you can't, she needs to stay here, on Earth." Shaking his head, Cassiel held up his hands as if he were going to stop Remi from walking away.

"I have no other way of keeping her safe. No matter where she goes, Xaphan and his merry band of unholy asshats will hunt her down. We still have no idea what's going on inside of her head, or why she's trapped, scream-ing and fighting in her sleep like she's possessed. But we both know this is not her version of normal." Pushing passed Cassiel, Remi realized he didn't care anymore what the ramifications of his actions were. It wasn't about his dire need to have her in his bed. It was so much more, went so much deeper. He couldn't leave her alone. She had awakened a part of him, and he didn't have the slight-est clue how to turn it off. How could one kiss cause such a shift?

Ferrian's head rolled into his chest, and he could have sworn her cheek nuzzled against him. Gazing down at her face, serenity had finally enveloped her, if only for a few moments. For the first time since she'd fallen unconscious she seemed calm, and he couldn't help but wonder what was causing her now peaceful repose. He held her body close to his chest, and he sensed the faint beating of her heart flutter. He pecked a kiss on her head. With one arm cradling her back and the other under her thighs, he eased out of the front door carefully

"Remi, she isn't ready for this, dammit! You could seriously affect her in a bad way. I mean, what if she loses it while she's up there? And shit, I don't even want to think about what the others are going to say if they find out." Cassiel kept pace with Remi as he descended the stairwell. His voice remained calm but assertive in true Cassiel nature, and strangely, it irked the hell out of him.

Cass was right. Yet he didn't care. It didn't matter what anyone else thought. He wasn't going to let Ferrian out of his sight until he got to the bottom of things. The idea of bringing her up Realmside was stupid, and possibly dangerous, but what else could he do? Leaving her in her apartment, even with him there, was no longer an option.

"Listen, man, I get that you want to protect her, but she doesn't even know who or what she is, let alone what we are. All she's ever known is what's here on Earth. I will agree, keeping her in the apartment isn't the best idea, but Realmside … I mean, c'mon. Surely you can understand the logic here."

Remi slowed to a standstill, taking a moment to let it all sink in. He knew all too well the possible repercussions of this. Closing his eyes, he inhaled Ferrian's sweet jasmine scent, letting it saturate his lungs. "What can I do? I can't let her stay here. She's not safe."

"I know, I know. What about hiding her away somewhere around here, like at a hotel or something? Somewhere she won't be too freaked out about, when she awakens, because she'll still be in a familiar city?"

Remi took a long moment to consider what Cassiel was saying. His gut still demanded he take her topside and tuck her safely away in his bedroom, but Cassiel was right on this one. "Fine. The Four Seasons Hotel is on the other side of town. I'll stay with her there, until we figure out this mess. When I know what's doing with her, I'll call you. Fair enough?"

"The Four Seasons, huh? Man, you must like this chick." Cassiel choked back a small laugh as he clapped Remi on the shoulder. "Yeah, I've got you covered. Call me as soon as you know anything."

"Sure. Hey … thanks. Guess my head's a hot mess right now. Do me a favor when you get back."

"What's up?"

"Tell Roc to wear a rubber next time. I'm pretty sure his dick is going to fall off at some point." Winking at his brethren, the first break of a smile subtly slipped out.

"What the fu—You know what, I don't even want to go there."

Nodding to Remi, Cassiel turn skyward and dematerialized from sight. He followed suit, as he held Ferrian tightly to his chest.

"My sweet Aingeal, please … wake for me soon," he whispered into her hair as they disappeared from human sight.

CHAPTER
TWENTY-NINE

S inking back into the red suede chair, Remi couldn't turn away as Ferrian thrashed back and forth on the king-sized bed. The hotel suite was roomy enough, and he had had the concierge stock up the kitchenette with food, leaving no room for error. He wasn't about to let Ferrian walk out of the hotel into the waiting stranglehold of Xaphan or his minions.

Getting passed the front desk and eyeing which room was available had taken only a moment of a well-worded mindful inception, followed by a quick bit of convincing the concierge his bride was drunk and simply fallen asleep. Placing a Do Not Disturb order on the room gave him the privacy they needed while Ferrian remained trapped inside of her head. He sat back and listened to the variations of her heartbeats and breathing.

His heart sank with each new onslaught of the torment her mind was going through. He had tried for hours to access her mind to see what she was seeing, and each time he hit a wall far beyond the reaches of her subconscious. Frustration ate away at him the longer she stayed asleep. Checking his phone once again for any new information by way of Cassiel's informant, Focalor, he sighed with its silence. It had been a mind-numbing wait as he turned his focus back to Ferrian's wincing expression.

She fought an invisible assailant, throwing punches and twisting into unnatural positions. He worried at some point Ferrian was going to snap her body in half from the odd bends of her limbs. There had to be something he could do to wake her. His heart seized as she launched up in the air, shrieking. Quickly jumping on her to keep her from slamming her head off the headboard, he held her as tightly as he dared, lowering her back down.

Holding her body close to his, he tried to comfort her as her eyes fluttered before closing to him. "Ferrian, shh, come back to me." His deep voice never rose beyond a whisper as he pulled her into his arms. His mind ran through multiple scenarios, all ending with tearing Xaphan's corpse apart with his hands, as he stared down at her pinched expression.

Pecking a kiss on forehead, he held her until she sank back into a deep, quiet slumber. Slowly he lowered her back down on her pillow, wishing more than anything he could understand what Ferrian was seeing in her dreams. The shimmer of her lips as they gently smirked back at him made his insides jump with a need to taste them. Brushing his lips over hers, the supple feel of her kiss ignited his desire, yet he held back; he'd only allow himself one small kiss.

"Remi," his name rolled out in a breathless taunt.

She's going to be my undoing.

It was as though years in Hell had passed. Each time Ferrian thought she had seen and been through enough, another round of torture began with fresh waves of excruciating pain exploding throughout her body. Then again, the bodies weren't hers, always strangers. Trapped in different bodies, male and female alike, taking the beatings for the innocent souls. Saving them from the shattering torments so they souls wouldn't be stuck in purgatory. The whole notion of it was bullshit, and pissed her off all the more with each strike. Why should she have to be the one to do this? What was in it for her? Sure, she always survived—beaten and broken down—but she got back up again, and walked on to another day. But at what expense? She had turned into a complete introvert, scared of her own shadow.

'*You were meant to save the innocent*'. The voice coated her psyche with strength. Sagging back against the cool, blood-dampened wall, she was teetering on the verge of insanity.

In those few brief moments when the sweet lull of a void consumed her, she wished she could feel the warmth of Remi's comforting touch. She could've sworn she heard him calling to her, his deep voice riddled with fear and longing, begging her to return to him. Yet, she couldn't break free of wherever she was trapped. Stuck in a dingy concrete room, with no windows, and only a few broken light bulbs swinging from ratty electric wires, she spun the inevitable questions around and around until her brain was on the verge of exploding. The darkness devoured light with covetous greed, swallowing it up like an addict needing its next fix.

Secretly, she knew the truth. It was building up inside of her gut each time that haunting voice reminded Ferrian she had been created for this. If she could save one soul from this, then she'd willingly take this on. It sucked nonetheless.

For a moment the pain was absent, granting her a few seconds of unsettling peace, as a faint voice pleaded her to return to him. Her heart leapt with the idea it could be Remi's voice, and her fingertips lightly feathered over her lips, remembering the soft crush of his mouth pressing against hers. The dizzying effects were spinning out of control, as a new intrusion of light and heat, surrounded her.

She couldn't tell what the hell was going on, but something warm filled her body with genuine hope, suggesting she would be released from the shithole she was trapped in. His face came into view. And her chains had dissolved away. The aches throughout her body had disappeared as well. She imagined being in a luxurious room with soft clean linens on the bed; rich colors accenting the room and the scent of fresh flowers filtering through the air. It was then she realized she was dreaming, as Remi's eyes, covered in worry, stared down at her. Running her fingers through his silky inky hair, she figured why not indulge herself a little and take the moment for what it was and let desires consume her.

His lips brushed over hers, and she pulled Remi down for an urgent kiss. Slipping her tongue past his strong lips, tasting rich, exotic flavors in his mouth, she reveled in the sensations, savoring it. Remi held her tighter, sinking deeper into her kiss. The heat in his kiss grew more intense, as Ferrian slid her free hand around his waist, pulling him down on her. The weight of his body as he sank into the cradle of her split thighs was welcoming and surprisingly lighter than she thought possible. His body shivered under her touch with the slightest touch of her fingertips grazing up and down his skin. Remi's sultry groan as he devoured her mouth made the liquid heat between her thighs well up with each passing second. Breaking their kiss, fear raced across his eyes, setting off panic in her belly. "Ferrian, what are you doing? This isn't you," he softly whispered, his voice oozing with desire. His gaze said something altogether different as he stared darkly into her eyes.

"Shh, Remi." Resting her fingers over his lips to stop his protest, she couldn't bear the idea of rejection. "I want this. I've wanted this since the first time I saw you," she replied breathlessly. Her heart pounded against her chest, and her lips trembled. "Please, let this happen." *Oh god, please let me believe that you want me even though we both know it's a lie.* "I know I'm nothing to look at, but I beg you, let me feel like I'm worth something more than a freak who holds as much beauty as a bag of dog-food." She stared long and hard into his brilliant blue eyes, and saw the hurt in them, matching her own.

"Ferrian, you're worth so much more than you realize. Each time I see you, I think of how amazingly strong you are. How beautiful you are, especially when you're dancing around in your apartment. Everything about you entices me, calls to me." Cupping her cheek, he watched as her breath shuddered and tears threatened to prick her eyes. "I don't want you to regret what you're doing."

Sliding her hands around to the back of his skull, Ferrian crushed his lips down to hers, capturing his kiss once again, only to break away panting. "I want this. I need you. I've never desired anything this badly before. I've been so afraid to get close to anyone for so long, Remi, and yet here you are, peeling back my layers, and I'm helpless to fight against it."

Her heart was racing like a freight train thundering down the tracks, while she waited for what seemed like a lifetime for his answer. Slowly, a smile spread across his face, as his fingers ran through the tangles of her hair. Every inch of her flesh craved to be touched. Sweeping his tongue over her lower lip, he playfully captured it between his picture perfect teeth. His eyes burned hot as an inferno and he claimed her lips once again, taking his kiss deeper, slower. Milking the moment until her body was quivering under his touch.

Her mind went blank as instinctual sense took over. His sweeter than honey taste was intoxicating her into a drunken lust. The longer Remi kissed her, the more she realized she could never tire of this feeling. Simple. Pure. Blissful. Shuddering against him, and arching up into him, Remi's hands captured her breast, gently thumbing over the hard little bead of her nipple, while he caressed the delicate bones around her face and jaw with his other hand. Her accompanying groans left a smile splitting across his lips, breaking the seal they had forged. Her core grew wetter, soaking her panties as the hard length of his cock rubbed gently against her body. She didn't want it to feel this good, she didn't want to want Remi this badly. It went deeper than the physical need. It consumed her body as her hips writhed sinuously against his body. His sensual groans mixed with her own in a beautiful melody.

The lovely friction their bodies created, grinding against one another, had her close to the edge. For the first time in her life, she was free. This time, she wasn't about to let this dream end by holding back what she wanted or wanted to give. Fierce need to strip him bare overcame her as she pushed him back.

His startled stare penetrated her while she lifted his shirt over his head. Her breath caught when she came face to chest with a wall of hardened muscles, perfectly cut as if he had been sculpted from the finest marble by angels. A series of intricate tattoos danced over his wide shoulders and thick chest, weaving a tapestry of scrolls and lettering, but she had no idea what language it was. *How do I even know that it's a language?*

Washing the question away, her eyes dance over the breathtaking sight, then reached up to trace the markings from the top of his shoulder down to his chest. Biting her lip, she steeled herself from tracing the markings with the tip of her tongue and tasting his skin. *This is my dream dammit. Who says I can't do what I want to?* Leaning into him, her small pink tongue licked and pecked kisses down the hard planes of Remi's chest as his breath sawed in and out, panting with low dark groans.

"Wait! M'aingeal, you don't want to do this." Remi pushed off her, heaving out breaths, as distress stretched across his face. But why? This was only a dream, so why was he resisting her?

Fire coursed through her veins as she stared back up at him from under low brows and a fan of dark lashes. Ferrian's inner vixen wanted to play, and releasing it for one night, even though she knew it was silly, was exactly what she planned on doing. She was dreaming, and dammit, she was going to own this shit! Displaying a devious smile, her nimble fingers quickly worked his black leather belt, ripping it out from around his waist, and tossing it across the room without a second thought. "Shut. Up." Her eyes darted between his hypnotic gaze and the button fly in front of her. Her hands shook slightly as she carefully plucked each button free from its hold, revealing a patch of inky groomed hair nestled around the dusky stalk greeting her hungry gaze. Biting her lip, a fresh wave of anxiety slapped her upside the head. *Holy shit, I can't do this*! She almost wanted to give up. Steadying her fingers, she finished popping each button free, carefully returning her stare to his longing mien.

Holding her breath, she slowly pushed him back on to the bed. The expanse of his body as he stretched out before her, seemed to go on forever. Never having expected to see a man appear as beautiful and terrifying at the same time, she had to gulp past the lump securely lodged in her throat. She had imagined this scenario so many times since first meeting him. What it would be like to have Remi under her spell, craving her, and trembling from her touch as his body begged for more. Where moments when her vulnerability and confidence merged, and swallowed her whole at the same time.

Her fingers quivered as she gazed into his heated stare, his eyes transfixed on hers. Slowly she slid his pants down his thickly sculpted thighs, springing free his thick shaft. *Oh, he likes going commando in my fantasies. Rock. On! Thank you subconscious, I effin' heart you.*

Slipping her hand around his hot flesh, she enjoyed

listening to him groan from her touch, as his hips arched into her hold. For the first time she could ever remember, she reveled in the intoxicating lure of control. The supple flesh she held, with its ridges and vein bumps, stoked a lust deep as an abyss in her as she stroked over the length of his cock from the base to tip. A sultry hiss broke from his lips when she thumbed over the plum head, rubbing over the warm crystal drop on top. Remi was a beautiful sight, with the way his body went taut and his eyes burned for her. Shallow breaths and guttural moans ripped haggardly from his lungs, sawing in and out the faster she fondled him. His hands clenched the edges of the mattress, and his hips bucked against her hand.

She never thought she would feel such a sense of power, or the rush of control, yet here she was, and he was helpless against her onslaught. Ferrian carefully timed her movements, fast and light to slow and deliberately tight. Thumbing over the weeping tip, curiosity struck her, wondering what a man like Remi would taste like. His eyes grew wide as she wrapped her hot mouth around the head of his cock, tonguing over the sweet spot and lapping up the droplet beading at the tip. The taste of his essence was exquisite as it danced over her tongue. His hand raked through her hair as he threw his head back into the pillows. "Oh fuuuuuuuuuuuck." The rush of her desire to tease him with long, wet strokes of her tongue played out a tune of hypnotic moans, singing praise to her, as she continued with her wet assault on his sex.

CHAPTER THIRTY

Ferrian had surprised the hell out of him when her eyes groggily opened. Tiny swells of hope emerged from his gut when his lips brushed lightly over hers, only to feel the heat of her kiss return the sentiment. He melted in her palms the second she raked her slender fingers through his hair. Springing his cock to life the moment she pulled him down on her to take their kiss deeper. He hadn't missed the delicious sounding little inflections of moans as they passed through her supple lips. She pulled back and shot him a smirk he hadn't seen before, and dammit if it didn't add fuel the fire burning in his veins. He wanted to taste her again, taste her from lips to hips. Melt between her thighs, and live in her heart and eyes. Her expression twisted from playful to downright sultry as she pecked kisses down the column of his throat to his shoulders and then his chest. Biting his lip, he couldn't explain it, didn't understand what had changed in her, but he hoped and prayed she was in her right mind, since what she was doing to him made him want to roll her beneath him and consume her wholly without a second thought. He only half-heartedly meant it, when he told her she didn't want to do this, because the inner desire deep within wanted her with a fire raging hotter than Hades.

The thundering of his heart was deafening in his ears as his body arched up from her sensual touch. Remi couldn't remember the last time a female had laid hands upon his body, and damn if his body didn't respond so fervently. Groans, thickly coated with undiluted lust, rumbled through his chest as his muscles coiled, ready to strike hard and fast. He should've fought her off, or begged her to stop. But at the moment, all he could say was the name of his goddess; the woman he would pay worship to each day he drew breath from now on, until eternity perished, "Feeeeerriaaaaaan."

His mind raced back and forth between what was right, what was wrong, it feels too good, and he would be the reason why she ended up in Hell. He could justify it a number of ways, but none of it mattered, as his body torqued from her softest touch. No, the only real question he needed an answer for was, *'Why now?'*

The answer would have to wait. Air hissed through his teeth as he lifted his eyes to focus on her. He wanted to say no, this can't happen, but in truth he didn't care about any violations to the code. Remi didn't know who wanted her more … his cock, his heart, or the entirety of his mind, body, and soul. If his brain hadn't been so wrapped around the pleasure and sensuality of Ferrian's loving kiss, south of his waistline, he would have had better instincts to pull away from her touch and walk into the bathroom. An onslaught of a cold shower would surely do the trick. It didn't matter. He was lost to her touch. The intensity she was ratcheting up inside of him threw his self-control right out the window and straight down into the dumpster.

He'd wondered many times what it would feel like to be with Ferrian, but he hadn't expected it to feel as incredible as it was. He knew she hadn't been with anyone willingly … ever, so why was he the lucky one? It didn't make sense. He tried to beg her to stop, but the hurt, mixed with dire passionate need in her eyes, convinced him to let Ferrian have her way. She needed this to happen. If he rejected her now, he knew deep in his gut Ferrian would lock herself away from the world. She'd carried the scars of rejection around like banged up armor, letting the weight of guilt consume her. No, if this is what she needed to find a sense of peace, he was willing to endure it. Smirking at the thought, he realized enduring it wasn't the problem. However, enjoying it immensely was.

Sinking back into the plush mattress, his body tensed with each succulent pull of her mouth. Her fingers slid over his thickly muscled thighs until she reached the contours of his hips. His body ached to feel her from the inside, and hold her in his embrace as he drove deeply into her wanting body.

A sudden fear assailed him. What if him coaxing her made her freak out on him? What if his unwanted advances made Ferrian retreat into the shell of her comfort zone? It was a dicey idea to play around with; he was walking a fine line of wanting to pleasure her, and worrying he might send her on a one-way spiral down. Resolving himself to one solution, he gripped the edge of the mattress and rode out her desires at her pace. He wasn't sure how far she was going with this, but he wasn't going to push her either.

Staring down from under a half-lidded, lust-fueled gaze, he watched the motion of her lips, her tongue on his erection. She flashed her glowing emeralds on him, and he nearly lost it right then and there. Biting back the need to release his hot seed, his balls cinched up tight as he fought the urge. In the single moment of connection between them, his mind became clear, with the truth in his heart. She was the only one he was willing to give up his wings for and suffer an eternity in Hell.

His jaw dropped as he watched her pink tongue languish a moment longer, circling the tip one final time, grinning the same sinful smile she had before. Her heated gaze ignited a primal and deeply carnal craving he had to covet. Her body moved sinuously back up his, like a cougar, locked on her prey. The nimble tips of her fingers grazed over the contours of his stomach, up to his chest, sending pulsating shivers coursing throughout his entire body. His breath hitched in irregular increments each time she nipped at his flesh. It was a side of Ferrian he'd never seen before, and he wasn't sure if she was possessed by some kind of succubus demon or if she'd finally accepted she was free.

Her hands found their way up to his neck, wrapping them around him as she crashed her lips down on his once again, taking the kindness out of their kiss and moving straight into the realm of urgency. He had never been so turned on by a kiss, but at the moment his whole body was ready to explode. Long moments of her body on top of his and his hands sliding down to her shapely ass, cupping her tightly, expelled more precious little mews from her lips. She fit perfectly in his arms. The only problem he found was she was still dressed. A temporary problem with an obvious solution, and one Remi was more than willing to help remedy. Focusing on the delicious contours of her body, he slid one hand under the hem of her tank top to test his welcome.

Surprise rocked him once more when she reared back and pulled it off without hesitation. His eyes flashed open wider, holding his breath as Ferrian reached behind her back, freed the hooks of her bra, and carelessly tossed it aside. He couldn't think, could barely breathe as he feasted on her exquisite beauty. Her bare, milky skin glowed. All signs of the scarring from violence had dissolved from view, leaving her appearing as untouched as a newborn. She was more beautiful than Aphrodite herself. His hands traveled around to the small of her back, lowering her back down to his chest. The sensation of her hard twin beads pressing against him shot another erotic wave pulsating straight down to his cock.

"Remi," she purred, her lips only a whisper away from his ear, "I want you." The words poured from her mouth thick with raw, carnal need. His arms ensnared her as she licked the fleshy patch beneath his ear, leading up to her sinking her blunt teeth into the same spot. He hissed at the pleasure and pain mixing. His hands sank into her back as he pinned her to him. It was only a matter of minutes before he lost complete control, between her biting him and her hips grinding against his. It wasn't a matter of taking the time to let her play anymore. His own desire took over, and with it, his sanity. Rolling her beneath him, his lips captured hers, locking her in a cage of his desire. Her returning moans as she clawed at his skin, demanding more from him, coaxed his own guttural groans to break free.

Ferrian's warm breath heaved in and out, skating over his skin as his hand slipped down between her warm thighs. Even through her jeans, he could feel the heat of her body feverishly building, and her sex damp with desire. He didn't know how it happened or when her fly had popped open, but he was damn glad she welcomed his touch to the soft, silken skin. Slowly he feathered a finger along her wet slit, relishing the feel of her body writhing under his. Ferrian's eyes flared wide with silent pleas as he thumbed small circles over her sensitive clit. Moans rose through the air in a symphony with each stroke, and he could only imagine what it would feel like to bury himself to the hilt in her well-spring of divinity.

His cock throbbing, and his balls squeezing harder than they ever had, he risked taking things further and dipped a finger between the silken folds of her wet hot core. His breath caught watching her body rock with pleasure before his eyes. Arching her back higher, her plump mounds jutted upwards and Remi seized the chance to latch on to one of the hard tips of her nipple, lavishing it with his tongue and lips. His own need twisted him tighter as she clawed voraciously at the blankets to keep herself from springing off the bed. He carefully worked her over, slipping in deeply between her silken wet folds while thumbing small circles over her soft nub.

Tamping down his growing need to sink in to her luscious body, he had to make sure this time was all about Ferrian. His desires would have to wait, at least until Ferrian was teetering on the edge of being completely spent. Her approving moans as her body demanded more made his cock bounce, slapping her thigh with its moist tip. Remi thought he knew the real Ferrian. He had been studying her since birth, and in recent months got to know her on a deeper level. She was a woman who buried all of her pain inside, hiding herself from the world, yet here she was. The epitome of a sexual goddess lay out before him. Not only letting him, but demanding him to satisfy her.

Her hands scrambled to push her jeans over her hips, squirming to slide them down her legs. He saw the dire need in Ferrian's eyes, lit with a frenzied fire. Lifting off her just enough to give her the space she needed, he caught her hands, and took over sliding her jeans down. Sure, he wanted to tear the fabric right off her, but why rush things? Nope, he was planning on taking it one leg at a time. Slowly and deliberately. He took it slow, pressing tender kisses down her thighs to her ankle before peeling the fabric off. Then moved over and repeated his intentional actions.

Resplendent wasn't a suiting enough word to describe the way Ferrian glowed before his eyes, spread out before him in nothing but her natural beauty. Taking his time, Remi grazed his fingers along her calves, and trailed toward the inside of her satiny thighs, until he reached the source of bliss before him. Ferrian's breath shuddered harder, as he delved between her wet folds, with one finger and then braved a second one.

"Oh god, Remi!" she moaned, reaching out for him. He wouldn't have minded staying where he was, pumping his fingers deep into her wet slit, but the sight of her sweet nectar gleaming from her southern lips on his fingers, made his need to taste Ferrian turn downright deadly. Licking his lips, his eyes caught hers raging with the same fiery need as she spread her thighs wider for him, welcoming his greedy kiss, with all of the delicacy of a blaring neon sign on a dark winter's night.

"Is this what you want, m'aingeal?" His deep voice was thick with hunger as his eyes darted to her sweet wet core in his palm, coaxing her to bloom for him. With a small nod, Remi took his cue and sank down between her moist thighs, kissing and licking satiny flesh along the way.

All it took was the first lap of his tongue slicing between the soft wet folds to send Ferrian jackknifing off the bed, moaning out his name and clawing his shoulders. Her hands raked through his hair, holding him in place as her hips met his mouth with a feverish need. Writhing from his touch, from his penetrating kiss, her body shivered with the pleasure he was giving her. His tongue danced eagerly along her silken folds, and delved into the core of their mutual bliss, savoring her sweetness with gluttonous greed. Thumbing over her sensitive nub, her tight body demanded his touch to stretch her in ways, which would leave them both in a tangled blissful mess. And he'd be damned if he was going to deny Ferrian anything she wanted.

CHAPTER THIRTY-ONE

Ferrian's ramped thoughts surrounded the delicious feel of Remi's ravenous mouth as it lavished her core with the flat of his tongue. He had her body torqueing in delicious ways she swore would snap her in two. She had never known pleasure like this. Reaching for the headboard, she needed to grab on to something familiar for dear sanity.

He handled her with such attention, making sure to coax moans out of her with perfect timing. Each kiss was full of passionate doting. She braved a glance down between her thighs in time to catch him staring back up at her. For being a fantasy dream, she had to admit, the vividness was far too real. Part of her wished it could be real, where she appeared as beautiful as moon rays on an October night. Then the other part of her feared if he saw what lay beneath the clothes, he would turn from her in disgust and run for the hills. No, if this were the only way it could happen, in the depths of her dreaming world, then there it would stay.

Nothing compare to the beauteous feeling he coaxed out of her. Well, maybe it wasn't entirely true. The kiss they had shared, his pliant lips soft against hers, as his tongue deliberately sliced its way into her mouth, had left a stain on her memory. The first kiss was truly magical, but nothing compared to what this dream kiss had over it. Here, she was safe and wanted. More importantly, and unexpectedly, she was ... desired for the first time in her life. "Remi." She almost wanted to laugh listening to her voice, thickly coated in lust as she murmured his name. Her body twisted and writhed to his will as her hips bucked against his mouth, riding out another shattering peak.

He had complete control over her body, and God help her, she devoured every second of it with covetous avidity. Her body had been starving for so long for a comforting touch, for what he was offering. With Remi taking up residence between her shaky thighs, milking her dry of every last drop, she couldn't imagine what real life would be like. To feel him, all virile and gorgeous six foot four male, built like a Roman warrior with looks to kill for, consuming her as if she were his cure to an unquenchable addiction. Stroking his arm, as Remi palmed the mound of her breast, she couldn't tell who was enjoying this more, her or him. It didn't matter. All she cared about now was getting him beneath her split thighs so she could take her control back.

"Remi," she whispered again as she pulled his hand to her face. The warmth from his palm as it caressed her cheek was a gentle intimacy she had longed for. Pressing her lips to the fleshy mound of his hand, she inhaled his rich dark scent, letting his natural spell pull her under further. The overwhelming sense she was dangerously close to losing herself completely jarred her back into reality. It was then she saw Remi glance back up at her. His brilliant smile slicked with her arousal and his sapphire blues beaming like electric lights.

Guiding him back up to her, Ferrian stroked her fevered hands around the back of his skull, and leaned in closely to his ear. She couldn't help but notice his pulse had quickened. Her swollen lips were but a breath away from his ear. "I want to feel you inside of me … now," she whispered, brushing her lips along the crest of his ear.

Remi took her cue and hooked his arm under her legs to pull her body closer. Pushing against his chest, she watched as anxiety shot across his face. "What's the matter, m'aingeal?"

The glint in her eyes didn't hide the craving clawing its way to freedom. She wanted him all right, but wanted him beneath her. Shaking her head, she licked her lips, twisting them in to a devilish smirk. "I want you beneath me."

Pressing her fingers to his lips, she urged him farther off her, and slid her legs to the floor, as he knelt before her. Her hand cupped his chin as she guided him back up. Her eyes stayed locked on his when she pivoted them around until his body was but a mere thrust backward onto the mattress. Her hand slipped down to his chest, feeling his heartbeat quicken from her touch. The thrill of feeling more alive in this moment than ever before in her real life, swept over Ferrian. With one impetus move, she quietly demanded Remi to follow her lead, as his body fell perfectly to the waiting luxury of Vera Wang's best mattress.

There was no way of telling when she'd wake up, but she prayed with every ounce of her soul it wouldn't be too soon. If this was to be the only tenderness, and frenzied moment of passion she would ever know or feel, she wanted it to last as long as humanly possible. *'Humanly possible'*. She had felt anything but a human since childhood. Slaking off errant musings, she dwelled over Remi's outstretched body, gulping past the growing lump lodged in her throat. What did she honestly know about seduction? Remi's approving gaze danced over her naked flesh. "Do you want me?" Her voice hung low, seductively raspy as she steeled herself for the moment she had been dreaming about. His returning smile ate up the last of the doubt scratching around in her brain.

"Yes." The vibrations of Remi's voice tickled the tips of her hard nipples. In one lithe movement he captured her tiny waist and moved back up to her, stroking the curves of her hips as he pecked small kisses along her ribs. "I want you." His voice hit her low, and straight to her core. Her sex welled up again, burning to feel him deep inside of her. "I've wanted you for so long. To kiss you. To touch you. God, the way you taste … is pure ecstasy." Rolling his massive frame up, his body towered over hers.

Cupping her ass, Remi drew her to his hard body, making her feel protected. His other hand lifted her chin to meet his gaze. "Ferrian, I need to tell you something. I—"

Cutting him off before he said the one thing she couldn't handle, she crushed her lips on his, sealing their fate. Shoving his thickly muscled body back down to the mattress, she landed on top of him, cradled in his embrace. She scrambled before he tried to break from their kiss, slipping back down to his hips. Gripping the rigid length of his cock, she thumbed over the crystal droplet weeping out in appreciation.

It was do or die time, and giving Remi the chance to object wasn't happening. She straddled him coyly, darting her eyes between his appraising stares and his pulsing cock. Sucking in a deep breathe, she slowly lowered herself down onto him. A split second of fear raced through her mind. She had no idea what she was doing. Ferrian was hardly practiced in the art of seduction and sex, still she wondered if she could go through with it, or if she could fit him in her. She carefully guided him in as his hands slid up to her hips, holding her in place. His body tensed beneath her when the head of his cock penetrated her inner sanctum.

Her breathe hitched as her brows furrowed tightly together. Closing her eyes, her nerves lit up like a live wire, searing down to a waiting bomb. Inch by inch she slipped farther down on to him, as Remi gently rocked his hips, probing her from under. He stretched her to the point of pleasurable pain. Her whole body raged on as she fell into a rhythm of her own making. Rolling her hips to meets his with sinuous inflections and deep thrusts; each buck brought with it, hisses, and ragged gasps. Her heart was racing, the higher she climbed the magical ascent to peaking.

His guttural groans vibrated through his chest, down to his cock, tickling her in ways she'd never thought possible. She was balancing on the precarious edge of oblivion when the first peak hit. Rocking and grinding against him, Ferrian rode out the first of many orgasms, littering the air with her cries of passion. Her fingers clawed at his chest as she tried to keep herself from floating up to the ceiling. She was completely in control, and at the same time spinning out of control. It didn't take long for her to lose count of the amount of orgasms she had experienced.

Yet, her hunger had ratcheted up more watching

Remi straining to keep it together. "I want to feel you deeper inside me," she purred. Her command lit another fuse, this time in him, and he smirked back at her.

Circling one arm around her waist, he rolled them over until she was flat on her back. Brushing his fingers down the length of her legs, he gently coaxed them up to rest on his shoulders. "Are you sure you want this?" His voice was pure sex as he eyed her with a new intensity.

Yes! No ... yes! Lifting her hips to meet his, she sucked in a quick ragged breath and welcomed the tip of his cock, bouncing eagerly against her swollen core. Nodding her head, she smiled coyly as she buckled down her emotions for the moment she had been waiting for. The delicious ache between her thighs wanted more, and with one smooth, hard thrust, Remi had buried himself to hilt between her slick folds.

Her body clenched around the erotic feel of his cock, plunging deep until she swore he was going to split her in two. Bringing her to new heights, her moans quickly turned into melodic cries with each thrust, taking her higher and higher. She wanted more, needed more as Remi set the rhythm. She was helpless against her body's craving.

Leaning down toward her, he shot like a piston at full throttle. Sweat beads trickled down his back, glistening across his skin. Feathering her hands up to his shoulders, she held on for dear life. *Oh, dear God, Remi, I don't want you to ever stop. Please don't ever stop!* Fluttering her eyes open until she finally focused on a pair of twin sapphires staring back down at her, she decided right then and there, that this one pure undiluted moment was as close as she would ever come to Heaven.

"I want to feel you come." It didn't matter if it was a

command, demand, statement, or request, she wanted to feel everything Remi had to offer. His half-lidded eyes popped open wider, and his smile turned downright wicked.

"Your wish is my command." He slid her legs down and around his waist, and lowered himself until the only space between their slick bodies was the trails of dew on their flushed skin. Ferrian's body ratcheted up for another explosion of ecstasy. His body was straining and she almost feared he's burst into pieces from the stress, but he never broke their connection. While he stared down into the windows of her soul, she was exposed in new ways. Before she had time to think it through, her body launched into an orgasm, blowing away all others as Remi released a roar capable of deafening a crowded room. With a final thrust, he sent both of them over the edge. Colors danced before her eyes as she tried to regain her focus. Dropping his head to her chest, the final few shudders of his pleasure rattled through his taxed body. Her approving mews quivered, along with her thighs as she slowly came back down from Heaven.

His breath, heavy from panting, skated over her heated flesh as his heart pounded against her chest and he sagged between her thighs. The moment was perfect, almost too perfect, as she combed her fingers through his sweat-dampened hair. However, it was only a dream. Nothing this real could be this beautiful. In the real world, she never would have been so bold. Especially not with someone like Remi; he wasn't the type to settle for a scarred up freak like her. Yet she wasn't about to let the thought take root as she relished in the feel of the delicious aches in her body.

"Remi," she murmured through the coarse feeling in her throat. All she wanted was to drown into his beautiful blue eyes for as long as it took until she found the famous satiated gaze she had read about in all those trashy smut novels. "Remi, are you all right?"

Lifting his head, his returning smile lit up the room as he whispered something she couldn't quite understand. "What did you say?"

"I'm in love with you, Ferrian." His words sounded so sincere and, dear God, she wanted to believe this was real, believe all of this had actually happened. *Damn you subconscious for playing such a bullshit trick on me. Jesus, you had to go there!* Anger ripped through her, as she pushed dream Remi off her.

"No, no you're not in love with me. This is nothing more than a fantasy, and you're not real." Climbing off the bed, she hated the fact her subconscious would play such a shitty trick on her and break up the blissful moment with a big dose of reality.

"Wait, what? What do you mean? Ferrian … Ferrian, where are you going?" His voice grew thick with alarm as he followed her frantic pacing around the suite.

"This, Remi," waving her arms around the ornately decorated room, the fear and resentment in her chest began to well up, "all of this is a dream. I'm not here, and neither are you! Whoever has me trapped in this warped version of reality will probably come back and sever this whole scenario before throwing me back in a prison cell. Beating the shit out of another innocent, while I'm the one who invades the innocent's body so they won't feel a good goddamn thing! Why the hell am I taking the hits for others?" Her anger roiled into full-blown hysterics, and she knew what she must look like. But, hey, it was all a dream anyway, so it didn't matter if she lost it in this surreal reality.

He launched off the bed, and pulled her to him. His massive hands grasped her arms, holding her in place. "M'aingeal, listen to me. You're not dreaming this. This is all real … this is all happening. I brought you here while you were unconscious. It wasn't safe for you at the apartment." Blowing out a ripe curse, she focused on him; the worry scouring Remi's face set her alarms off. "Please, listen to what I'm saying. You're not dreaming this." A prick of dread ran down her spine.

What if she wasn't dreaming all this up, what if she was here, acting like a looney-tune? What if? *Nope! I'm not crazy, I might be ugly but I'm not friggin' crazy!*

"Please," she hissed. "The real Remi wouldn't profess his love to me! No one loves me. I'm a fucking monster! Just look at me." Snatching her arms out of his grip, she twirled around him, giving her dream man full viewing of each mark on her body. "See this, I'm covered in scars. No man alive, let alone a man like Remi, would ever touch me or say he's in love with me. Not when I resemble a bad patch-up job of Frankenstein's bride!" Agony bled from her eyes as she slid down to the bed, rocking from pure frustration and questioning her sanity. She was losing it for sure, even in the dream state.

Kneeling before her, Remi cupped her face between his strong hands and kissed her before she had a chance to pull away. His soft lips tasted like the same sweet honey from the first time they had kissed.

Oh shit, I'm not dreaming! Shoving him away, she jumped off the bed and made for the bathroom. What she needed was some alone time and a big dose of oxygen ... and maybe a sledgehammer to put her out of her misery.

"Where are you going?" His voice, laced with worry, followed her.

"I-I need to be alone." Racing for the door, Ferrian closed herself in and locked the world out.

CHAPTER
THIRTY-TWO

" All I'm saying is if Xaphan succeeds in killing the Darkling, then you better prepare for a fall out like you've never seen before. I overheard Lucifer and him talking about sending Vepar in to lock your Darkling in a subconscious prison. I've seen Vepar at work, and I'll tell you what, I wouldn't want a crazy bastard like him screwing around in my head." Leaning fists down on the oversized cherry-wood desk, Focalor leveled Cassiel with a deadly serious stare. His chocolate eyes showed no signs of jest as he let the weight of his admission hang in the air. The tension in the room was suffocating. There was no mistaking the sullen tone running rampant, as Amitiel and Cassiel shared worried glances.

"Jezzzuschristalmighty! If this dickhead gets into Remi's Darkling's mind, we're all screwed." Roc blew out a stream of curses that would make Satan himself cringe. Their odds went from fifty-fifty to ninety-ten. "His chick is a disaster magnet. With Vepar jumping into her cranium, she doesn't stand a snowball's chance in Hell."

Searching the room until his deep chocolate eyes found the source of profanity, Focalor's leer and not so subtle doubts about Nisroc's ability to serve in the brotherhood did nothing to loosen the wedge between them.

"Listen, I'm not saying one way or the other how this could or will play out. What I am saying is, I think it's best to keep a close eye on her. If she falls into an unconscious state and can't wake from it, then it's safe to assume Xaphan has Vepar working on her. It can last for minutes, hours, even days."

"Can a person be conscious and then be pulled under, falling into an unconscious state?" Cassiel waited on the edge of his leather wingback chair, appearing as though he was ready to bust out of his cardigan.

"Yes, I've witnessed it personally. One minute they're awake, usually in some sort of panicked state, then they seem to collapse into sleep. Why do you ask? Has something already happened?"

Blowing out a ripe curse, Cassiel shook his head in despair and leaned back in his chair. "Yes." The ante had been upped, and the dark side was using everything they had at their disposal.

"Why didn't you say anything about this before, Cassiel? It's not like you to keep secrets from us."

"I wasn't keeping secrets, Am. I was waiting to talk to Focalor about this first. Get his take on this. And yes … it happened earlier today. I was watching over the Darkling. I heard her screaming from inside of her apartment. So, I went in half-expecting to find Xaphan or one of his Hellistics in there, but the place was empty. She came running out of the shower and blew right past me, didn't say a word. It was as though she was in a trance. Then she fell to the floor. Out cold. I called Remi, and now he's taking care of the situation."

Her amethyst eyes were mere slits, and fury radiated off her the longer she listened. "And why are you getting around to reporting this now?"

"Like I said, I wanted to talk to Focalor first. Knowing he's a Watcher and has free reign to travel both sides, I needed to find out if what I thought was even probable."

"Now, you know." Ezekiel's stoic expression wasn't hard to read. "Where's Remi and the Darkling now?" His voice—cold as ice and cutting—left little to the imagination.

"Last I heard from him, they were at the Four Seasons off of Delaware Place."

Wagging his pierced brows, Roc cracked a crooked smirk. "Four Seasons, eh? Guess our boy wanted to make an impression on his little Darkling. Hope she's at least putting out a little sumthin' sumthin' for good old Rem-dog. Feel me?"

"Can it, Roc," Kakabel's voice, normally melodic, cut a sharp demand. "Should we send someone down to inform Remi? I mean, he does have the right to know what's going on."

The long silence stretching out before them, left the feeling that this news was going to set off the ticking time bomb they called Remi. Five pair of eyes shot straight to Am's as she mulled over the idea. Informing Remi of this new piece of intel would only drive him to protect Ferrian at all costs. However, keeping him out of the loop until they had a better understanding of Vepar's abilities, maybe finding a way to turn things around in their favor, was also a possibility.

"Yep, we're completely screwed. Either we tell him and he goes batshit crazy, or we don't and he finds out, going atomic on us then on the fucktards of the Underworld. Awesome choices." The sound of Roc's teeth grinding together as he flicked his tongue ring against the backside of his teeth grated Focalor's nerves, and he shot him an irritated glare. The whole situation sucked. If they lost Ferrian to the Underworld, there would be little chance of redeeming herself.

Amitiel had tried to stay on the 'good side' of the Big Boss. Lord knows she had her own demons to deal with, and had lost more than she could bear to stand. She had nearly fallen from grace during her darkest time, forsaking everyone. But this time she couldn't afford to fail. Struggling with her inner demons, Am had fought through the darkness, and tried to redeem herself, for the good of humanity. Although she'd be damned to admit, the darkness she had tried to run away from still lingered deep in a corner of her heart.

"Gimme a few minutes." With a wave her hand, Amitiel dismissed the group. "Not you two." Cutting a stern glare at Cassiel and Focalor, no other words needed to be said to suggest the gravity of the impending conversation.

The oversized study was suffocating as she stepped over to the leather chair. Her shoulders weighed heavier than they had in many millennia as she sank into the supple coffee-colored seat. Realizing the impasse they were at, she scrubbed back her short, spikey hair and waited for her brethren and the Watcher to take their seats as well.

"Pull up a spot, kids, cuz this isn't going to a quick game of poker."

The silent minutes following left her nerves on edge as she tried to figure things out. "I need more details," she blurted out, not directing to either one in particular. "So?"

Grunting back a cough, Focalor sat pin straight, leveling her with a cautious stare. "What else do you wish to know? I can only inform you of which I know about."

"Well, first let's start with—why were you downtown cozying up with the dipshits of the Underworld? And how do we know you're not setting us up?"

"Lest I remind you, I am a Watcher now, it is my duty to check in with both sides. I cannot take sides, but I can inform either side of what is going on, should they ask or need to know."

"So, again, how do we know what you tell us is the truth? How can we trust you? What if you're running your mouth off to the bad guys as well, huh?"

"I understand your reservation, but I assure you, my only goal is to earn my way back into the good graces of the Big Boss. I realize if Satan wins, we're all screwed, for lack of a better word. I have no intentions on feeding any information where it will benefit the destruction of the world."

"I thought you said you couldn't choose sides?" Ezekiel's ice-cold voice sliced through the air from the corner of the room.

"Dammit, Z! I told you to leave. Get the hell out of here. This doesn't concern you right now." Shooting Ezekiel her own version of an icy glare, Am's voice was laced with frustration. The contention heard with each syllable she spoke.

"The hell it doesn't! And why would you keep this from the rest of the brethren? Don't you think you're doing the rest of us a great disservice by keeping this from the group? With intel like this, we could form a better strategy and be two steps ahead of those assholes!" Menace rolled off Ezekiel as he stepped farther into the room. Am slipped a sideways glance over to the Watcher, and noticed the way Z's presence made Focalor's fine hairs stand up on end. Ezekiel's reputation for snapping the wings off fallen angels, and sending them down to Earth to face a mortal death was well known throughout the Angel-Realm. Amitiel almost pitied the fool who crossed him.

"Listen," Focalor began—if he couldn't win over the hardest angel brethren, he wouldn't stand a chance in leaving the Angel-Realm with his legs intact … never mind the vacant space awaiting the return of a missing set of wings, "I agree with you. The Guardians should be made aware of this. And, for the record, I chose to inform you rather than the Underworld. I, too, have a conscious. I would rather see a fight where we stand a chance instead of allowing Lucifer, Xaphan, or anyone else to gain the upper hand. If any of you have a problem with it, then I see no other option than for me to take my leave and wish you the best of luck. You're going to need it." Rising from his chair, Focalor made no effort to play nice.

"Shit, wait! Focalor, wait a sec." Cassiel caught Am's hesitance as he slowed the Watcher's leaving. "Am, we need him. He's a great source of information, obviously. Whether you choose to see it as such is entirely up to you. I do, in fact, trust what he's saying."

"I'm leery about the Watcher, but I will admit, Cassiel is right. If he does as he says, informing us of Lucifer's plan of attack, he could prove quite useful."

Am stared at the faces of her two comrades, and knew what Z had said was true. However, her faith in the Watcher had yet to be tested. Biting back the fire in her gut, she cursed, realizing Focalor was right. "Fine! But if so much as one of my men gets his ass handed to him because you betrayed us, Z here will be the least of your concerns. Got me?" She squared off with the Watcher, and her hardened expression gave him no reason to think she was anything more than deadly serious. "Z, if you're going to lurk in dark corners, then at least make yourself useful and grab me a Grey Goose on the rocks. We have some planning to do from the looks of it. Focalor, I need you to stay put for now."

"Am, I think it's best if we send him back down to find out whatever else he can from the Underworld."

"Whoa, whoa," throwing his hands up, Focalor stepped away from the group, "I'm not going to be some errand boy. Got it? I'll pass you whatever information I can, but don't think for one minute you have any say over me."

"All right! Christ on a cracker, will you all settle down? I thought we were here to find out what the bad guys know, not whip out our dicks and see whose is bigger." Slamming his fist down on the armrest, the crack of his anger slapped the air as Cassiel's normal calm façade slipped past pissed and straight into furious. "I asked Focalor here to help us. I didn't think making him our bitch, running interceptions when we should be doing *our jobs*, was part of the job description here."

"You're right." Heaving out a heavy sigh, Am sank back into her chair and motioned for Z and Focalor to do the same. "I apologize, Focalor. You're here to help and it's appreciated. Tell us what you can. We won't keep you any longer than necessary."

The clank of ice dropping into a crystal glass brought her head around, as if she knew Z was purposely dropping it as loudly as possible to piss her off. "Z, get your ass over here with my drink."

"Yes, ma'am." The lost love between them wasn't a new story, but now wasn't the time to rehash old wounds. Passing her drink over, Z pegged her with a harsh glare, seeing the storm brewing behind her eyes. Slipping down adjacent from her, his shoulders pulled back as he rested his wide hands on his knees. "So what else can you tell us?"

CHAPTER THIRTY-THREE

If she had to guess, Ferrian would assume she had permanently worn a pacing track in the oversized marble bathroom. It didn't matter if she had shut the door and locked the most beautiful man she had ever known out. Smacking her cheek over and again, the red welt grew angrier with each strike. Frustration, fear, nausea mixed and mingled as fresh crystal traitors slipped past tightly shut eyes.

"Ferrian, please open the door. Let me in. Talk to me." Remi's voice was coated with concern as he lightly knocked on the door.

Hell, what could she say? *Sorry I lost it out there, and locked myself in this bathroom. How am I supposed to believe any of this is real and you're not some insane delusion that won't stop trying to convince me it isn't?* No. There wasn't a damn thing about this that made sense. Sagging to the cold marble floor, red and silver inflections scattered in rivulets through the black stone, shone like rivers of blood pooling around her. She had hoped smacking herself hard enough would wake her. But it didn't.

"What's happening to me?"

"M'aingeal, come out. We'll figure this out together. Please, unlock the door. Don't shut down on me now."

Her heart ached, listening to the sincerity in his pleas. She questioned herself, over and again if it was possible, but deep down, she knew the truth. The little hope she retained for rare and special occasions screamed maybe this was real, and Remi was here. And she quite possibly had had the most incredible sex she could have ever imagined with the only man on the whole damn planet that made her abandon her self-loathing, and free her from the prison of her mind. The short answer wasn't as easy as she thought.

The wonderful ways her body ached as she tried to pull herself up wasn't enough to convince her this was all real. Feeling lost for days, she recalled the time spent in that dank hellhole, each crack of a whip or paddle—which had holes drilled through it for the ultimate searing pain—she'd unwillingly sustained for others. It didn't matter if Remi stood on the other side of the door, pleading with her to open it. She knew it was only a matter of time before the cruelty she had been facing at the hands of some sick bastard would resume. Like the rest of the things in her life, her dreams were as cruel as reality.

Her own reflection didn't resemble the monster she knew herself to be. Aside from a red cheek, she held a blush of color over her body. Staring intently at the woman in the mirror, confusion rode her the longer she stared. Blinking back the tears from her eyes, the pull of surreal reality reeled her in. "What the?" She traced the outlines of faint wings in the mirror, a soft glow surrounding the image, and she found herself mesmerized by the sight.

Disbelief rippled through her as they faded from view. *I should promptly check myself into Bellevue's*

Psych Ward. Slapping the faucet on, a cool splash of water on her face calmed her. "Relax, you're going to wake up any minute in your shithole apartment." Inhaling a few deep breaths, her resolve to touch back down to reality was steadily upon her.

Twisting the lock free, she eased the door open, glancing around the edge to view the scene. The darkness enveloping the room gave her a sense of normality, and she exhaled another breath of relief. Ferrian sidled around the edges in search of her bed. Shadows danced over the walls, making simple objects appear more sinister than they were. Cautiously craning her head back and forth, she scanned the darkness for anything lurking in the night. Anxiety struck her hard, leaving her frozen in place, when she saw the outline of a tall figure standing in front of a large bay window. Her hands searched her pockets for her knife, and quickly cursed under her breath when she realized she was standing in the dark, in an unfamiliar room, buck-ass naked.

Curling her hands into tight fists, the unmistakable burn of fear and fury roiled through her like poison, infusing the cells in Ferrian's body with the do or die trying survival instinct. Slowly, she stepped closer to her clothes lying scattered around the bed. Her footsteps whispered over the soft pale carpet. The shadowy figure stood, stone still. Focusing intently on it, she swallowed back her panic the closer she crept.

"Ferrian" The soft voice struck her like a sucker punch.

Oh shit! She knew who the deep, raspy voice belonged to without guessing. The moon's rays gradually outlined his body, and the immense size of her visitor became clear. Her heart hammered behind her ribcage, and she swore it was going to burst out of her chest. "This isn't happening."

"Yes, m'aingeal. It is. It's all real. I need you to come to terms with it." He swiveled his head around to meet her stunned stare. "What's it going to take to make you understand you're awake and here, with me?"

Ferrian tried to shake off the angst tightening around the growing knot deep in her belly. Her lips became numb as she panted out short bursts of air from her struggling lungs. "No, God, I thought … you can't be serious. Please tell me I'm dreaming. This isn't real! Why would someone like you want to be with me? Unless—" Ferrian's eyes darted from Remi's confused expression to the suite door. Fear assailed her hard from every angle.

Remi held his hands out, walking over to her, as he tried to comfort her. It didn't work. Her trepidation ratcheted another notch as Ferrian's internal warning system convinced her she needed to bolt. Ripping her clothes off the floor, she shoved her legs into her jeans, yanked on her tank top and hoodie, grabbed her boots, and made for the suite door. Her heart jackhammered harder in her chest. Anxiety stormed in her stomach, fighting back the distinct flavor of acidic bile rising up her throat.

How could she have been so careless to think it was a dream? She'd spent what seemed like days trapped in a dank, dimly light hellhole, chained up like a dog. Beaten and assaulted in ungodly ways. So how did she end up in some upscale hotel with the one male who could completely unravel her?

"Ferrian, no! You can't leave. Please, come back." His voice sounded strained as she thundered down the hallway, unsure of which direction the closest elevator was. Hauling ass, she cut a corner to find the set of six gilded doors, closed and quiet. Repeatedly pushing the down button, her worst nightmare slapped her in the face. She ran away from the one person who had cared for her and about her, for no conceivable reason.

Guilt washed over her as she turned to find the stairs. Waiting for the elevator wasn't going to work. She needed air and lots of it, before her breakdown turned into a some-thing ugly. Turning the corner, she saw his half-dressed body rushing past people in the hallway. "I need to be alone, Remi. I'm sorry. I didn't mean for any of this to happen! You need to get away from me right now! I'm evil."

"No, please, Ferrian, come back! It's not safe out there!"

Catching sight of the eloquently designed exit sign, she pumped her legs as hard as she possibly could to reach the door.

Her throat constricted as she thought about the people she had loved and the violence behind their deaths, all be-cause of her. "Remi, get away from me!" Slamming the door lever down, the hollow echo splintering the air screamed more like a death sentence. Her feet slapped against the cool concrete floor exiting into the stairwell. Vaulting down the stairs tow at a time, there were more floors between her and freedom than she could handle. Shoving her feet into her boots, she jumped the railing, hoping she didn't break her ankle on the landing. "Shit!" Her hands shook as she gripped the railing, listening to his voice echo down the stairwell.

Gulping back the panic eating away at her rational

senses, she shot out into the hallway and made for the elevators. If God held any love for her, he'd have an elevator ready and open to for her to slip into. Sending a quick prayer skyward, she cut around another corner and caught sight of the bank of golden gilded transports to her freedom.

The dinging of doors opening to the first one sent a small wave of relief washing through her as she bit down into her run, hurling her body in between the closing doors. Heaving heavy breaths, the doors sealed her in alone. She couldn't believe all she had done. Not only her crazed dash away from Remi, but she had also completely lost it on him in the suite, even though he'd tried to comfort her. Punching the button to the first floor, and sagging against the mirrored walls, she let the flood gates open as fresh hot tears stung her eyes. She was dead tired, but it didn't stop another round of mental gymnastics from ensuing.

"What is wrong with me?"

CHAPTER THIRTY-FOUR

"**D**amn it!" Scrubbing his face with his hands, the weight of fear sank his shoulders as Remi gnashed his teeth in frustration. He had no idea which floor Ferrian had managed to get down to before disappearing from him. He hadn't expected for things to go so terribly wrong. Sure, he'd had reservations about telling her the truth, knowing she might possibly shut down, or worse, not believe him. Denying his feelings for her stung more than any amount of lashings. Had he known she would run away terrified, he might have reconsidered the timing. "Good going, dumb ass!"

There was no undoing this.

Anger exploded deep in his gut as he launched a crushing punch into the concrete stairwell wall, leaving behind a spider web of cracks trailing across the wall. How could he have been so stupid to believe she would've been all right with his admission? Why did she think she was dreaming all of it? How could she not tell the difference between reality and a dream—what was happening and what was impossible? None of it made sense, and yet, here he stood; alone, half-naked, and exasperated wondering where she took off to.

Pushing open the emergency exit door, his heavy footfalls ate the length of the hallway. The soft vibration of his cell in his pocket snapped his attention. Palming the small device, he grimaced, glancing down at the glowing screen. *Great ... just what I frigging need right now.* Half tempted to send it to voicemail, his shoulders blades twitched. Oh, this was not good. "Hey, what's up?"

"You need to get your ass up Realmside stat. Got it," Z's flat voice drawled. Ice flinted over his skin as his gut churned. Something wasn't right. In fact, something was wrong in so many ways.

"Why? What's going on?"

"Get up here, and I'll explain. Secure your Darkling and be up here in five minutes. Understand?"

His palms grew slick. How was he going to explain this one? He had lost his charge; he was half-naked and reeling from his last encounter with Ferrian. Yeah, great place to be in. Between the proverbially rock and so screwed hard place. "Yeah. Got it." Ending the call, he slipped the small device into his pocket and made for the suite. His mind was splintered into a million places. The five-minute time limit would have to wait. He had to find her, and convince her to return to the hotel with him.

Bursting through the door, he summoned his clothes on, and braved a glance back over to the mussed bed. He wanted to regret everything that had happened between them on it, but he couldn't. It was something he wouldn't ever apologize to anyone for. Except to Ferrian, herself. His cock twitched as he pictured her lying across the bed, her milky skin resplendently glowing with need and her hunter green eyes smoldering like twin emerald coals.

His skin grew taut as a fresh wave of terror rode in. He had to find her and quickly. She was nothing short of a dead-man-walking with a neon target painted on her back, beckoning the Hellistic demons. There wasn't anything he wouldn't give, or give up to have her here safe with him and in bed once again. The glint of stainless steel caught the corner of his eye, and he leaned down to retrieve a small folded knife. Blowing out a ripe curse, his heart ripped into high gear. It was Ferrian's pocketknife. She hadn't left home without it since she ran from her last foster family nine years earlier.

It was her source of comfort, her only tool to defend herself, and it was in the palm of his hand. Thumbing over the worn out Celtic cross design, he wondered how many times she had done the same thing. Ferrian's mental state was already a huge concern, but he feared if she remembered what she left behind, she would altogether lose it. Crushing the metal knife in his hand, he held it to his forehead and begged for the strength to convince Ferrian she was safer with him, than anywhere else. It was a long shot, he knew it, but there was no other option.

Stashing it away in his pocket, Remi dematerialized out to the street below and listened for any sign of her. Nothing. Flashing to her apartment, he prayed he'd find her there—alone. Nothing. His gut turned into one big knot as he flashed back to the docks, hoping he'd catch her there. She wasn't there either.

Grinding his teeth, his mind ran rampant. "Where the hell are you, m'aingeal?" He checked every spot he could remember being with her. Hope twisted into morbid fear. She was gone, vanished into thin air. His blood ran cold as he tried to sense her once again. Nothing. "Feerrrrriaaaann!" The roar of his cry thundered through the city, and God, he hoped she would hear him.

Hitting the hard pavement running, she couldn't put enough distance between her the man she'd left calling out for her. Her boots slapped against the concrete, leaving echoes of her fears lingering in the pre-dawn hours. She had no idea where she was going, yet her body wouldn't let her stop from propelling forward. Slipping a glance over her shoulder, her heart trip over itself as her hands slickened with sweat. *Please don't let him be following.*

A small moment of hurt pricked her before disappearing. Ferrian wanted to feel completely relieved Remi wasn't following her, hoping her abrupt exit was enough to dissuade him from coming to find her. Wiping her fingers over her cheek, little trails of wetness trickled down. How could she have been so stupid? She loved every moment Remi had his lips, and hands on her. Her body seemed cold from the absence of his warmth covering her, screaming at her for being a traitor and running away from tenderness of his touch.

The familiar wave of crushing self-hatred and despair unmercifully crashed down on her, choking the air from her lungs as she hurled herself into the first vacant doorway she could find. Trembling, she couldn't fight the feelings from creeping up inside of her. She didn't want to feel anything, not for anyone. Loving people only meant death would follow soon. Shutting down the thought, she angrily wiped away the tears with shaky hands. Pushing Remi out of her life was more painful than stabbing a stake through her own heart. She sunk down against the creaking wooden door and numbness set in, swaddling her in a suffocating hold. Wrapping her arms around her legs, her body trembled as she fought away the memory of her time with him. Her breath shuddered, as did her heart, picturing Remi's body spread out before her, awaiting her touch.

She hated herself for believing him when he'd said he loved her. She wanted to believe him, but every instinct she harnessed screamed to run. Ferrian steeled herself against the onslaught of pain she knew would inevitably follow. Burying her face in her hands, soft sobs ebbed out as the wind carried the sound of Remi calling for her name. The hurt in his plea hit her like a wrecking ball. Throwing back her head, she strained to listen for his voice again. *No, this isn't possible!* How could she hear him? Glancing down the street, not a single person could be found. *You're going crazy, woman! Losing your damned mind.* Fresh hot tears stung her eyes as she lowered herself back and into her shell.

She didn't hear the door open behind her, or notice the wood peel away from her back, until the musty odor of a decaying building plumed around her. Fear clipped her heart the second two cold, clawing hands ensnared her in a bear-tight hold, dragging her backward. The scrapping of her boots across the old wooden floors danced in the cold air. Trying to rip away from her captor, Ferrian lashed back trying to strike the unseen being. "Reeeeeemiiiiiiii!" Her screams riddled the empty room, before another hand clamped down on her mouth, stifling her cries.

CHAPTER THIRTY-FIVE

"**Z**, call his ass again! It's been thirty damn minutes. What the hell is taking him so long?" Am paced the room, agitation rolling off her in droves. "You did tell him we needed him here stat, didn't you?"

The last place Remi wanted to be was Realmside, waiting for Amitiel's tirade to chew his ass out for disobeying her command ... again. He could picture her amethyst eyes glowering violently purple at him, as she worked over the tick in her jaw. For a place that was meant to be all serene and shit, he cringed hearing Am's voice bellowing out like boulders crashing against the earth. *Awesome, she's in fine form for tearing my ass a new one. Get in, get out, and get back to finding Ferrian.*

His nerves were lit up like live wires as he continued to stalk toward the great library.

"What's his problem anyway?" Charo's voice sliced through the ebbing silence of Am's bitchfit, hitting everyone's mind.

"Seems like old Rem-dog has the hots for his little Darkling, what else?"

"Not now, pinhead." *Well at least Am had something right for once.*

"Hey, I'm calling it like I see it, Boss-lady."

"Roc, cut it out. Now isn't the time for your antics. I think it's time to revisit the last time we faced off with Vepar to see if and where we can cut him off before he latches onto the Darkling."

Vepar! This can't be happening. His heavy footsteps sounded like thunderheads crashing as he stormed into the library. Frustration rolled off him in waves, thickly coating the air. "So, what's so friggin' important I had to leave my charge? And what's this about Vepar?" His muscles bunched beneath his shirt, ready to destroy the holy hell out of anyone stupid enough to stop him from leaving. "I have a charge to protect, or did Cassiel forget to mention what happened to her?" Cutting his brethren a glare, he knew it wasn't fair to snap at the guy; Cassiel was all about duty and honor and blah, blah, blah. However, every minute he spent Realmside, was another lost minute, where he should've been searching for Ferrian.

Every pair of eyes in the room purchased a piece of his ass as he stepped deeper into the chamber. Slaking off their stares, he bee-lined it toward Am. His shoulders squared, ready for a verbal throw down. "Spill it." Ice edged his voice as his eyes locked onto his superior.

"Next time you're summoned, you better get your ass back up here on the double. Got it?" Am folded her lean muscled arms over her chest, standing toe-to-toe with the walking menace of the moment. "Our little Watcher spy has informed us what Lucifer and his crew are planning to do to your charge."

"And?"

"The word is they're planning on attacking your Darkling using a new tactic. Vepar is being sent in to mentally mindfuck her, if he hasn't done so already."

A steady stream of curses spilled from his lips as he combed his hand through his hair, certain he was about to pull out half of it on the first pass. The idea had crossed his mind while he'd watched Ferrian fight in her sleep, but he hadn't known for sure. His skin grew tighter the longer he stood there. It was too much to ask of him to stay put. Turning on a heel, Remi rushed past Amitiel, with his heart pounding against the cage of his chest.

"Wait! Where the fuck do you think you're going?"

Stopping dead in his tracks, the hair on the back of his neck stood up straight. He sensed something off, but knew this conversation wasn't leading in the direction of *'Okay-do-what-you-have-to-do-but-be-safe-out-there'* range. "I'm going to see my charge." It didn't matter what any of the Brethren thought. He didn't serve them.

"The hell you are! Bring your ass back here, Remiel. There's more to discuss. Your Darkling will be fine for an hour or so."

"She's not safe alone, remember?" His body vibrated, but he had no idea if it was because his temper about to explode, or if he was picking up Ferrian's signal. Either way he was a loose cannon.

"We need you to stay here. That's an order."

"I'm going." He made for the door, and came up to Z's lean frame blocking his exit. "You need to hear this first, Remiel." Per usual, Ezekiel lacked emotion when he spoke.

"Kiss my ass."

"Seems like our boy Remi needs some Pamprin to

cure his PMS."

"Shut it, Roc, before I shove my size nines up your ass." Bels didn't hesitate to lift and inspect her stiletto boot, just to make a point.

"Oh yeah, you know how I like, baby. Come to daddy!"

"Piss off, Roc."

Spinning around to find Am coming up to him, wearing a grim slash cut across her face while she trained her livid amethyst eyes on him. "Fine then, if I'm needed so badly up here, let me bring her topside. At least that way we could question her while keeping her safe from those bastards."

"No," she said sharply. "You know the rules. No humans—ever. Not until she's transcended." Yes, he knew the rules … the constantly-in-your-face rules. No human shall enter the Realm of the Angels until death welcomes them. No Darkling shall be permitted unless deemed appropriate or allowable by the Council of the Seven. Only Dark Angels may enter upon being summoned. Getting the council's approval wasn't going to happen, since they considered Darklings as a potential threat. Even if their memories could be completely erased, something lingered deep in the recesses of their mind, making them a valuable prize should they be kidnapped by any demon, and forced or coaxed to talk.

Remi had gone before the Council only once in his existence. Standing before the Council of the Seven Archangels: Michael, Gabriel, Uriel, Raphael, Raguel, Saragael, and Oriel. It took every ounce of courage and humility he had. He had proven himself worthy during the Angel/Demon wars when the Earth was still young, arguing

236

the point he had served his time as a Battle Angel and would live up to the expectations of the Council as one of the brethren.

Remi had been around long enough to understand and rationalize the 'No Humans Allowed' rule. Humans aged faster than dark angels. One hour in the Angel-Realm equaled a day to the humans. Bringing Ferrian topside for a week would stop her aging, until she landed back down on Earth. Once she was back, she'd age within minutes. He found solace in the promise of when she turned, she'd stop aging until the day she was released from duty. Darklings only had two options for getting out of *'their duty'*. Either by getting killed by a true angel, or a true demon. Daemons were Darklings who turned into darkness, holding the same power as a Dark Angel. They had the ability to kill each other. Everything in the universe had to have balance. God and Satan, angels and demons, down to the Dark Angels and Daemons. It was the way it had always been since the universe first exploded into multiple dimensions.

"Unless they break the rules first, we can't intervene any more than we have. Keep an eye on her from a distance. If, and only if, shit hits the fan and they go after her, you should get her out of there. Understand?"

His knuckles begged to pound into flesh. Gnashing his teeth, a low snarl rumbled in his chest. His returning nod said all he was willing to agree to.

"Remi, I think it's best you familiarize yourself with Vepar's tactics. They are going to come at her any way they can. We need to be prepared for anything, should she turn, or worse." Remi, refusing to consider the 'or worse' idea, pierced Cassiel with a don't-you-even-think-it glare.

"Listen, I understand. But I want you to fully appreciate and understand what we're going up against." Sliding the Angel Tome of Demonology to him, Cassiel flipped open the gilded pages, and tapped the section on the newest player in their proverbial game of chess. "You should read this."

"And what about Focalor, what else did he have to say about all this?"

Am cleared her throat, slightly nodding her head at Cassiel. "We should try to focus on Vepar for now, and he'll keep us informed about what's happening underground." Her words were clipped as she reached over, tapping the book. "Read on. We need all hands on deck."

The stark muscles in his jaw ticked as he eyed her. "What aren't you telling me, Am? What else did the Watcher say?"

"Am, you need to tell him."

Considering Ezekiel with a cautious eye, she scrubbed her head roughly and nodded in agreement.

"Tell me what? Am ... Z, what the hell do I need to know?" When she didn't open her mouth to answer the question, the distinct sensation of his anxiety spiking up his blood pressure heightened the longer he waited. Sweat permeated from his pores and stress seeped into his bones, as he eyed the pair. Cracking his knuckles down on the hard mahogany desk, little fissures of his frustration decorated the previously unblemished surface. "For chrissake, what is it?"

"Team fucktards have a secret group of bigger fucktards swiping humans off the street and torturing them somewhere underground." He might not have been eloquent with his words, but Remi didn't care how it was put, and for once, he was thankful for Roc and his absurd vocabulary.

"What does this have to do with Ferrian?"

"If she's close to changing, then she can feel their pain. Hell, she'll be drawn to it. Their cries as they call for God, will be her summoning. Taking over their mortal body, and kicking their soul out so the innocent doesn't go through the trauma or even death in some cases." All of the blood in his face drained as he thought about what Ferrian had said back in the hotel room, amidst her frantic pacing. *"All of this is a dream. Whoever has me trapped in this warped version of reality will probably come back, and throw me back in a prison cell. Beating the shit out of another innocent, while I'm the one who invades the innocent's body!"*

Cassiel's voice as solid as it could ever be, hit him straight in the balls. Jesus Christ! He couldn't remember if he was breathing, or if the room had decided to warp on its own accord. One thing was for certain … someone was going to die.

"Hey, man, are you okay? Wanna beer or something?"

"No thanks, Roc." Craning his head back toward Cassiel, his eyes trained on his brethren; he wanted answers and nothing was going to stop him from going after Ferrian. "So, you think she was summoned to the innocents while she was out cold? Wait, isn't that one of Vepar's tricks?"

"Truthfully, I have no idea what your Darkling was experiencing. Unless we talk to her and find out what she was dreaming of, there's no way to fully understand what or who we're up against. If that's what was truly happening to her, then I'd say she's real close to turning."

Another steady stream of curses spilled from his lips as he tried to stop the mental gymnastics from doing the floor routine. "What do we do? How do we stop them? Do we have any information on the whereabouts of these innocents?"

All eyes focused on him, setting his edginess on full seek and destroy mode. Locking sights one at a time with each one of his brethren, he read the answer loud and clear.

Kakabel quietly walked up to Remi, her black boots softly crushing the Atlantian rug. She slipped her hand over the thick flesh of his shoulder for a gentle squeeze, but it did nothing to soothe him. All he had left in him was the anger coiling beneath the surface. "Focalor has a team of Watchers scattering out around the Chicago searching for any Hellistic demons, Daemons, and minions Xaphan might have sent out to kidnap the humans. He said he'll be in touch as soon as he hears anything."

"Oh hell no! We need to get down there. We need to find them and destroy them." Electricity shot through Roc, lighting up his electric blue eyes like bolts of heat lightning. For once, he was on the same page as the youngest member of the League of Guardians. There was no point to standing around talking about the what-ifs when he needed to find his Ferrian and keep her safely tucked away until she turned. *She's not your anything, asshole. Remember the scene from the hotel? She wants nothing to do with you.* A deep, cold ache etched out a hole the size of a bowling ball the longer he stood there, not sensing where she was or if she was okay.

"Z and I have been discussing our next plan of attack

here. I need everyone's head in the game."

Remi spun around, hoping for any good news. "Find the innocents, find my Darkling, and kill the bastards behind this. Sound about right, or do we need to whip out the tea party set and discuss each detail in painstaking precision while we lose precious time?"

"Calm yourself, Remi! As long as your Darkling is safe, then we have—"

Curling his hands into tight balls, he launched forward, coming toe-to-toe with Am once again. "She's not safe." His muscles bunched, ready to unleash his fury on those who deserved it.

"No shit she isn't. She's a buck twenty soaking wet and insanely accident prone? The chick can't walk across a flat surface without falling on her ass. So please do tell me, if she was supposed to be with you at the hotel, how can you stand here and tell me she's not safe?" the tension in the air grew thicker by the second when she met his pissed-off stare with one her own,.

Leaning in closer so Amitiel could feel the heat rolling off his chest, Remi snarled, "Piss. Off." He had no desire to stand around and play one of the merry band of puppets bullshit.

"Touchy, aren't we, Remiel? I wonder why exactly? I mean, if she's locked in the hotel suite, then we'll send someone down to guard the exits. You need to get right in the head. Right now."

A guttural growl rumbled through his thick chest, and he folded his arms tightly over himself to keep from striking her. "She's not safe. End of story. I need to get back down there."

"No. We need you up here," she snapped.

"You have Cassiel, Roc, Z, Bels, and Charoum up here. I think you can handle things without me for a while. Show the boss that you're not as useless as a bag of dicks on a deserted island."

"Day-um that was good! I'll have to remember that one."

Now wasn't the time for a cheering section, and he shot a sardonic grin at Roc to let him know that.

"Until you get your fucking head clear, I want you to stay away from your charge, understand? It's not a request, numbnuts, it's an order."

"Fuck. You. I'm going to find her, and when I do, I'm bringing her somewhere safe."

"Whoa, whoa, wait one damn minute. What do you mean 'when you find her'? I thought you said she was at the hotel with you."

The furrow line between his knitted brows clenched tighter as he considered what he was going to tell them. Sure, he messed up. Messed up huge. He lost his charge all because he had to taste her, touch her. "She took off."

"Why did she run, Remiel? What could've happened to set her off?"

He had dug his grave. Admitting the truth was a fate worse than death, but the heat of six sets of eyes burning a hole right through him, all anxiously waiting for the juicy gossip, wasn't enough to make him spill all his secrets.

Deciding the little-as-possible route was his best option, he said, "She woke up, saw she wasn't in her apartment, and freaked out."

"That's all? I don't know, Remi. I'm sensing some bullshit here. Why didn't you go after her then?"

"I did, but I lost her when she hit the stairwell, brainiac. Anything else, or am I free to find my Darkling now, mother?"

"JesusHChrist, you really know how to treat a woman, don't you?" Shaking her head, Am decided she wasn't going to win this round of whose dick was bigger contest. Waving him off, she turned away and focused on the ancient tome again. "Go, get the hell out of here and find her. I hope to God you find her before Xaphan does. Otherwise, we're all screwed."

He didn't think twice; he stalked away, shouldering his way past Charoum and Z. Now wasn't the time to talk. He considered what Amitiel had said when he pushed the oversized mahogany doors open wide. The hallway remained quiet as he made his way down to his personal quarters. A quick stop in his closet armory to load up on the essentials, then he was in full on hunting mode. Finding her was mission critical. Destroying Xaphan, Vepar, or any other demon stupid enough to get in the way was secondary.

The vibration from his cell snapped his head up. A streak of dread skated down his spine, as he pulled the device free from his jeans pocket. *'Hey, man, be careful. Charo and I will be down to help in thirty. Don't do anything I wouldn't.'* He wanted to be annoyed with Cassiel, but he couldn't. Cass knew the deal with him and his growing obsession with Ferrian. However, bringing Charo meant only one thing. If Ferrian was caught, she was going to be seriously psychologically screwed up, and Charoum would be the only one who could mentally shut her down long enough for Remi to figure out what to do to help her. He made for the back of his walk-in closet, ready to get the show on the road. Punching in his passcode, a small puff of air plumed out as the door swung open, displaying shelves of weapons—new and relics—which gleamed from the overhead lighting.

Carefully smoothing his fingers over his favorite swords, he reached for his modified weapons vest and backpack. Tossing in demon grenades, angel-blood tipped throwing knives, and DMT bullets into his pack, he zipped up the bag shut. He hadn't dressed for battle in centuries, and when he glanced in the mirror he saw that though his appearance hadn't changed since the dawn of time, his eyes told a different story.

Scrubbing his face with both hands until he was clutching his head between his hot palms, he thought back to Ferrian's expression the moment she had realized she wasn't dreaming. Fear initially covered her, but he could've sworn he had seen a hint of a smile trying to peek through. Dammit, if it didn't make his cock spring to life thinking about it. Pissed off with his body's reaction, he smacked his crotch to bring himself to heel and promptly yelped. *Pull it together, man!*

Reaching for the next shelf, he pried his Sig Sauer pistols from the velvet-lined casings and threw them down the line of sheaths. Carrying six on his chest wasn't a problem; making sure he had enough pre-filled clips would be. His hands went into autopilot mode as his mind wandered off again. His thoughts pulsed to life picturing Ferrian's delicate, milky skin and fiery green eyes lighting up like emeralds. Her soft lips and the sound of her delicious mews spilling from them, echoed in his ears. "No!" he snarled, stuffing semi-automatics and fixed blades into pockets and sheaths to distract himself and cut off his train of thought.

"I will find you, m'aingeal. I promise." Kissing his last pistol, he tucked it into his waistband and stomped out of his closet into the wide-open bedroom. Closing his eyes, he envisioned her bedroom, dematerializing within seconds. Whatever it'd take, he was going to find her. Protect her at all costs, and make her believe he wasn't lying to her when he'd told her he was in love with her. God help him, he loved her more than his own life.

Remi's absence left the room in a brewing storm of chaos as Am sagged her shoulders, heaving out a hard exhale. Cassiel watched Am slip into a reverie and knew the dark place she was dancing around. "Okay, so let's get this show on the road." Slapping the Angel Tome closed, snapping Am out of her thoughts, he shot her a subtle nod. Whipping out his cell, he punched in the only digits needing back-up whether Remi wanted it or not. He wasn't about to let Remi run loose after what Cassiel saw brewing beneath the surface. "Charo, you and I will head down to meet up with Remi and scour the city. Bels, Z, Roc, I need you to gear-up and hit every hot spot for demon activity. See what you can drum up on intel. Am, can you go speak to the boss and see what he wants us to do considering the game has changed? We'll converge at dawn back here."

"Hells, yeah! Let's go kick some soul-sucking demon ass! Woot!" The lightning flashed in Roc's eyes as he clapped the shoulders of Z and Charo.

"Get your hand off me," Z snapped, casting an arctic

glare to his brethren.

"Dude, chillax already, this shit gets me pumped is all. Maybe you should consider getting laid while you're downtown. I know a great dive-bar where the beer is lousy and the women are easy, whatta say?" Waggling his brows, Roc was prepared to take a punch to the face when it came to Ezekiel. "Okay, girls, like goldilocks said, let's get this show on the road."

"Get locked and loaded, kids, it's time to seek and destroy." The eerie chill to her voice littered the room as another round of shouts of approval rumbled through the air. "Cass, make sure you keep a tight eye on our loose cannon, got it? I know you saw the bloodlust in his eyes. Don't say a word to anyone about it. Do you understand?" Her voice was low; her eyes pegged his with intensity.

"Understood." Cassiel knew about most of Amitiel's past issues with bloodlust, but how far she had gone off the deep-end was never spoken of.

"If he shows signs of losing it, you drag his ass back up here. No questions asked. I don't care how you do it."

"Understood."

"Good. Now get ready. I got a feeling it's gonna be a long night."

Cassiel knew this all too well. Patting her arm, he was well acquainted with the ramifications if things went wrong. He had seen too many angels give in to bloodlust killings, and he'd be damned if he would let the same thing happen to any one of his brethren.

"Yes, ma'am."

CHAPTER THIRTY-SIX

er mind was racing as she thrashed against the arms hauling her backward. The clammy, claw-like hands dug into her flesh, and she knew without a doubt, soon she'd have new scars covering the old ones as the jagged nails scratched across her skin. The scent of coppery liquid trickled down her arms.

Panic overrode her, and she screamed out the only name she could think of, "Reeeeeeemmmmmmmmiiiiiii!" A heavy hand clamped down on her mouth. Biting down into the thick pads, the acrid taste of a mixture of metallic and something she could only assume was bile hit her tongue. Her stomach rolled in disapproval as her teeth cut deeper. *Oh my god, I'm going to puke!*

"Bitch!" the voice snarled, as another hand flew toward her face, backhanding her with a loud crack. Stars danced before her eyes as she tried to register what was happening. *Shit!* This was so not good. She couldn't see where she was being dragged to, and the faint light peeking in through the cracks under the door gave her no hope. Escaping was not going to be an easy task.

Rank breath blew out around her face, and she begged

her nostrils to close off from smelling the cloud of sewage. Kicking her heels into creaking wood, her body was hauled farther into the room. The scent of age and decay was a welcomed distraction from the thick, moist breaths fuming against her throat. Her blood ran cold when her vision was blinded by a black bag. A second set of hands came around her when the first finally decided they were deep enough into the room to stop.

The steely clap of handcuffs snapping into place around her wrists had Ferrian curling her hands into fists, as she tried to uppercut with both balls of rage to the enemy standing in front of her. The satisfying 'oomph' she heard as a result was short lived. A hard crack against her cheekbone made her eyes instantaneously water, knocking her backward until she fell over something hard, spilling her to the floor. Another set of cuffs clicked into place around her ankles while she tried to clear her head from the crushing blow. Biting down on the inside of her cheek, she attempted to keep from screaming; she was so over this bullshit business of getting the crap kicked out of her on a regular basis. Had the whole world decided to use her as a personal punching bag?

"Well done, lads."

The voice quickly registered in the deep recesses of her mind. *Xaphan*. Her body shot to life as though a super surge of electricity shot through every cell in her body. Before she could mentally command her body to stand, Ferrian had launched forward at the one person she would see die by her hands. The resulting chortle as she fell forward—thanks to her newest accessories—enraged her more with each passing second.

"My dear child, don't go hurting yourself, that's my

job. Really, my sweet, is this the way to greet your kind host?"

She sensed the evil grin spreading across his chiseled face, and the pleasure he took in terrorizing her. "What do you want, Xaphan?" she snarled as fiercely as possible, hoping she sounded more menacing than an angry cat taking a bath. Two sets of hands clamped down on her arms, pulling her vertical. In situations like this, you would think fear would pool from the inside until it spilled freely from each pore, ranking the air. But it wasn't fear surging through her body. It was pure, undiluted hatred for the enemy standing before her. "What's the matter, dickhead, are you afraid of little ole me? I bet you are. No wonder why your moronic friends bagged my head."

In the resulting few silent moments the air shifted while Xaphan and his buddies stood stone still. Her heart jumped into triple time, as the sound of rushing waters filled her ears and new scents assaulted her nostrils. The loud smack of thick soles slowly filtered in around the room, and a bone-chilling coldness swept over her exposed flesh. The temperature dropped quickly. If she hadn't been wearing a cotton bag over her head, she would've sworn winter had tripped and fallen in her path. Shivers rippled up her spine as the faint sound of screams permeated the air.

"Vepar, it's time to put her under," Xaphan commanded. The distinct memory of her whereabouts knocked the breath from her lungs.

"Get her inside the room," the abnormally deep voice said. Panic flooded her core as she swiveled her head back and forth. How in the hell had she ended up here? One moment, she was in a dilapidated house full of dirt, dust, rats, and vagrants' shit. So how was it even possible she had ended up in the one place from her past she feared with a deathly grip?

"How ... how did we get here?" She tried hard to keep her voice steady. However, the dank smell of cruelty and malice coated each word with dread. The two males holding on to her forced her to walk down the long, dimly lit corridor. As the heavy wooden door accented with iron bars swung open, a new frenzied fight for survival ratcheted up to a whole other level. She had to get out, and now. She knew the room they were pushing her toward. Ferrian knew every crack in the concrete walls and floor, and each toy of torture, hanging from the wooden racks screwed into the sidewall. It was a room designed for one thing: pain.

Rearing back, she kicked as hard as she could until her foot connected with a body part. Tearing her arms free from the second male's hands, she twisted hard enough to land a crushing blow with her elbow. The spray of an oily liquid hit her in the face, covering the wall in the explosion. She couldn't wait another second. Running was her only option. Hobbling into an awkward run-hop combo, the shackles gave her only a couple of feet of chain for movement. Ferrian had one chance and one chance only to try to make a break for it. If she ended up in one of the cells, she would never see daylight again.

The sound of ripe curses echoed off the stone concaved corridor walls. She tried to make it down the length of the hall, glancing back to check the status of her enemies. Hitting a wall of solid flesh, she fell backward again with a hard thud.

"Don't struggle; you'll only make it worse," the

haunting voice murmured low as he pulled her back up.

She slowly lifted her eyes to see the biggest male she had ever seen in her life. His head about grazed the ceiling and his legs resembled tree trunks. Gulping past the lump firmly lodged in her throat, she tried to focus on his face for any identifying marks. All she could see in the darkness were a pair of glowing amber eyes staring back at her. He kept himself hidden, behind shadows, but he didn't make a move to hurt her.

Two massive hands clamped down on her shoulders from behind her, crushing her bones with his grip. She wanted to cry out and wriggle free, as the sensation of her body starting to freeze from the inside out beckoned her attention. The deep chill sprung from her toes, traveling up her legs, and her hands followed suit locking her muscles in place.

"She'll be more compliant now," the harsh baritone voice said. Her eyes caught a glimpse of his yellow irises flickering like flames as the second male spun her around to face him. Terror consumed her.

"Good. Now take her inside. Vepar will explain to you what's going to happen." Xaphan barked orders like he owned the place, and the males standing before him were nothing more than underpaid minions there to serve him.

"No," the male spoke sharply, cutting off Vepar's protest with a wave of his hand. The returning grunt of disapproval dissolved into the darkness along with the limited lighting. Ferrian rolled her eyes back and forth to watch the confrontation, as the four males ate up the space around her and the darkness devoured what little light speckled the damp stonewalls.

Xaphan sucked in air through his teeth, emitting a sickening hissing sound as it echoed off the surrounding stones. "What do you mean no? I hired you to follow orders, understand? Do as I tell you to, or I'm going to cut your balls off and feed them to the barghest. Are we clear?"

The air was thickening from the tension between the male standing behind her and Xaphan, who stood a few feet before her. The little hairs on the back of her neck prickled up while staring at the man she wanted to kill, and she hoped that if their verbal combat came to blows, she would be able to move out of the way fast enough. The idea of two big males—one who could easily kill her beneath his monstrous boot—scuffling, and either pummeling each other on top of her, or crushing her in the melee against the floor or walls, jerked her mind into action. She didn't mind the idea of them killing each other, but she didn't want to end up as collateral damage in the process.

"My place, my rules," he stated sternly as he crossed his heavily muscled arms over his chest.

Ferrian knew this place all too well, but she had no idea who the steroidal monster was. Scared was an emotion best used for haunted houses or horror movies. However, freaking-the-fuck-out was closer to her reality right now.

"Is that so," Xaphan clucked, and she guessed he was cocking his perfectly manscaped inky eyebrow while checking out the status of his manicure. "Well then, I guess I'll be taking my business elsewhere. In the meantime, please send the Dark Lord my regards before he rips your intestines out with a rusted knife and feeds it to his pets. Those nasty things will chew on your internal organs for hours." The subtle excitement in his voice led Ferrian to believe, finding out whatever a barghest was, wasn't going to make her top ten things to see list. The only thing she could assume was that it was some species of animal.

"If she's going to stay in my keep, then I say which room she goes in and no one, I mean no one, goes in there. Understand? As it were, I had her cell prepared. It's the last one open."

The sound of Xaphan clapping his hands together in amusement shot a new degree of fury through her veins. She imagined the smirk slicing across his face, and dammit if she didn't want to carve a red smile across his throat to match. Her survival instincts began searching through the darkness for any signs of a secondary exit, or at the very least obtainable weapons.

"Why didn't you say so? Vepar can work his magic from outside the cell. But please keep her close to the others. The radius will make her suffering so much more delectable."

CHAPTER THIRTY-SEVEN

Her frozen body hit the concrete floor with a hard thud, like a sack of rotten potatoes. There was no telling what was colder, her body or the floor. The musty scent of decay engulfed her while her eyes searched for a way out of the darkened cell. Pointless, she quickly realized, since she knew each detail with vivid clarity. Six months in this hellhole years earlier had bestowed a lifetime of nightmares and scars on her.

The heavy door shut her in, and strangely, it was the one thing out of place. In all of the time she had been trapped and chained inside the subterranean cell, never once was the door quiet as a summer's breeze. A sickening feeling, like death was waiting for her, clamored in her chest. The muffled sound of voices, all male, standing outside her cell door set her teeth on edge, as she strained to listen. *Dammit!* She couldn't discern exactly what they were saying, but her spidey-senses were tingling. Ferrian was in the deepest lake of shit ever, wearing concrete shoes and sinking faster by the second. Minutes later came the menacing knock on the door. Steeling herself for what was coming, Ferrian focused all of her energy on trying to squirm free of her frozen state. Cocking her jaw, she tried to swivel her head to the side. Barely able to move an inch, she inhaled a deep breath and pushed her body harder to work.

"Oh, princess, look at you! Trapped, not only in this disgusting cell … but in your body as well. Pity. You can thank me later." Her stomach rolled seeing Xaphan's sex strain against his pants and his face light up with enjoyment. When it hit her that not only was he was aroused by her confinement, but seemed to revel in it. The bile in her gut rose higher, making it harder to keep down.

What she wouldn't give for the use of her hands … and her machete, which she kept hidden under her mattress. However, wishing for things wasn't going to get her out of there any faster. She kept her face as stoic as possible, staring up at him through lowered lashes. Whatever it was going to take, she would see Xaphan's life extinguished by her doing.

"I would like you to meet your new playmates." Xaphan slightly shifted from the doorway, revealing two more males. "To my left is Vepar. He's here to make sure you have an unpleasant sleep." The sickly way he rolled around those words in his mouth, made the stomach acid climb higher until it hit the back of her throat. "He'll help your dreams feel livelier. To my right is Carnax, your host for the time being. I hope you'll behave with some decorum while you're in his keep. Now, my lovely, I must attend to other matters. Please make yourself comfortable. Vepar, please help our guest rest." Cocking his chin toward the oversized Ken doll, Xaphan spoke softly in a language unrecognizable to her. Slipping a quick glance back to her, his casual smirk returned. "Please don't forget to call me with her progress." He spoke to know one in particular.

Unsure of their next move, she stared carefully at the three males. Whatever was coming wasn't going to be pleasant. It never was. The door slowly closed, and she exhaled a breath of relief. Small spots began to de-thaw around her body. The sound of two sets of heavy soles smacking against the stone floor made her wonder who had left with Xaphan, if Vepar and Carnax were expected to stay. A cold lash of dread whipped her, realizing she hadn't seen the fourth male's face. She only recalled he was taller than Xaphan, with an unusual scent, reminding her of the ocean. His hood had stayed in place, even as she jerked and kicked against his crushing hold and rock hard body earlier. The only defining details she could see was an embossed black tattoo down his ring finger, reading *Амитиел*, and those eyes, unlike anything she had ever seen before. He didn't hold the same menacing ire about him as the others did. The male's concerned nature struck her oddly when his hands did not.

Exhaustion filtered in, replacing the foreboding. As she fought against the feeling, another powerful wave of somnolence washed over her. The more she tried to fight it, the harder it was to focus on the two remaining males' voices on the other side of the cell door. She knew what the purpose of this place was and quickly figured out what Carnax's job entailed, but she couldn't quite get was what role Vepar played. Xaphan's words, 'Help our guest rest' rattled around her head until it ached.

Slowly her mind wandered into the one place she didn't want to go, yet she couldn't deny it was easy to slip into it. Like a heroin junkie seeking a quick fix to their addiction with the drug full of promising bliss, she fell into the same old comfort spot in her mind with ease. Closing her eyes, she figured it was no use. Unwanted sleep was luring her under and there wasn't any way of stopping it. Slipping into old habits, where her fantasies mingled with dreams, Ferrian soaked in the one thing which made her feel anything other than the truth she knew too well.

Remi's image gradually became clear, seeing him standing at the bay window in the hotel suite. His supple skin shimmered in the soft moonlight. The velvety crush of soft carpet beneath her footfalls as she quietly moved in closer was a welcomed feeling beneath her feet. Her body began to warm up with each step she took and beat of her heart. Resting his hand against the side of the window he didn't move; his eyes stared down to the street below. She couldn't have imagined a more perfect man to free herself with, and yet the crushing feeling when she had flipped out earlier raked her from the inside.

What had she done? Why couldn't she tell it had been real? The soft caress of his hands traipsing down her curves, and sensual way he used his tongue when he took their kiss deeper, made her skin flush with desperate need all over again. He had been everything she wanted in a lover, and still she couldn't believe he wanted her the same way. Letting her eyes wander, she went from his well-muscled calves up to the rigidly cut muscles, starting from his thighs and traveling up to his shoulders. She gasped, taken back when she saw the impossible. The gleam of transparent wings clinging to his back had her gaping in disbelief. *You've completely lost it now, time to fit you for a strait-jacket.* She stared closely, picking out more little details, and wondering if they were as soft as she believed they were or if they were even tangible.

She wanted to laugh at the oddity of it, shriek hysterics at the sight of them and demand answers, when it hit her. She was dreaming. Recalling the previous night's events vividly, she shouldn't have been surprised with this small inflection of surrealism. Too many times, her dreams were as vibrantly real as the reality she woke to. Each scent she smelled, the humid air she breathed in, even the cooling sensation of her skin, held as much reality as walking down to the pier and feeling the icy kiss of winter's wind. "Remi."

When he slowly twisted his chiseled torso to see her, an ominous glow sprayed over his bare-naked skin. The heat of his gaze pitched a fire deep within her core. It hadn't taken but a millisecond for her to lock eyes with his sizzling blues, momentarily rendering her immobilized.

He exuded a radiance raging from an internal fire, unwittingly burning her with desire, thick as sin. In those few moments, Ferrian swore an eternity had passed. She unknowingly understood everything she needed to know. Opening the floodgates, Remi spilled all his secrets to her. Her breath hitched as cliché images depicting angels flashed before her eyes. It was all she could do to remain in the present when it struck her ... hard. Remi wasn't real. He was something between her wildest fantasy and a supernatural being. *Angel.*

Cautiously slipping on a smile, he stood stone still as she sauntered closer, worry creasing his eyes. "I thought you were going to stay in the bathroom all night," he teased. Extending his hand, his wide palm called out to her, and became more inviting with each step she took. Slipping her hand into his, her breath quickened, with each ragged inhale.

"What are you?"

He gently coaxed her closer still, until their bodies were but a few mere inches away from each other. He radiated heat hotter than a furnace, welcoming her body to wrap around him. Goosebumps prickled her skin with desire, revealing the truth she refused to deny as butterflies created a tornado in her belly.

She wanted him. She wanted to feel him like this, pulling her closer, and pressing their naked skin together, until they melted into one another. Even in dreams, she trembled from his touch. With each pass of his gentle fingers down her spine, her knees grew weak. His other hand cupped the small of her back, pinning her body to his.

The thick stalk between his legs poked at her stomach, leaving a droplet of his desire on her skin. "I am whatever you want me to be, m'aingeal," he whispered across her skin, sending more shivers racing down her body until they punched a hole into her will. His lips purchased the fleshy spot below her ear, hitting the right bundle of nerves, causing her sex to well up with liquid heat. Although they were only words filling the space between them, they weighed heavy like a promise he was willing to wrap around her heart as he whispered it once more against her lips.

She hadn't realized she was biting her lower lip, until his coaxing kiss demanded to taste it. Gently tugging it, she gave in. His warmth slowly consumed her from head to toe, when his greedy tongue sliced its way in, taking their kiss deeper. How could anything feel so unspoiled, and at the same time have her stomach twisting in knots as a nagging pull jerked her backward? Her fingers reached for his skin, trembling with need as she fought the nuisance tug. Feathering her fingertips over the hard planes of his chest, her eyes searched his for the truth. "Are you an angel?"

His devilish grin spread like wildfire across the plains as he nodded once to her. Dropping her hand to her belly, the twisting feeling grew as dread seeped in. "Why didn't you tell me?"

"I wasn't allowed to, m'aingeal. I knew you'd figure it out sooner or later."

Nuzzling her cheek into the warmth of his palm, she thought wryly, *Paradise couldn't touch this moment with a ten-foot pole*. Another quick jerk backward jarred her back to the feeling of foreboding.

"What is it, Ferrian, what's wrong?" The concern in his apprehensive eyes scoured her face for answers, and she wished she knew how to explain it to him. Slipping her hands over his shoulders, she found some comfort, holding him in place.

"I'm afraid I'm going to lose you. I feel like there's a cable inside of me, pulling me away from you."

"Nothing is going to take you away from me again, Ferrian. Understand me?" Propping her chin up with his finger, his lips grazed hers. She relished his sweet taste each time she licked her hungry lips, and she whispered another kiss over his mouth. Closing her eyes, she sank deeper, coaxing him to take more from her.

The hard snap ripped her away from him as darkness enclosed her. "Remi!" she screamed, wrestling her way back to him. The cable tethering her from the inside, broke her from her dream, hastily dragging her through the void. This was it. What was coming next wasn't going to be a surprise to her. Steeling herself, Ferrian awaited for the onslaught of torture and traumas beyond comprehension.

"Welcome, Darkling." Her head was spinning as she shook off the dizzying effects. A dark voice spewed acid, chilling her to the bone. They were the only two words she was going to hear, as a set of yellow eyes zeroed in her. Braving a glance around him, she recognized where she was. In a dream state version of her cell, where Hell began and any hope for freedom dissolved into the ethers.

Screams littered the air, echoing off stonewalls as she watched the corner of the room light up, revealing a young girl. From what she could tell, the girl—who was chained to the wall like an animal—was not much older than sixteen. Her delicate features were covered in blood and fresh bruises. Tamping down the deadly desire to destroy their captors, she sank back into the darkness, focusing on the keys jingling from his belt. Although she tried to fight back the fury, a deep roar rumbled through her chest, exposing Ferrian as her body shook, rattling the chains tethering her to the cold damp walls.

The vicious sneer of the male, who she assumed was Carnax, tore away any sense of forgiveness. She pictured his head between her palms as she detached it from his body. Smirking at the thought, she reveled in the idea of Carnax's blood pooling all around his lifeless body as she sloshed barefoot through the inky liquid, leaving wet foot prints while making her way toward the fire pit. Her intentions were to dispose of his head in the fiery flames.

Her mind ran amuck with new ideas the longer she was forced to watch the disgusting display he was taking great pride in. She tried to close her eyes, shut off her hearing. She had seen enough in her twenty-four years on

Earth. Hell, she had lived through most of it personally. Yet, watching some innocent soul suffering like she was, enraged Ferrian to new levels. It left her with a deadly desire to dispatch monsters—like her host—to the ranks, which she hadn't experienced before. Her body grew taut and she sank into a pre-launch crouch. Survival instincts kicked in again, as she quickly formed a plan of attack. Realistically, her chances of success in nailing one of the males were slim to none, but she had to try.

Snarling loud enough for Vepar to hear, she waited patiently for him to step nearer. Her hands wrapped around the chains, and she sucked in a quick breath. The scent of his acrid cologne wafted closer, stinging her nose. "What did you say, Darkling?"

When she didn't respond immediately, he yanked her hair back by the base of her skull, forcing her to look at him. Sneering the moment their eyes met, he snarled back at her, "What's so funny, bitch?"

She waited a moment longer before launching her body up and kicked his face with the sole of her boot. Vepar stumbled backward a step, releasing her hair. Following through her attack with a cross-kick to the side of Vepar's head, she watched his jaw swinging as his large frame tumbled to the floor. Landing back into a crouch position, she waited for the male to climb to his feet and come after her.

Vepar reared back, gripping his head between his hands. A shrill sound howled from his twisted lips, giving her some brief satisfaction. But it wasn't enough. His evil scowl when he pushed himself off the floor raged with fury as hot as lava burning from his eyes. Curling his jagged lip, she noticed a thick, ropey scar running from one ear to over his lips, and trailing down his chin. The look on his gnarly mug suggested he was about to make his move. *Predictable,* Ferrian thought sardonically.

"I don't think so, asshole!" Jumping quickly as he swiftly swatted for her leg, Ferrian came crunching down on the limb with a heavy thud, snapping the bones in his forearm and hand. His ripe curses screeched through the dank room, alerting Carnax to the scene.

Carnax's head whipped around and she half-mused about it completely spinning around like he was Linda Blair from *The Exorcist*. The seething stare of his flaming eyes told her he wasn't amused in the slightest by her antics. "What?" she taunted, eyeing her cellmate, hoping the girl had enough sense to sneak away before their gracious host turned back around. "You can't do shit to me here."

"And why is that, exactly?" His voice was dark, and so deep, she wondered if there was an octave range he would fit in.

"Because we both know this isn't real. It's nothing more than a dream," she stated, jutting out her chin in defiance. She knew better than most; even in dreams, you can be tortured and feel the pain. However, what if she wasn't dreaming, what if this was like what she experienced back at the hotel with Remi? A cold sweat broke out on her skin, as all hope this was a dream rapidly dissolved.

"That's where you're wrong, little girl." Shaking his head, Ferrian watched him with a wary eye. "He pulled you out of your dream in time for you to see what I have in store for you." The bitter chortle rumbled off the stone walls. Tiny reverberations rattled through her body, sending another round of frozen fingers curling around her limbs.

"Shit!" she yelped, as her body torqued in an odd position of her undoing. And there it was, the other shoe not only dropped, but had been savagely ripped off her foot.

Swallowing back the panic clawing its way up her throat, she refused to show him what was going on inside of her head. She was freaking out, completely and totally. Hysteria would soon have a new name, and it would be Ferrian. Fear mixed with fury as she locked eyes with the innocent across the room. Curled into a ball, her body resembled more of connect the black and blues than what should have been a healthy young woman. Carnax followed her gaze, looking back over his thick shoulder to his latest victim.

"Thing of beauty, isn't it? I get to play with her until she breaks, and you get to feel all of her pain, her fear, until the beautiful moment I finally allow her to die."

Vepar climbed to his feet, a grimace curled his lip over the elongated fangs he had hidden too well earlier and revealed the full spectrum view of his dental work. The smell of wrath he was about to unleash on her, suffocated the room as she braced herself for the first hit.

Curling his fist tight, Vepar pulled back his arm, ready to launch it toward her. *Three ... two ... one!* "Remi," was the last word she said before the crushing blow knocked her backward and out cold with one hit. She didn't stand a chance in Hell against the male while she was tethered like a dog on a leash. A surprise attack was one thing, but full on engaging was a no win situation.

CHAPTER
THIRTY-EIGHT

The endless veil of night had securely closed in as Remiel and Charoum stalked down the back alleys of Chicago's West End. Debris ridden streets and cracked asphalt from too many years of negligence carried promise of finding either Hellistics demons or Daemons. He searched for Ferrian in run down and vacant buildings, and came up empty each time. Stopping by the bus and train depots elicited much of the same.

With one mission set to mind, he dived in and out of buildings. Much of the night had been spent clearing one vacant building after another. Charoum followed suit, ducking in and out of urban decay, while Cassiel searched by air for any signs of Ferrian, entering or leaving any buildings, block by grungy city block in the district. The group of his brethren had met up to discuss their plan of attack. After considering the size of the city, they decided on doing a clean sweep from each end of west side until they met in the middle. Breaking into two teams, Remiel lead his team and Z lead Bels and Roc on the far end of the city's West End district.

The sounds of the city pulled him back to the present.

He couldn't change what had happened, but from here on out, he was going to make damn sure he didn't put Ferrian at risk in any way again. The sickening feeling plaguing him earlier, thinking Xaphan had somehow tracked her down and captured her, had proven absolutely correct. Reading the text Focalor had sent Cass, they found out he had dug up a small piece of information; Xaphan had hidden Ferrian and she was still in the city, but where she was being held was under wraps. Cursing at the bit of news, the crushing weight of guilt came crashing back down on him. He should've tried harder to keep her in the suite. He shouldn't have held her closely, making love to her. *Dammit!* How could he have been so stupid to think she'd be okay with it? She was his charge, his sole purpose was to protect her, guide her when she was lost, and help her when she asked for it. Granted she never would ask for help, but tangling with her in the sack was not in his job description. He was in too deep. And regardless if he lost his wings, he couldn't abandon her, not even if she turned into a Daemon.

The scent of death and sulfur filtered in on the back of the cool air, stinging his nostrils as if he had snorted bleach. "Hellistics." The odor grew stronger, promising a fight once they came across one of the Underworld's signature demons. Although the smell thickened with each new block they passed, he held no illusions they would happen to stumble upon one lonely demon. Each step he took in the direction of the scent cranked up his adrenaline a notch higher. His thick muscles bunched beneath his Guinness tee shirt and black leather coat. Palming his Sig Sauer P250, he swore he would find Ferrian alive, or destroy anything in his path until he found Satan himself and crushed the Demon God beneath his boot heel.

Word came in from Ezekiel periodically with updates on what they had or hadn't found, while hitting known demon hotspots downtown. Chicago was slowly turning into a battle zone, and the fear of all-out war was on the verge of breaking out, was quickly becoming their new reality. Each new place their team hit, and demon they questioned, came up as dead ends. Whoever had Ferrian wasn't taking any chances by sharing the information, and nothing had been leaked up until this point. Raking his fingers through his hair, frustration mixed with determination to keep searching gnawed at him the longer he went without finding her.

Since hitting the streets, they had destroyed four Hellistics demons who were trying to lure a small group of underage girls into a vacant building. In human form, the breed appeared like any other human. Created in the pits of Hellas, by the Demon Lord Baphomet, they were intended for seducing the weak-minded, spitting out promises of sex, drugs, and music to the unaware. In their demon form, they resembled skinless lions with rabies and a bad case of scabies.

Charo had artfully sliced one of two Daemons they'd found savagely devouring a vagrant in one of the city's retired mill buildings, from neck to naval with his Tachi sword. With Cassiel on his heels, Remi plugged a hole the size of his fist through the chest of the second one.

"Remind me again how Daemons have survived for this long, yet we lost all Darks?" Charo only spoke through his mind, as he plugged his question straight into both Cassiel and Remi's heads.

"Because Lucifer was smart enough to hide them until all of the Dark Angels died away. Makes me wish we had done the same thing." The action was heating up as they turned down another back alley. The sickening feeling they were getting closer to finding her began pooling in his gut. Time was not on his side and the stakes were high.

Things had gotten worse over the past two and half decades. Demons were rising more frequently than centuries past, to cause havoc and chaos in all over the world. Modern technology had equipped them with the tools necessary to take out anyone who got in their way with little exposure to the Underworld. Somewhere in the depths of his heart, Remi knew Ferrian would rise to the occasion and prove herself to be a true Dark Angel. In turn, he hated to admit it … if only to himself, he slightly feared she might not choose the right side. With the threat of another apocalypse on the horizon, and panic sending stinging signals down to his balls, he doubled his efforts to find her quickly, and tuck her away in the one place demons couldn't enter.

The faint tingling sensation running down his spine, gave him some hope he was getting closer to Ferrian. Signaling Charo to follow his lead inside of the decaying building, he crept along the street, hugging walls. Whipping his finger around in a tornado signal, he motioned for them to materialize inside. It would be their best option, if not their only one. The element of surprise was crucial, should they happen to come upon any type of demon or minion alike.

Charo gave a quick nod, clutching his Tachi tightly, his twin emeralds locked on Remi, awaiting the moment. Cautiously they split up, searching around the outside of the building for any signs of recent entry. Charo chose to search the backside while Remi took the front. Everything he saw reminded Remi of death; from the dried up remnants of bushes dotted along the side of the building to the grey wooden slates, cracking and breaking right off the building with each passing gust the wind. He moved soundlessly toward the front door. Glancing down the street from one end to the other, there was not a single soul was in sight. His eyes searched for the little details of anything out of place. However, given where they were searching, the only thing out of place was the Aston Martian Rapide S sitting adjacent to the building they were surveying.

As quickly as the thought had hit him, Charo popped out to join him in front of the vacant house in serious decay, which sat on the street amidst so many others time had forgotten.

"Anything?"

Charo gave a subtle shake of his shaven head. His brown brows knitted together, alarming Remi. Charo had been created with a special communication quirk. Lacking a voice to speak with, he had the ability to speak directly into the mind of any being, and control their emotions, too. As if the first wasn't a total mindfuck, the latter had the capability to seriously twist a person inside out. He had yet to find someone other than the big boss man who could read Charo's personal thoughts. Putting words into another's head was one thing; someone else reading his mind was quite different. Sure, his quiet nature came in handy most of the time. Yet as much as it was convenient, it was also irritated the hell out of Charo when Remi could tell the guy wanted to scream at someone.

"What's up?" The soft vibration buzzing from his jean pocket caught both of their attention. Pulling the device free, he showed Charo the screen. Ezekiel had sent him an update. Reading the text, his inky brows popped up. "They've got some information for us, and will be here in a minute. Let Cass know to get his ass down here, pronto."

Charo nodded once and sent the message skyward. Remi slipped the device back into his pocket. Letting out a sigh, the tingling sensation grew stronger the longer he stood there. Anxiety had worn him out. Aiming for the front stoop, Remi hauled his body over to find a spot to plant his ass for a moment while they waited for the second group to show up. As he was deciding which step would be strong enough to hold his weight, something odd caught his eye. Faint drag marks on the tiny deck. "What the..." Studying the marks, he could feel his heart dropping into his gut as the scent of jasmine wafted around him. "Shit!"

He knew the lingering scent all too well. Drawing his gun, he searched the door for any signs she'd entered freely, but that hope quickly disappeared the longer Remi studied the doorway. His eyes zeroed in on the few strands of raven hair, stuck on a jagged piece of the wooden doorframe. Launching up the steps, he kicked in the cracked wooden door with a devastating blow. In the back of his head, he heard Charo tell him to wait for the others because they needed to figure out what was going on, but he was far past rational.

He wasn't surprised in the least when he sensed his two brethren had followed in behind him. Staying close to the walls, Remi searched the entryway, and down the hall.

Heel marks from being dragged all the way, ended in what he could assume was the living room. Carcasses of dead rodents, cats, and a few birds littered the area. Torn wallpaper peeled effortlessly from fragile walls, riddled with holes. Biting back the bile from the stench of death and sulfur, with a hint of fecal matter scattered about, he quietly made his way to the end of the line.

Studying the last of the marks, he couldn't find another trail indicating where Ferrian's abductor had dragged her to. The fresh prints of two sets of footfalls decorated the dust and drywall floured floors. His heart sunk a little more as he knelt down to touch the last place she had been. The thrumming in his head ran straight down his spine, signaling him she was still alive. *Where are you, baby? Talk to me.*

The creaking wood gave way to silent footfalls, as he brought his attention back up along with his gun. "Whoa, easy there, little fella, wouldn't want you to shoot the wrong guy." Roc threw his hands up in surrender, but he stayed the gun on him, until he confirmed it was the king of the pain-in-the-asses. "Yo, Rem-dog, it's me. You can lower your pea-shooter anytime, buddy."

"Just checking. You never know if one of those soul-suckers will try and impersonate one of us."

"Fair enough."

"So what's the word? Any leads on my charge?"

Z stepped forward wearing a grave expression. He didn't know if his heart was going to stop beating entirely or jump out of his chest, waiting for someone to answer his question. "What is it? For chrissake, will someone tell me before I start tearing down every friggin' building from here to the bay?"

"Yeah," Z spoke. "Word is she's being held nearby, but no one is saying where. The Watcher overheard some talk, Xaphan has—Remi, where are you going?"

"To find her," he barked, pushing his way through the group. "If Xaphan has her, there's no telling what he's going to do to her!"

"Wait! There's more."

Cassiel stepped in front of him, with his hands held up. "Remiel, listen to him. You can't go charging after her half-cocked without knowing all of the details."

"Like hell I can't! See those marks are the floor? They're hers, and I can sense she's near."

"Listen, I get it, I do. However, you won't do her any good if you go all Hulk on us without a back-up plan. Breathe, my brother." Z's grim tone lashed the air, slicing some sense into the reality of their situation.

He let those words sink in. Dropping his head, Remi realized Z was right. He still had no real idea where she was being held. All he had to go by was the tingling sensations racing down his spine, which were growing stronger with each passing minute. "I hear you, but you can't expect me to stand-by idly when I know she's so close. If I could figure out where she disappeared to ... shit, the tracks end here."

"Seriously, man, she weighs all of a buck-twenty soaking wet, wouldn't someone toss her over their shoulder and hightail it out of here?"

"Roc," Z shot him a cutting glare, "shut up. You're not helping."

The fury he carried mixed with cold fear since there was a possibility Roc was right. Rolling his head back on his shoulders, he let it enter his brain, knowing it would quickly fester into toxic mixture of revenge and bloodlust.

"Remi, how do you know?" Cassiel cupped his shoulder, reassuring Remi he would stand by whatever he had to say.

"It's the sensation I get when she's near. Sort of like electrical currents running down my back." He let out a long, low sigh when he could felt five sets of eyes staring him down as though he were a dead man walking.

"Remi, a little word of advice ... don't tell anyone else about this again. If the Council of the Seven ever got wind of this—" Remi lifted his hand to cut Z off, because he knew exactly what the Council would do. "Listen, we'll figure this all out. Hang on a minute and listen to me, okay?"

"I'm trying to, Z. Every second that I'm not searching for her, feels like my insides are tearing apart." The weight of his admission coated the air with sworn secrecy as guilt for including everyone except for Amitiel struck him with a low blow. He had unintentionally put a price on all their heads should the Council catch wind of things. Now he owed a lifelong debt to each one of his brethren, for the unsaid promises they each made upon his confession. Never mind if they ever found out about what happened between him and Ferrian in the hotel. Even thinking about it was like a prison sentence where both of them were doomed to serve an eternity in the inferno pits of Hell.

Silence befell the room, deafening his thoughts. The growing knot in his stomach continued twisting tighter, sickening him with dread, panic, and a murderous rage welling up by the minute. The longer he stood there trying to focus on those around him, the further he fell into the abyss of his mind. He could sense her; the vibrations were his only connection to finding Ferrian. He didn't need intel to help him, not when Ferrian could lead him right to her. Scrubbing his face nearly raw, he mentally berated himself. How could he have been so stupid to think any of this would be okay?

Each caught in their own reverie, no one made a move, not a single word was spoken as though they all considered the gravity of his circumstances. He wondered how long it would take before Roc popped off another snarky comment, when a round of vibrations brought each of the members reaching into their pockets for their cells. The flashing of incoming text beeped bright green. **'Top-side ASAP'**. "Shit." Slipping the small device back into his pocket, he knew there was no way of getting out of this. Yet leaving Ferrian unfound wasn't something he couldn't handle right now. Z caught on to his thoughts, and locked him in a showdown of stares. The subtle shake of his head spoke volumes. There would be no getting out, not without one massive fight. Five-to-one odds, even in his about-to-go-apeshit state, he didn't stand a snowball's chance in hell. "I thought we had new intel?"

"We were summoned based on it. We were coming to find you guys. We know little at this point."

"You don't expect me to leave now? I-I can't. Not when she's so close. I can—"

"Remi, no! Now's not the time. We need to find out what's going on first! A few minutes longer isn't going matter." Z was edging around a tricky corner with this one, as Remi's rage began to thicken.

"Are you trying to tell me Ferrian's safety *isn't* my first priority? Because I was under the distinct impress from our *boss*, she is my first and only concern. So do you expect me to leave here, without her? I don't think—"

The loud crack echoed around the stark room, silencing Remi, and his body fell lax to the floor. "Damn, he's got a hard head! Think I almost dented the butt of Shangri-La knocking him one." Shoving his Smith & Wesson .45 back into his chest holster, Roc grinned wickedly, staring down at the unconscious one of the group.

"Roc, that was completely uncalled for." Cassiel, sidestepped around the walking mohawk, and bent down to check on Remi. "Great, you frigging moron, he's out cold! How the hell do you suppose we explain this to Am? I swear, you act before you think. Is there anything you use your head for?"

Wiggling his dark brows and licking his lip until his tongue caught his lip-ring, Roc cocked his head and shot Cass his best, you-better-believe-it smirk. "I can think of plenty of things I use my head for."

"I wasn't referring to your shrimp dick, dickhead. Now can you be somewhat of a decent angelic being and get over here to help me carry him Realmside, or is it too much of a task for you to manage?"

"Well, I don't know. I might break a nail or something, your assholiness."

"Enough you two!" The thunderous crack of Ezekiel's voice sliced the air with his intentions. "Roc, help Cassiel get Remi Realmside. Charo, Bels, you should head up, too. I'll be right behind you."

The air had taken on a sullen note as Z weighed all of the new information. Given what he had found out from Amitiel already he hadn't had a chance to tell Remi with the way things were going—he knew this wasn't going to end well. Regardless which way it went, somebody was going to get hurt, and angels being immortal can carry pain for eternity.

Catching on to his thoughts, Charo stepped up, cupping Z's shoulder, and with a subtle nod, he left Ezekiel to do what he knew he couldn't talk Z out of.

"Be vigilant, my braća". Returning the gesture, Z bowed once and set his mind to task. He was limited on time, and wasting any more of it, sharing quiet moments with his crew wasn't in the plan. "Make sure someone revives him, but keep him tethered until he calms down. And, Roc, you can fully expect a beat down when he's freed."

Lightning flashed in Roc's eyes. Rolling his shoulders back, he cocked one pierced brow, tilting his chin over his shoulder. "Good! About damn time one of you pansy-asses tried to take a piece of me to the floor."

"Be careful what you wish for, young-blood. You might get more than you bargained for."

Roc's throaty laugh echoed off the decaying stark walls as Cassiel dragged Remi's body to the center of the room. Throwing his hands in the air, he mockingly surrendered to Cassiel, but there wasn't a hint of jest in Cassiel's return glare. "Okay, okay. I get it, man, for chrissake. Chill!" Without further argument, Roc looped an arm under Remi's arm and hefted him off the ground with Cassiel.

CHAPTER THIRTY-NINE

The repulsive effluvium of sulfur mixed with the coppery tang of blood—fresh, and drying—hitting her nostrils slapped Ferrian back to reality. Working her jaw out from the last crack Vepar had hit her with, left a growing drive for his demise escalating throughout her body. Shaking the sleep from her head, she tried to focus on anything solid as her blurry vision fought to clear up. A quick check of the female chained in the corner, slumped over in a heap, gasping for breath reminded her of the days she had spent trapped as a teenager.

Silence coated the room as thickly as the clammy air, stirring memories Ferrian long wanted to forget. The heavy thud of boots walking down the hall as fresh screams littered the hallway, set her fury into inferno mode. Balling up her fists, she struggled to wiggle free from the bonds tethering her to the floor. As she lifted her body up from the cold stone floor, the niggling feeling of someone evil coming crawled up her spine moments before the heavy wooden door slammed open. *Vepar*. Gritting her teeth, Ferrian was more than ready to go another round with the oversized gym-rat.

"I see the little bitch is awake. About time." She didn't have to see his face to sense the sneer curling his lip, like she was nothing more than a rabid animal needing to be put down, or the disgust he wore considering her, but she did. Staring up at him from under disheveled hair and fresh bruises, a guttural rumble shuddered through her chest. Begging him to come closer, her hands curled tighter into boney balls, ready to strike.

"Ooh, am I supposed to be threatened by those pathetic growls of yours, Darkling? Save it. By the time I'm done with you, you'll have no fight left inside of you."

Readying herself for what was coming, he stared her down, raising his hand in an odd wave. Blackness swallowed her whole as frigid air abraded her flesh. *What the hell happened?* Pusillanimity wanted to creep in, settle in the familiar place inside of her stomach and sink its claws in as permanent anchors when subtle flashes of lights flickered in the distance.

The room sluggishly lit up, revealing the worst of her memories. Trapped and tethered to stone walls by her wrists and ankles. Enough chain hanging loose to wrap around her as her tormenter turned her body to face the wall. "Holy shit!" Hysteria climbed up her throat as she shrieked. Her voice cried out in under gravel-lined voice. She had fallen back into a sixteen-year-old girl, tortured at the hands of her foster father and brother. Rivulets of crimson trailed down her pale flesh. Stinging pain from the slices left on her arms caught her breath, and a set of pitch black eyes of a man she thought she knew approached her.

"Noooooooo!" She knew without a doubt who those eyes belonged to. *Xaphan.* It had been him who caused all this, trying to destroy her since childhood. A swell of fury erupted within her. Gripping the chains, she thrashed as violently as she could, trying to break free. The scowl on his lips, and heat in his stare, the closer he came set a wave of impending death across the room. "This isn't real, this isn't real!"

His chortled laughter bounced off the thick walls, and with one nod, she knew the term *'I'm fucked'* was a complete understatement. "Welcome back, Ferrian." Acid layered each word he spit at her while reaching for a white sand-like substance. Ferrian's stomach twisted tighter into knots as she observed his blood-covered fingers idly running through it, before cupping a handful. *Holyshitballs!* She knew what was coming and it was going to pure agony.

If this dream was any indication of what was going to happen, she was reliving her life with all of the pain and anguish, as fresh as the day it happened. With a heavy slap of his hand, he smeared the substance over her bleeding wounds, and she bit down to hold in the howl begging to come out. Salt, and not the ordinary Morton's table salt, oh hell no! He went for the coarse sea salt kind of shit, made to burn the hair out of your nose.

"That's right, Ferrian. Scream for me. I can make this pain last for hours, even days. So let's hear my favorite beautiful sound."

Gnashing her teeth harder, she wondered if it was possible to be even more worried about breaking her teeth than she was before. The longer she held out, the harder the past pulled her back. Slipping from the present, where she knew someone was purposely screwing with her dreams, she slid head first into the past. She had had some messed up dreams before, but the moment she became her sixteen-year-old self again, she lost all sense of the present. Fighting against the invisible attack, she tried holding on to one face. *Remi.*

Her hair clung to wet skin as tiny rivers of blood ran wildly down from her brow and the gash on the side of her skull. Gravel had ripped her throat raw as another round of slices made by her foster brother around her legs and hips shredded the last of her clothing. How long had she been chained-up in this dungeon? How much longer did she have before they killed her? Panic rose in her throat as the boy swung her around, slamming her face first into the damp, cold stonewall. The warmth from her blood spilling from her latest wound dripped carelessly into her eyes, filling her vision with red death. "Boy! Back away. Give this filly some time to rest." Begrudgingly he did as he was told, grumbling curses under his breath as he threw a handful of salt at her oozing wounds.

Darkness closed her in with the slam of the heavy wooden door. Releasing her pent up breath, she wanted to break down and cry. Scream for help. But it was no use. Her voice was lost and the tears had since dried up. Sagging against the only comfort she had, the cold stones were a welcomed relief as the swelling set in.

She had lost track of time. Had it been hours, days? There was no way of knowing. All she could feel was the longing for death, even as the pain dulled. Through all of the beatings, and when he strapped her to the table to carve odd lines down her arms, Ferrian had secretly begged for reprieve, asking God, or anyone to save her. No one came. No one knew what was happening to her, except the man responsible. "Dear God, please, I beg you, please help me. Free me or let me die. I don't want to die by his hands. Please ... please." Rolling the words around in her head, exhaustion swaddled her, luring her under. She feared her prayers were going to be ignored. After all, God didn't help the unwanted. The ones who've caused the deaths of two innocent people, who only wanted to protect her. They paid the price with their lives. No, she was damned, and maybe this was what she deserved. Death would be too easy. Too tired to care anymore, her body lacked any warmth, nor craved it. She closed her eyes and imagined what death looked like. Time ceased to exist.

She was the reason her mother was dead. She was the reason her foster mother died. She caused their deaths. They tried to protect her. They loved her. What was left of her heart had shattered and fallen to dust the moment her foster father came home. Sneering, he picked her up by her throat and slammed her into the drywall, cracking it around her scrawny body. "You did this! You caused her death, you little bitch! It's all your fault!" His breath reeked of Jack Daniels, as spit splashed her in her face with each word he said. The memory flooded her aching chest as she tried to pull her quivering arms to her body. Desperation rattled through her. She didn't know what she longed for more ... freedom or death. At least in death she could find her birth mother and foster mother, beg them for forgiveness on her knees.

The searing pain of his whip lashing her skin brought Ferrian out of her reverie with a pained cry. "See, boy, catch them when they're sleeping and they'll always sing when you wake them." The deafening sound of laughter from the boy hooting and hollering as the next lashing came made the terror twist in her stomach. "Spin the bitch around, son. I think it's time we make you a man."

"Oh God no!" She struggled to pull away from him. His coarse hands grabbed her first by her thighs, splitting them wide as he kneed her core, causing her to wince against the pain. He chuckled and dragged her around by her breast, ripping at it like it was nothing more than a handle. "No! Dear god let me die, please! I beg you, let this be the end! Don't do this. Let me go. I promise I'll never say a word to anyone. You'll never have to see my face again. No, no—"

Her pleading cries were cut short by the master's hand crushing her throat.

"There's no God here to save you, slut. No amount of begging will save you either." When he backhanded her across her swollen cheek, tears shots to her eyes against her will. His hand raked through her blood-stained hair, yanking her head backward until she couldn't struggle anymore. "Go on, son. See, you have to know how to treat whores like this one. She's all yours."

Biting against the fear, she fell silent as the void consumed her whole.

Coppery smelling blood crusted the corners of her dry mouth. Screams had raked the inside of her throat raw as if she had swallowed shards of glass. All she could do was lie there, on the damp, cold floor, curled into a ball to keep from losing it completely. Her prayers for death had gone unanswered. Swimming in the emptiness, she didn't care about anything anymore. There was an odd comfort to the abyss now consuming her. It didn't matter what had happened, or would still come. She didn't have to feel any of it. She was nothing more than a shell filled with noth-ingness. Closing her eyes, she decided she wasn't going to fight against the agony anymore.

"Holy hell," muttered the dark, smoky voice, soft as a whisper and leaking with disdain. She was too tired, too far gone to care if he was here to hurt her. She tried to open her eyes, barely lifting the lids halfway, but it was enough to see a pair of silver wings shimmering in the dim light. The mysterious male leaned down, and caressed her cheek. "Shh, you're safe now. I'm getting you out of here. Dear God, M'aingeal, I'm so sorry."

She tried to speak, ask what he was planning on do-ing to her. Instead, she could only mouth the words, 'I'm broken'. As his face came into view from her blurred vi-sion, Ferrian let the hope of being rescued die away. There was nothing left of her to save.

Two warm arms slid under her battered body, rattling the chains. She froze as the manacles freed her wrists and fell to the floor clanking. Had God decided to answer her prayers after all? Had she been put through enough to satisfy her past crimes? She could only hope so.

Hot sand stung her insides as she tried to speak once again. "Who are you?" The words sounded like grit to her ears, barely a whisper. Finally lifting her eyes to meet his, a pair of sapphire blue eyes gazed back down at her. Hid-den under a fringe of inky lashes were the most brilliant blue eyes Ferrian had ever seen. Hypnotic. A pained mien crossed his face, furrowing his brows.

"My name is Remiel, I'm your guardian. Close your eyes now, rest." Pressing her shivering body to the warmth of his rigid chest, she reveled in the heat his body gave off. Her swollen and bruised cheek rested against his soft as feather and silk shoulder. Her eyes closed even as she tried to keep her gaze on the lines of her savior's per-

fect profile. His warmth seeped into her aching muscles, relieving her, and comforting her in ways she hadn't known before. This couldn't be real, nothing could feel this good. She had died. This was it, and he was bringing her to Heaven. "Thank you."

Pressing a kiss into her hair, he whispered back, "I don't deserve your gratitude. I failed you, m'aingeal, and I mean not to do it again. I will never be able to make this right, but I promise you, I'll never let anything like this happen to you again."

CHAPTER FORTY

The sensation of being ripped in-half tore through her with the gentleness of a Sherman tank. Pain exploded in her head as her eyes darted around the room. The hazy image of a woman standing by—staring horrified, with her hand covering her mouth—didn't seem real. Her slender fingers reached out to touch Ferrian, until she glanced down at the body. A horrified expression etched across the female's face, as Ferrian realized what the woman was seeing. It was her body and Ferrian was now occupying it.

Another searing sting laced behind the soft tissue of her eyes. It was happening again. She was ripping souls out of their bodies and enduring their agony. How was this happening so fast? One second she was her sixteen-year-old self, locked in a hellhole to waking up here, in someone else's body in the blink of an eye. All memory of the warmth she'd had, curled up in the arms of the male who had saved her, dissolved away when the hard crack of knuckles struck her face. This was only going to end one of two ways. Either this body she filled was going to die or be tortured beyond repair, leaving the body's soul to return without memory of what had happened. Steeling herself for the next hit, she bit down on her lip, coiling up her muscles, ready to launch before the strike. The stench of sulfur and death ranked the air as a pair of yellow eyes, flickering as flames burned brighter.

"Carnax," a scoured voice called out from the shadows. Glancing sideways, she assumed the male had to be one of the other prisoners held in the underground dungeons.

Carnax's flaming eyes bore into hers knowingly. The hair on her host's body rose in alarm until she realized why he was standing there, staring and smirking. "Darkling, you can't get away from me. Try as you might."

Shrinking away from the bloody gore laid out before her, Ferrian swallowed back down the rising vitriol to keep from revealing her disgust. Each lashing that sliced through her host's skin stung with agonizing licks. Ferrian bit down on the inside of her cheek to keep from crying out, until the coppery tang of blood trickled down her throat. She refused to give Carnax what he wanted. The excruciating wounds crusted with salt made all of the other pain dull in comparison. Carnax wasn't only doing his job … no, he enjoyed his work. Pride etched across his jagged features, as the flickering of orange and red flames licked blood-soaked skin.

The cruelty in which he delivered his tortures, and the viciousness of his handiwork was growing with each new host Ferrian was called to. She couldn't help but sneer at the words dancing through her mind. *You were made for this, taking the place of the innocent souls and their miseries. You're saving my mortal children from a hell they weren't meant to suffer. You, and you alone, have survived for a purpose."* The ethereal voice spoke the words over and again until the vibration of the first syllable bounced around her skull. Those words had haunted her day and night for too long. They wore on her each time her soul was ripped from her body to consume another's. Was this God's intention? Was her life so meaningless, held so little value that enduring the pain for others was all she was good for?

Her jaw ticked; gnashing her teeth she silently cursed the life she'd been given. Fury replaced compassion. Anger roiled deep within her gut, as she stared at the first person she'd happily destroy if she could break free. Soaking in the warped images, Ferrian envisioned in perfect detail what she would do to Carnax, Vepar, and especially Xaphan. They were all going to die before this was over. And God would have to accept she was a broken soul after all.

"You won't win." The swell of hatred grew in her chest, tingling down her body, spreading through her arms and legs. Her eyes burned into his, seething with vengeance. "You and your scum-sucking asshat friends are going to die!" Her voice didn't waver, even as her legs buckled from exhaustion.

With one long step, Carnax came an arm's length away and crushed her shoulder with his fingers. Ferrian winced, but refused to scream. A fiery ball of fury licked at her insides; she imagined it bursting from her body and slamming into his with all the placidness of a tsunami. The harder he dug his fingers into her flesh, the more her internal ball of white-hot heat grew. One second she was nearly on the verge of shattering when poof, the throbbing disappeared. Slowly she peeled one eye open, followed cautiously by the other. Carnax shook off whatever had thrown him into the far wall, knocking his senses offline for a split second. She seized the chance to scan the room for anyone else hiding in the shadows. How in the hell had Carnax ended up on his ass, across the room?

She only found one other living being in the room. A male, chained to the far wall. His hair was grimy, caked in blood and grease, and his clothes were in the same condition with a few well-placed rips and tears. His dark, haunted eyes latched on to hers as if she were his life support, silently begging her for help. He struggled to pull his hands from the metal manacles shackling him to the stone wall.

"What did you do to me, Darkling?" Carnax let out a stream of curses, glaring at her. His teeth bared and a menacing scowl curled at his lips.

Her heart was pounding, frantic to break free of her chest. Sweat trickled down the back of her neck as she tried to figure out what had happened herself. Breaking eye contact with Carnax, she quickly assessed her options for escaping. Breath sawed in and out of her lungs as fear crept into the pit of her stomach. Whatever had happened, whatever had caused her ungracious host to bounce off the far wall like a sack of potatoes was going to cost her dearly. The rattling of chains and racing heartbeat of her cellmate, made her wish she could enter his body next and spare him what was coming for both of them.

Swiveling her head around, she found Carnax climbing to his feet, his teeth bared and fresh, glossy black blood coated his hands. Her dread twisted in defiance. "You're going to pay for that, bitch!"

Her heart raced faster as the ire in Carnax's eyes

flared up. Climbing to his feet, Carnax pulled the heavy wooden door open. "Vepar," he called. "It's time." Her eyes darted between Carnax's cruel smile and the innocent male trying to break free. Two oversized steroid freaks—with a discernible taste for torture and blood—against two chained up beings left no room for wonder. She knew without a shred of doubt what was coming for her, for both of them. Death. And it wasn't going to be the easy, fall asleep and drift away kind everyone wished for. No, it would be cruelty beyond anything the John Wayne Gacys and Christopher Wilders of the world had caused.

She couldn't let the male suffer the way Carnax was willing to do to him. Her mind sprinted for ideas. How could she drift into other innocent's bodies without thought and yet she couldn't do it on sheer will? Could she only enter a host's body if she were asleep? The questions didn't have a simple answer.

To her surprise, her cellmate's face grew taut and anguish quickly dissolved into sheer determination. Who was he, a wannabe superhero or something? Subtly shaking her head, with her quick warning she dropped the gravity of their plight on him hard, mouthing '*No*'. When he refused to stop, she saw the desperation in his mirrored eyes.

Vepar's heavy footfalls echoed down the hallway. Still unsure what his purpose was, other than being a royal douche bag, she crouched lower. Backing up against the wall, her eyes darted between the doorway and the innocent. The instinct to fight grew stronger, and her hands balled into fists. The eerie creaking of the door widening upon Vepar's entrance left the cheesy horror movie sounds lingering in the air.

"Ah, Darkling, I see you found your gift." Flames

glinted off his pearly whites, leaving traces of reds and oranges to soften his twisted smile. "Don't worry, he won't feel a thing. But you will." Vepar's cold laugh stung like acid on wet skin. "You'll feel everything. Now close your eyes."

"No!" she snapped, low and deep as, she fought the exhaustion rapidly consuming her.

"Leave her alone!" The male's thick Irish accent was a stark contrast to the gritty rasp she had grown accustomed to from the voices of the other captures. Whipping her head around, she was just in time to see the chained male lunge forward, kicking Vepar to the ground. She wanted to cheer him on and throw out a round of 'Hells yeah!' to show her support, but her lids grew heavy, even as she demanded herself to stay alert. Watching through half hooded lids, she saw the male strike Vepar over and again. Then the crushing blow of Carnax's fist cracked him in the back of skull, knocking the male to the ground. With one final breath, darkness swept over her and the pull of the void overpowered her desire to stay awake.

CHAPTER
FORTY-ONE

"Ferrian!" Sweat dripped from Remi's temples as he called out her name. She had been within reach, close enough that his fingers could grasp her hand, but before he could touch her, Ferrian's small body was ripped away from him. Lunging for her, all he came up with was vacant space. Her eyes flashed with absolute fear as she flew backward in a display of flailing limbs. Darkness blanketed the light with a heaviness, leaving him crushed under the weight of his failure. He swore he'd protect her, even from herself. As the lingering shadow of her face streaking across his eyes began to fade, terror mixed with a rising rage burning through his veins.

Whoever was behind this was going to die. Releasing the frustration of losing her once again, his roar broke him from the mental prison as he faced his worst fears. Tearing his gun free, he threw open is his eyes, surveying the threat around him.

"See, I told you he'd come around sooner than later. Glad to see you're awake, cupcake. Wanna cuddle, and you can tell good old Roc all about your bad dreams?"

He ground his teeth together, deciding that telling anyone the hell he had played out in his head wasn't on his top disclosure agenda. Pushing himself off the buttery-soft leather couch, he scanned the room, wincing as he palpated the back of his skull. A sizable lump seemed to appear out of thin air, bringing a hiss with it. His eyes zeroed in on Roc, already assuming he was behind the reason why Remi now had a headache from hell to match the tension coiling in every damn muscle. "You're a real twatwaffle ... I'd say sometimes, but I'd be lying."

"Be loud be proud, that's my motto. Not my fault you got your panties in a twist."

Crossing the room, he fisted the cuff of Roc's shirt, getting all up in his brethren's grill. "Listen up, and get this through your thick skull. I have one job to do. Protect Ferrian. Finding her has become mission critical. So I'd say she is my top and only priority, got it, asshole? Stay the fuck out of my way."

"And you fail—"

He didn't give Roc a chance to finish the statement before letting him meet the business end of his right cross, and following it up with a left uppercut.

Cassiel jumped in to break up the melee as he barked at Charo to follow suit. "Get Roc out of here, before Remi tears his head off!" Throwing a choke hold on Remi, Cassiel peeled him off swinging, trying to show Roc how much he truly appreciated the guy's opinion.

"Get off me!" He tried pry Cassiel's arms away.

"Not until you calm down."

"This doesn't concern you, Cass." Grunting as he spoke, he reached behind him and flipped Cassiel over his head, breaking free. "Keep captain asswipe far away from me!" Casting one final glare at Roc, still struggling in

Charo's hold, they locked heated stares, and the unspoken 'screw you' pulsed in the space between them. He turned to leave, when Z stopped him in his tracks. Thick arms crossed over his broad chest and death pooled in his eyes.

"Get cleaned up. Then come find me. We need to talk." Ice coated each word, making Remi's heart drop down to his stomach. Z knew something and whatever it was, it wasn't good. Otherwise, he would've spoken what he needed to say right then and there. He knew without the slightest doubt where Z had been and he, too, would need some space for a few minutes to collect his thoughts. Nodding to him, Remi agreed before stepping around him. Anger still licked fire through his veins as he stomped out of the library, making his irritation well heard.

Roc's comment rolled around his mind, ratcheting him up once again, and as true as it might be, the sting of it speared him with suffocating guilt. However, it wasn't Roc he was pissed at. Sure, Roc called him out and it was seriously an assholish thing to do short of kicking him in the nuts. Nonetheless, the anger belonged to the one who actually deserved the ass-kicking.

Stopping when he reached his suite, he wondered how many times he had thought about bringing Ferrian Realmside only to lay her down on his bed. To make love to her, and curl her close to him as she slept. Too many times. And now he was on the verge of losing her to infinite darkness and losing himself to insanity if he couldn't locate her soon. How long had he been out cold for? *Friggin' Roc*. Maybe he couldn't be pissed off for the truth his brethren had spoken, but the lump on the back of his skull definitely deserved a return gesture. Pushing open the door, the icy tingle of despair skitter over his skin. What could he do? He had a vague idea of where she was, and the only real source he had to rely on was his strange connection to her like an internal GPS system.

Glancing around his suite, as beautiful and spacious as it was—accented with timeless relics he had collected over the course of time, mixed elegantly with modern features like his big screen TV—he decided none of it mattered. It was all useless shit taking up space. Emptiness covered every square inch of the room as he stepped in farther. What was the point of all of this, of his existence if it wasn't to protect Ferrian? The crushing weight of failure assaulted him harder than before as he slumped down to his knees. Burying the heels of his palms in his eye sockets, he realized it wasn't the emptiness of the room that was bothering him so much. It was the tidal wave of hollowness echoing inside of him, missing her presence. He knew he loved her, with each beat of his immortal heart, but it hadn't hit him with the voracity in which he truly did until all he had left was the desolation overwhelming his senses.

Find her, dammit. Find her and never let her go again! Remi had no idea how he was going to locate Ferrian. The undercurrent of electricity, which sang over his skin and down his spine whenever Ferrian was near, was his only indication he had been close to finding her before, when he was in the vacant building. However, pinpointing her exact location was proving difficult.

A soft knocking caught his attention, jerking him out of his mental gymnastics. "Remiel, I need to speak with you." Z's soft tone set him on edge as he willed the door open. Pulling himself up, a small recognition of the night had descended upon him, spiking up his need to save Ferrian. How long had he been wallowing in self-disdain? How many more hours would he have to wait before he could begin his search again? He knew this conversation had to happen with Z, but it didn't make the waiting any easier to stomach.

"Come in." His throat was dry, like the mid-summer desert, when he tried to find his voice, hoping it didn't sound as rough as it did to him. Barely lifting his eyes to meet Z's, the hollow feeling swelled up inside his chest and began to fill with dread the longer Z stood before him, not speaking, not moving. Finally meeting his icy gaze, all he found was the haunting air of death dancing around the edges. *Oh shit, this isn't good.* Panic bubbled up from his gut, like scorching lava burning up from the pit of his stomach to the back of his throat. "What is it? Speak, man, for God's sake!"

Z's time travelling to the Underworld had taken its toll on the male as he leaned against the wall, dropping his head to his chest. The sound of four sets of footsteps approaching the door to his suite made the uneasy feeling grow, which came with bad news, and covered him with foreboding, thick as concrete. With the brethren standing by on the ready, he knew whatever Z was going to tell him was bound to send him over the edge. Gulping past the boulder that had lodged itself in his throat, he knew he wasn't going to last up here long, sitting idly and allowing nature to take its course.

"I got word about your Darkling."

"And? Tell me she's alive? Tell me I'm free to track her down and bring her back up here, where she'll be safe?"

"Remi, I need you to remain calm until—"

Remaining calm was a request he couldn't do. Any sentence starting off with '*you need to remain calm*' was always followed up with a '*yep, this is messed up kind of situation*' type of statement. Shit. Raking his slick palm through his hair once again, he commanded his feet to stay locked in place. Whatever Z needed to say, he had to listen. "How can I remain calm, when my charge is out there somewhere, and I haven't the slightest idea where she is?"

"I understand your concerns, honestly I do, but I need you to focus here. You can't go flying off the handle and think you'll be successful at finding her. I need you to listen and think rationally for a moment." Ezekiel's voice softened a hair and Remi sensed for the first time his brethren finally understood what was going through his head.

Sucking in a deep breath, he made his way to the wingback chair in front of his unlit fireplace. "So she's alive, right? Is this what you came here to tell me? Or has she transcended while I was out cold?" Silence befell the room. He considered Z's silence as bad news. "Speak, man! Jesus, say what you came here to tell me!"

Slowly Z moved to the chair adjacent from Remi's, and his eyes purchased a piece of the ground as he sank down into the coffee-colored leather. Resting his elbows on his knees, Z brought his eyes to meet his. "Yes, she's still alive, but for how much longer I'm not sure," he offered. "The word is they've sent in their Prime Master of Torture, Carnax, and that little shit, Vepar, to work her over."

"What? And you're getting around to telling me this now! What the hell, man? Why would you wait so long to tell me? I need to get to her!" His voice broke into hysterics. The door to his suite opened as hasty footsteps clamored in. "What do you guys want? I suppose you are all aware of this news?"

Ezekiel rose to meet his accusations head on. "They know little. So don't get pissed off at them. I wanted to talk to you first. I asked them to wait outside, in case you decided to do something stupid, like not listen to me."

"Well, is there more then?"

"You're not going in alone. Understand?" Z's eyes pegged the group, nodding to them. "Guys, get in here, we have much to discuss and little time to work with." Charo, Cassiel, Roc, and Kakabel proceeded in until the group made a half circle around Remi and Z.

He shot Roc a heated glare, warning the angel not to piss him off. "So what did you find out?" Each muscle in his body coiled tightly as he swiveled his head back around to Z's flat expression.

Z's moments of silence were starting to wear on him as he waited for his brethren to speak again. A soft buzzing caught his attention, and he followed the sound to Kakabel. "What the hell does Am want now?"

"Not sure, hang on." Pulling the small device free from her jeans pocket, her hand subtly trembled as she glimpsed at the glowing screen. "I've got to go, boys."

"Wait, what's up? What does Am want?" Ezekiel slipped her an incredulous glare.

"It's not Am." Her voice shook slightly as she stepped away.

The remaining group eyed one another; each curious to know who it was sending their sister a message. A slick coating of apprehension had covered him when the big boss had summoned him, and given him his current assignment. He never did understand why his summoning for Ferrian had affected him so, but now he wondered if Kakabel was getting called in for the same reason. Had Ferrian found the next Darkling? *Impossible.*

"Okay, back to order, guys. Word is Remi's Darkling is being held in an underground prison cell. Long story short, Xaphan hired Vepar to play with the Darkling's mind while the Underworld's Prime Torturer, Carnax, tortures innocents, knowing the Darkling will be mentally tethered."

His knuckles cracked, imagining the hell Ferrian was suffering. Xaphan had been at the helm the last time she had been set to be tortured as a teenager. Years had passed since he found her chained up like some kind of rabid beast, bloodied and beaten. Another wave of guilt washed over him as the gravity of his reoccurring failures to keep her safe surfaced again.

"So did you find out exactly where she's being held?" Cassiel approached Remi, squeezing his shoulder for comfort.

"Yeah, we were close. She's underground though." Hearing those words fall from Z's mouth, knowing he was right, she had been so close all along, made his blood boil that much more.

"Well let's start there. What are we waiting for?"

"Because you are waiting for me." Whipping his head around, he watched as Amitiel squared her shoulders in his direction. Her eyes burned into his. "I want you guys to infiltrate and grab the Darkling. Remi, you are to bring her up here."

"Wait, what? I thought it was forbidden? Didn't you tell me there was no way I would be allowed to bring her topside?" He cursed under his breath as he stared her down incredulously.

"I know what I told you. This isn't coming from me. The Council called for this. Seems team underscum has broken a few key rules, and went above and beyond what they were allowed to do. Plus we need to wait for Bels to come back. This is going to be a team effort. And don't think for one second this mission will be easy. There's more at stake here than one little fragile Darkling."

His chest rumbled with disdain as he let Am's term fragile sink in. "Watch yourself, Amitiel. She's not as fragile as you believe she is."

"She's still human, which means she's still breakable in a human kind of way."

"Shut your damn mouth, Am, or I'll do it for you."

Sliding in front of Remi, Z locked eyes with him. "Listen, now is not the time for bullshit. She needs you, and we need you to focus. Drop this shit and get your head in the game. Got it?" Turning toward the group, Z held their attention as he continued. "Am's right, this isn't going to be some cake walk. Xaphan has Hellistic demons surrounding the area now. Our presence didn't go unnoticed apparently."

"What did I miss?" He couldn't break away from Z's information, even as Kakabel's sing-song voice split the air.

"We're about to be up to our asses in demons to find his Darkling. Well, I don't know about the rest of you guys, but it sounds like my kind of party!"

"Seriously, Nisroc, could you at least display some sort of maturity? I swear you are nothing more than an overgrown child sometimes," Bels shot back.

"Enough!" Z's voice shattered the banter. "Go gear up. We leave in ten minutes."

His skin itched, tightening all over. He'd make Carnax's work look like child's play when he was through with him. He didn't know what he desired more, killing the sick prick who was torturing the woman he loved, or bringing Ferrian Realmside. Tough call, but first things first, it was killing time, and nothing was going to stop him from finding her.

His internal war-dance shot off when the group roared as loudly as thunder claps. He stared back at Z, knowing more needed to be said, but the time wasn't now. Nodding to his brethren, he left the circle to load up. When he felt Z on his heels, he waited for the male to enter his oversized armory closet. Sealing the door shut, and cutting off the sounds littering his suite, he didn't bother to turn around as he proceeded to pull on his weapons vest. "So what aren't you telling me, Z?"

He let out a low curse, and it was then, he knew what Z had been keeping from him, and it wasn't going to be pretty. "I'm not going to beat around the bush. Even if we find her, there's a chance she could be stuck in the dream world. Xaphan has Vepar keeping her locked in her subconscious from my understanding. Letting her wake up to see the destroyed remains of the bodies she had been in. They figured out her secret."

Spinning around, Remi wasn't sure what he was hearing. "Wait, what secret?"

"She's more than just the next Dark Angel, Remiel. She was chosen by God to serve as a protector of sorts. When she sleeps, she's called to innocents in need. Taking over their bodies, and basically kicking out their souls.

Your Darkling takes the brunt of the physical pain and emotional anguish, so the innocents aren't traumatized and can safely move on to Heaven."

"This is some sick and twisted shit I'm hearing! And how in the hell did you find this out? How come I wasn't made aware of this? JesusHchrist! This explains so much."

"I know this is a lot to take in, but believe me when I tell you, no other mortal could have handled this like she has."

A swell of pride erupted in his heart as the raging disgust for their Creator echoed in his mind. Why would anyone bestow such a gift on a mortal being, let alone his Darkling? But she wasn't his, was she? No, she had run away from him at the hotel. Fear stretched across her face as her feet pounded against the floor in a full out sprint to get away from him.

"Remi, get out of your head and focus. Don't dwell on the things you can't change. You can't undo what's been done to her. But if she survives this, should she turn into a Dark Angel ... well, I think we'll all be astonished by what she'll be capable of. I want you and Bels to grab Ferrian and get your asses back up here. The guys and I will deal with the rest. You need to protect her."

"I understand." With a quick nod, he slammed two DMT covered knives into place and turned to walk out of his closet armory. "And Z ... thanks, man. I know how shitty it is for you to go down there. I appreciate this." Clapping Ezekiel on the shoulder, the unspoken love between brothers became crystal clear.

"You'd do the same for me."

"Damn straight I would."

CHAPTER
FORTY-TWO

T he unmistakable feeling of her soul getting ripped out of one innocent's body and thrown into the next, had her stomach on the verge of purging, if it had anything in it to vomit. With each new host, she suffered a fresh barrage of assaults. Forcing her host to wake up, she braved a glance over to her listless body lying in a heap on the blood-dampened stone floor. The male's body she occupied couldn't have been any older than eighteen. Sagging against the wall, she relished the small reprieve from the constant stream of punches, kicks, and slices the body had already endured, but she feared it wouldn't last much longer. The cool stone against her back soaked up the blood, and momentarily relieved the aches. She knew there was no chance of this body surviving. The other bodies she had occupied had faded quickly in front of their owners' ghostly eyes. The male who once lived inside this current form watched horrified, pacing the floor. It was only a matter of time before he, too, would end up staring at his lifeless body brutalized in this hellhole, never to be laid to rest. She could hear his shrieks as he swung at Carnax. It was no use. A ghost couldn't harm the demon-like man.

No, there would be no reprieve as Carnax pulled a metal rod out of the roaring fire. "Oh shit!" This was something new from the realm of torture and it was going to test her will not to cry out. Movement out of the corner of her eye caught her attention, and she tilted her swollen jaw toward the other body lying in a heap across the room. Vepar and Carnax had gone a few rounds with the wanna-be superhero, until his fight had left him unconscious. She wasn't sure if he had died from the beating, and prayed for his sake, he had.

Peeling one eye open, he found her staring back at him and winced as he tried to smirk at her. Her heart fell watching him struggle to push himself off the floor. He had lost so much blood, and had so many broken bones, it was a wonder he wasn't screeching like a banshee.

Hatred continued to grow deep within her soul, and she partially considered killing her host body to save both of them from any more pain. How long had she been trapped in this state? How many more bodies would she be called to? Time seemed to disappear as perpetual night lasted in the dark cell.

With each new host, a fresh round of desire to kill erupted stronger than before. She could feel it taking root again and growing stronger each time. She had to wake up. She had to break free, and kill the males responsible for this. But how? How could she snap out of this? How could she be so alert—as though she were awake—yet see her body sound asleep? What the hell was she, what was happening to her? Nothing made sense. She had assumed her dreams were nothing more than horrible reminders of what life had to offer those undeserving, or possibly caught in a cycle of hellish imagination, even when it all appeared real. Distinguishing dreams from reality had become impossible.

"How is our guest doing?" Snapping her head up, Ferrian locked gazes with Xaphan. "Is she in this body?" His tone sounded as though he was already bored with any answers he'd receive. Xaphan's presence grated on her nerves as she thrashed against the chains tying her to the floor. Vepar followed behind him. His twisted smile as he eyed her gave her a renewed sense of revenge coursing through her veins. Carnax pulled his big body vertical, a glowing rod in hand as he stepped toward her.

"Yeah, she's in there. Not for long though."

A sickening smile split Xaphan's face. Straining against the chains, the warm feel of blood trickling down her hands as the metal bonds cut into her host's skin, electrified her need to destroy the three males. Fire licked up her body, yet at the same time it was twitching. "Wake her up, Vepar."

"I'm not done with the host."

Grabbing the rod out of Carnax's hand, Xaphan plunged the burning metal into the heart of the host. The body shook uncontrollably, until all signs of life had dissolved. "There, now the host is dead. You may take a break."

The burn of her soul tearing free of the dying body stung worse than a thousand scorpions. Settling back into her body, she wondered how much more she could handle. Didn't matter much in her mind. She wasn't planning on surviving this.

The cold skin of Xaphan's hand cradling her jaw when he pulled her upright, jolted her awake. The sleep in her eyes blurred her vision, yet she tried to focus on anything solid. "Look at me." His voice was low and demanding, his hand crushing her jaw as he tilted her head back farther. "I'm not done with you yet, Darkling. Not until you realize what you are."

Ferrian struggled to pull her chin away, refusing to settle her gaze on his. "And what am I, huh …aside from pissed off?" She wanted to rip her hands free from the metal bonds, and cold-cock the sonofabitch back to the Hell he came from. His acidic laugh rang in her ears as he tossed her back into the wall, bouncing her skull off the stones.

"What? Haven't you figured it out yet? I'm surprised your guardian hasn't given you any hints. Pity. I guess I get the pleasure of telling you after all. How delightful! You were created to destroy all things good on this forsaken planet."

Sucking in a rapid breath, she shook her head in disbelief. *Guardian, what guardian?* She didn't have any guardian. Shit, she didn't willingly spend any time with anyone, except for … "Remi." His name had slipped past her lips before she could call it to heel.

"Yes, him. *Your guardian.* And I see he has once again failed to keep you from me. You are meant to kill, Ferrian."

"The hell I am!"

"Tsk, tsk. You can't tell me you haven't been planning our demise since you woke up in this cell."

Clamping her mouth shut, she clenched her teeth to keep from spilling the truth. Yes, she wanted to tear each of their limbs apart and dance upon their shredded remains. It was a no-brainer, but the glint in his eyes read he knew so much more. Each time she saw an abused child, or an animal being kicked by some scumbag, she had imagined what killing the perpetrator would feel like. To watch the life in their eyes slowly die as she crushed them. Her hands ached even now thinking about gauging out Xaphan's eyes from their sockets.

"Release her."

"You can't be serious. I mean, look at her. She's got a feral look in her eyes." Vepar glanced over his shoulder to show Xaphan what he was asking him to release.

"Your point being? I said to release her."

Her heart thundered in her ears as she quickly planned her escape. Three huge guys, to one of her, and she'd be damned if she was going to leave her cellmate behind. Upon Carnax's mental command, her metal bonds fell to the floor, clanking an ear-piercing sound when they hit the damp floor. "Get up, Darkling."

Slowly pulling herself up, she caught her cellmate's eyes and silently begged him to stay quiet long enough for her to distract the group, so he could somehow free himself and get away. "Bring me him." Pointing to her cellmate, Xaphan's command went undisputed.

Shit! Think fast, dammit, think! Fury burned deep inside of her gut again, building with each passing second as she pictured it hurling a fiery globe of hatred toward the group of males.

"It's time you accepted what you are. Don't worry, my precious, I promise you'll love the way taking a life feels. I wouldn't be surprised if the sensation doesn't intoxicate you."

Swallowing back the fear, as hatred boiled over, she pushed the ball of fury out of her body, like an explosion of light blinding every corner of the dimly light cell. The force was so much stronger than before, throwing herself backwards and the three males across the room crashing to the floor. *Good night, Lucy!*

CHAPTER
FORTY-THREE

Night was closing in fast while Remi, Z, Roc, Cassiel, Charoum, Kakabel, and Amitiel stood on the roof top of a vacant mill building half a block down from the last place, he had sensed Ferrian. "So where is this little prick, Focalor? Thought he'd be here by now," Roc barked out as he crushed one fist into the other.

"He's on his way, and you would be wise to curb your tongue, juvie. He's been around much longer than you, so I suggest you show some respect."

"Yeah, ain't happening, Am. I'm not the one who went batshit crazy and tore apart every living thing in his path for kicks."

Knocking Roc's shoulder with a swift punch, Cassiel stepped up, ready to get to business. "Shut up, both of you. Roc, stop talking shit about things you don't understand. Am, what should we do about Carnax and Vepar? I'm sure once Xaphan knows we're in the vicinity, he'll jump ship to save his pasty ass."

"Bels, Cass, come with me. Z, you and the rest come in from the opposite end of the street. Charo, you stay with them, in case we need a heads up, you can call out to us."

With a sharp nod, Charo accepted his role as an angelic walkie-talkie. "Seems like Xaphan has his minions crawling around everywhere. Something tells me that he was planning on us showing up."

"So, you're saying he's trying to trap us?" Charo's silent words filled everyone's heads as he zeroed in on Remi.

"Yeah, I am. I'm thinking if we attack from both sides, we stand a better chance of one of us gaining entrance and tracking her down. If you guys can hold off the outside, we'll make a run for the holding cells. Everyone clear on this? We don't leave without her." There were no more words to be spoken, as a round of nods agreed to the plan. "Bels, Cassiel, are you guys ready?"

"Yes."

"Yes, I'm good to go. Am, what about Focalor? What's his deal?

"Don't worry about him. He's here as merely a Watcher for the Council." Glancing down at her watch, Am counted down the seconds. "And he should be arriving in five ... four ... three ... two ..."

Focalor's wings flapped soundlessly when he settled down on the rooftop. "Somebody call for witness?"

"Yeah, go perch yourself somewhere, parrot, and leave the real work to the big boys."

"Roc, didn't we have this discussion already?" Amitiel cast him a stern glare, warning him to behave.

"No. You decided no one was allowed to bust his balls, because it might damage his sensitivities."

"Enough!" Z's chilling voice cut across the rooftop as fiercely as a winter's wind. "We're not here for a pissing match. Now stuff your dicks back into your panties and let's get moving."

"You heard the man, move out! Focalor, keep an eye out for any demons and the like who might be following us."

"Yes, ma'am."

With a final nod, Remi, Kakabel, and Cassiel took their leave, bounding off the six story rooftop, landing silently on the wet pavement below. "I think she's being held in the basement of the building we were in before. I felt her close by."

"What do you mean, you felt her?" Bels stopped short, staring incredulously at him. "Well?"

"I don't know how to explain it. It's like, whenever she's near, I get these vibrations, like a sixth sense."

"Has this happened with previous charges, Remiel?" Cassiel's voice didn't waver as he gripped Remi's bicep, pulling him to a stop.

"No. Only with her."

"Interesting."

"What? Cassiel, what aren't you telling me?"

"It's nothing. Listen, let's talk about this later. I have a feeling we're not alone."

No sooner had the words fallen from Cassiel's lips than a group of Hellistic demons walked around the corner. "Ready, kids?" Bels crouched low, and carefully pulled free her twin Katana blades, as Cassiel slipped his Sigs free from their sheaths.

"Ready as I'll ever be." Remi charged for the group, firing bullets coated in DMT into the skulls of two demons, and kicking a crushing hit to the sternum of a third. Tearing through the group of seven demons, his adrenaline rose higher with each kill. Scanning around to find Bels and Cassiel, he saw the same desire to destroy evil in their eyes. It had been ages since they last fought together. He stopped for a moment to watch in amazement as Kakabel swung around in an artful dance with her swords, slicing down two Hellistics, and Cassiel plugged perfectly squared shots between the eyes into the remaining two demons skulls.

Nodding to them, a familiar tingling traveled down his spine. "We're getting closer," he whispered, rounding the next corner. Night had enveloped them, and sparse street lamps spread halos of light down the long alleyway. "Incoming."

Preparing his pistols for another round, he slowly edged around the corner tightly. Keeping a close eye on the sentinels making the rounds around the house, he was last in. "We were right, there are minions everywhere. Cass, I want you to flank my left, Bels, the right. We get in and find a way down into the cells."

"Remi, how can you be so sure the entrance we need to find is in the same house?"

"I need you guys to trust me. There are two minions crossing back and forth every two minutes in front of the house. I say we cut them down quickly and quietly. Hide the bodies in the dumpster and get in the house ASAP. Got it?"

"Let me handle this one. You guys watch my back and get ready to haul ass."

Remi didn't argue as he stepped back. The squealing of leather bindings in Bels' hands meant she was ready for business, as she tucked her twins behind her back and step out into the street.

"Be ready, Cass."

"I'm good, but keep an eye on her." Seconds dragged on like hours as they watched Bels saunter up to the first minion. Down the street, he saw the second coming closer with deliberate steps. Flicking her hair in her classic girly behavior he had come to accept, he held his breath as the two minions stopped dead in their tracks to eye her.

His muscles were tight, like hardened steel coiled and ready to strike. With a gracious twirl, Kakabel had sliced the heads off both minions and slipped her Katanas back into their sheaths before the heads had hit the damp pavement.

"Damn, she is good!" Cassiel gave in to a small laugh as Bels turned toward him. "Remind me again why we think she's the weaker sex?"

Slipping from the edge of the building, they collected the bodies as Bels picked up the heads. "Over there is a dumpster. Bels, flip the lid."

Tossing the corpse into the rancid smelling dumpster, another stinging sear of electricity raced down Remi's spine. "I've gotta get in there. Something's wrong, I can feel it!" Kicking off the wet asphalt, he bounded into the air, landing with a heavy thud on the steps. He didn't bother to wait for Cassiel and Bels to follow. Busting the door open, and causing the hinges to protest with a metallic hiss, he scanned through the darkness. Each step farther into the house, the pull to Ferrian became stronger. His spine painfully sang a tune he knew too well. Gripping his guns, he leveled them in each direction, as he waited for another minion to jump out and try to get the drop on him.

The tender groans of the wooden floors bending beneath his shit-kickers could've set off the alarms, warning any demon within a block radius of his presence. Cursing quietly, he edged down the dark hallway, following the scent of sulfur. The sound of trailing footfalls behind him ratcheted up his adrenaline more as he spun around, guns fixed on whoever was coming up behind him.

"Remi," Cassiel's voice whispered out.

Sagging back a half step, he called out to his brethren, "Down here." His eyes stayed locked on to the bodies coming down the hallway until he saw the whites of their eyes glowing. Taking in a deep swallow of breath, he slowly lowered his guns, nodding to them. "She's here, I can sense her."

"Have you found the entrance? Focalor said she was being held down in the cells. So how do we find the door down?" Bels whispered into the still air. "Shit, the stench is unbearable!"

Turning back around, he inhaled another deep breath, letting the acidic scent guide him. "I guess we follow our noses." The revolting odor of sulfur fumed thicker the farther he made his way down the long hallway. Each step brought with it another tick of desperation to find her. He had to stop, as searing pain shot straight up to his head like a thousand spikes trying to stab through from the inside out. His skin sang to life with her energy. The powerful current ran like lightning through his veins. He stumbled to the side and he gripped the wall for support. The wall bowed then popped as the floorboards creaked beneath his feet. "I think I found it." Carefully peeling back the false-wall, more acrid sulfur assaulted his nostrils as he scanned down the stairs for any signs of life.

The splintering of his focus and fear didn't leave room for second guessing as he rushed down the stone stairwell. He made it halfway before the first of the

Hellistics ascended the steps.

"What the hell?" one called out, baring his teeth and pulling free a fixed blade.

Hell bent on finding Ferrian, he launched after the male, crushing it under his shit-kickers, as the demon writhed and clawed his way to freedom. Snagging free his DMT tipped dagger, Remi stared deeply into his victim's eyes. The growing need to destroy Hellistic demons and minions alike consumed him as he sank his knife into the frontal lobe of the screaming pile of rotting flesh.

"Remi!" Cass yelled, as he hurled down the stairs, and landed in a crouch. Pulling himself upright, he unloaded his mag of bullets into the oncoming crowd of demons climbing out of the darkness.

Not wasting another second, throwing himself forward with Bels flanking him, the three angels descended upon the horde of evil offspring, spilling guts and plugging holes into the mass of bodies. In a flash of bone crushing punches and kicks, when the last of the demons fell, his insides screamed louder to find her. He didn't waste another moment as the sting of electricity shot straight up to his brain. He stormed down the darkened hallway; the sound of his heart pounding in his ears drowned out Cassiel's voice. "I need to find her, have to find her, where the hell is she?" he chanted, kicking in door after dingy wooden door. The crushing blow from his boots splintering the aging oak wood cracked like a whip.

"Any sign of her?" Kakabel called out.

"No! Dammit! Where is she?" His spine tingled stronger the farther he descended down the hallway, kicking another door in half. Punching through the next door, his hands trembled with rage.

"Remi, focus dammit! Concentrate on what you're feeling. Sense her."

Panic rose in his throat and he tried to listen to Cassiel's words. He was right. Wasting time kicking in random doors like some kind of frenzied Neanderthal wasn't going to help him get to her any faster. Slowing his pace, he let his rapid breathing calm, and closed his eyes to concentrate on her delicate face. Counting to ten, Remi allowed the electrical current to indicate Ferrian was near, abrading his skin from toes to scalp. With every breath, the vibrations grew stronger. With each step, the magnetic pull tugging him from within guided him. "Ferrian." Her name whispered off his lips as he let the strange current of electricity feather over his flesh. "Down here." His feet scrambled into gear as he stormed down the dim hallway. "She's close."

"Are you sure?" Kakabel fell in line behind him, wiping the black bloody gore off her sleeves. "You'd think these asshats would be less messy when you rip out their intestines."

He didn't want to admit it, but Bels had a way with words. She always made him want to burst out laughing. "Yeah, Bels, I am. Cass, are we cool back there?"

"Yeah, man. Clear so far. I think we got all of them."

Nearing another door, the ripping pain of fire tore through his brain, dropping him to his knees. His hands clutched his head as agony spread through his veins. Cassiel rushed to his side, trying to pry his hands from his skull. "Remi! Remi, what's wrong?"

"I ... don't ... know!" his pained cry stabbed him deep as he tried to focus on anything. "Sh-she's hu—rt!"

"Remi, focus on me." Pulling his face to meet his

stare, Cassiel saw the agonizing sensation covering him like a blanket of steel spikes. "Breathe, dammit! Focus. You need to pull it together, for her. She's going to die if you don't!"

Sucking in a ragged breath, he lifted his eyes, and swallowed back the anxiety rising in his throat. Long moments passed until he could steady himself to climb to his feet. "I won't let her die," he swore, and by every ounce of love he had for her, he made the one promise he had no way of knowing if he could hold to it. Didn't matter; if she died, he'd slice off his wings and fall just so he could join her in the afterlife.

He didn't think, he allowed the magnetic pull to tug him down to the last room. Cassiel and Kakabel kept to his flanks. He listened momentarily for any sign of movement. It was quiet, too quiet, except for the rattling of chains. *Shit!* Pushing the door inward, he found that the limb of a male's leg was unmoving on the other side of the door. "There's someone up against the door." He pushed harder, wondering if the male lying motionless on the floor was already dead.

Scanning the dimly lit room, he sucked in a shallow breath. Dread sucker punched him sharply in the balls. "Holy shit!" Diving for Ferrian's listless body, he pulled her into his arms, crushing her frail body to his chest. Kissing the top of her bloodied head, he murmured his pleas. "Ferrian, please, m'aingeal, wake for me." He could feel her sporadic heart beating against his chest as he climbed to his feet. His desire to destroy the unconscious males, bled from him as the dire need to get her to safety overwhelmed him.

"Is she alive?" Cassiel cupped his shoulder.

"Yeah, I hope she stays this way though. Her heart sounds like it's about to give up. I've got to get her topside immediately."

"Go, man, get out of here. Bels and I got this covered." Cass let out a low whistle. "What I want to know is, what the hell happened in here?"

Glancing around the room, he saw that the bodies of Xaphan, Vepar, and Carnax were tangled in a solid heap of limbs and blood. He couldn't imagine what had caused this, but thanked God for the small reprieve. "Are they deceased?"

Cassiel stepped closer, checking for any signs of life. "No, I think they were knocked out. Seems like they're breathing. Better get her out of here, before sleeping dickheads wake up. Bels, get in here."

Remi watched as she silently slipped around the door, tossing her hair over her shoulder. "Is she okay?"

"Not sure, taking her topside right now. See you guys in a few." Bels clutched his forearm and smiled sweetly, nodding her head.

"Okay, and watch your ass. I heard Z and the crew coming down."

"Good, maybe they can take care of these assholes. Bring Xaphan to the cillés. I want to deal with him myself." As he strode for the door, something caught the corner of his eye. Movement. "What is that?" He nodded but didn't stop, as he carried Ferrian's limp body back down the hallway. He trusted his brethren to clean up the mess. Leaving her lying on the floor so he could slam his dagger through the chest bone of each one of males, although appealing, wasn't a viable option. She needed healing, stat, and nothing was going to stop him from giving her exactly what she needed to survive.

"Holy shit!" He heard Bels voice ring higher than ever before. His heart stopped for a split second as he considered turning around.

"You found her, how's she doing?" Z called out.

"What? Uh, not good. Check on Bels, something's up. Not sure what's doing." With a quick nod, Remi ascended the stones stairs two at a time, until he reached the creaking wooden floors. His eyes darted between her bruised face and the darkness of the hallway as he stormed down the length, not willing to slow down until the cold air slapped his skin.

"Help … me," Ferrian softly rasped from swollen lips.

His heart beat wildly as he pulled her closer to his face, hoping she would utter another word.

"Ferrian, can you hear me? It's Remi, I've got you. I'm taking you somewhere safe." He waited for her to recognize him, to start arguing with him, screaming she didn't need to be saved, anything. Nothing. Fear twisted in his gut once again as he pictured the worst things her mind could be showing her. "I've got you, m'aingeal. I've got you," he murmured into her hair, kissing her gently as he reached the front stoop. Unfurling his wings, cascading with white and silver tipped feathers, he didn't hesitate a second longer as he bound into the night sky.

"Holy shit!" Sucking in a ragged breath, Kakabel locked eyes on the thin frame and sunken eyes of a male chained across the room. A soft buzzing down her spine sang to life and intensified the closer she got to him.

"You must protect him." The words filtered through her head as though they were whispered in her ear. Taking in his fragile, beaten body, her heart sank as she knelt down beside him. "I don't know who you are, but something tells me finding out is going to be critical." Smoothing away his sweat-ridden hair, Bels hoped their arrival hadn't been too late, as she sensed his thready heartbeat and labored breathing. The unconscious male lay awkwardly against the stone wall, and fresh blood stained his forehead and cheek, and she silently wondered why this male was so important the boss wanted her to keep an eye on him.

"Bels, what is it? What did you find?" Cassiel's voice called out in a rush, echoing off the stone walls. The rustling of bodies stirring across the room set her internal warning systems off on a level five urgency to get this chained male out stat.

"It's an innocent." She spoke in a low voice, and turned at the sound of Carnax rising, shaking off Vepar's leg. "Cassiel! He's waking up!" she shouted, lunging for the innocent, and landing next to him, covering him with her body. Beneath her palms, his heartbeat was racing as she checked his pulse.

Charo was the first to slide around the open door, followed by Z, Roc, and Amitiel.

"Hey, guys, looks like it playtime," Roc jovially barked out as he kicked one of the males lying in a heap on the cold dirty floor. "And seems we have a few chumps to play with. Whattyda say we wake these fuckers up?"

Turning back to the male, Kakabel ripped the chains from the wall. Scooping up his inert body into her arms, she ran for the door.

"Who is he?" Am called after her.

"Not sure, but I'm not letting him get caught in the crossfire." Bels stormed up the stairs, following Remi's lead, not slowing until she hit the night air. "Who are you?" she whispered.

CHAPTER FORTY-FOUR

"Please, wake for me." His soft pleas caressed her ears as his lips pressed a soft kiss to her forehead. He longed for the moment Ferrian would wake up, and start fighting with him for bringing her here. And knew there would be repercussions from the Council of the Seven, even if they supposedly allowed it. Nothing with the Council was ever cut and dry. Still, he didn't care. Careful not to jostle her in his arms, he swallowed hard and prayed for her to wake soon. Her skin had grown more pallor by the minute, and dark circles appeared deeper as the glow from the overhanging crystal chandelier splashed golden light down upon them.

The servants scurried around, trying to offer help to Remi when he kicked the door open, scuffing the ivory coating without concern. "Sire, is there anything I can do to help? Would you like me to fetch Annika to help madam with the bathing?"

Cutting a sharp glare to his head servant, Andros, he shook his head without stopping. "I don't want anyone coming to the suite. Do you understand me? No one. I'll take care of her myself." His command cut like a knife, leaving the unspoken threat lingering between them as he climbed the stairs two at a time. She hadn't said a word since they had left the cells, let alone moved a single muscle with the exception of her eyes fluttering wildly behind her soft lids. Without wasting a moment, he entered the room, willed the tub to fill, and warily stripped her down to bare skin before lowering her smoothly in a tub of warm honey-milk. His eyes darted over all of the cuts and bruises stretching across her skin. Dipping the soft terrycloth into the honey-milk to wash away the blood and dirt, he realized she was covered from scalp to toes. Gnashing his teeth, he watched the liquid turn to the color of a red desert with each gentle wipe.

With slow and deliberate passes, he swore he had seen those wounds before. She had suffered enough, and he'd be damned if he caused her anymore pain as he gently sponged away the fresh marks left by Carnax. He silently prayed the asshole was still breathing, because he was planning a special kind of death for the demon. Spinning images of torture around in his mind, his ideas revolved around unrelenting pain, and a hell of a lot of it. Each new picture stirred the fire simmering in his gut.

He stared at the soft planes of her face, and winced as splotches of swelling and bruises replaced her resplendent blush. "Concentrate, dammit!" Focusing his healing ability, he hoped the memories of what she had faced—trapped in the cell—would disappear as easily as the marks left upon her skin. Relief soon came, as her dusky pink color returned to her lips, which were knitting back together. Long moments brought with it the optimism she'd wake, only to be dashed when she didn't.

Slipping his arms underneath her body and lifting her

out, Ferrian's healing skin softly glowed to life as he cradled her closely. He could feel the gentle beating of her
heart against his, and her warm breath evened out the
longer he sat on the marble floor with her cradled in his
arms. Something about the way he held her was comforting and incredibly intimate. The small thought she would
probably want to kick his ass for holding her like this, tickled him as he reached for a towel to drape over her skin.
There was no way of knowing how long she had been
knocked out, or how much longer he would have to wait
until she woke. Never had time been such an enemy and
right now, Remi cursed each passing second.

Hours had passed by since he'd washed away any
signs of the hell she had been trapped in. Why wasn't she
waking up? Why couldn't he climb into her dreams and
pull her out? Irritation rode him, reminding him of how
helpless he was. He had attempted to enter her dreams, to
coax her to wake. Each time he came upon a barrier of
darkness, like a fortress made to keep her locked in. She
was nowhere to be found inside of her head. Gulping past
the fear he might have lost her to the void, he reminded
himself of Cassiel's words. *"She needs time to find her
way back. Like Alice in Wonderland, she's lost to her
mind's idea of reality."*

Knowing Ferrian, it was going to be a long road of
treacherous mazes to find her way out. He couldn't sit still
for long, switching from sitting in the golden tapestry
wingback chair next to the bed, to pacing laps around the
immense suit. The whole time he kept an unwavering eye
on her slumbering body. Each small inflection she made
with her facial expressions, to the small pained cries echoing through the suite, stabbed him with another blade of

guilt for not protecting her better.

Why hadn't he found her sooner? Oh, right … because Roc knocked his ass out. *Asshole!* Crushing his fists into his eyes, his anger grew more intense as he wished he could use the sonofabitch as his personal punching bag and relieve some serious stress. But what good would it do? He couldn't undo what had been done. He couldn't change the course of history. Or what's to come. The what-ifs were tearing him apart as he launched across the room, throwing open the glass French doors that overlooked a serene lake with mountains dashing across the horizon.

"Remi." The soft rasp nearly stopped his heart, and he spun around quickly. His eyes nearly popped out of his head, as he watched Ferrian prop her slender frame up onto her elbows. The stark contrast of her raven hair and delicately radiant pink flesh against his silver sheets made his breath catch as he drank her in.

Rushing to her side, his hands trembled, wanting to pull her close and wrap her in his embrace until the next dawn. "Ferrian, oh my god, are you okay?" His voice shook, as he slid down beside her. "I've been so worried. I mean, you've been out for—" He didn't want to think of how long. Swallowing back against the lump in his throat, a fresh wave of sweat broke out across his skin.

She didn't speak as she stared back at him with those gorgeous hunter green eyes. Entranced by her, he hadn't noticed when she reached up to touch him, until the warmth of her skin caressed his cheek. Inhaling her sweet jasmine scent, his heart pounded against his ribcage, beating solely for her. His eyes didn't miss the way the satiny sheet fell away as she closed the distance between them, exposing the luscious curves of her body.

"I knew you'd find me," she whispered against his ear, sending erotic shivers dancing down his spine as she wrapped her arms securely around his neck. "I knew you'd come for me."

His chest seized up as the sincerity of her words hit him like a hammer. She had been banking on him coming for her. Even though she had lost it back in the hotel, it was he Ferrian counted on to find her, and save her. His arms embraced her tightly, and he sank into the warmth of her body.

"I'm so sorry I didn't find you sooner. I wish I had some way to make up for it." For the first time, it was he who was fragile, and on the verge of breaking wide open. But she held him tighter, stroking his hair, comforting him. The first tear fell, trickling down her skin, followed by another. He clutched her tighter, as though she was his life support. "I'm so sorry I failed you."

"You didn't fail me. You came for me." He wanted to see her face while she said those words, but he buried his wet eyes into the sinuous curve of her neck. Inhaling another lungful of her sweet beautiful scent, his lips grazed the soft patch of skin of the last place he kissed making love to her.

Her hands caressed him, traipsing up and down his back in soothing waves. She didn't try to pull away as he nuzzled into her. Long silent moments passed. Only the sound of their breathing and heartbeats dotted the silence.

"Remi." Her breath whispered against his heated skin, and he couldn't help but detect a hint of something different in the way she said his name. The sultry tone of her voice as her lips grazed his earlobe shot liquid fire straight to his groin. She pulled him closer, guiding him down as she lay back against the puffy pillows.

Oh. My. God. Her core was so hot, so wet, and so enticing. His breath caught as he pulled back to gaze into her eyes. "Ferrian."

Lost to the moment, her heart skipped a beat, feeling the first of Remi's tears trickle down her back. She should've been pissed off as hell. She was in a strange room, naked beneath the sheet with the last man who had seen her in all of her buck-ass nekkid glory. But none of it mattered anymore. She was where she wanted to be. Wrapped up in his arms. When her mind would normally flip on the panic button and send her freaking out to find clothing to hide behind, she let the dread of being seen naked slip away, and allowed a moment of feeling beautiful to the one person who mattered soak in.

When she had woken, she watched him from behind half-lidded eyes. The expression of fear and worry stretched haggardly across his face. She held her breath when he stormed to the doors, and threw them open without a single damn care if the glass shattered around him or not. He wasn't the same man who rescued her like a sexy knight in shining shit-kickers. No, here sat a man, wrapped up in her arms, letting down his guard and exposing his raw vulnerability to her. Her heart swelled a little more as the next tear trickled down his cheek, onto her shoulder. He didn't see her scars, or the ugliness hidden beneath the surface. She knew this now. He came for her, not knowing where she was being held, and pulled her from the depths of Hell like a damn angelic mercenary.

How could she have been so wrong about him? She had sensed his nearness even when she thought she was alone. So many times while lying awake in bed, his richly dark aroma lingered around her, spraying wishes and dreams with a vitality she thought were nothing more than ridiculous wanting. Yearning for the kiss, she thought had been only a dream. Yet here she was, cradling him as he opened up the fresh wounds of his soul and spilled it freely for her.

The heat radiating off his body warmed her from the inside out, comforting her in ways she didn't fully under-stand. Listening to the pain in his words as he apologized shot a wave of guilt through her veins, for running away from him in the first place at the hotel. Nothing was going to make the moment right, but she'd be damned if she made the same mistake twice.

Her body hungered to feel his weight on hers. And for the first time, she didn't think about what she looked like. She couldn't feel the nagging pull of the monster who tormented her daily; ripping her apart and driving her self-hatred to new levels.

Thinking back to each encounter she had had with him, she couldn't remember a single time when he saw her as a monster. Catching her breath, she realized Remi only viewed her in reverence and beauty. As the first inkling of self-doubt crept in, she embraced the feel of his body pressing against hers. And reveled in the feel of him want-ing to be there with her. Remi didn't shy away from the unwanted decorations marring her skin, as he smoothed his hands down the lengths of her arms and back.

Tamping down the rising fear, she whispered his name, as the tug of desire pulled her under its spell. Her fingers sank into the thick flesh of his shoulders, guiding him down with her. The fear twisting in her gut disappeared quickly when her eyes flipped up to meet his, smoldering with the same building heat. Breathing in his dark, spicy scent, the burn of wanting him more coursed through her body, pooling liquid heat in her sex. Splitting her thighs wider to cradle him, her core ached in feverish ways, welling up with unquenched fire. Nothing about this was wrong as the pulsing need between her thighs throbbed uncontrollably when he slid the ridge of his erection against her sensitive moist slit. Even through the thin fabric of the satin sheet, she could feel the desire building with his sex, growing more rigid with each breath he took.

She wanted to push him off her, beg him to strip down and stand there, so she could admire the statuesque perfection of his hard body. But there would be no separating them, from touching the warm flesh of each other's bodies. Relishing the feel of his weight, she coyly wrapped one leg around his, as he slid his hand along the length of her from toe to hip. Hooking her other leg around his back, she silently refused to release him.

Slowly he rocked against her, ramping up her need to feel him deep inside of her. With each pass, the head of his rigid length tapped against her sensitive bundle of nerves, sending another electrifying pulse shooting through her body. "Remi," the sultry, raspy voice whispered against his mouth, followed by the tip of her tongue tasting the seam of his lips.

His hand raked through her hair until he cupped the back of her skull, taking their kiss deeper, gentler. His eyes stayed locked on hers. The longer his tongue explored her mouth, the more intense her need to feel him deep within her body and soul grew.

He caressed his way down her arm, sliding over to palm her breast. Arching into the feel of his warm skin, peaked her small rose buds into hard little beads. The rigid length of his cock and the delicious friction it caused, stirred a frenzied need as she tugged roughly at the sheet. A smile spread across his handsome face, and his hand slid over hers, to help her in her mission to bare herself to him. Pulling back, he slid off his leathers and knelt down before her. The glistening droplet tapped against her sensitive bundle of nerves. Glancing up she saw the heat in his eyes as he stared down at her, naked and completely exposed for his taking. Biting down on her lip, her heart raced as his hands glided from her hips to the tops of her knees.

"You are so beautiful, m'aingeal."

Her heart swelled as she reached for him, hooking her arms around his neck and sinking into the depths of his wanting mouth. She didn't know what tomorrow would bring, let alone what the next hour did, but right now all she wanted was what she had right in front of her. She was his, and he was hers, if only for the night. She let the thought soak in as Remi lead her back down to the soft billowy mattress, never once breaking from their kiss.

CHAPTER
FORTY-FIVE

The golden shimmer of the ascending sun, painting the walls and floors in warm light, glittered against his skin as he stood on the balcony. Another stirring of desire punched her square in her sex as her eyes traveled down the length of his body, lingering longer on the towel slung around his waist, which hung dangerously low.

Remi stood stone-still, his eyes staring far off in the distance, deep in thought. Biting her lip to keep from revealing she was awake, she marveled in the breathtaking view. He was majestic to see, from the cut muscles from his shoulders, to the wet, inky hair sweeping down below his collar. Curling deeper into the pillows, she figured her hair was a messy halo, and her body ached in blissful ways. She inhaled his scent until her lungs nearly exploded. Burying her face into the linens to prologue the moment, she wanted to make certain it would be secured in her memory bank for the long nights ahead of her. She couldn't imagine not sleeping next to him. Feeling Remi's statuesque body curl around hers all night, as his thick arm wrapped around her waist, safeguarding from the world. A twinge of anxiety pricked her as she wriggled across the bed. What if she couldn't handle being alone again? What if he walked away and never returned? The pain of those thoughts clenched her heart, momentarily knocking the breath from her lungs.

Time held no value or meaning as she idly wondered how long had they been in bed. They had taken meals in his suite and the maid service was pretty outstanding, bringing them whatever they desired. Sinking deeper into the soft ivory duvet, she observed him with a cautious eye. The room was as silent as a tomb except for the rhythmic beating of their matching heartbeats. Her eyes stayed transfixed on his gleaming skin and the hard planes of his back, when the faintest sight of something unexpected appeared out of nowhere.

Gradually sitting up, Ferrian wasn't sure of what she was seeing. Maybe it was an optical illusion from the shadows playing gently with the sunlight, or she maybe was on a serious acid trip. The more she focused, the clearer her surroundings came into view. Feathering her fingers over her kiss-swollen lips she tried to prove to herself she was awake, but the outline of white wings with silver tips hanging from shoulder blades to mid-calf solidified with each blink. "Remi?" Her breath shuddered as she tried to convince herself she was seeing things again.

He slowly turned to face her over his shoulder. The blue irises of his eyes sparkled in the light like brilliant beacons welcoming her home. "Yes, m'aingeal? What is it?" The purr of his dark, erotic voice skittered over her sweet spot, ramping up her desire to feel him sink into her body once again.

Considering how to answer him, she took a long,

deep breath and twisted the sheets in her hands. "I think I'm going insane. I'm seeing impossible things. Maybe you're right, maybe I did hit my head harder—" Ferrian struggled to recover herself before the hysteria crept in and shattered her control.

"Wait … Ferrian, calm down." His muscles rippled as he turned his body toward her. The cut lines of his abdominals reminded her of an Adonis statue she once saw in an *Art International* magazine while waiting to be seen by a triage nurse. Adonis perfectly carved for all time, couldn't hold a candle to Remi's magnificence. "What's the matter? What do you think you're seeing?" Alarm grew in his voice, echoing her own.

"I feel like an idiot saying it. You know what, forget about it. I think I need something to drink." Climbing out of the bed, her head spun and stars flashed before her eyes. Taking another deep breath, she closed her eyes, yet the familiar pull of darkness beckoned her. She wouldn't give in this time, fighting it with every ounce she had. Popping her eyes open, the warmth of Remi's arms scooping her up and holding her closely to his chest shot a flurry of emotions racing through her. Overwhelming her until the emptiness she had always known, filled her in new ways.

He walked with her in his arms toward the balcony. She wanted to ask how he had caught her so quickly before she fell to the floor like a fool. Hell, she had so many questions she wanted answers for, but they would have to wait. Soaking in his warmth, she nuzzled her cheek and nose against the soft sinews of his neck. The golden sunlight warmed the areas his skin didn't cover, as the cool wind caressed their bodies.

"Tell me, what did you see?" He gently pressed a kiss

into her hair.

Pulling back to look at his face, she gnawed on her lip, wondering how she could admit she had seen a pair of angel wings slung from his back? Sure she had wondered many times before if he secretly was one; Remi seemed so damn saintly at times. But to ask him flat out, she knew it was going to sound crazy. "Um, I thought I saw wings on your back. Sounds nuts, I know. Like I said, I must've hit my head pretty hard. I mean it's not possible, right? I'm los—"

Cutting off her rambling with a kiss, Remi crashed his lips down over hers, as his arms tightened around her slender body. Long moments passed, while his tongue sliced into her mouth. Her fingers combed through his hair, pulling him down on her fiercely. The longer they kissed, she swore she could feel his heart about to burst out of his chest.

Breaking free, panting breath brushed across heated skin. Remi stared into her eyes, sending another wave of fire licking down her body. "Yes, you saw what I am. You saw the truth." His smile curled up as he continued. "I've wanted to tell you for so long. God, I hated keeping this from you, but I had to. Orders and all. I'm so happy I don't have to hide this anymore!"

"So, I'm right? You're an angel? Like heavenly body, under the command of God and whatnot? Is this how you've been able to find me? And wait a minute … um, we … the bed—Are angels allowed to … well, you know?"

Nodding, Ferrian reveled in his wide, beaming grin. "Even angels like to indulge in a little sin." His guttural laugh rippled through her body, causing more erotic vibrations to electrify her growing need.

"Holy shit! Oh crap. I mean ... I don't know what to say. So demons I assume exist as well?"

He carefully set her down and placed her hand over his heart. The hypnotic beating pulsed beneath their flesh, slowing the longer her hand stayed there. She sensed he didn't want to answer her even when she pressed further. "Demons do exist, don't they? Those men who held me captive, they were demons, right?"

His smile faded, and he nodded once again. "Yeah, they were. My brethren handled them after I got you out. I don't think they'll be bothering you again." He turned around to admire the vast expanse of vibrant green, speck-led with flowers of various colors of the rainbow. Advert-ing her gaze, she had no doubts Remi was the reason she was alive and standing on a grand balcony. What she didn't know is, where the hell she was. The scenery was too vibrant in color, too beautiful to be Chicago. Sardoni-cally she guessed maybe she was in the Heavenly realm. *Right. As if.* "So where exactly are we?"

"My suite." He spoke low and softly.

"Well, no shit. But where is your suite located?"

"In the Brethren's mansion, we all live here. Well, except for Nisroc. He prefers to keep a place downtown."

"This doesn't look like any part of Chicago I've ever seen before," Ferrian shot back, growing annoyed with Remi's lack of full disclosure.

"Because it's not."

"Let me guess, we're in Heaven right now?" Prop-ping her fist on her hip, she stepped closer until his rich, dark scent swam around her head.

Spinning around to meet her stare, Remi, cupped her

opposite hip and dipped his head low. "No, m'aingeal, not Heaven. The Angel-Realm," he whispered, brushing his lips over her cheek. Sidling around her, he walked over to the French doors, stopping in the doorway. His massive shoulder leaned against the doorjamb as he folded his arms over the thick bands of rigid muscle of his chest.

Knowing she should be freaking out, because nothing made sense, she sucked in a deep breath. And yet, it all made perfect sense. He had saved her too many times. Found her in places no man alive would've attempted to search. Remi saw beyond the scars and stared down into her soul. How could she have been so blind before?

Her breath caught as the outline of his wings appeared once again; translucent, and yet she could see them as clearly as she could see her hands. His glow was magnanimous as she closed the distance between them, and smoothed her hands down the supple skin of his chest and abdomen. The simple act of touching his flesh gave her renewed sense of hope that this was all real. Her hands traipsed up the rigid planes of his chest and down until she reached his towel clad hips. Circling him, until the expanse of his back blocked her view, she bit her lip, soaking up the view. Sensing a slight strain, she encircled her arms around his waist, pressing her cheek to his skin, and pecked a small kiss to his spine. "I knew there was something different about you. I'm glad I know now."

Ferrian's warmth wrapped around more than his body, as he sagged into the feel of her skin pressed against his. He knew they couldn't stay locked up in his suite forever, but he would have been happy trying to. He had ignored all incoming texts and calls. And placed a 'Do Not Disturb on Pain of Death' sign on his room … unless it was for food.

Although it had been nearly a week in the Angel-Realm, time on Earth moved much faster. A twinge of worry furrowed his brows as he wondered how she would take the news that a month had passed downtown. If he was being honest with himself, he wanted her to stay with him, for the rest of his life. Swaddling his arms around her while she slept peacefully, inhaling her sweet jasmine scent. And waking each morning, staring into her eyes as a beautiful smile spread across her lips. But it wasn't going to last, and it sucked donkey dick!

His cell had been vibrating every five minutes for the past two hours and he knew full well what was happening. All he had to feel relieved about was, Carnax wasn't going to be able to utilize his hands for torturing others anymore. Z had made damn sure Carnax had watched as his arms burned in the fire. As another text came buzzing through, and his nerves frayed a little more as he tried to think of a good way to explain to Ferrian, she would have to go back down to Earth.

Like a stab in the gut with a rusty knife, he knew the hurt it was going to cause. How could he make it all right? "Ferrian." His voice cracked as he smoothed his hands over hers. "I need you to get dressed."

With his request, her body subtly tensed against his. "Why? What's wrong? Did I do something wrong?" Her sultry rasp strained as she unfurled her arms from his waist. "Remi, what did I do? Please tell me."

Turning around to face her, in her twin emeralds he saw the first round of hurt poke through. "It's nothing you did. I have to talk to the group. They've been texting and calling for days. I need to find out what the status of things are." Caressing her cheek, he tilted her head to meet his gaze, pressing a soft kiss to her lips.

"Days? How long have I been here?"

Realizing the time thing, his small chuckle startled her. "We've been here for six days. It's been almost a month downtown."

"A month? But how?"

"Time moves much slower up here. Come on, I think Bels left some fresh clothes for you." He followed Ferrian's eyes as she stared down at herself wrapped in a sheet. Her small laugh made his heart swell, as she smoothed her hair down.

"Did she happen to bring a brush, too?"

"Yeah, I'm pretty sure every toiletry you can think of is in the bag." Walking to the front hallway of his suite, he reached for the pink and black Louis Vuitton bag Bels had left a few days earlier and smirked knowing Ferrian was going to hate whatever Kakabel had packed for clothes.

CHAPTER
FORTY-SIX

C ombing her fingers through the long tangles of her wet hair, she fidgeted as they made their way down the length of the hallway. She stopped and stared at each painting, before moving to the next. Her eyes grew wide with each statue they passed, and she marveled over the exquisite attention to detail. The light and airy corridor seemed to go on forever, which was fine with her. Her nerves were on edge.

Remi slid his hand to the small of her back, cupping her tenderly, and pressed a kiss into her hair. "Everything okay?" Patting her shirt down, she slipped her gaze up toward his, only to find Remi was smirking back down at her.

"You could've warned me you lived in Heaven's version of a museum."

"I know, it's ridiculous … too much." Waving off the ivory decadence, Remi clasped her hand tighter.

"No, no it's beautiful. I've never seen anything like it. I kinda feel like a scrub being here." Staring down at the clothes left for her, she remembered she would have to thank Kakabel for bringing her a set of black jeans and long sleeved Henley. It wasn't sexy, but not as oversized as she was used to either.

"Scrub?" He cocked a dark slash of brow at her, as she curled into his arm. Her wide eyes wandered across every painting, and each crystal chandelier in awe.

"Yeah, you know, a lower class human minion mingling with the rich and famous." A thick sigh carried her worries into the open, as the truth weighed heavily on her shoulders. "I don't belong here, is what I'm trying to say." Sucking in her doubts, her nerves were frayed, unsure of where Remi was leading her. She had offered to wait in his suite while he attended his meeting, hoping he would agree to her request. But he didn't. Instead, he had waited patiently as she took an obscene amount of time getting ready. And yet she barely brushed her hair, never mind doing make-up. All of the Cover Girl and Maybelline crap scared the hell out of her.

As if on cue, Remi pulled her hand to his lips, brushing a kiss over her knuckles. "Don't worry. They need some information from you. I swear, they aren't scary. Well, Nisroc is kind of an asshole at times, but don't worry about him."

Don't worry? Riiiiiight ... what was he smoking? Each step they took twisted the growing knot a little tighter until full-out dread assailed her as they hit the top of the grandest staircase she had ever seen. Her eyes danced over the intricate scrollwork lining both sides. Gilded over ivory ivy vines swirled around balusters with each step, guiding them to the front foyer.

Sliding her eyes over, she caught a glimpse of Remi staring back at her, clearly amused by her different expressions as she processed what she was seeing. "I-I feel like

I'm in a dream. Almost like I'm the villain walking into all this beauty."

The seductive turn his laugh took caught her off-guard, and he crushed her in a massive hug. One second she's oohing and awing over the banister, and next she's face first, pressed against his steely pectorals. If she didn't require air, she would've been happy to remain right where Remi had planted her. Inhaling another lungful of his naturally decadent scent, the alluring idea of pulling him back up the stairs to his suite and locking him in until she had her fill of him sent a flutter through her stomach.

"You're too funny."

"What do you mean? I don't get it?"

"You see all this," waving his hand in display, she followed its trail, "and think it is beautiful. Have you looked in a mirror lately?"

Scoffing, she tugged her hand free and folded her arms over her chest as a deep-set furrow emerged between of her brows. "Yes, I have."

"Then you've seen what true beauty is. It's here." He gently pressed his palm to her chest, covering her heart. The warmth of his touch eased her as she dropped her arms in a subtle surrender. When she glanced back up at Remi through lowered lids, the sincerity in his expression made her swallow hard. He hadn't made her think any-thing less of herself, yet she still couldn't break free of a lifetime of thinking she was a monster. But what could she say in rebuttal? *'I think you're a bit delusional? Have you not seen your sister? She's drop dead gorgeous. I'm a sewer-rat compared to her.'* Arguing how he saw her wasn't an option. The honesty in his eyes told her all she needed to know. Rolling her shoulders back, she lifted her chin to meet his gaze head on. Remi had been right. Her heart, even when she hated herself, refused to hate the world. Her heart yearned to help the helpless like a shaggy orange tabby-cat who followed her around the docks in hopes of finding food.

A smile slowly spread across her face as she reached up to cup his cheek. Her breath caught when she saw down to his soul. It was as though a bad horror movie played out before her eyes, from his point of view. She was stunned, as a flood of memories assaulted her with each new vision.

"Holy fuck!" Rearing back, her head spun as she tried to ground herself. "You-I … no way, not fucking … possible!" Her heart raced like a freight train screaming through the darkness. Gasping, her fingers covered her mouth as she stared incredulously at him. With eyes full of hurt and questions, the words spilled out, "You saw it all, didn't you?" Her smile fell quickly as her disbelieving eyes searched his. However, she knew the truth. It wasn't the first time she had seen down into a person's soul. She had seen some the vilest things mankind could be, and she's seen the innocent beings passing through life without a care in the world.

His voice came out in a humble, low, "Yes." As much as she wanted to hate him for standing by when those terrible things had happened to her, the pain and guilt for his in actions, and the anger that resided within him, washed over her, as she soaked up his emotions coming along with the visions. He hated himself more than she could understand for not stepping in and saving her. "I'm so sorry, m'aingeal."

"Why didn't you stop it then? I mean, you were there. Why, Remi?" Cradling his face once again, she refused to

341

let her anger control her. "What stopped you?"

"God did." He delivered his answer stoically, sending chills down her spine.

"But why? I don't understand. Tell me, why?" Fighting back the sting of tears, she planted her feet firmly in front of him and placed one hand over his heart. "Please, tell me why?"

"I can't."

"Bullshit!"

"I wish I could, but I can't." The tick in his jaw worked overtime, as he considered her. "Ferrian, believe me, if I could've stopped it from the beginning, brought you here years ago and saved you from all you've been through, I would have in a heartbeat. I wasn't, and still am not, allowed to interfere with the course of your future."

"What the hell does that mean? You're confusing the shit out of me."

"Listen, we need to get to the meeting. There are things you need to hear. I promise you," cupping her face gently, his eyes burned into hers, "I will tell you everything I can, as soon as I'm allowed to. I hate keeping things from you. I can't protect you like I should. I hate—Gah!"

He wasn't the only one who hated it. She wanted to be pissed off, instead her body sagged into his, craving to comfort him. She watched as frustration rolled through him, the harder he clenched his teeth.

"Listen, we'll figure this out. I'm not gonna lie and say I understand any of this. I'm more confused than a transvestite nun, but I'm here. I'm not going anywhere." She gently pressed a soft kiss to his lips, only to feel his quivering upon her touch.

"If I could undo everything you've been through, take it all into myself and erase all the memories and nightmares, believe me, I would do it without a second thought." His voice cracked as he tried to remain strong, but she could see it was eating away at him.

"I don't know why, but I think I was created for this, to take on all of the bad things like I have. I can't explain it, and I sure as hell wouldn't wish my life upon another living person. My only regrets are those who died because they loved me." Her eyes fell, purchasing a piece of the ivory and green rug-lined floor. "My mother. My foster mother. They died because of me."

"No, they didn't!" Remi reared back, holding her face between his palms. "They died because they were protecting you. It's not your fault. Don't you ever think like that again! Do you understand me? Their deaths weren't your fault."

Anger rifled through her veins as she tried to make him see sense. "But they're dead regardless! Whether it was because they loved me or to protect me, they still died and I'm the cause of it. I can't change the facts." Pulling out of his hands, she shrank away from him. The familiar rumbling of energy balling up in the center of her body built up faster than before. Her hands shook almost violently as alarm crept up her throat.

"What is it? Ferrian, what's wrong?" He rounded on her, alarm growing in his voice.

"Remi, get away from me! Do it! Now!" She didn't know where she was going, but ran anyway. The undeniable sense of foreboding consumed her, as the sizzle of electric vibrations multiplying by the second devoured her senses. Her boots smacked against the ivory marble floor, echoing down the hallway as she hauled ass in search of any door leading outside. Passing one door after elaborately carved door, she didn't register the beauty surrounding her as she followed the trail of golden light shimmering through a set of French doors. Fleeting hope surrendered as she searched for a place to release what was building before Remi caught up with her.

"Ferrian. Wait!" His apprehensive plea fell on deaf ears. She could hear him closing in behind her as she reached for the golden doorknob. Pushing the heavily paned glass door wide open, a warm wind welcomed her outside as wisps of raven hair fluttered around her head in a chaotic dance. The vibrations rippled down her spine, and through her arms and legs. She had to expel it quickly before she hurt someone … or worse. Darting down a set of stone stairs, she hit the steps two at a time before landing securely on the emerald blades of grass. To her right, a rock wall blocked off the entrance to an ornate garden. It would have to do.

Grounding her feet solidly, she pulled the energy from her center, manipulating it into a basketball sized orb. Holding it between her palms, the heat licked up her arms greedily demanding attention, as she focused her intentional destination. Remi's voice called after her, and it was only a matter of moments before he caught up to her. Panic surged down her spine. Launching the sphere, she sent the orb hurtling through the air. The sound of smashing rock reminded her of a cartoon sonic boom as it collided with the top corner of the rock wall. A small explosion of concrete and carved rocks exploded in a halo, littering the air in a powdery flume.

Before she even realized the extent of the damage she

had caused, the hard crash of Remi's body crushing her to his chest knocked the wind from her lungs.

"Ferrian! My God, what the hell was that? How are you able to push energy out the way did?" His voice was strained; she braved a glance up to his expression of complete disbelief.

"I'm not sure, exactly. It's the same thing I did in the cell. I can't explain it. The energy forms into this ball inside my body and I … have to push it out. Except when I do, it destroys whatever it hits. I was afraid it would explode on you. So I ran."

Wrapping his arms around her tightly, he surveyed the damage, and she stayed focused on him as he did so. He let out a low curse. Her body tensed as his fingers sink deeper into her shoulders. "I've never seen anything like it before. I mean, holy shit!"

She wasn't sure if it was a good thing, or if she was in serious trouble. Craning her head to see the remaining rubble, she wasn't sure what to make of it herself. As if she didn't feel like a freak already, but a destructive one, was another nail in her coffin. Worry lines creased her forehead, the longer she watched Remi's expressions morph from disbelief to devilishly sinful, as he smiled back down at her.

"Holy shit! By far, the coolest damn thing I've ever seen. Let's see you do your little parlor trick again." Roc's booming bass voice shattered the moment as Remi whipped around. Her heart thumped loudly when she saw a large, menacing male, with nearly every inch of exposed skin covered with tattoos, and piercings sauntering up to them. His green mohawk and sharp blue eyes cut her down the closer he came. "How the hell did you do that?" She got the distinct feeling the male was deciding whether or not to put her into a Magic Monkey show.

"I didn't," Remi snapped, as he turned his gaze back to her. "Ferrian did, however."

Smoothing her hand over the hard cut of his jaw, she wondered if it was possible for someone to break their teeth simply by clenching them as tightly as Remi was.

"Get outta here! The Darkling did that much damage? Hells yeah! Good going, kid. The shit was fugly anyway."

Studying Remi's tight smile, there was no denying the imposing male wasn't among his top ten favorite people. Slowly she slid from his embrace, ready to make another run for it as the tension between the males thickened the air around them. Sidestepping away, Remi ensnared her wrist and gently tugged her behind him. Why was he protecting her, from what she assumed was one of the good guys, even if he appeared like he belonged to one of Chicago's toughest biker crews?

"What do you want, Roc?"

"Well since you've decided your job interests lie elsewhere, I was sent to get you." Patting himself on his stomach, she wondered if Nisroc had the same thick sheet of ripped muscles hiding beneath his grey tee shirt as Remi did. "Yup, I'm a glorified dog, sent to fetch you. So get your asses up there before Am decides to send another winged one to summon you."

Blowing out a heavy sigh, Remi scrubbed his jaw and scrutinized her until her insides jumped with anxiety. Was she ready for the official meet and greet bullshit? She swallowed down the lump sitting in her throat, imagining a room full of scrutinizing stares, all considering her. "Are you ready for this?"

Nodding her head she knew her voice would betray her.

"Hey, Darkling, for the record, what you did there," Roc pointed to the rubble, as his eyes lit up with blue flames, "is some seriously awesome shit. I wanna see you do it again later."

Blood rushed to her cheeks as she wrapped her arm around Remi's, securing herself to her anchor of sorts. A crooked smiled slipped out as Remi's body went rigid with Roc's request.

She struggled to make out what Remi was saying. Speaking in a language she had never heard before, he spoke so low and quick, she didn't have to time sort out the context of it. All she had to go by was his body's reaction. Whatever he was saying had Remi tensing up and cautious to keep her from finding out. A long moment passed in silence as she watched the request weighing on biker boy.

"What the hell?"

"What?" Remi slipped his gaze down to her suspicious stare.

"Why do you need to speak in a different language around me? I thought you weren't going to keep secrets from me?" She pulled away. Pissed off was the tip of the iceberg as she pegged him with a suspicious glare. Whatever he had said to biker boy, she wasn't allowed to know.

Roc's loud whistle, followed by a throaty chuckle, grated on her. The simple fact the male enjoyed egging on Remi rankled her more. "Somebody's making promises he shouldn't be." Roc's grin flared out in a knowing way, and had her on the verge of backhanding him.

"Nisroc." Remi's booming voice rumbled through her

body, startling her as she waited for a verbal beat-down to ensue.

"Sup?"

"Piss off. Like now."

"Whatever, dude. Get your funky ass inside already."

Long moments lingered in silence until the sound of Roc's grumbling had fully disappeared. Relief washed over her with the male's departure, but her frustration level shot up a notch, refocusing on Remi. "What did you say to him? What aren't you telling me?"

"Remember when I said there are some things I'm not allowed to tell you?"

"Yeah, and?"

"Well this was one of those things I'm forbidden to tell you."

"But you can discuss it freely with biker boy?"

He barked out a laugh, alarming her, and leaving her to wonder what he found to be so funny. "Biker boy, eh?" Oh, okay, he was scoffing at her new nickname for the male. "Please, m'aingeal, as soon as I can tell you, I will. I wish I could now, seeing how much this upset you. I … can't right now. Please don't be upset."

Screwing her face up, she considered him as the tendons in her jaw were ready to snap in half. "Fine," she finally ground out. "Let's get the rest of this circus over with."

Taking her hand into his, she was tempted to jerk it back and bury her hands deep into her jeans pockets. Instead she chose to let his fingers interlace with hers as he guided her back to the mansion museum. His eyes grew soft as their palms connected. Dipping his head low, he whispered a kiss over her lips, murmuring something she couldn't understand.

"What did you say?"

"I'll tell you someday, my beautiful angel."

CHAPTER
FORTY-SEVEN

"The Council says Xaphan and Vepar are our problem. They won't send in Fallens to scout them out. We let them slip through our hands, now we need to clean up the mess." Amitiel's voice resounded down the ivory hallway as they strode toward the study. "Such bullshit!"

"So the fact we were ambushed by a fleet of Hellistics during all this means nothing?" Cass stepped up, his voice growing with contempt.

"I'm not saying they aren't right or wrong, but your crew did in fact let them live instead of destroying them. All Watchers out there have their eyes peeled for them, but no one is getting anything. And forget about me slipping underground for intel. The demons are on strict lockdown. No one is saying a word. So what do you want me to do, huh? Honestly, if you have any ideas, I'm all ears. I'll happily round up a crew of Watchers loyal to the cause. So?"

"For the record, we were keeping them alive to lock them down in them cillé. We planned on interrogating them."

"Doesn't matter much now, does it?"

Remi cursed under his breath listening to Focalor serve Am a new ass. Although he knew Xaphan had slipped away, he hadn't been given all the details, clearly. Stopping short, he pulled Ferrian closer. Dipping his head low until his lips were a breath away from her ear, he sensed her anxiety levels rising. "It's okay, m'aingeal. I promise you'll be safe in here. Everyone's a little high strung right now." His heart raced, and lungs burned as he slowly read her eyes. She was scared, and he didn't need to see the worry crossing her face to know it. Thumbing the curve of her cheekbone, he studied her, wondering if he wasn't making a huge mistake bringing her in. A long moment passed until he realized one thing was for certain, she wasn't breathing. Cupping her face with both hands, he whispered a kiss to her forehead. "Breathe, Ferrian, I'm right here with you. I'm not leaving your side." Letting his hand slide gently down the length of her arm, interlacing his fingers with hers, he wasn't sure she was truly okay with this.

Ferrian squared her shoulders; put on her brave face and God didn't he love her all the more for her bravery. His eyes stayed locked on her as she gave him a slight nod. He didn't care how long he had to wait for her to relax before pushing through the slightly ajar doors. "Ready?" Nodding once more, she stepped toward the door.

The heavy inlaid ivory and mahogany doors swung open wide, spilling out more booming voices and exposing a room full of angels and one aggravated Watcher. He slowly led them in, and the din of voices fell silent the deeper they walked into the room. Positioning Ferrian slightly behind him, he guarded her from inquisitive stares.

"Well? Where's Xaphan holing up? And how in the Hell could you let him live after what he did to Ferrian?" Anger boiled in his veins the longer he waited for an answer, glaring at each set of eyes, one at a time. "For chrissake, will someone answer me already?"

"If you would pick up your phone once in a damn while, you'd know what the deal is." Sidling around Cassiel and Kakabel, Ezekiel to come eye to eye with him. A curt snarl laced with ire flashed over his face. "Next time you want to take a vacation, you'd better make damn sure it's not in the middle of a friggin' battle. The Underworld is unleashing Hell on Earth, Fallens are being taken out left and right by Daemons, minions and Hellistics are killing innocents, all the while, you're sitting back with the Darkling while we try and sort this shit out."

His eyes bulged and his stomach flopped to the floor with the new information. Why hadn't anyone texted him all of this? Or knocked his door down and dragged him out kicking and punching? Oh yeah, because he was being a selfish ass, making love to his charge for a week. Instant regret crashed over him as he dropped his gaze from Z's.

"He wasn't sitting on his ass," Ferrian snarled. "He was taking care of me. In case you forgot, that piece of shit Xaphan decided to make me into a voodoo doll for some sick shit! If he hadn't come for me, I'd either be dead or close to it by now. He came for me," she stepped away from his protective stance and got right up in Ezekiel's face, "you didn't. So back the fuck off him. Now. Understand, dickhead?"

"Actually, I did. We all did. So how about you simmer that attitude down a notch." Z snapped, and eyed Remi with a subtle silent warning.

He wanted to reach out for her, pull her back and sink down into her mouth as a swell of pride surged through him. The fiery spirit she held deep within, radiated out through her sparkling eyes, beaming like lasers in the night at Ezekiel. Grasping her arm, Remi tensed feeling a slight vibration surged down to her fingertips. It was the same vibration of energy he had picked up on, building as before. Panic crept in as he tried subtly shifted her behind him once again.

"Whoa, Darkling served you, bro. Way to go little lady!" Roc's chortled laugh grated on Remi's nerves, but he had to agree. She had single-handedly shot down Z like a tigress defending her cub, pouncing and tearing into him without a single hesitation.

Reaching for her hand, he realized the vibrations had grown in intensity. Leaning down to her ear, he sensed she had stopped breathing again, as her eyes stayed transfixed on Ezekiel's. "M'aingeal," he tried coaxing her to look at him, cupping her chin with his fingers. When she didn't budge, he did the unthinkable. "You need to leave." Kissing her head, he figured there wasn't any more reason to hide his feelings for her. "Roc, take her outside." He couldn't believe what he was asking but there was no other choice. Roc had witnessed what Ferrian was capable of and hadn't said a word to anyone … yet. "But I warn you, you lay one finger on her, and I'll finish what we started," he snapped, leveling Nisroc with an 'I-will-not-only-kill-you-but-make-you-wish-for-a-slow-death' warning. All he got in return was a simple nod.

The vibrations grew stronger the longer she stood there. Consciously he realized her anger was setting it off, and as livid as she was with Ezekiel, it made him wonder how far she would go. Fear shot down his spine. She had a weapon, and in all his existence he had never witnessed another being—human, hybrid, or supernatural—who had ever possessed it. Gently he urged her to follow Roc. "Please, go with him for right now."

"No!"

"Please." Dipping low, his lips brushed her earlobe. "I don't understand this gift you have, and I can't have you hurting yourself or anyone else. They won't understand it, and I worry what they'll do if they find out." His voice danced with desperation for only her to hear. A small amount of relief slipped out when her breathing slowed, and she finally glanced back up at him. Kissing her forehead, he gently pushed her toward the door. "I'll be with you soon."

She didn't say another word, but she didn't have to. He held on to the overwhelming sense of pride as he watched her walk away; her shoulders pulled back and ready to launch if necessary. Ferrian, his charge, had stepped up to defend him, when dread had riddled her minutes earlier. As much as he wanted to follow her outside, and watch the destruction caused by her energy again, now wasn't the time.

Sending her with Roc made his stomach roll. Who knew what the angel would tell her, and the secondary concern scared the hell out of him. However, he wasn't ready to discuss this new revelation about Ferrian's gift with anyone. Tamping down his desire to run after her, he craned his head back around, pinning Z with a stern stare. "You didn't have to go off in front of her the way you did. She's freaked out enough by all this already." Hoping his own anger didn't shake in his voice, he slowly crossed the room and sank down into one of the two matching coffee-colored wingbacks.

"Like I said, maybe if you had picked up the damn phone, then going off wouldn't have been a problem for your Darkling," Z countered. "Seems she can handle her shit pretty well to me."

"Enough! For chrissake! We have enough going on with Fallens disappearing, humanity being taken out and you two numbnuts wanna have a my-dick-is-bigger-than-yours contest. I'm warning you both—all of you—we don't have time for this shit. Get tight in the head right now!" Amitiel's alto voice echoed off the cathedral ceilings, making the sound rattle through the room like thunder.

"She's right. If what I've told you isn't enough of a reason to get focused, then honestly, what is the point of the Angelic Brethren?" Focalor moved to the center of the oversized room, flaring out his translucent wings, which was a sign he hadn't fully earned his way back as a true angel. He held Remi's hard gaze. Locking him in like a heat-seeking missile. Remi's brain itched in the uncomfortable showdown, the longer Focalor stood there.

"Are you going to catch me up to speed, or do I need to patch this shit together from the messages on my phone?" Leaning his elbows down on his knees, he decided he wasn't interested in playing, 'Oh-let's-make-him-wait-in-suspense' any longer. "What are we talking about, Daemons taking out Fallens? Minions going after innocents, what?"

Shifting in his throne-sized chair, hands clasped together Cassiel coughed, grabbing his attention. "It's only part of the problem, I'm afraid."

If his expression was anything to gauge things by, then it was safe to say shit had hit had the fan. His gut twisted tighter. "What? I know Xaphan got away. And when I find the piece of shit, I'll personally see to his demise. What of Vepar? How did he slip through you guys? I thought the plan was to go in, get Ferrian out, and you guys destroy those low-life pieces of shit. What went wrong?"

"The other innocent in the room."

Not understanding what some poor bastard had to do with anything, he cocked his brow. "Okay, so what of it?"

"Bels, I think you better handle this one." Cassiel motioned for her to step up and start explaining. He watched as she reluctantly swiveled around to meet his curious stare.

"What am I missing, Bels? What gives with the innocent?"

Clearing her throat, her hands slightly shook as she folded them discreetly in her lap. The oh-shit meter was edging on the high end, ratcheting up him up tighter. With a heavy sigh, Kakabel met his stare. "I was contacted by the boss. He wants me to keep an eye on the innocent."

"I'm sure it's only a precaution. Interrogate him and see if he knows anything more than we do?"

"Not quite, Remi. I need to speak to Ferrian about this, too."

"Why? What is so important about this human?"

"He wouldn't say. Boss-man told me to keep an eye on the innocent and talk to her and find out what she knows about him."

Getting pretty damn sick and tired of all the half-assed answers, he considered her with an incredulous stare. Whatever. Surrendering up his hands, he was ready to strangle someone, anyone, and he didn't care who it was at this point. "By all means, she's outside. Go talk to her." With a dismissive wave, he scrubbed his chin with his other hand and sank deeper into the supple leather. "What else?"

"Carnax has been taken out of the game," Am offered, but it didn't feel like much comfort considering.

"So he's dead? I thought you guys cut off his hands, am I missing something?"

"You're right, Charo and Z made damn sure he couldn't use the tools of his trade again. But we've detained him for further questioning. He's down in the cillé right now, and as far as I'm concerned, he'll stay there until he rots."

"Has he said anything useful?"

"Not since he bit off his own tongue." Focalor approached him, arms folded tightly over his chest. "He's only a pawn in Lucifer's plan, like Xaphan."

"So why aren't we going after him then? Don't get me wrong, I still plan on tearing Xaphan apart with all of the delicacy of Mr. Hyde on coke, but why not get to the source first?"

"It's not as simple as you think. We have no proof Lucifer is behind all this. Granted I know differently, but the Council doesn't take the word of a Watcher too seriously. Feel me? They demand hard proof, and until one of those pansy-ass bitches gets off their high angelic horses, we're stuck going after the low man on the totem pole."

"So what now? What do we do about the Fallens? We can't stand aside and do nothing."

The room fell silent as a tomb. Eyes darted around,

waiting to see who was going to answer this.

Kicking off the table, Am lifted her chin and cursed. "Nothing. For now, we can't do a damn thing. They're fighting the lower level demons and we're not going to intervene."

"Are you kidding me? So we're to watch them die? Why? Please tell me why, because this is some messed up bullshit!"

"Because we have to. Until your Darkling turns, we will do nothing. She's the key to unlocking all our fates." He knew all this, but somehow he didn't expect the world to go to hell in a handbag in a matter of days. What else could go wrong? The niggling feeling the conversation was about to take another dive into the realm of fubar-land was pressing him hard.

"Remi, there's one more thing," Am began. Shifting in his seat, his skin tightened and his heart raced, waiting for her to finally spill it. "It's time she goes back. She's getting closer to her transition." And there it was. He had sensed her changing more by the day. Hell, she had stood up to one of the hardest angels in all of existence and had developed a gift he hadn't seen coming.

"No, no she isn't ready to go back yet. I mean, you saw her. She's still nursing some psychological wounds. Give me a little more time. A week … please, Amitiel."

"It's out of my hands. The Council has spoken. She goes back today. It's time."

"Please, give me one more day then?" Am was hard to bargain with, but he had to try. There was so much to say, and so much more to still learn.

Considering him with a calculating stare, her eyes told him no. "Why?" Her tone was flat as she concentrated her sights on him.

Like a beacon of light cutting through the midnight sky trained on him, Remi stood up to meet her glare head on. "Because I'm asking. One more day, and then I'll bring her back."

Her single nod was all the answer she was going to give, but it was all he needed. He released a pent of breath. "Thank you."

"All I can say is day-um, Darkling! That was one hell of a shot." Ferrian turned to peg biker boy with a slicing glare. She wasn't in the mood for props, or the hooting and hollering from some dumb-ass. Her muscles coiled tightly, as if she was going to snap from the tension alone. Her shoulders ached horribly and she rolled them back, hoping to find some relief. Knots doubled in size in her stomach as she marched past biker-idiot and headed for the forest line.

"Wait, where ya going, little lady?" Ignoring him, she sped up her pace, hoping to make it to the entrance before he decided to follow her in. "Don't make me follow you in there! I hate trees. Darkling, get your ass back out here!" Roc's voice thundered across the distance, but she refused to stop.

For the first time, she wished her ability to be invisible applied to angels as well, instead of the humans around her. "Piss off. I need to be alone."

"Fine. Don't come calling on me when you can't find

your way back."

Didn't any of them understand the desire to be alone once in a while? She didn't need or want a damn babysitter, and stomped onto a pristine footpath. Noticing the trail ahead, and that the snake-like path weaved around the lake, the driving need to run kicked in. She took off like shot, searching out a nice rock to perch herself on by the water's edge. For the briefest of moments, she relished in the feel of the wind in her hair, as it danced behind her, and the burn of her thigh muscles when she pushed herself harder. Pumping her arms as breath sawed in and out of her lungs, she ran deeper into the dense forest. Her mind replayed what had happened in the meeting. Why had she gone off so badly? Remi was a grown man, so why did she feel the need to protect him? How had her anger caused the energy to ball up so quickly? Twice in less than a half hour, she had pushed an orb of destruction from her body. The farther she ran, the more she wanted to keep running and hide from every living being on the planet. Yet she wasn't necessarily on the planet, now was she? Her head spun as she tried to wrap her thoughts around what she had learned, and what she still needed to understand.

The trickling daylight speckled the ground through the leaves as she caught sight of a promising boulder to climb up to. Spitting out the last spurt of energy she had, she made it to the base of the rock wall. Her lungs burned for oxygen and she heaved her body up, climbing higher, faster as if ravenous beasts were nipping at her toes. She hit the top in time to see the fading sky blue gradually dissolve into darkness.

"Hey."

Whipping around, her heart nearly burst from her

chest as she searched for a voice she recognized. "Kaka-bel, right? Where are you, I can't see you."

"Yes, it is I." Slowly the angel lowered down beside her. Her hair shimmered with silver in the waning sunlight. "I came to talk to you." Her melodic voice was soft and somber as she motioned Ferrian to sit.

"Talk about what?"

The way Bels's eyes gazed upon her, as though she had seen sadness at the core of Ferrian, made her insides cringe. "You. Well, the time you spent in the cell with the other innocent. I need to know some—"

"Okay?" Cutting off Bels, she stared at the female with a cautious eye. Rehashing what had happened in the prison was the absolute last thing she wanted to talk about. "Are you wondering if I was forced to do things to him? Or are you more curious to know if he was forced to have sex with me … well, the host body I occupied anyway, like the others? What do you want to know?" Fury licked up her veins as she tried to tamp down the desire to search and destroy those who had held her captive.

"Oh God." Kakabel covered her mouth with her dain-ty fingers. Horror crossed her face, and she gazed at her with sorrowful eyes. "I'm so sorry. We tried to find you sooner. Honestly. Remi was going crazy. He wasn't going to stop until he found you."

"I know." The thought comforted her. She knew down to her soul that Remi would search Heaven and Hell to find her and bring her home. Exhaling, she sank down to her knees, and stared out over the vast lake. "It's so beautiful here."

"Yes, it is. Ferrian, I'm sorry, I didn't mean to upset you. What I need to know is, did he, the innocent I mean, did he ... have any strange abilities? Did he say how he got there?"

Cocking her head, she racked her brain for any details she could remember. "Aside from the fact his brainiac scheme to get himself nearly killed, while those sick shits brought in others to beat and forced me to jump inside their bodies and endure the beatings ... yeah, can't help you much there. I was a bit preoccupied."

The news came as a disappointment. Bels screwed up her face and concentrated on something hard. "Did he say how they abducted him? Or why they chose him?"

"He said the last thing he remembered was pulling a dog out of the garbage bin. Some kids had dropped it in there after taping its legs together. He jumped in and pulled it to safety, and then he ended up in the cell like me. Doesn't know why, then again, I don't think any of the people who were brought there knew why they were chosen. Why?" She watched Kakabel's face as she studied her feet closely, purposely avoiding eye contact. "Why?"

"I'm not allowed to say."

"I'm so sick and tired of this 'not allowed to say' bullshit. What does he have to do with me or my knowing?"

"I don't make the rules, sweetie. I was asked to keep an eye on him and to ask you what you know about him. And to be truthful, I'm not totally sure I understand it either."

A spark of recognition flashed in her memory as one peculiar detail screamed out at her. "Wait, there was something kind of odd about him. I don't know, maybe it was lack of lighting or something, but ..." She let the thought roll around in her head before she said it. It was crazy. It had to have been an optical illusion. The way his eyes flared bright golden amber like the sunshine on a summer's day, then dimmed to black holes she could barely make out.

"What is it? Please, Ferrian, if you know anything, anything at all no matter how insignificant you think it may be, I want to hear it."

"Well, I don't know how accurate my memory is, but I'd swear his eyes lit up with this weird amber glow when he was angry. I thought I saw it happen after one of his beating sessions, and then, his eyes became dark again. I thought it was because of the way the firelight was playing on his face. I don't know. Sorry. Told you it wasn't much."

"No ... no. Oh my god that's was more than enough. Thank you, sweetie." Kakabel leaned over to hug Ferrian with a vice grip. Her arms slightly shook as she tried to straighten out her smile. Something was off, but she wasn't about to question the Victoria's Secret Angel on all the details. A simple answer would suffice.

"Why does it matter? What does it mean?" Leaning back, Ferrian wrapped her arms around her legs, like she was holding on for dear life while waiting for Kakabel to respond.

"Not sure yet, but I aim to find out. Surely eyes like his have some significance. Okay, young lady, I'm sure Remiel is half batshit crazy trying to find you right about now. What do you say we head back and find him, and get something to eat while we're at it?"

Food did sound tempting, but solitude held much greater appeal at the moment. Slipping a small smile to her unlikely friend, she shook her head. "I'm gonna chill here for a few. I need to adjust. I'm still trying to make sense of all this stuff and I feel like I'm on a tilt-a-life-whirl still spinning out of control."

"You sure you should be alone right now?"

"Yeah. I am. If Remi asks, tell him I needed a few minutes to myself. I'll be back in a little while. 'Kay?"

Patting Ferrian on the shoulder, Kakabel rose graceful as a ballerina, and returned the nod, silently agreeing to her wishes. She partially wondered if the Victoria's Secret designers had come up with that bra line because of Bels. With her beauty, it was a wonder that the female didn't have a line of suitors trailing behind her constantly.

CHAPTER
FORTY-EIGHT

So much had happened, and still she hadn't been able to wrap her head around all of it. Surges of power rippled through her mixing with pain and panic as she struggled to stand up. Night had set firmly in place as she glanced over the edge. It would be a miracle if she didn't break her neck climbing back down to the path below.

From her earliest memories, Ferrian had only known fear. It was a constant living, breathing element of her daily life, until Remi came along. She had for so long been forced to walk the Earth and accept she was only worth what someone would beat into her. The more she swam in those thoughts, the more she seemed like she was drowning again. Anger raged, as she ripped herself away from the rocks and cursed the pain of the past. "I am not her anymore!"

She didn't want to admit it to herself, much less anyone else, but the power of manifesting the sphere of energy and hurling at an object of desired destruction fueled a need to do it again and again. The fact she could muster it up when she was angry didn't scare her. It was her lack of ability to push it back down. Something she would definitely have to work on.

All of her life she knew there was something different about her. Never quite fitting in, and not sure where she truly belonged. She kept to the shadows and hid from the world, all the while toying around with an energy source she thought was a cosmic joke or quite possibly a delusion. After hurling the first orb at her captures, her doubts of it only being in her head were promptly dismissed. Not only dismissed but utterly destroyed. It was more than anger that spurred it on. It was the delicious desire to extinguish life, which had caused so much pain. Not only to her but to the others trapped in the hellhole.

It provoked a new question. If she could manifest it when she was under duress, could she muster it when she was clear headed? With her feet firmly planted on the ground, she focused all of her attention on creating energy again. The first tingle skittered down her arms and over her chest as before. Taking a deep breath, she poured more of her concentration into making it stronger, bigger. Her fingertips tickled with the sensation as it slowly worked free from her abdomen, pulling it out of her body. The soft glow she had seen before, while trapped and chained to the wall, radiated with a spectral of hues from baby blue to emerald green and sunny yellow to lipstick red.

"Ferrian, what the hell are you doing?" Remi's panicked voice cut away her attention, dissolving the energy.

"Remi, I did it. I made it ball up again, and not while I'm angry. Hold on a sec." Flexing it between her palms, she concentrated harder, pouring more energy into her orb. Glancing back up, his eyes grew wide. "What's wrong?" A small inkling of hurt came when he didn't respond the way she had hoped. The simmering energy slowly faded as he stared back at her, his eyes full of questions.

"I don't know what to say. Can you dissolve it, I mean without throwing it and it destroying anything?"

"I'm trying to. Hang on." Carefully she rolled her hands around, closing in on the orb until all that was left was a golf ball sized sphere. She pushed the orb back into her body, and a current of electricity stung her nerves as it absorbed back in. "Owwww, geeeeezus!"

Lunging for her, Remi crushed her to his chest. "Ferrian, promise me you won't try it again. Not at least until I understand what exactly this gift is."

A squished face wasn't exactly was she was expecting, but the panic in his voice jarred her from the fascination of her accomplishment. A small victory, one she had planned on reveling in for a while, until he cut it short. "It's okay, I did it. I backed it down and sucked it back inside. See!" Pushing back from him, she lifted her palms for his inspection. He studied her hands while deep creases etched his forehead.

"How? Earlier, you bolted from me only to hurl it at a wall. And now you have some control over it? Are you playing games with me? Have you been able to do this the whole time?" He pinned her with a suspicious stare, and Ferrian wanted to crawl back inside her skull and hide. How could he think she had been pretending or hiding this from him?

"I'm not playing games. I thought ..."

"Thought what? You could play around with something that could destroy anything you set your sights on?" His accusation made the joy of her moment shatter into a thousand pieces. He was right. She was a force of destruction. Biting back the tears, the overwhelming shadow that she truly was created to kill, made her stomach roll.

"I won't," she murmured. "I'm not evil." Tears stung the back of her eyes as the pain of the past washed over her. "I wanted to get a grip on it. I don't want to hurt anybody with it." Soft sobs coated each word as she covered her face with her hands. His reaction was all the conformation she needed. She was walking a fine line between good and evil. "I won't hurt anyone, I promise."

Fear raked him, watching Ferrian manipulate something beyond his understanding. The power in her eyes as she toyed around with it, and the thrill she got from freeing a side of her, scared the hell out of him. However, as much as he wanted to be afraid, or down right pissed, she also entranced him. The way Ferrian handle her gift, practicing and honing her skills with it, far away from everyone, he couldn't blame her. Still, he wondered if she had any idea how dangerous she could be. How dangerous she would be if the wrong people found out about it.

He hadn't meant to snap at her, and instant regret followed when the first signs of crystal tears hinted at the corners of her beautiful green eyes. "Hey, I'm sorry." Clasping her shoulders, he gently tugged her in. Pressing a kiss into her hair, he cursed softly, and realized he had become the biggest asshole on the planet. It didn't take a genius to figure out what he said had sent her spiraling back down into her dark past. In a matter of a few seconds, he had successfully convinced Ferrian she was a source of death. With one sentence, he had backtracked everything she was trying to overcome.

Sobs rolled through her as he held her closely. "Shh, shh, you are not evil, m'aingeal. I'm so sorry for what I said." Regret sank in bone deep. Smoothing his hands up and down her back, as her tears slowly eased, he tried to comfort her. "I'm an asshole. What can I say, I panicked."

"No, no—you're right. I cause death and devastation. But there's something I can do about it." She pulled away from him, as the last of her shimmering tears fell silently down her cheeks.

His heart stopped, thinking the worst. Remi could only imagine what Ferrian's idea of stopping herself from causing anymore death would only include … more death. Her death. Cupping her face between his shaky palms, dread filled his throat. "Ferrian, listen to me, you don't have to do this. You don't have to figure this out on your own. I'm here, let me help you." He knew his plea sounded desperate, but he didn't care.

"What are you talking about? I'm lost." Drying her eyes with her sleeves, she stared into his eyes. Concern rimmed her tear stained lids. "All I meant was, I don't plan on using it to hurt anyone, ever. But I need to learn to control it better so it doesn't try to explode out of me like before."

He didn't know how to respond. She was right. However, she had a gift or tool which could be used to kill. A flash of recognition lit in her eyes as she reared back from him. "You thought I was going to kill myself, didn't you?" She stared him down with an accusatory glare, and rightfully so.

Exhaling a heavy breath, he nodded sheepishly. "Yeah, I did. I'm an ass, forgive me."

"Why? Because I'm a walking disaster? I know I have nothing to offer you or anyone else on Earth, but killing myself would be my last resort. Besides, it didn't work—"

Subtly he shifted, reaching out for her. He didn't need her to finish that statement. They both knew the truth. Ferrian made no movement to welcome his touch. Shame rippled through him as he wished he could take back every damn word. "I really am sorry. Please forgive me. I'm as scared as you are. I'm not sure how to handle all this, but …"

"But what?"

"But maybe I'm wrong. You seemed like you were able to get a handle on this energy sphere thing. Maybe training yourself to harness it and suppressing it will be the best thing. I mean, it's a gift, right?" Extending out his hand farther, until he could feel her hesitation on his fingertips, he waited for her to respond.

Quirking her lip, she stared back at him with a skeptical expression. Gradually unfolding her arms, she slipped her hand into his. "I can do this," she stated with conviction, leveling him with an intent to match her words.

Grinning, he couldn't help but fall more in love with her by the second. Picking herself up over and over again, as though she was permanently proving herself to him and everyone else what she was made of. And here he was being an ass, making her believe she needed to prove herself to him. Kicking himself, he couldn't help but wonder what had he done? "I know you can," he murmured, winking at her. "You can do anything, m'aingeal. I believe in you and all you can do."

A smile carefully unraveled across her face as she slid up to him. She locked him in her gaze, and it was there, deep in her soul, he saw the truth. Pulling herself from the depths of her past, to confront him with self-assured resonation. He was quickly learning not to underestimate her. *Too bad for you underworld dickheads, you're not getting my Dark Angel.*

Her hands smoothed up his chest and over his shoulders as Ferrian wrapped her arms around his neck, crushing him to her. "Thank you," she whispered in his ear, burying her face against the crook of his neck. Pecking a trail of soft kisses down the sinews of his throat, she turned him on, and his body went instantly rigid with want. Heating up like a fire on the verge of combustion, he sensed her body's desire growing stronger as she straddled his thigh, hooking a leg to keep him locked in place. "What do you say we …" The sultry groan as she nipped at his earlobe, sent erotic shivers down his spine, and he fisted the hem of her shirt.

"Finish saying what you want," he taunted.

"Finish what we began back in your suite," she purred, curling a finger around a tendril of his inky hair.

"Finish?" Cupping the small of her back, he cocked her head back by her chin, lowering his lips until he barely brushed against hers. "I've barely started with you, darling."

CHAPTER
FORTY-NINE

Hesitating, he swallowed back the distaste of what tomorrow would bring as he sank down into her lush mouth for what would be the last time. His heart raced, the deeper he explored Ferrian's mouth. Urgency to consume her was overshadowed by his longing to hold her close forever. Each time her slender fingers grazed his skin, he promised to remember the warmth of her touch, and the gentleness of her caress. His hands trembled as they sank into her hair, holding her close to him. He wanted to close his eyes, and fall into the abyss of pleasure, but he refused to. Drinking up the sight of her, he decided he wouldn't risk losing one second of his time with her. Soaking up her natural heat and inhaling the flowery jasmine scent wafting from her skin, his senses collided with his desires.

Pulling away from her, he gazed into her eyes. He wanted those twin emerald eyes to burn him until he was nothing more than a mortal man. "What's wrong?" The subtle rasp of her voice trickled with trepidation. Smoothing away the worry crease between her brows with his lips, he knew he had to tell her. His heart ached to say it, but dropping it on her last minute would tear her apart.

"I-I have to bring you back tomorrow." He hoped his voice didn't shake as much as his insides were. "It's time, Ferrian." Kissing her forehead, he sensed the unease rippling through her.

"Why?" Her voice trembled as she stared into his eyes. "I don't belong there. Down there, I am nothing more than a monster. Why do you want me to leave, Remi? Please … tell me." Her plea swallowed him up, and chained him to the inevitable drowning he would face when she left.

"It's not my choice. I have to bring you back down. The Council—"

"Screw the Council! Do you want me to leave?"

"No!" He sensed she wanted to pull away, but Ferrian stood there, arms locked around his shoulders. "I don't. I'd keep you here forever, if I could. This isn't about me, Ferrian. You need to go back. Please, m'aingeal. We have tonight." Releasing a heavy sigh, he lifted her chin up to meet his lips once again, and tenderly caressed them, asking to be let back in. "I'm not going anywhere tonight. Tonight, I'm yours and you are mine." He had barely finished the last word before Ferrian sliced her tongue between his lips. The resolve in her kiss to devour him overwhelmed him, and he gripped her tighter. He wasn't sure if she understood what he was trying to say, but pushing her anymore on the topic was out of the question.

Sinking down in to her kiss, his blood pulsed to life, searing through his veins. His muscles went taut under her touch as Ferrian pushed her body into his, molding to him like a second skin. He reveled in this moment, the feeling of Ferrian's body pressed against his, until the idea she wouldn't be with him come dusk ate away at him. It took all he had to keep from whisking her away and hiding them in some distant cave. But the Council was right. Ferrian was the key to saving humanity, and she didn't even know it. Reining in his ramped-up mind, he forced himself to focus solely on her being here with him, right now.

Breaking away from his kiss, she impaled him with a heated stare. Her lips curled into a sinful smirk as her eyes darted from his gaze to his lips and back. "Damn straight, you're mine." She cradled his face between her palms, as she seductively moaned what he was to her, and then crashed his lips down onto hers. Damn if she didn't stoke his fire up to inferno levels, sending all of the blood in his body straight to his cock with brutal force. The harder she kissed him, the harder he grew.

The scent of her arousal spiraled around them as she crushed her breasts against him. Her body demanded to be seduced and devoured, and who was he to deny his angel's demands? Scooping her up in his arms, he walked them to the soft sands of the lakeside, willing a blanket to appear on the moonlit shoreline. The stars twinkling above them like diamonds speckled against a black velvet backdrop, as he laid her down gently.

Her black hair shimmered in the moonlight. The resplendent flush of her cheeks made her natural glow brighter as the reflection of silver rays lit up her eyes. A small laugh slipped out, watching her shimmying out of her shirt quickly, exposing the soft curves of her milky white skin. Sucking in a ragged breath, he leaned over her, and drank her in.

Lowering his lips down on to hers, her body shivered under his touch. Gently palming her breast, he rubbed over the soft lace, coaxing her tight rosebud to peak. Her approving gasp as he thumbed over and around it, sent a surge of erotic pleasure down his spine as he replaced his thumb with his lips. Staring up at her under a half-lidded gaze, he saw that her chest rose and fell in rapid waves, and she was watching him.

Raking her fingers through his hair, he succumbed to her touch as her short nails dragged back, sending more shivers over his scalp and skating down his body. He needed more of her to taste, greedily lapping up her sweet essence until his craving faded. And there was the greatest cosmic joke of all. He never thought his body could want for anything as badly is it did for Ferrian. From the feel of her fingers raking through his hair, to the way her hips sinuously moved beneath him as he suckled on her nipple through the thin lace, had Remi on the verge of ripping her clothes off and ravaging her right then and there. Her voice, thick with lust, was music to his ears as little mews escaped her when she bowed upward, jutting out her breasts.

Seizing the moment, he hooked his arm under the small curve of her back and arched her body up higher. His mouth danced over her tight, hard little bead once more before traipsing hungrily down the supple planes of her body. Lavishing slow, tender kisses down her body, until he reached the valley between her lithe hips. The heat of his breath moistened the spot her jeans covered as he nuzzled the tip of his nose along the seam. His body ached with gluttonous need, demanding him to tear away the obstacle separating him from his desire.

Biting the edge corner of the waistline, he popped free the top button of her jeans. Her body went rigid, and when he glanced up he saw that she was staring at him with the same heated desire. Licking at the zipper until he secured it between his teeth, he tugged at the metal jailor, releasing her body from its cloth-covered confines. Her breath hitched as he slid his hands over her hips, gripping the rim of her pants and sliding them gently down her legs. In one smooth sweep, he uncovered her body, jeans and panties, exposing her natural beauty to him.

Rising on to his knees, he beheld her, his goddess who he needed to pay worship to. He could see it in her eyes; Ferrian wanted no other male, and God the little bit of knowing shot an arrow of prideful love straight to his heart. Hunger burned his tongue when his eyes finally landed on the glistening slit waiting for his touch. There was no fighting it any longer. His body coiled. Desire for her sinuous body overruled his gentle nature.

Drinking in the sight of her moonlit body, he tucked away another memory of her in his heart as he lowered his mouth down to her sex. His goddess had learned to trust him, opened herself up to him in ways he couldn't have imagined and gave herself willingly to him. Tears stung the back of his eyes, as she stroked the curve of his cheek, glancing back at him with eyes so clear and full of promise and love. Gripping his chest, it swelled to the point he thought it would explode. He fought back his own desires, because her happiness was what mattered to him. He'd happily spend the rest of his existence making sure she knew she was loved, even if he wasn't allowed to be around her.

The cool night air enveloped them as tiny goosebumps abraded her skin. With a small nod, she coaxed him to go on and devour her until he had had his fill. But it wasn't going to be about him or his wants. No, he'd make damn sure Ferrian was fully satisfied before taking care of his needs. Lowering his wet lips over the warm slit of her sex again, he tested his welcome with the tip of his tongue. Skimming the length of her moist folds, he trailed along the seam until he hit the small knot of sensitive nerves, evoking a raspy moan from Ferrian. Her body writhed as he pulled her closer. Circling the small knot, then slicing his way between her silken core. Fire pulsed though his body with each droplet of her silky, liquid sex dancing across his tongue. Sinking his mouth down on her, she bucked and wriggled against him. Her moans sang to life, littering the night with a song of pure ecstasy.

He hungered for her, coveting each droplet as his tongue lashed wickedly into her sex and then trailed back up to tease and suckle on the bundles of nerves. The feel of her nails scoring his shoulders and down his skin, leaving red streaks behind in their wake, made his cock as hard as steel, and his hips undulated with want. The harder his mouth swallowed her down and licked up her, the higher her cries became. Slipping a finger into her wet slit, he pumped slowly into Ferrian's sex, letting wetness from her arousal coat his chin and hand, as he lapped at the liquid heat dripping from her. Her body pitched harder when he entered her with another finger. Meeting his intrusion with the roll of her hips, she ground her core against his hand, and clenched around his fingers tighter with each thrust. Her skin flushed the higher she climbed to peaking. Lapping at her, his body shook inhaling her scent making the rigid length of his cock throb. She was close, but so was he.

Tamping down his sex's demand to plunge into her,

he focused solely on her face, her pleasure as she raked through her hair with one hand and gripped his hair with the other. The sultry mien in her eyes, as he glanced up through half- hooded lids, said she had him right where she wanted him, as she rode out the first climax. His hips rocked into the sand, as her body jerked, tensing and releasing in undulating waves. He relished in her melodic cries as they echoed off the water in a glorious symphony, before bringing her back down.

The ripples of her descent had barely waned when he plunged his fingers back in, thumbing over her clit as he slid back up to kiss her. Filling his mouth with her moans, she clung to his back by her fingertips, arching into his touch. Strumming her sex as she struggled to keep her body on the ground, he licked inside her mouth, tasting her. The delicious feel of her body clenching him, as he sank deeper into her kiss had his body rocking his hips against her, demanding attention.

"Make me come for you," she panted, fisting his shirt as her body begged for more. "Please." The utterly sinful tone of her voice electrified him, and his body jerked in response. His own release was edging around the dangerous zone.

Abiding her request, he pumped into her faster, lifting her body higher each time. She was so wet for him. His cocked twitched, begging him to spring free and feel her body from the inside. The higher he brought her to peak, the higher her voice grew. The sound of her pleasure, even as he filled her mouth with his tongue, was pure divinity.

He could feel her close to the edge, as he slowed down to drag out the moment longer. Her breath hitched, making her chest jut out and jerk to his delight. Her hand reached up, cupping the back of his skull, as her eyes drilled into his. "Now," she whispered.

Without further coaxing, he ramped her up, bringing her to orgasm as he halfway rolled on top of her to keep her from bucking him off. God she was glorious to behold as she rode out her climax, calling out his name. Her body trembled as he brought her back down carefully. Slipping his fingers free, and refusing to waste a single drop, he smoothed them over his lips, tasting her as she caressed his face. A resplendent smile stretched ear to ear across her face as he licked the remnants of her essence away.

She lifted her head to meet his kiss, nipping at his lips as her hand stroked down his chest and tugged at the hem of his shirt. "I want you naked ... right now," she murmured against his mouth, licking the seam. The erotic growl in her voice shot another wave of throbbing need straight to his swollen sex as he met her kiss head on. Pulling her up with him as he slipped his shirt over his shoulders, he hated the idea of breaking from her kiss, even for a split second. Instead he artfully slipped it over his head and down over hers, draping it over her shoulders to cover her goose-pimpled skin.

Her giggle as the fabric slid down her flesh warmed his heart. She wasn't relenting on her demands. Fumbling with his belt buckle, she quickly unfastened his button and pulled hastily on his zipper. Her desire to get him naked as fast as possible was becoming reality. And he was helpless against her wants. Well, almost helpless, he corrected himself.

He wouldn't fight her off, as she cocked him a sultry smirk and pushed his jeans down his hips while simultaneously springing free his sex. The cool wind caressing his heated flesh as it bounced between their bodies played hell on his senses. A hiss slipped past his lips as she palmed the hard shaft, thumbing over the sensitive tip. Her hand was as soft as heaven stroking him. His body grew taut as her nimble fingers worked him over. He was already at his breaking point before she had popped his fly. How much more he could handle was questionable. "Ferrian," he breathed into her hair, as she lowered her lips to kiss along his collarbone.

She had him under her spell; working her magic on him—from her kiss to her touch—and he was completely hypnotized. Sinking one hand into the tangles of her hair, and the other gripping her hip, he wasn't sure how much longer he would last staying as they were. As if she read his mind, Ferrian pulled his body down with her. Splitting her thighs wide, he knew she wanted him as much as he desired her. He needed to fill her body to the hilt and lock himself there forever. Her body opened for him, ready to cradle him between her thighs, as though God himself has designed their bodies to be a perfect match. Positioning his head, she slid the tip against her wet slit, coaxing another groan from his lips. Accepting her invitation, he plunged deep with one long stroke. Nearly lifting her body off the ground, the overwhelming sense of pure ecstasy swallowed him whole.

His arms strained, holding himself up as he charged into her. His control was shot to hell as he concentrated on her face, displaying her pleasure. He couldn't get enough of this. Feeling the warmth of her body, swaddling him tightly, and her glorious face as she cried out for him. Driving hard into her, her legs wrapped tightly around his back. Her wet core clenched around the swell of his cock.

Slowing down his pace, he didn't want send them both over the edge before either had time to fall to pieces. He slid back, holding her hips in his hands, causing a delectable friction, as he locked his eyes squarely on hers. Each thrust brought with it a wonderful new melodic moan creeping higher. Playing with the depths and speed of his thrusts until her body's demands to peak sent a shiver of anticipation to new heights. The sight of her licking her lips, as she gripped his ass, fueled him for another round of let's-take-this-up-a-notch. Gripping her hips tighter, he delved deeper, harder. Grinding into Ferrian's exquisite body, she rolled her hips to meet his intrusion with just as much fervor.

"Owwww!" she howled, lifting her shoulders from the ground. A small tear trickled down her cheek as Remi dropped her hips and leaned over her.

"What is it? What's the matter, m'aingeal?" His eyes darted over her face, and his heart stopped short, fearing he had somehow hurt her.

"It's okay, my shoulder blades are a bit sore. Must've dug into the ground too hard is all." Rolling her hips, Ferrian's way of coaxing him back was nothing short of sexy. While he wiped away the single tear, he wasn't completely convinced her shoulder blades were the only things aching her. Cocking an impish smile, he kissed her softly, slipping an arm under the back and hoisted her body up with this. Refusing to break the connection from her, he proceeded to encircle his waist with her legs as he sank back on to his ass. He propped her up in his lap, and the tip of his cock bounced eagerly to dive back into her sex.

She slid down sinuously, moaning with each inch she took, which made his body surge with fire. She fit him like a glove, and damn him if he didn't want to stay inside of her like this forever. Cupping her lush ass, he let her set the pace as she rolled her hips like a snake charmer, gliding effortlessly up and down the length of his thick stalk. While biting back his own moans, she worked him over to the point he wasn't sure he could last much longer. Sliding one arm up her back, there wasn't enough skin to touch, until he reached her source of her pain. *'Oh shit!'* Panic stabbed him a thousand times over when he realized what had happened.

Twin mounds pulsed to life, growing as he feathered his fingers over them. She was closer to transitioning than originally thought. His heart stilled, even as Ferrian continued in her carnal pursuits. His mind raced, and he wondered how much longer she had until the time came for her to choose. He hadn't realized he had stopped breathing, or was even enjoying the moment with her until she cupped his face between her warm palms. "Remi, what's wrong?" The alarm in her voice grew. "Breathe, dammit! Don't make me do CPR on you."

Squeezing his eyes tight, he didn't want to envision her with black leathery, hellfire wings. He didn't want to wonder if his love for her was enough to make her choose the right path. He could feel her panic rising with each passing second he didn't answer. Oh God, was this to be the last time he was with her, loving her like this? Did she have the faintest idea of how deep his love for her went?

Her body trembled against his, as her voice pitched higher with worry. Slowly opening his eyes, hers were there to greet him, with shadows of what could be passing beneath them. Only a small recognition registered in his mind. It wasn't her trembling, it was him. She spoke, asking question after question, but his fear deafened him. "Remi, you're scaring me. What's wrong? Come on, answer me!"

"You can't change what is it be. Don't waste what time you have left with her. Show her your love." Snapping his attention back, the deep male voice boomed in his head like a wrecking ball, easing him back into the present. Taking his first deep breath in who knew how long, it was clear his lungs didn't appreciate the temporary abandonment of oxygen.

"It's okay. It's all going to be okay," he murmured into her hair, crushing her body against his. The warmth of her core, still swaddling him, and the deep embrace as she held him closer, washed over him, bringing him back to the moment. She gently pushed back from him and stared into his eyes. The expression on her face said she needed to say something. Whatever it was, he couldn't be upset with her if it was along the lines of *'What the hell is wrong with you?'* As though she was figuring out the best way to say whatever it was, he caressed her cheek, pressing a soft kiss to her lips.

Whatever and however long he had been in his mentally-frozen state, it was clear to him, it affected her more than he thought possible. Before he could utter a single syllable, she feathered her fingers over his lips to stop him. "I need you to know something. I, ah, I'm ..." Her hesitation made his stomach twist as he waited for her to finish, and he readied himself for rebutting any argument she was about to lay on him.

"Ferrian, what is it?"

"I'm in love with you." Her eyes grew softer, and she pressed her lips gently against his. He succumbed to her as she left him defenseless with one statement. Of all of the things he was expecting her to say, *'I'm in love with you'* wasn't one of them. Brushing his fingers through her hair, he held her closely, sinking down into her kiss as a tear fell down his cheek. Blissful moments passed before they came up for air. Panting, the heat in her stare warmed more than his body, but his soul. Those few simple, powerful words, 'I'm in love with you' filled him completely, sealing any doubts in his heart.

"You have no idea how much I needed to hear you say those words," he whispered, not only to her, but to the universe. "I love you, too.

CHAPTER FIFTY

L ying with Remi on the soft, sandy shoreline, his body curling around her small frame, she savored the warmth of her heart filling completely for the first time in her life. Dawn broke through the dense night-shade as her eyes fluttered against the soft intrusion of light. Snuggling closer to him, and wrapping his arm tighter around her chest, his soft snore tickled the curve of her neck. His grey tee shirt covered her body like a blanket, and yet the heat from his naked chest pressing against her back warmed her more than the shirt.

The delicious aching of each muscle reminded her of how beautifully their bodies fit together. Losing herself momentarily to the memories of what had happened between them, Ferrian filled her head with swirling thoughts for their next encounter. She opened her body to him as they sank down to the ground, embraced in each other's heated embraces. Along with her body, she had finally opened up her heart to him, as though she had no other option.

The feeling of time waning rode her from the moment she had stormed out of the meeting, leaving her frustrations to linger in her wake. What was so pressing, time had her counting the minutes? Whatever was coming made her feel like today could well be her last. She had faced death so many times, and walked away ... or as of late, been carried away. Yet, the overwhelming sense of foreboding skated over her, unrelenting as she tried to push it away and continue to fill her mind with tiny reminders of the night's turn of events and how intensely intimate each moment had been. Revealing the truth to Remi, she never thought those words would ever spill from her lips. She had done the unthinkable and exposed her soul to him. It didn't matter to her how scared she was, or how much she wished the timing could've been better. She had finally admitted it to herself, but more importantly, to him. And if today was to be her last, then she'd die knowing she'd loved another for once in her wretched life.

Remi became her light in the darkness to guide her, and the warmth her body unknowingly craved each night she slept, curled up alone and afraid. Stroking his arm, she couldn't imagine not being with him like this. It was the first time she was unafraid of being herself. The first time she wanted to be seen and touched. So many first times danced her head and she feared for the last times to come. Dread seized her stomach in a cruel wanting for a life she wasn't sure she could have.

With a head filled with questions, and a heart full of love, she struggled to relax enough to rest her satiated body. She still didn't know why Remi had stopped breathing, stopped moving, as his eyes became vacant while they made love. Something niggled at her, something she was afraid to ask. She needed to know. But could she handle the answer, especially one she might not want to hear? It was too much already. Her head was on the verge of exploding.

Her lungs seized. There wasn't enough air to suffice neither her needs, nor enough space to for to breathe.

Wriggling free of his embrace, she carefully climbed to her feet, nearly falling on top of him in the process. Padding around searching for her clothes, she silently prayed her departure would go unnoticed. When she located her black jeans, she slipped them on and followed it up with her boots. Glancing down at Remi, who had barely shifted, she blew him a small kiss and walked away.

She had no idea where she was going, but she needed to leave. Once she had reached a reasonable distance from the shoreline, she kicked it into high gear, stretching out her legs and pumping her thighs in a flat out run. Like a deer running from a predator, she sprinted down the winding path around the lake. It didn't matter to her where she was running to, nor how far she'd go, because there was nowhere for her to truly run away to. She wasn't totally sure where she was, but it was safe to say, running down to the corner market for a hot coffee wasn't possible. Her heart was thundering as she pushed herself harder. Clearing the bend, the sun broke free from the horizon, momentarily blinding her long enough for her to run into a log. Her fall came with a hard hit to the bracken-ridden ground, skidding and scraping-up her arms and face.

"Are you all right? What hurts?" The panicked voice barely registered as she shook out her head, waiting out the visual dance of stars before her eyes.

"What? Oh yeah, I'm fine," she offered, blinking back against the bright golden light, the dark outline of a massive figure approached her, crouching down to his hunches. "Remi?" Wincing against his gentle caress to her cheek, the new bumps and bruises made their presence known. "Shit."

"What were you doing running out here by yourself? Are you trying to get yourself killed or something?" She sensed he was trying to keep his voice soft but his accusations still bit her.

"What? No. I-I needed." She fumbled for words, wondering how she was going to explain the way her mind was racing with impending dread when she didn't quite understand why? "I wanted to run." Sure, it sounded legit. Feeding herself a heaping scoop of bullshit, she pushed herself off the ground, wincing again as dirt and tiny pebbles sank into her tender flesh.

Trying to keep her face stoic, she braved a glance up, and saw he wasn't buying her pathetic excuse either. Smirking back at her, Remi offered a half-hearted laugh as he pulled a leaf from hair. "You wanted to go for a run, huh? Okay then. And where is it you wanted to run to?" There was no answer she could give that held any fiber of truth, until she saw her ace in hand.

The soft whoosh of water falling called to her, as she spied a waterfall off in the distance. Pointing her chin toward the rushing water, she waited for him to follow her gaze, and prayed he bought her story. "I was running to the waterfall. It's a secret obsession of mine. I love them. I heard the sound on my run, and was following it. When I saw it, I knew I had to get there." Puffing her chest out, once again, her bullshit lie sounded legit. What she didn't expect was, her lie held too much truth. She had loved waterfalls for as long as she could remember, yet she hadn't ever been to one.

"Do you wanna see it from the inside?"

"You can't see a waterfall from the inside, goof. The water rushes over the top." Pointing with her explanation, she pondered what he could have been thinking.

Reaching for her hand, Remi pulled her close, and smoothed back her tangled mess of hair. "That's where you're wrong." His wings flared out, expanding over six feet on both side, and all she could think was a gracious, *Holy shit!* Sure it wasn't eloquent, but it fit perfectly. In the few seconds her eyes grew wide, gawking at the sight of his white wings with silver tips fully expanded, Remi was lifting them into the air. His mighty wings flapped as gently and soundlessly as a summer's breeze when he carried them toward the waterfall.

"Amazing, isn't it?"

She wanted to answer him, opening her mouth to speak, but she was lost for words. Amazing was an understatement. When a meek, "Yes," finally slipped out, he squeezed her tighter.

"Wait a second," he offered.

Clenching him tighter, and closing her eyes to feel the wind brush against her skin, Ferrian wondered if this was Heaven. To her this was her perfect idea of it. Embraced by the man she loved, and flying free as a bird toward the rushing turquoise waters of something only nature could claim, swallowed her whole.

The wind caressed her face as Remi circled in flight. Opening her eyes, she was filled with a rich mixture of awe and excitement as he dipped them lower. "Um, you might want to close your eyes for this." His handsome smile widened in amusement as they skimmed through an opening between the rock wall and rushing water. The mixture of terror and exhilaration was short lived as he dived deeper into a hidden cove, before setting them down without so much as a thump.

The air was much cooler than it had been during the night. Moist, yet smelled of magnolias. Her breath caught glancing beyond the edge and saw things as they actually were. She was in fact standing inside of a waterfall. A fleck of a rainbow shimmered in the spray as she reached out to touch the translucent wonder.

"Careful!" he called out, catching her off-guard. "The ledge."

"Oh crap! Okay, yes, you're right. Long drops and I aren't the best combo." Slowly she stepped back, one eye focusing on the distance down to the pool of water and jagged rocks below.

Taking a few deep breaths, she inhaled the sweet, flowery scent as if she could lock this memory away for the future. The swooshing roar of water spilling over the ledge above them echoed around the rocky room, as slices of sunlight cut through small openings between the water and rocks.

She didn't hear him walk up to her, and jumped a little when he wrapped his arms around her. "Sorry, I didn't mean to startle you, m'aingeal." He pressed a kiss into her hair, and she leaned into his natural heat, soaking it in as the cool air prickled her exposed flesh.

"Have you ever seen anything so beautiful before?" she asked quietly, reveling in the astounding views. Even through the rushing water, it appeared as a wall of water covering a window. It was surprisingly clear as she gazed through it and visually explored the mountains and valleys laying beyond the lake.

Cupping her cheek, he gently coaxed her to eyes to meet his. "I can honestly say, in all my existence, I have never witnessed anything more beautiful than what I see before my eyes right now."

She didn't need a mirror to see the blush in her cheeks glowing fire engine red, even as she shied away from his gaze. Desperately, she tried to come up with some snarky retort, chiding him on the cheesiness of his compliment. Instead, she decided it was best to let him have this moment, and nuzzled her cheek against his chest.

He pulled away from her, dropping his arms. Had she done something wrong? Should she have said something, anything? His eyes fell, as did his smile, sinking her moment of joy when he turned away from her. "Remi, what is it?" Placing her hand on his chest, she found that Remi's heart was racing at an uneven pace. Thumping wildly against her palm. Alarm shot down her spine as she searched his eyes for the truth.

"I would never let you fall." Oh man, this wasn't going to be one of those unnerving talks leading into something wonderful conversations. The reluctance on his face shadowed her anxiety of what was to come. Nodding, words failed to find a way out. "Ferrian, I mean it. And if by some small chance you did fall, I'd be there to catch you. I promise you, regardless of what happens in the future," pausing, he sucked in a haggard breath, lifting her fingers to his lips, "I'll always be there."

Heat and sorrow filled her heart with his sincerity as his lightly kissed her fingers.

Smoothing her free hand over his heart, she reached for his, placing it on hers. "It's in here where we live. I know this now. And I will be here to catch you, if you fall as well." She didn't know if he believed her, but it was a promise she would keep. "It's in here, where you'll stay, Remi. Nothing could ever change the way I feel about you. You see me, not my scars, not my past, but who I am inside. You breathed life into this soul and made me believe love is a living, breathing thing, and I can have it. You've made me feel things about myself I never thought possible before, and surprised me to all hell when I found the feelings I feel for you are mutual." Closing her eyes, the hot sting of tears welling up made her wish for once she could hide them. "I-I trust you."

The weight of her words, *'I trust you'* caved his whole world in. She had never trusted another living soul, and here she was confessing her heart to him. It made what he had to say next feel like he was being stabbed a thousand times, by a thousand rusted blades and rolled in salt and broken glass all at once. He hated himself for what he was about to do, knowing it was going to either crush her, or drive her over the edge.

Feeling her heart beating against his palm, and her hand trembling from his in return, had been the richest experience since the day he took his first breath. Gradually she let go of his hand. Reaching up, he brushed back a long tendril of raven hair from her face. He didn't want to miss a single inch of her beautiful blush, or the small trail of droplets shimmering down from her stunning green eyes. He was going to miss this. This closeness. Her touch.

The quiet moments when the world around them disappeared, leaving them to slip into a reality where nothing bad ever happened. No one wanted them dead or sought out a soul for a higher calling. It was only Ferrian and himself, lost in paradise.

A long moment passed—as hearts beat a little faster and breaths jostled around in ragged ways—before he had to finally accept what needed to be done. His stomach twisted and his sac tightened, knowing this was going to hurt him almost as much as her. He waited a second longer, seeking the right words to say. The truth was, nothing he said or the way he said it, was going to make this sound right.

Her face quirked with a curious expression as if she understood what was coming. "What it is? What's wrong?" Had he been so easy to read all this time? Cupping her shoulders, he lowered his head, unable to meet her eyes. "Please, talk to me," she whispered, but her voice wavered on the verge of tears.

"I have to bring you back. It's time."

"What? Now?"

"Unfortunately, yes," was all he could bring himself to say.

"But there's nothing for me there. Please, Remi," she plead, and her eyes shimmered with hurt and tears. The more she said, the more he wanted to hold her close and lock them away where no one would find them. But it was true, it wasn't his decision. She was close to transitioning, and he hated having to leave her alone through this time, but it was what had to happen ... the way it had always been.

"Don't make me go back there. I don't belong there, I

belong with you." Her eyes glistened with fresh tears, and she angrily wiped them away. Betrayal fell with each droplet, landing on the person who provoked them. As suspected, the sting of a thousand rusted blades began stabbing him over and over again as he rolled in salt and broken glass. Enveloping her in his embrace, the tears he hid behind centuries of duty, breeched the walls of self-containment as he swallowed her hurt whole.

"Shh." Whispering, he wasn't sure if she'd listen or not, but he had to get it all out in the open. Well as much as he was allowed to. "I love you, my sweet, m'aingeal. It isn't about you standing up for me against Z. Frankly, I found it brilliant. However, you can't stay up here forever. There are things you're meant to do, a being you're meant to become, and those things won't happen if you stay here."

"So come with me," she begged. "Come stay with me. I don't want to lose you, lose all this." She wrapped her arms tighter around his neck, pinning him to her for life support.

"I can't. Please understand, this isn't my decision. I'll always be with you, even when I can't be. You won't lose me. I promise."

Rearing back, anger flared in her eyes. "Don't you dare make me promises! I don't give a damn for pretty promises wrapped up nicely to make me feel better about this. You're leaving me. Be honest with me for once. You don't want me ..." She let her words trail off, as her eyes fell from his, followed by more angry tears.

"No! God no! I'd keep you forever and a day from this point forward if I could. I swear to God and all things holy in creation and the universe." Cupping her face, he lifted her eyes to meet his. He needed to make her see what he said was coming straight from his heart and not his ass. "I love you and I will not lose you. I won't let you lose me. I am yours and you are mine." In a single moment, he knew, without a shred of doubt, each word he said to her was the absolute truth. And somehow, someway he was going to show her how much his promise sealed their fates. He crashed his lips over hers and promised her with a kiss, locking away any fears.

Ferrian fought against him as her fists beat his chest away, until the tip of his tongue licked against the seam of her wet, salty lips. His fingers sank deeply into her hair as she little by little melted against him. "I love you," he whispered over her lips, sealing another promise he'd keep for the rest of time.

CHAPTER
FIFTY-ONE

Pacing the basalt rim of the Underworld, sulfur and brimstone assaulted his nostrils as Focalor was left waiting for Gadreel, the Underworld's prime Watcher. He always hated these little info exchanging meetings. The sounds of Hell's fury and agonizing cries from souls paying penance for their life choices reverberated around him like a rock concert off-key tenfold.

Focalor prayed his presence went unnoticed by the resident demons, all whom had a greedy desire to tear a chunk out of his ass. After a century, he thought they'd have something better to do than plot to take him down. Morons. As far as Watchers go, Focalor thanked his lucky stars only high-born angels and demons could kill them. However, it didn't stop the remaining Daemons and Hellistics demons from trying to any time he ventured down to meet with Gadreel. Couldn't they have met at a local bar and talked over a pitcher of beer?

"What's the matter, angel ass-kisser? Afraid someone will figure out where you're hiding and throw you in the Desmoterion for punishment again?" The sardonic voice caught his attention, snaking past the symphony of screams below. "You do realize you deserve to rot in a cell for betraying Lucifer, don't you." It wasn't a question; Focalor knew where Gadreel's true loyalties lied.

"You know, as a Watcher who's not supposed to choose sides, it seems to me your choice has been clearly made. And I'm not in the mood for your games. So let's get this over with."

"What's the rush? Got a hot date waiting for you at the Blue Moon Bar or something? Yeah, I bet those boys are missing Mr. Perfect Hair right about now."

He ground his teeth together; it wasn't so much the insinuation bothering him, rather it was Gadreel's love of provoking him into a pissing contest each time they met. Glaring, Focalor stood across his opponent, ready to cold-cock the bastard to shut him up. "You done?"

"Why? Does your boyfriend have you on a short leash? I bet you're shackin' up with the tall ass, pretty prick, Ezekiel, aren't you?" Gadreel's fire-red goatee lifted into a snarling smirk. The shine of his pristine pearly-whites was a stark contrast to the tattoos decorating his face and arms.

Glancing down, the damned serpent inked across his shoulders, turned its arrow-shaped head toward him, like a living breathing snake. Winking at Focalor as an insidious smile spread wide across its black-lined lips. "Seems Eval doesn't like you much either."

Focalor remembered hearing the story when he had fallen. Gadreel loved telling anyone who would listen about his role in the fall of mankind, claiming he was the reason Eve bit into the apple. He was the serpent who coaxed the stupid, hungry-ass chick to bite, while filling her head with nonsense. *Good going, Eve.* Brushing off

Gadreel's bullshit, Focalor held his gaze, ready to get the show over with before the scent of death made his stomach roll again. "What's the word on Xaphan and Vepar?"

"Cut to the chase why don't you? All right then, still nothing on Xaphan. All I've heard is Lucifer is full-on pissed off with your pansy-ass, winged warriors kicking the shit out of Xaphan, and he's been in hiding ever since."

"What about Vepar, what's his deal?" Considering Gadreel with a suspicious eye, the tick in his jaw worked overtime as the Hellion Watcher decided what to say and what to omit. "Come out with it. I know you know some-thing."

Clucking his lips, Gadreel leaned forward, and the scent of his acidic odor made Focalor want to vomit right there on the spot. Swallowing back against the horrid smell, he balled his hands into tight fists and hoped this meeting wasn't going to end like the last one did. The last time he came down on business, Gadreel had a surprise waiting in the wings to jump out at him the second he turned to leave.

"He's alive. That's about all I know."

"Bullshit!"

"My, my … you don't believe me? Now why would I lie to you, my fellow Watcher?"

"Because you're an asshole. So where is the jack-ass?"

"Why should I say anything? I mean, all you're going to do is run back to your boys' club and spill the beans like a good little boy scout."

"Please tell me you have some brains left in there af-ter smoking that brimrag shit. Where is he, Gadreel?" He knew the Watcher loved to indulge in brimrag, the Underworld's version of heroin and ecstasy mixed with brimstone ash.

"Piss off. You now know as much as I do. No one's talking. But if I had to guess, I'd say the Darkling better not close her eyes for too long."

"What are you saying? Is Vepar is going to go after her again? By whose orders?"

"I didn't say shit, and you know what? You're frigging lucky I know what I know. So suck my dick, asshole. We're done."

"You know the rules. This isn't a game."

Gadreel's laughter ricocheted off the charred rock walls, as he stepped up in Focalor's face. Nose to nose. Balls, the bastard had some set of balls on him. His muscles were coiled tightly; the edge of tension was on the verge of snapping. "Isn't it? Isn't this all one big fucking chess match of souls? You better get shit straight in your head, boy. Time is running out, and you better decide pretty damn quick which team you should be playing for." The stench of Gadreel's breath lingered between them, as Focalor subtly shifted, readying for a fight. "Now piss off, I have shit to do." Gadreel turned toward the ledge and leapt off.

"Shit!" He knew it, had heard the whispers of Lucifer getting Vepar doing his dirty work again. Time was against him, and reaching Remi before the Angel brought his Darkling back down to Earth was now mission critical.

Scanning the area, the rock walled cave fell eerily silent as he awaited any potential threats to come at him. A minute passed ... nothing. Casting his portal, Focalor stepped inside, ready to head back to Angel Realm, when it hit him. The thud he had been waiting for. A hit so hard, he fell to the ground in a heavy heap of flailing limbs. As the world around him grew dark, he hoped the portal closed before whatever had knocked him off his feet had a chance to make a grab and go with his listless body. *Shit!*

CHAPTER FIFTY-TWO

"N o! Dear God, let me die, please!" Ferrian's screams were deafening, as her eyes popped open. "Dammit! Another friggin' nightmare. When will this end?" Her heart was thundering and her breath caught. She tried to forget the grisly images of a life ruined before it even had time to live. The same pair of black, soulless eyes had haunted her since she was sixteen years old. They had occupied the deepest crevasses of her subconscious, and penetrated her mind like a hellish Sherman tank, pushing fear into every cell of her aching body. Reminding her of the piteous existence she was condemned to endure. The cold sweat trickled down her brow in thick ropes of moisture, leaving her pillow soaked as she gripped it closer, trembling. Exhaling a heavy groan, she faced the sad reality … a good night's rest was a luxury she would never be afforded.

She rolled onto her back, and blinked back the intrusion of light cutting through thin slits in the heavy maroon curtains. Stretching out her arms brought on another round of *Holy Hells*, as she winced against the throbbing in her muscles. Rubbing the last of the nightmares from her weary eyes, nothing could ever take away the truth of who she was. Bathed in blood from birth, she was the mistake, and too many people had paid the ultimate price for with their lives.

With a heavy exhale, she closed her eyes, and tried to envision Remi. A mountain of thick muscle, golden skin, and sapphire blue irises, lying on the sand next to her. *"M'aingeal, I'll always be watching over you."* His voice was but a whisper in her head, though she could've sworn he whispered it in her ear. Jolting up, Ferrian spun around in hopes of seeing him sitting there with his devilishly impish grin smiling back at her. Nothing. It was another memory of him, as it had been since the night he left her standing on the pier, alone.

It wasn't only his voice stalking her. Remi stretched out in her mind when her dreams tried to fight off the memories. As she laid back down, her fingers brushed over the last place his kiss had touched. Tingles of his warmth still danced across her lips. The rich taste of his kiss, once intoxicating Ferrian with heated desire, now left the emptiness to swallow her whole. As quickly as the sensation came over her, it was gone again. The emptiness swelled in her chest, capturing her in its dark void she had grown comfortable with once again. She didn't like it, but it was her security blanket.

It had been two months since the last encounter, and each day grew more difficult to hang on to the scent of him. Ferrian strained to remember the feel of him cradling her in his thick arms. He had made each day tolerable and now he was gone. The sinking feeling consumed her all over again. He wasn't coming back, no matter how hard she begged and prayed for it.

A spark of anger flickered in her gut, as Ferrian glanced back down to the cellphone he had left for her. How many times had Ferrian texted him? Not once had he replied. Not even with *'Hey, I'm okay, hope you are, too.'* He had abandoned her. It was nothing new to her, except this time the bite of it was too much to bear. The darkest and most vulnerable parts of her begged him to return to her, pull her into his waiting arms, and promise her forever. But it wasn't going to happen, was it? He wasn't coming back, no matter how hard she pled and prayed. Remi wasn't going to return to her.

Her fists hit the mattress as she twisted and turned, trying to find a comfortable spot to lure her back to sleep. At least in her dreams, she could be with him. In her dreams, what they had had was real and she was whole once again. She hated missing him, and the ache in her chest grew more by the day since the night he'd said his good-byes. Slamming her eyes shut, she demanded her body to relax. Images of him splashed across her mind until one memory finally sank its roots in.

The cool wind coming off of Lake Michigan bit into her as though it was the middle of winter. Her shoulders ached and her body grew sluggish with exhaustion while she clung to him. He held her tightly, as though letting go wasn't an option. His eyes penetrated hers with compassion, and he traced the jagged scar down her brow with this finger. The simple act sent fire coursing through her veins. It had been the first time Ferrian had allowed anyone to touch her scars so intimately. Steely herself from cringing, her eyes flooded with tears as this one gesture broke down the nightmares she wanted to leave behind.

She had finally freed her heart to him, opening it completely as though she had released the floodgates, and pure love crashed down on her like the rushing waterfall they had hidden behind. Her heart sank deeper with each passing moment. She knew he was leaving her behind, abandoning her because he had to. Such bullshit. *"I will always be with you. I will always be watching you, even if you can't see me." His promise filled her with hope even when she didn't want to believe him. "There's more to my feelings than should be, so now I must leave." Gently he caressed her trembling lips, holding her close as her silent sobs shuddered through her body. Remi's thick arms embraced her tightly. She willingly soaked up every bit of warmth, allowing it to seep down into her bones. "I will miss you until I see you again," he murmured against her ear, his warm breath sending shivers over her scalp and down her spine.*

"Why must you go?" There was no telling which shook more, her voice or her heart as she locked her watery gaze onto his. The warm pools of his soul welcomed her with one last gentle kiss and she prayed to drown in his eyes and never come back up.

"Because I can't stay, I've been here for too long as is. I'm sorry, m'aingeal." Tilting her head to the side, she stared at him. She had heard him call her the pet name before, but for some reason it registered in the back of her mind, painfully shocking her memory from the deepest recesses possible. She pulled back, questioning him with her eyes.

"I swear, I've heard someone else call me the same thing." Fingering away her crystal traitors, her eyes could barely meet his. "What does it mean?"

"I hope to tell you someday." Pressing a soft kiss to her wet lips, Remi embraced her closely, letting his love radiate through her. It hadn't dawned on her how much she sensed about him until the love he had given her broke down the tower walls with all the grace of a dozen wrecking balls. "Do you feel my heart? It beats for you and only you." He smiled innocently at her, and lifted her chin to meet his stare. "Always." His eyes danced upon her soft features once more, brushing a final kiss on her lips before he turned away and left her standing on the pier.

The ache in her heart splintered with small fissures. By the time her hand reached for him, there was nothing left to touch. He was gone. Launching after him, she realized she couldn't imagine her life without him. He had come to mean too much to her. The pounding of her feet against the concrete echoed off the water, yet she couldn't catch up to him. Her heart thundered in her ears as hot, salty tears fell from her eyes but it was useless. His body dissolved into the thick fog, leaving her alone in the waning velvety cover of night. "No!" she cried out, as she dropped to her knees.

Jerking awake once again, the deep seated aching his absence caused made her dream feel more like a nightmare. Sadness consumed her, swallowing her more as each day. Some days, she fought with herself, as the anger of his abandonment crept inside and clawed at his memory. There had been so many times since the night at the pier Ferrian had sensed his presence. She smelled his rich, dark scent lingering around her. And thought she was imagining his gentle caress on her cheek as she slowly roused from sleep. Her emotions battled it out in the silence, like a tennis match between love and hope and anger filled with despair. Her mind had returned to the battlefield she had walked before, only this time she was armed with knowing. And she wasn't sure it was a good thing. Knowing what she had when Remi was around. Knowing the coldness his absence brought.

She rubbed away the last of sleep from her eyes, as the last remnants of sunlight sliced through the curtains. Pushing herself off the bed had become an agonizing chore. Letting her anger fuel her ambition, Ferrian climbed to her feet. Fire licked in her belly even as her shoulder blades screamed they were on the verge of snapping into a million pieces. Biting back the round of curses brimming on her lips, Ferrian reached for her black hoodie. The scent of him still lingered on it as if his smell was stitched into it.

Nothing seemed real, except she was becoming more aware of the world around her, as life resumed almost back to normal. Seeing into the souls of anyone who passed by her had become a natural habit. With each new shadow taking on a demonic form, and the scent of sulfur wafting from skin when she passed by a particular human, she wasn't sure what was happening to her. But one thing was for sure, nothing was what it seemed to be. Even the orange tabby cat had changed. Growing as big as a lynx, he followed her home from work and camped outside of her door.

After a few days, she decided it was time to give him a home. Something only weeks earlier she would've shied away from. His glowing yellow eyes watched her intently as she stumbled around the room getting dressed for work. Staring down at the cat, the connection they had formed became unmistakable. He was meant to be with her. Meowing as loud as possible to get her attention, she swiveled to see him stretched out on her favorite chair. Stepping over to him, she leaned down, and scratched his chin. Whipping his tail side to side, she received an approving purr.

"What's up, Beast? Hungry?" Licking his lips, he jumped up to his paws, and hopped off the chair. "Guess so. Come on, big guy. I think there's a can of chicken and gravy in the cabinet. Let's get you fed before I take off for work." His purr grew louder with each step, as Beast kept pace with her, nearly prancing in excitement. "You are a strange one." She wasn't sure she knew what it was, but each time she stared into his eyes, she swore he had been placed in her life to watch over her. His kind eyes seemed to follow her wherever she went, and guarded over her when she was asleep.

Licking his paw to wash his face, Beast had found his seat on the corner chair and waited patiently for his plate. "You know, not for nothing, but it's kinda nice having you around." Glancing back, she laughed as he gave her the 'gimme-a-break' look. "Don't get a big head about it, furface." Some small part of her heart had opened to Beast, feeling him next to her as she fell asleep gave her some comfort. It was there, in his yellow eyes, his solemn promise to stay by her side. And for some reason, aside from the free meals and warm bed, she believed him.

CHAPTER FIFTY-THREE

"You can't keep doing this to yourself, or her. It's not fair to either one of you," Kakabel's sing-song voice rushed out, as she stepped in front of Remi, cutting off his view of Ferrian walking down to the same pier he had left her at.

In the two months since he'd left her, he watched her from afar as she resumed her normal day-to-day routine. Yet it hadn't resumed normally, had it? The nightmares returned with vengeance and he couldn't stay away. She cried out in pained screams, thrashing about, and he was helpless to stop them. It was another stab to the heart. He had promised to protect her, even from herself, but it was exactly what he couldn't do. With orders hanging over his head, there was only so far he could push it before the Council would call him back and make him explain what he was doing.

The only blessing he could be thankful for was the fact no one had tried to kill her since her return. Remi told himself it was the reason he still hung around, watching after her. Deep in his gut, he knew it was a bullshit excuse. He was her guardian, sent to watch over her and keep the demons at bay until she transcended, sure. Except the demons attacking her now were of the mental type, residing solely in her mind.

Each day it grew harder watching her walk alone, back to hiding from the world behind her black hoodie as the loneliness covered her like a second skin. He listened to her cries at night as she fell into a restless sleep. He had hoped the familiar he had sent to stay with her would fill some part of the void his leaving had caused. It hadn't. He realized it too late; forcing himself to watch the downward spiral she descended the moment he walked away from her. Every day she fell farther away from him.

Shaking off Bels' hand from his shoulder, he cringed. Even an innocent touch by any other than Ferrian was unwanted. The longer Ferrian stayed on Earth and away from him, the harder it was to think of anything but her. He should have been trying to track down Xaphan and Vepar, but he couldn't leave her. Even if she had no idea he was there, he wasn't willing to walk away now.

"Hey. Bro, come on now. You can't change what's going to happen. Stalking her like some sort of pervert isn't doing you any good. Besides, I heard Focalor went down underground to— Well, I guess it doesn't matter to you, since you obviously don't give a two-craps about anything else right now."

He didn't miss the thickly laced sarcasm Bels had unleashed on him. A rarity for sure, and maybe even a little deserved. However his mood wasn't up for the verbal chess match. "Get to the point, Bels. Not in the mood for playing games."

The audible humph as she crossed her arms tightly over her chest, almost made him want to laugh. Almost.

He knew damn well he should care about what news she needed to relay, but his head wasn't in the game. "So, are you going to tell me, or stand there like a stubborn child who didn't get a pony for Christmas?"

Screwing up her face, Bels belted out a tinkling laugh, nodding her surrender. "Yeah. Word is Focalor went to meet with Gadreel to get some information on your demon."

It was the best damned news he had heard in weeks. Now he needed to find the bastard before Ferrian ended up as his plaything to torture again. The thought of Xaphan getting anywhere near her again twisted the sickening feeling in his gut into a pretzel. Xaphan wasn't capable of staying away for long, and he'd make his presence known in time for Ferrian to turn. "Let's hope that the Watcher brings back some tangible information. Xaphan's been on the run for too long, dammit!" Anger rolled through him for not ripping the demon to shreds before he carried Ferrian out of the hellhole cell. "I should've killed him for what he did to her."

"Don't beat yourself up about it. You did the right thing. You got her out of there. She's alive and breathing because of your hard-headedness to find her." She offered a small smile, glancing over her shoulder to follow his point of interest. "I know you love her."

"So? What's it to you?"

"Don't bite my head off, all right? Sheesh. I'm saying, it's written all over your face. But I'm curious about one thing though."

Her question piqued his curiosity. Then again, with Bels, her question could be anything from what was his favorite color to what is the chemical make-up of Elmer's

Glue. "Okay, what do you want to ask me then?"

"What does it feel like to be in love with someone?"

Taken back, it was the one question he wasn't prepared for. He considered her for a few moments, thinking of the best way to explain how Ferrian made him feel. "The best answer I can give you is, it's ... well, it's phenomenal. She means more to me than my own life, and I'd willingly give mine for hers. Without question." How could he deny it? The longer he was forced to keep his distance, the stronger his need to be with her grew.

"Wow! Jesus, talk about intense." Letting out a relieved breath, Bels swiveled around, shoulder to shoulder with him. "I can see it in your eyes, and feel it radiating off you. I know it doesn't mean much, but I'm glad someone has captured your heart. I wish circum—"

"Don't say it. Don't you dare say it." What he didn't need was another reminder of the cock-sucking rules. Blowing out a heavy sigh, he came to terms that she was trying to show some empathy for his plight. "And thank you. Coming from you, it means a lot to me."

His eyes zeroed on her Ferrian, observing her like a hawk. Something was off ... well, more than usual. Her walk was more hunched over than usual, and her eyes were rimming with pain. His instinct to run after her, scoop her up in his arms, and bring her back to his suite overwhelmed him with longing.

"Is she hurt?" Kakabel's voice fell to a whisper. She was seeing exactly what he was.

"Yeah, I think she's in pain." On so many levels was she in agony. Guilt saturated every fiber and molecule in his body. Why did it have to be her? Why did he have to fall in love with her? He wanted to regret the choices his heart made, but he couldn't.

"You want to go to her, don't you?"

Tilting his head, he shot her a sarcastic glare, saying what he wasn't about to. Hell yes he wanted to go to her! It took every ounce of his willpower to remain standing where he was. Shifting his eyes back to Ferrian, as she waited for the number nine bus to show up, his heart ached. Missing her was the understatement of the year. "I miss you, m'aingeal," he whispered under his breath.

"What did you say?" He could see Bels trying to figure it out, as a suspicious glare eyed him. It didn't matter; it wasn't for her to hear. Shrugging his shoulders, he gazed on, watching as Ferrian hugged into herself, lifting her eyes in his direction. His heart skipped a beat, wondering if she knew he was there, hidden on the corner of an old Brownstone across the street from her? The words "I miss you so much" echoed in his ears as a soft wind carried her message to him.

It grew dangerously difficult to stay away. She needed him. Barely feeling whole himself anymore, he rubbed away the aching in his chest. He had given his heart exclusively to her and to her alone, and not being with her was the cruelest torment he could think of. Flashes of her, curled up against him, staring down into her eyes as she laughed at one of his stupid jokes stung him with a tidal wave of yearning. Nothing was going to make their time apart any easier. He was driving himself to madness, becoming her personal stalker when he had important things to attend to. Like tracking down a couple of demons and destroying them. He didn't care about any of it, not anymore.

Remi heard a soft vibrating sound coming from Kakabel's pocket, soon followed by his own cell. "Perfect timing," he grumbled, not bothering to read the text. He was positive Bels would fill him in if it was important.

"Shit, we gotta go, bro. She'll be fine, right?" Offering him half a smile, he read the uncertainty in her face. "I mean, she's going to work, what could possibly happen?"

Chuffing out a cynical laugh, he spun those words around a few times before he could bring himself to answer. "Bels, she has the entire team of the Underworld douche bags after her. What do you think?"

"Right. Sorry, I'm a dumbass. Come on, we better get topside before Am decides to hand us our asses on a silver platter."

Folding his arms tightly over his chest, he kept on eye on Ferrian, as the screeching of airbrakes brought the metal beast to a halt. "So what's got her panties in a bunch now? Is Roc being a bigger asshat than normal?"

"No. I'll explain on the way." Unfurling her silver wings, Kakabel lifted skyward quickly. It didn't surprise him when Bels refused to answer him. He held tight, remaining where he was, while he waited for his angel to climb onto the city bus.

He observed her attentively as she stumbled down the aisle, wincing as she slid into one of the hard plastic seats. She was definitely off. He waited for her to slip her ear buds in as per her usual ritual. Nothing. Her body twisted as though she was trying to get comfortable, leaning over the seat in front of her. Her pained expression was rife with agony. He couldn't stand keeping his distance, but it bothered him more knowing he couldn't take her pain away.

The bus jerked forward; Ferrian's brows knitted

tighter and she curled into herself. He needed to get closer, find out what was going on. However, thanks to Am's timing, his plan was interrupted with another text buzzing through. "What now!" Ripping the small electronic device from his jeans pocket, he hoped it was indestructible, because he was about to lose it under his boot heel.

Glancing down, all he saw was the emergency code flashing across the screen. "Oh shit." As much as he wanted to be pissed off, he also knew Am wouldn't pull the old 9-1-1 trick without cause either. Checking the time, he saw that he had nine Earth hours to get back down before Ferrian left to return home from work. A quick trip to find out what was so important wasn't a choice anymore. Blowing it off would mean his wings, and if he had any hope of helping Ferrian through her transition, he needed the tools of his trade. He had seen many Darklings turn, but none could compare to her. Her gifts ranked her among the high-born angels, yet she was a hybrid. Maybe it was time to check deeper into her biological parents.

Spreading his wings wide, he bound into the evening sky. With his plan set, he hoped he had enough time to figure things out. But first, he had to deal with the angel emergency.

CHAPTER
FIFTY-FOUR

Each night during her lunch breaks, Ferrian found herself searching for something she didn't quite understand while she walked to the end of the boat-loading docks, where tankers full of imports came for vendors. Staring out across the dark waters of the bay, she found solace in the last place she expected … her mind. As much as she detested it, it also offered her a place run to.

The nights grew colder by the hour, as Ferrian waited for some small sign he would just happen to show up randomly as he did before. Praying desperately to see him, to talk to him again, she was devastated discovering he had been nothing more than a figment of her imagination. Ferrian's hunter-green eyes searched the tiny breaks in the water for answers she knew would never truly come. *Damn it! Why couldn't you have stayed with me?* She folded her arms over her chest to ward off the blast of cold air; it wasn't only the winter winds freezing her to the bone. The sting of time, and lack thereof, crept up in her mind.

"I wish I could've, m'aingeal. I miss you." His dark voice danced in her ears, and Ferrian begged her sanity to

tell her he was standing behind her with his strong hands on her waist, drawing her to him instead of her imagination playing tricks on her again.

Each time it grew harder to walk back into the loading docks. The noise of the machines drowned out normal words, but Ferrian's ears heard every single syllable as it spilled directly from his lips. *Stop doing this to yourself*! If he had cared about Ferrian, or missed her, then why did he leave in the first place? The truth was, Ferrian loved her solitude and she didn't want anyone near her, ever. Except for him. Tonight the feelings gnawed at her like hungry rats seeking a long overdue meal. "Shit." Kicking off the cement wall, she walked back to the docks. What good was it doing her to dwell on the how-comes and whys? It was pointless.

Ferrian needed to forget him, needed to stop letting herself drift back to the memories of his strong hands holding hers softly to warm them. The way he saw into Ferrian's soul without flinching at the ugliness surrounding her like a black aura, had set something in motion. And she wasn't overly convinced it could be stopped. Nevertheless, he was gone, and letting go was proving more difficult than she realized.

A wave of unbearable pain dropped her to her knees on the cold concrete. Ferrian wrapped her arms around her waist, trying to keep her body from blowing apart. Her head swam in visions of death and blood as her stomach pitched wildly. "Reee-mi," she strained to cry out, falling over.

Pulling the oversized ivory marble doors open, the din of voices spilling out from the Grand library echoed into the foyer. Stepping over the golden inlaid compass, he waited for Cassiel to come down the hall to meet him. If there was one angel who could help him track down information, Cassiel was the guy.

"Hey, man, I got your text, what's up?" His sandy blond hair shimmered under the chandelier lighting, leaving Remi to half wonder what styling products the guy was using.

"First, I need you to keep this between us. Got it?" Pinning Cass with a serious glare, the subtle nod said all he needed it to. The guy was straight decent, and he thanked the Heavens his trust wasn't misplaced with his brethren. "I need to find out about Ferrian's birth parents. I know her birth mother was a mortal, but I don't believe her father was."

"Wait, didn't you say her father went mad and tried to kill her when she was a baby? Wouldn't that make him, oh I don't know, human?"

"Here's the thing, I don't think the piece of shit was her real father." The memory of the day he'd first held Ferrian, covered in her mother's blood, burned behind his eyes, as the movie reel in his mind replayed it with graphically precise accuracy. "I think her real father was one of us, or at least, used to be."

"What makes you think he was?" He watched as Cassiel tried to process what he was saying. Sure, he knew it was hard to believe. Then again, all Darklings had bloodlines of angels. Most were highly diluted down with human bloodlines over the centuries.

When Darklings first showed up on the Angelic map, they were revered as the human embodiment of angels. Considered hybrids, they had capabilities to do extraordinary things. As time marched on, angels were forbidden from mating with humans for fear their offspring Darklings would start a war and take over. He wasn't sure what to think where Ferrian was concerned, but it was clear to him, she was far from the typical Darkling.

"I'm not sure. Something's different about her, I can't explain it. Can you do this for me, please?"

"Sure. You got it. Give me an hour, I'll see what I can find out. Meantime, you need to get in there. Shit's about to hit the fan and it concerns you and your Darkling."

Blowing out a ripe curse, he shook his head. It wasn't surprising he had become the topic of conversation. "How bad is it?"

"Let's say, things are up shit's creek right about now without a paddle. Focalor has gone missing, and we suspect Gadreel's behind it, but we don't have any hard proof. He claims Focalor never showed up to the meet."

"What a crock of shit. Focalor sent me a text earlier saying he was there. Said as soon as he had any information on Xaphan or Vepar, he'd hit me up. Obviously it didn't happen. I don't know the guy too well, but I don't think he'd lie about going there."

"He wouldn't. There's no doubt in my mind he went. The question is, where is he now? But right now you need to get in there. Let me work on your request and I'll meet you in the kitchen in an hour."

"Yup, got it. See you in an hour. Text me if you find out anything sooner. I need to know what the deal is."

Cassiel nodded, knocking knuckles with Remi before heading off to his private office.

Turning back to the rising voices, he sucked in a deep breath; he didn't exactly want to be the focal point of the room upon entering. His gut twisted, searing as though he was on high alert. A deep sense of urgency rattled him to the bone. With his nerves vibrating, matching his fleeting thoughts, finding out what was doing and getting the hell back to Earth was mission critical.

Some days, he wished the heavy claps of his shit-kickers hitting the delicately designed floors would break into the silence and shatter it. Pushing the doors wide open, he saw Ezekiel pacing, pinching the bridge of his nose as Amitiel carried on. Hoping his entrance would go unnoticed; he slipped into the leather wingback and waited out the shitstorm tirade.

Tensions were running high, and even Charo, the resident peacekeeper appeared agitated. What the hell had he walked in on? Bels glanced over to him, shaking her head with worry dancing in her silver eyes.

"If we can't find Xaphan before she turns, we're completely screwed! Let me repeat this one more time. We. Are. Screwed!"

Snapping his head up, Am's ranting ceased as soon as he jolted out of his seat. "What are you saying? Do we know where he is? Tell me, dammit. I'll cut down the bastard right now!" His body coiled tightly, ready to snap bones and tear apart limbs.

"No," Am screamed skyward, raising her fists as though she was going to beat the piss out of some invisible assailant. "Can't find Vepar either."

"We've got word from a Daemon we caught yesterday, you'll want to hear. Xaphan and Vepar are gearing up to go after your Darkling. But we haven't a clue when, or if what the shitbag said was true."

"But we must treat it as though it is, Z. And for chrissake, with the rigging Roc put on him, the bastard's lucky he's still alive."

Roc's booming laugh broke the shouting as he leveled Remi with a smirk, waggling his pierced brows. "Or really unlucky, depending on how you look at it." The gleam in his Mohawk-headed brother's eyes read like a book of warfare. The Daemon wouldn't make it out of the cillé alive.

"So what do you want me to do then? Bring her back up here?" His heart fluttered at the idea, as he secretly prayed for the chance to get his way. The grimace on Amitiel's face read otherwise.

"No. It was a mistake in the first place. We'll send out a few Fallens to see what they can find out. Try and track down those bastards. Listen, Remi, I know you've been following her." Raising her hand, she cut off his argument before he even had a chance to utter one syllable, but he wasn't ready to give up his fight. "You know you have to maintain distance. But, yeah, stay close. If Xaphan has a beat on her, then it's safe to say he'll take her down the first chance he gets."

The knot in his gut loosened, but only by a fraction, as the rolling feeling of sickness slowly seeped in. "Thank you. I'll head back down in a couple of minutes then." He made a move to walk out; the last place he wanted to be was in eyeshot of Am, given she was in her volcano mood.

"Wait!" she yelled sharply. "You are not to interfere whatsoever … unless Xaphan shows up. Then call out to Charo. He'll alert us, and we'll come and get him. Understand? You are not to take him down by yourself."

"Are you serious? Do you think I was born yesterday? The scrawny dickhead doesn't stand a chance."

"I'm not arguing this with you, dammit! Do as I say.

If Xaphan is close to the Darkling, then there's a good chance Vepar isn't too far away." The audible grind of her teeth as she ground out Vepar's name grated like nails on a chalkboard in his ears. The seething hatred she had for him echoed in the shadows in her eyes.

Nodding to her, he reached down for his cell, pulling it free to see another text from Ferrian come through. "Got it. We done?"

"Yeah, get out of here before I send Roc down there to keep an eye on your Darkling."

He didn't waste any time lingering. Making his way down the hall and heading to the kitchen, he hoped the Cassiel had some information waiting for him. Lifting his cell to eye level, his heart thumped wildly as he read it.

"Hey I know you're not going to answer this one either. I need to know why, Remi. Why did you walk away? What did I do wrong? I should've known, I wasn't good enough for someone like you. Was it all some sick game to you? Or was it all a dream and I'm left wondering if this damn cell even works. Maybe I've completely lost my mind and this reality isn't real. I loved you, not like it matters to you, but it matters to me. How could you walk away so easily? Please, let me know you're okay. I think I'd be able to move on if I knew you were okay. Please, text me back, okay? I don't know how much more I can take. I don't know what hurts more, my heart or my body. Let me know if you're alive."

She sent a text each night, knowing she wouldn't get a response. Most nights his heart cracked a little more reading the sadness laced in her words. Then there were the nights when anger pricked her words as she harshly accused him of abandoning her.

So many times he had wanted to reach out to her, reassure her it wasn't the case. He was with her every second of the day, but he couldn't communicate with her. There was no mistaking the downward spiral she was in. The guilt was twisting the knife deeper in his heart for aiding in it. He read and reread her texts until his eyes wanted to bleed. He slid his thumb over the keyboard, ready to text her back, sensing her pain as sharply as his own.

"Hey." Cassiel's voice broke his concentration. Lifting his eyes to meet his brethren's, he clicked the screen off and slipped the small device back into his pocket.

"Yeah, what did you find out?" Clapping Cassiel on the back, they strode toward the kitchen. His stomach rumbled in relief of their destination as he silently cursed his need to eat.

"Not sure. I mean, there's something, but I'm not exactly sure what it means."

"Um, you've lost me, bro. Did you find out anything useful or not?"

"Let's put it this way, I found her birth records, but the only identifier I found in relation to whom her biological father is, was a small symbol. However, I can't seem to place it. I've run it in the database, and it does belong to the Angelic hierarchy."

"Wait ... I've seen that before. On Ferrian. I thought it was some wonky birthmark."

"Interesting. I wonder—"

"I don't understand. Is she one of us or not? Do you think her father is a Fallen? I mean, those guys are known for screwing any human."

"Again, I'm not sure. Upon further inspection, the symbol appears pretty ancient. If I didn't know better, I'd almost say it's been around since the time of Lucifer. All it states is her biological father is of angel bloodlines. What little I could find suggests her blood is the purest amongst Darklings, since the time of the first Darklings many millennia ago. However, if she bares a mark similar to this symbol, I think it's worth investigating deeper."

"So what you're saying is she's a *pure hybrid* then? Half angel, half human—not the watered down version?"

"If I were to listen to my gut—"

The soft buzzing in his pocket alerted Remi to another incoming text. Slipping it free again, he glanced down quickly to see another text from Ferrian. Sensing the urgency, he held up his hand to stop Cassiel for a moment as he read the text.

"I feel like I'm dying. The pain ... I can't take it anymore."

The hair on the back of his neck pitched straight up as a chill ran down his spine. "Oh shit."

"What is it? What's going on? Remi. Remi, are you okay?"

CHAPTER
FIFTY-FIVE

Staring down at her cellphone, her hand trembled so hard she had to hold it close to her body to steady it enough to read the time. *Breathe, Ferrian, breathe dammit. Fuck me, let me die!* It was close to midnight, and she wanted to laugh at the silly idea she was only minutes away from her twenty-fifth birthday. Pain laced throughout her body as she struggled to walk to the head office. She rolled her shoulders in hopes of finding some relief but it was useless. The agony pulsed with the gentleness of an earthquake in San Francisco. Sweat beads trickled down her brow, stinging her eyes as it mixed with the salty bite of tears ready to break.

What the hell was happening to her? Rage pooled in her belly as she clung to the wall for support. The more the agony seared through her, the more she wanted to rip apart anyone who crossed her path. The screams of those she had seen—when she had taken over their bodies—hit her like a wrecking ball all over again. Her anger turned into an inferno of fury, hating what she had been put through. Why her? Why did she have to be the one who took all their pain? Weren't they strong enough to handle their own misery? None if it mattered. Not the innocents she had helped as she stepped into their bodies to absorb all their pain to keep them from misery. It was all too much.

The more the thoughts spun around in her head, the more the clawing desire to destroy every person who had ever wronged her swelled in her gut. She screamed out, falling to her hands and knees on the concrete floor. It wasn't a surprise when no one came to help her. Hell, she barely knew any of her co-workers names, and doubted her screams could be heard over the sounds of the heavy machinery thundering to life. Slowly she managed to climb back up to her feet, as the sweat broke completely free down the back of her neck.

Her head was pounding and the overwhelming sensation of suffocation consumed her. *'Run, Ferrian, run!'* was the last thing she heard in her head before she let the electrical charge of energy start to engulf her. "Shit!" She knew what was coming, the familiar tingle of energy balling up in her gut. She needed to get away, and fast. Sucking in a deep breath, she pushed past the main doors and out into hallway. Her vision grew blurry, the harder her head throbbed, and left her struggling to find the main exit. Stumbling, she tried to run, but the pain had taken over. She grew more furious by the second, and pushed herself to the point of wanting to vomit. Using the bank of lockers for support, she followed the beaten to shit orange doors to lead her down the long corridor.

Pushing open the heavy metal door, the crisp October air cooled her heated skin the farther out she walked. Her mind raced, trying to out think the pain, while trying to quell the building energy within her body. Wrapping her arms tightly around herself, each quivering muscle sapped all sense of hope for relief away as she stumbled her way to the bus stop. She didn't care if she got sacked for leaving her shift. As the pain sliced through her head, the fury seared like liquid fire through her veins, burning her from the inside out. It was hard to breathe, as she labored on, sawing oxygen in and out of her lungs.

The longer she was vertical, the more she feared she might drop dead in the middle of the street. Refusing to sit on the empty bench, anxiety impaled her. She wouldn't be able to climb to her feet and manage getting on the city bus if she sank down onto the iron seat. Deciding to lean against the metal beam of the streetlight, she pulled free her cell. She wasn't sure why she needed to send him the message. Remi hadn't shown her any kind of response since he left her. Right now, she didn't care what his reasons were. She only hoped he'd get it before it was too late.

The device shook in her hand as she struggled to send out one last text. **'I feel like I'm dying. The pain ... I can't take it anymore'** was all she could manage before she crushed the cell in her hand from the pain slicing down her body again. The waves were growing stronger by the minute, as was the ball of energy sitting in her gut. The burning orb was waiting to explode from her body and destroy whatever was in its path.

The city bus pulled up a few minutes later, screeching its airbrakes to a halt. She grabbed onto the railing to pull her pain-crippled body on board as more sweat broke from her brow. "Hey, hey, buddy, you all right?" The bus driver's voice was drowned out by the voices riddling through her head. She waved him off and punched her bus ticket, letting it fall to the floor as she climbed into the nearest seat.

"You don't look so's good." What was he, some kind of Good Samaritan or something? Leaning her head against the cool glass window, a small sense of relief washed over the aching as she rested her head. Closing her eyes, she tried to focus on her breathing and calming the orb, which was growing bigger by the minute. Screams echoed in her ears as another wave of torturous agony shot down her body. She had to be dying, no human alive should be able to feel this much pain. Curling into herself, Ferrian hoped she'd make it home to die instead of keeling over on the city bus. She could picture what the police report would say. "*Local ghost dies of unknown causes on a city bus.*"

Counting the bus stops, she sucked in another deep breath. Three down. She was two stops away from home and the need to rip apart the driver for driving so slowly crept up as she envisioned the perfect way to snap his head off. The bus sputtered as it slowed to the next stop. The lights flickered, and even through her closed lids, the harsh fluorescent lighting stung her eyes.

"Not again! Base, this is bus four-o-three. Send out the mechanic. We ain't going no-wheres." His voice barely registered as she brought her head up. The radio static reminded her of nails on a chalkboard, scratching her nerves as cringed from the sound. It wasn't until her eyes caught the driver's in the oversized mirror above his head when panic set in. His eyes shone as black as polished coals, and his lips peeled back in a twisted smile, revealing a set of pointed teeth.

Shaking the images from her eyes, disbelief seized her like a deer caught in the headlights of an oncoming truck. *This isn't real, it can't be.* The longer she stared at the image in the overhead mirror, the more she cringed as his face morphed into evil. A charge of energy rocked through her and she shot out of her seat. Undiluted rage pulsated through her coiled muscles as she gripped the seat backs to keep from doing the unthinkable. This was it, she was losing her damned mind. Slowly stepping down the aisle, the putrid odor of sulfur ranked the air. His eyes followed her movements, stalking her from the driver's seat. She was the only passenger left on the metal beast, and with her shitty luck, she wasn't taking any more chances. Palming her pocketknife, she shoved off the pain as she considered her odds for getting past her newest threat.

"Don't worry, pal, I called for help. You should take a seat. Might be a while." A hint of something she couldn't mistake for anything other than malice riddled each word the driver spoke. Glancing down at his radio, her eyes flared when she saw the mic cable had been ripped out of the panel and was dangling down to the ground.

His eyes followed hers, as a sardonic laugh split the air. "Bitch, take your seat, I said." He sneered, his nostrils flaring. He jumped out of his seat to lunge for her, disdain dripping from him like a sheet of pouring rain.

Whipping out her pocketknife, she kicked the driver square in the nuts, instantly dropping him to his knees, cupping his jewels. His black eyes welled with tears, as his face strained with pain. The fueling rage shook her entire body. Planting her feet firmly, she hauled back and released a punch straight to his face with knife in hand. Slicing his cheek wide open in the process, as dark blood wept from the wound.

Trying to catch her breath as it sawed in and out

wasn't the least of her concerns. The sweet intoxication of what she had caused and the inexplicable desire do more damage, devoured her with want. The seductive power to control someone else's destiny sizzled down her spine, ignited something deep within the recesses of her mind. It didn't all together scare the living shit out of her as it continued to hum throughout her body. It was quite the opposite. She was enjoying the feel of causing pain; relishing the sensation of hurting others as her chance for retribution. Landing one final kick straight to the male's brainpan, she laughed at the new senses vibrating from her body. Stepping over the male's body, she threw open the bus's door and took off outside, feeling taller, stronger, and deadlier. Until the crushing weight of pain overcame her once again, sinking her to her knees on the cold, cracked concrete.

"No!" she snarled. Her body shook uncontrollably. How could this be happening? One minute the pain was swallowing her whole, then she's kicking ass only to twist back into a trembling mass of flesh. The agony intensified with each movement as she forced herself to her feet. Singing to life with renewed vengeance, her misery was a reminder that life comes at a cost.

Every little sound and each stinging bright light of streetlamps she passed on the long walk back to her apartment throbbed throughout her body. Robbing her of any hope for relief. The orb growing inside of her burned hotter the longer she held it within. Panic skating over her, she searched for somewhere to launch it. Somewhere safe where no one would see her.

The sound of shrieking cut through the night air, catching her immediate attention. She whipped her head around at the screeching noise, which was without a doubt the sound of terror. Stalking toward the wounded cries, she couldn't control what her body was demanding. The source was coming from down a dimly light alleyway. Following the current of energy vibrating through her body—like a magnet dragging her to the cause—she closed her eyes, and stretched out her mind as everything quivered around her and through her. The energy pulsed through her veins and down every nerve. The dim recognition of the crippling she had experienced moments earlier quickly disappeared, as she stormed toward the screaming female. With her head dropped low, and her hood covering her face, she gazed into the darkness, to find three males pinning a young, blonde-haired woman against the dank, grimy wall of yet another decaying building in Chicago's dying district.

Mascara tears streaked her face, as blood trickled down her brow, nose, and lips. She was held against the wall by her throat and arms as she struggled to wiggle free. The cruel taunts of the males echoed down the empty alley, muffling her cries as the leader tore her blouse away, exposing her lace covered breasts.

The fright in her eyes glowed brighter with each passing second. The female's screams followed as the leader dragged his knife down the length of her body, slicing little marks across her ribs. The sight sent Ferrian to new heights of frenzy as she stormed down the alley. "Stop," she commended. Her voice cracked like lighting, and the three gangly heads whipped around to stare at her, wide-eyed in surprise.

"Or what?" While the male spoke, the sinister malevolence riddled his voice, lingered in the air, as he brought his knife up to the female's throat. "Come any closer, and well, you get the picture. Unless you wanna come suck my dick, bitch." He didn't wait to see if she would leave. But one thing was for damn sure, his eyes shone black as death, as did his friends. *Kill! Kill them all!*

Fury exploded within her since this woman replayed a part of Ferrian's life she had tried so hard to bury away. Spreading her arms open wide, the sensation of her body blowing apart as exquisite pain consumed her mixed with a wrath she had never sensed before. This was it, the moment she had been waiting for was coming. She was dying and God was lifting her up to Heaven.

The energy within her finally pushed outward, and she held it between her hands. If she was going skyward, she was going to make damn sure these bastards were going straight to Hell. Hauling back, she launched the glowing sphere at the male holding the knife, sending his body flying backward. He hit the brick wall hard enough to break through it.

Dropping the blonde, the two remaining males stormed toward her like twin sentinels. Hatred laced expressions spread over their faces, as they each drew knives and a pistol. Their huge frames dwarfed her, as they sauntered up to her, taunting her with plans of her demise.

"Well looky what we've got here. A Darkling who's sprouted her wings," the male on the left said. His lips twisted into a snarl as he spit at her in disgust. "Whatta say we break in those wings for ya, Darkling?" His acid tone coated each word with malice.

Staring past them, she eyed the blonde lying in a heap, eyes caught like a deer-in-the-headlight. "Get out of here now!" she called over, to no avail. Too scared to move, she remained huddled up against the wall, and shaking as fresh tears ran down her face. Ferrian knew the mien, and understood all too well the feelings coming along with it.

Squaring off her shoulders, a new sense was stirring deep inside of her. Calling to life her source of energy as she touched back down to Earth. Glancing over her shoulder, she saw a set of large black wings had sprouted from her back. The weight of them was more than physical as she considered her next move. Training her sights back on the two males, she realized it didn't matter if she was going to Heaven or Hell. There was no way she was willing to risk the female's life by walking away. The female was an innocent, and she refused to leave the girl behind to face a life she herself had already lived.

Power pulsed throughout her body like electricity building up, as another orb pushed outward from her body upon a simple mental command. Harnessing the vibrational vitality, she rolled it between her palms, grinning at her newest playmates. It was time to put an end to their madness.

CHAPTER FIFTY-SIX

Closing his eyes, he let Ferrian guide him by sensing her, pulling him closer as he flew over buildings. His heart thundered in his chest as a cold sweat broke over his skin. *Where the hell is she?* Something was happening, and he had no idea what kind of condition he'd find her in. Racing thoughts only ramped up his worst fears as he pictured her writhing in excruciating pain, tears staining her face as she called out for him.

His body gave in to the magnetic pull to her the closer he got. Landing on the street between two vacant mill buildings, his eyes grew wide as fear rippled through his body. "Ferrian, nooooo," he screamed, as his feet smacked against the concrete and he barreled down the dim alleyway. She wasn't in pain, but his second worst fear was playing out in live action as he lunged for her. Her black shimmering wings expanded fully behind her, as she cupped a glowing orb of energy. "Stop!" But she didn't listen.

He jerked back, horrorstruck as the two males stalked her like predators after their prey. Malice seeping from their expressions, they marched on with their weapons drawn and ready for use. He reached out to pull her away before it was too late, but caught only air as she lifted skyward, her wings fluttering in the air. Ferrian hurled the ball of energy at her intended victims. The blinding cataclysmic explosion following it blew him off his feet, sending him tumbling backward. "Ferrian!" he yelled over the sound of a bomb going off. Smokey debris clouded the air as someone choking on fumes yards away caught his attention.

Rushing to his feet, he shook the bits of brick and concrete from his hair, stomping down the alley. His pulse raced faster than a hummingbird's wings. Where was she? He prayed with everything in him Ferrian hadn't killed herself in the process of destroying the two humans. Clutching his chest, despair caved it in. He had lost her. Even if she had lived, anger and hatred had won out. He wasn't going to give up on her, unless she, too, was dead. Searching through the thick layer of fog as it slowly dissipated into the sky, and with each step he took, dread crept in unleashing a round of curses. "Ferrian, where are you?" Nothing. This was not happening. Anger in turn pricked him, stinging his red-rimmed eyes.

A long moment passed until he stumbled upon the listless body of a small blonde. Clothes torn, covered in soot and blood, he leaned down to examine her, feeling for a pulse. Thready, but she'd live. "What were you doing here?" he murmured. Folding the torn sides of her blouse back over, as she slowly stirred, fluttering her eyes open at the sound of his voice. "Easy now. You hit your head pretty hard."

She pushed off the damp pavement, lifting herself to sit up against the wall. "Oh dear God, no!" She trembled, curling into herself as fresh tears trailed down her swollen cheek. "Please don't hurt me."

Taken back, he gawked at her, wondering what Ferrian would have been doing down here with a girl who was suffering from—what he could only speculate from the evidence—being accosted. "No, quiet now, child. I'm not going to hurt you. But I need to know, what happened here? Are you okay?" Smoothing his hand over hers to calm her, he saw it there, in her hazel eyes. Fear. He had seen it on Ferrian's face too many times. Flashes of the past came back to him with vengeance, as he sank back on his haunches. *Oh shit.*

"Sh-she saved me. I swear she's an angel or something. Not like a typical halo and bright white wings, but she saved me. She stopped those men from hurting me." Thrusting her palms up to cover her eyes, sobs rolled through her body. He let her explanation spin around in his head. Placing his hand on her forehead, he willed her mind to forget everything she had seen and been through. Coaxing the young woman to slip into sleep, he'd see to it she was brought home safely before too long. Whipping out his cell, he shot a quick text to Cassiel, asking him to join him on the double. "Rest, young one. You're suffering is gone, find peace in your dreams."

Scanning the length of the alley, the smoke and rumble dissipated enough for him to see Ferrian was nowhere to be found. "Shit." Where had she gone? Had she blown herself up when she hurled the energy ball at the two males? The thought sent a shiver of dread traveling down his body until it reached his heart. The pull was so much stronger than he thought possible. Whipping his head around, he searched skyward for her, his Dark Angel. Relief splashed over him, realizing she killed the males, not to save herself, but to save an innocent. He only hoped the Council of the Seven would agree to the notion as well.

"Hey, man, what's going on? Why the 9-1-1?" Catching sight of the little blonde lying unconscious and covered in blood, Cassiel blew out a ripe curse. "What happened to her? Hellistics or human scum?"

"Ferrian happened." Pinning his brethren with a hard glare, he could read what Cassiel was refusing to say as clearly as the daily paper.

"She turned into a Daemon, didn't she? Damn, man, I'm sorry." Cassiel clapped him on the shoulder, he brushed off his attempt to soothe him.

"No, she saved the innocent and blew two males into oblivion." He could see Cass trying to process everything, but he was playing catch up himself. Glancing skyward again, there was no telling where she was.

"So let me get this straight … she blew up two human males in order to save this one female innocent. What the hell could have set her off this badly? And, how in the hell did she blow them up in the first place? I mean, look around you. If what you say is true, then where is she? Better yet, why aren't there any signs of body parts anywhere? Are you so sure she didn't toss a grenade or something and book it?"

"Cass, do you see the female lying here? Do you want to know what could set Ferrian off? How about watching another female get tortured, on the way to being raped, and most likely murdered?" Rising to his feet, he didn't like the insinuating glare Cassiel was giving him. "Think about everything she's survived."

"Yes, but it doesn't explain about the explosion part,

Remiel." Folding his arms over his chest, Cassiel leveled Remi with his disbelief.

"Yeah, I was meaning to talk to you about this *gift,* or rather ability she has." He waited to see if Cassiel was going to stick around long enough for an explanation or take off and convince the Council to lock him up in the cillés. "I know how this is going to sound, but trust me, I'm not the only one who can vouch for it."

"Go on."

"She can produce raw energy from her body, and manipulate it into a sphere of sorts. Hell, she can do some serious damage when she launches it at something."

Cocking his golden brow suspiciously toward the char marks left behind, Cassiel nodded for more of an explanation. "Clearly. Aside from black marks on the side of the buildings, there's nothing left of the humans she incinerated. Why the hell didn't you come to me sooner about this? I mean, how long have you known about this?"

"A while. It doesn't matter. But I have yet to see her blow herself up. I know Ferrian, and she wouldn't randomly kill people for shits and giggles. The female told me what happened and I believe her."

"Then where is she? Regardless of the reasons why she did it, your charge still killed two humans. You know there will be ramifications for this."

Throwing his head back in frustration, he silently screamed that the last thing he needed was yet another rant about rules and ramifications should things go wrong. Clearly things went wrong, but he didn't give a shit at the moment. All he wanted to know was where Ferrian was. "I didn't ask you to come down here to lecture me." The longer they stood there, the more he regretted his decision calling Cassiel in the first place. Bels wouldn't have busted his nuts this badly.

"Then why did you text me?"

"I need you to return the female to her home. I erased her memory. Please, do me this one favor and see to it she gets home safe and sound. I'll find Ferrian, don't worry about the rest."

The sardonic glare Cass shot to him riddled Remi with an edge of frustration as he waved down to the blonde lying deathly still. "So, are you going help me, or not?"

"Fine, but I'm still on the fence regarding your charge. When I return, I expect a full sit down and I want to talk to her myself and find out exactly what went down. JesusHchrist! The Council is going to have a field day with this one!" Shaking his head, Cassiel bent down to pick up the female. Cradling her in his arms, Remi handed him her purse, rifling through it for an address.

"She lives down off of Heritage and Wall St." Slipping the bag over Cassiel's shoulder, he quirked a smile, half amused by the sight of his six foot six, golden God look-alike brethren sporting a bright pink Coach bag.

"What are you smiling at? And don't say the purse."

Lifting his hands in surrender, he stepped out of punching range before he answered with a wiseass remark. "I don't think pink is your color. Maybe a vibrant orange or something."

"Hey, man, screw you. I'm a blond. I can wear any damn color I want." It was good to see a smile spread over his face. Small and lacking in sincerity, but it was something to break the tension rising between them. "Now go find your charge, before it's too late."

Nodding, he slowly realized there was a chance it was

already too late. Cassiel lifted skyward, carrying the small woman back to her apartment, leaving Remi to refocus his efforts of finding out where Ferrian had disappeared to.

Walking the length of the alley, he followed the charred trail leading to the end. What he expected to see was maybe a hole from one of her energy balls hitting the wall instead of the males. What he didn't expect to find was the broken body of a Daemon split in half at the waist. "Oh for all that's holy in Hell!" It was a trap, this wasn't her normal bus stop, and she had been in debilitating pain. Why would she get off the bus at the wrong stop? It didn't make sense. Ferrian was nothing if she wasn't a creature of habit.

Seeing the Daemon, as its inky blood wept down the cracks, it all made sense to him now. It didn't surprise him; the two males Remi saw Ferrian hit with the energy ball had disintegrated into thin air. His heart tripled in time as he launched skyward. This had all been too coincidental. She happened to get off on the wrong stop, only to walk right into a potential murder by three Daemons? No way. It was a pretty crystal clear sign someone was after her. Someone, who obviously knew too much. Someone, who had been watching her far too closely.

Ice shot down his veins and panic consumed his rational thoughts. "Xaphan." Whipping out his cell, he punched in Ezekiel's digits. "Hey, we've got a problem. I think I know where Xaphan is going to be and time is against us. Round up the crew, I'll text you as soon as I find Ferrian."

"What do you mean, *find Ferrian*? Aren't you supposed to be on guard dog duty with her?"

"Yeah, I am. Hence my urgent need to find her. Now

get locked and loaded and get your ass down here." Clicking off, Remi shoved the small device into his pocket. He closed his eyes, allowing her magnetic pull to guide him to her. Succumbing to the feel of his body being lulled, he opened his eyes in time to see her standing at the spot he had last left her side. Her raven hair whipped around in the crisp night air. Lifting enough for him to see a trail of tears streaking down her softly glowing cheeks.

"Ferrian," he called out to her. Landing without a sound, he rushed to her, crushing her body to his. "Oh my God, are you okay? Are you hurt?" His hands couldn't touch enough of her, even as he feathered over the curves of her newly formed black wings. His eyes scoured her body, searching for signs of trauma, until she stilled him.

Cupping his face between her warm palms, she subtly pulled back, considering him with a wary eye. "Is it really you? Am I dreaming?" Her voice was low and trembling as she gazed up at him.

His hands reached out, smoothing her hair down and cupping the back of her skull. "I'm so sorry for everything. I-I—"

When she pressed her fingers over his lips, he sensed her pulse beating rapidly. "It's okay. I understand. I'm going to wake up soon, and you'll be gone once again. Can you stay here with me until then?"

His heart cracked a little more. She had no idea he was there with her. Had so much happened to her too fast? Had she lost all sense of reality?

"No, m'aingeal, this isn't a dream. I got your text."

Her breath caught and her brows furrowed deeply as she pulled back more. "What do you mean, you got my text? If this isn't a dream, then why the hell did you stay away for so long? Why didn't you text me back and let me know you were at least, oh I don't know, alive? Jesus, Remi! I've been going out of my mind for months and you think you can walk right back into my life like nothing ever happened?"

Tears pricked at her eyes, as he tried to pull her closer. "Please, Ferrian, it wasn't by my choice. And I didn't exactly leave you alone. I was never far from you." Pulling her fingers to his lips, he gently kissed each knuckle.

CHAPTER FIFTY-SEVEN

S he considered Remi warily as his lips brushed over her knuckles. She wanted to believe him. Thinking over the time he had stayed away, she could've sworn she had sensed he was near her a thousand different times. Sometimes when the pain of his absence over-whelmed her, bringing her to tears once again, she found herself often hoping somehow he knew what he did to her. How he had come to mean so much to her, so quickly. As she curled into herself and tried to drift off to sleep on her nights off, his dark scent swam around her head, making the aching in her heart swell until she was sure it'd finally give out and shatter from the emptiness filling her.

So much had happened, so much she still didn't un-derstand, and here he stood, showing up and expecting her to run into his waiting arms. Tugging her hand free of his, she turned from him, moving farther down the pier. Her heart was heavy and her head was throbbing, thinking about everything happening around her in days past. "What am I?" Glancing back over her shoulder, she saw the hurt in his eyes, but it was nothing compared to the pain of watching him walk away that night. Anger pricked her as she waited for him to speak. "Dammit, answer me! What am I? Because, it's pretty obvious I'm not human!"

"I don't know yet," he confessed. His voice hung low as he dipped his head down.

Swiveling her lithe body around to face him again, irritation pricked in her gut. The familiar tremors seared through her once again. Shit. Now wasn't the time to let the energy fly. Sucking back a deep breathe, she tamped down the vibrations to a low buzz simmering beneath the surface.

"I don't understand what this means. What am I?" Her voice was laced with acid. Stepping out of his grasp, she moved away, but he tried to reach out for her. The last thing she wanted was to be comforted, let alone touched. Even by him. Throwing her hands up to stave him off, she took another step backward. "Don't."

Folding his arms over his chest, he planted his feet firmly, squaring his shoulders off as he leveled her with a stern gaze. "I need to know what happened in the alley. Why did you get off at the wrong bus stop? Why did you walk down that particular alley?"

Sucking in a deep breath, she knew the explanation wasn't going to be a simple story to tell. Turning her back to him, she leaned over the railing post, and focused on the distant lights across the bay, to keep herself from falling apart. "I-I don't know why or how. The bus broke down and something seemed off about the driver."

"What do you mean, *'off'*?"

She sensed the reservation in his voice. Brushing it off, she continued. "When I saw his eyes in the rearview, they were black as death and hollow. I was in so much pain, I-I honestly thought I was dying. I tried to get off the bus, thinking if I could get home, then no one would see my dead body lying on the ground. Then the guy jumped at me, and I don't exactly know what happened. It's like a surge of power shot through my body. And it was like I could do the Superman, leap over tall buildings in a single bound kind of shit. He came at me, so I reacted and kicked him on the nutsack, then nailed him with a right cross to the face." She heard his faint steps edging closer to her, and sensed his anger and frustration growing the further down this story road she traveled. His hand gently caressed her shoulder, momentarily jarring her. Her heart slowed as his warmth soaked into her body.

"What next?" His tender touch was a complete contradiction to the words falling from his lips.

Clasping her hands tight, she pulled up every detail she could remember. "So I got off, and the pain hit me harder than before. I couldn't focus on anything but the agony. Everything was so blurry, and I swear I thought I was going to drop right then and there. I stumbled down the sidewalk, trying to figure out if I was going in the right direction, when I heard a blood-curdling scream. I don't know what made me stop. My head was fuzzy, like I drank an entire bottle of tequila."

Taking another deep breath, Remi leaned up against the railing next to her. His hand smoothed down her arm as she focused on telling him what had happened, instead swimming of in the delicious scent of his natural dark spices.

"Something overcame me and I had to find out where the screams were coming from. Like I had no choice but to obey and follow the sound of pain." Rolling her head back on her shoulders, she let the wind carry her hair up like a tornado as she considered what to tell him and what was better left unsaid. Finally deciding it didn't matter, she continued.

"I saw those guys about to rape the woman. She was hurt and crying and it set me off. I succumbed to the rage pulsing through my body, and all I could think about was destroying each one of the guys for what they had done. When I saw into their eyes, all I could see was the evil in their souls and the malice living inside each one of them. They had no intentions of letting her live. I couldn't walk away, and leave her to die." Kicking off the railing, the feelings stirred once again as she replayed each detail with vivid clarity. "I couldn't let her suffer as I have. So I shot them with an energy ball." She braved a glance up to him, wincing as his concerned expression stared back at her.

"Then why did you disappear after? I called out for you and you were gone."

"Because, I didn't want you to see me as some freak! Killing those men ... Hell, Remi, it felt good. Better than good, it was incredible. And let's face it, all of a sudden, in my moment of fury, a set of wings popped out of my back! I mean, come on. So again," squaring her shoulders off, she tugged him to face her, needing to read the truth in his eyes, "I'm going to ask you, what am I?"

A small prickle of icy knowing skated down her spine as the wind kicked up around them. Her senses launched into full-blown search and destroy mode as she spun around to face the coming threat. Her muscles coiled tightly, ready to spring into action as soon as she laid sights on the one male she wanted dead above all others. Grinding her teeth, she snarled, "Xaphan." Remi stepped in front of her, pitching her infuriation to new levels. "Get out of my way," she demanded, trying to push past him. But he held her back.

"Awe, isn't this sweet. The Darkling has sprouted her wings. What a happy day this is." The acidic tone of Xaphan's voice rankled Ferrian. Her hands twisted into claws, ready to rip his throat out as she leveled her gaze intently on him. "So, please do tell me, which way has she turned? I'm as enthusiastic to find out as you are, I'm sure."

Heat radiated off Remi, as he tried to keep her hidden from the object of her destructive desire. "Piss off, Xaphan," he shot back. "You can't have her." She sensed Remi's protectiveness as a low guttural growl rumbled through his chest. His last words to her, before he left her standing on the pier, hit her in the softest part of her heart. 'I am yours and you are mine.' Those words seared down her spine as the vibrations grew stronger.

"Oh you misunderstand, Angel. It's not I who wants her. Although, a creature as lovely as she, wouldn't go untouched if it were up to me. Anyhow, it seems she's become quite the valuable commodity after all."

A freaking prize is what she had been reduced to? Oh hell no! That was all it took to ignite her internal energy into an inferno, ready to burn down every building within a ten-mile radius.

The vibrations continued to well up, as his bitter laugh littered the air. "So why don't you step aside, boy. There's no denying what she is capable of. We've both seen her little display tonight, down in the alleyway. Quite impressive, Darkling, if I do say so myself. So let's not fuss over whose side she belongs to. I would think it was pretty clear which side of the fence she's meant for." He glared at her with those soulless eyes, and she wanted to reach deep inside and show Xaphan the true meaning of pain. "Let me ask you, my dear, did it feel good to destroy those lowlifes? I mean all this power at your fingertips, ooh, the thought of it sends a tickle down to my balls. It feels good, doesn't it? You can admit freely, Darkling."

She focused all of her intent into the thickest sphere of burning energy she could muster. The copious desire from Xaphan to secure her to the Underworld, as their resident slave, shot her to apocalyptic hatred proportions. What she didn't expect was to see Remi lunge after the male in a vicious rage, teeth bared and roaring. His movements were so fast, she barely had blinked before he flew at Xaphan.

"Fuck you!" he snarled, barreling down Xaphan. In one fluid movement, Remi had lifted Xaphan up by the waist and landed both of them down on the ground as Remi struck him with a hard crack to the face.

An inkling of being watched was soon confirmed when two more males appeared from the darkness, hurling fireballs and lightning bolts at Remi. Rearing back, Remi's body coiled tightly, straining against the firepower he'd sustained. His body went rigid when the hits rendered him immobilized; his veins bulged and his eyes glowed red. "Ferrian," he forced out between rounds of labored breaths, "run!"

She wanted to listen to him—the old Ferrian would have—but she wasn't the same person anymore, was she? She had changed into something beyond reasoning. Powerful and fearless. Fury consumed every fiber of her being, twisting the inferno into pure hatred and wrath as she pulled the orb from her body. Her eyes fixated in on

Xaphan clumsily climbing to his feet. His eyes trained on her in return, and a twisted smile curled at his lips. "Get her, boys," he ordered the two males. The pounding of their boots smacking against damp pavement echoed over the water as she steadied herself, ready to launch a surprise of her own.

"Noooooooooo," Remi shrieked in terror.

"Isn't this sweet? The angel's still trying to protect his charge." Craning his head around toward Remi, the glower on Xaphan's face fueled the building shitstorm inside of her all the more. "She isn't yours anymore." He laughed harshly, smoothing his black cashmere sweater down as though he had risen from a chair.

Spinning the sphere in her hands, she closed her eyes and focused all of her intent on destroying him. This was war, and he'd be her first real causality. Cocking a devious smile, she quickly envisioned his head sitting atop a pike, showing his disgrace for all to see. "The hell I'm not." Hurling the sphere with all of the force she could muster, she watched as the glowing ball slammed into Xaphan's torso, cutting him in half before impaling the fireball male behind him. With a snarl, peeling her lips from her bared teeth, she succumbed to the exquisite intoxication of death. Her body sang to life as she watched gleefully while the dark light in Xaphan's eyes slowly began to fade. Black blood sputtered from his mouth as he reached down for the missing half of his lower body.

She couldn't resist; she needed to watch him die, staring back up at her and knowing she was the one who killed him. Sauntering over to what was left of him, the buzzing of energy skated over her skin and sang out loud and clear, as she relished the feel of this power. Her eyes flared with emerald flames, burning Xaphan with a single glance. "I told you, you would die by my hands and my hands alone." She let the ice in her words coat him in pure disdain as he reached out to grab her leg. Stomping as hard as she could, the sickening sound of bones cracking beneath her boot heel fed the gratification she had been starving for. "Your hands will never hurt another soul, you sick bastard."

He had been the demon that she had feared since birth. He was the reason she wore her scars like armor. And now, his death would be the reason she could finally sleep at night. Her glowing smile was reflected in Xaphan's black eyes as they glazed over. Moments passed, but she wasn't ready to walk away. This was the moment she had waited for her entire life, and now she let the satisfaction of it swaddle her like a new set of armor.

A harsh cough caught her attention, as Remi struggled to breath. "Oh shit." Rushing to his side, she didn't hear the pounding of footsteps run up to them, calling out his name. She sank to her knees and pulled Remi's upper body into her lap. "Are you okay?" The words fell from her mouth hastily as she stroked his hair back.

Nodding his head to her, she could feel his lungs forcing to work. "Shhhh, don't try to speak. Catch your breath first. I'm not going anywhere." She offered a soft smile, as her eyes caressed the hard planes of his worried face.

She couldn't stop her fingers from lingering on the supple curve of his lower lip, or retain the growing desire to strip him bare and climb on top of him until both of them were perfectly sated. "I missed you so much," she murmured, searching his eyes for something she had missed for too long. Luckily she found exactly what she was seeking, beaming from within … his love. Shining back at her as brightly as ever, guiding her to back to where she belonged.

"Are there anymore around? We caught one trying to escape." She didn't bother to glance up at the huge male, towering over them. She knew the voice behind her. It was the one member of Remi's group she would eventually have to come to terms with.

"No. Xaphan and the other dude are dead," she offered stiffly. "So where were you guys, while he had his buddies throwing lightning bolts and fireballs at Remi, huh? Aren't you guys supposed to be like some sort of team, watching out for each other?"

"We came as soon as we could. And, Ferrian," she tilted her head over her shoulder, offering half a glance of recognition, "we saw what you did for Remi. Thank you. You have our eternal gratitude." Z's voice trailed off, as he bowed his head in respect.

Stepping forward, Amitiel nodded to them in agreement. Her violet eyes scanned the area, then back down to Ferrian, but she never seemed focused on what was in front of her. Ferrian caught something, something hidden deep inside. A knowing she was quite familiar with. Deep seated anguish and guilt. Amitiel wore it like an invisible shield, but she saw right through it, to the core of Am's being. Her heart instantly hurt, recognizing Amitiel's odd behavior wasn't due to ADD, but rather a never fully healed broken heart.

"So, it seems Armageddon has officially begun," the female said flatly, looking around once again. "After the light show you put on, all I can say is I'm damn glad you're playing for our team." Clapping Ferrian on the shoulder, she sensed Remi's disapproval with anyone touching her, almost as much as she hated the idea of it.

He shifted awkwardly, pulling his body upward. Slipping under his arm, she wrapped it over her shoulders to help him up. She mused about how well she fit there, like she had belonged there since the dawn of time. His body trembled as he tried to stand straight. "Easy there, big guy. I've got you."

"I'm fine, I'll be all right now." Draping his arm tightly around her, he spun her into him, and sank down into her mouth with a new urgency. The heat blooming from his actions had her sex welling up in seconds. Refusing to fight him off, she welcomed the invasion, matching it with the same intensity as she raked her fingers through his inky hair. Feeling his body respond to her, the hard stalk between them grew stiffer the longer they stay locked in each other's kiss. He cupped the small of her back, pressing her body closer until all that separated them were the fibers of their clothing. "Easy, big guy," she murmured against his lips. "Wouldn't want to put on a show for your friends, now would we?"

The not-so-subtle chuff coming from the crowd made her break from his kiss reluctantly, leaving her to face the group with cheeks flushed a deep crimson. The night had been long, but her loneliness had lasted longer. A small prick of sadness stabbed her heart as she wondered how long she had with Remi this time, before he was forced to leave her again.

As if he picked up on her emotional gymnastics, he caressed her face. She could see him searching for answers to an unasked question. "What is it, m'aingeal? What's wrong?" Concern wept with each syllable as he gazed longingly into her eyes.

"I guess I need to know one thing first." The topic was uncomfortable at best, so she tried to put a few inches of distance between them. Trepidation laced her thoughts as she considered the fact she might not be able to handle answers she didn't want to hear. Needing to know, she sucked in another deep breath. Laying her fears on the line in front of a group of variable strangers, she focused her eyes solely on his. "How long do we have this time? How long before you leave me again?"

Pressing an urgent kiss against her forehead, his huge body trembled against hers as he embraced her.

"Maybe I can help." Cassiel stepped forward, his voice gentle as he clapped both of them on their shoulders. Man, what was it with these guys being all touchy-feeling? Didn't they understand the concept of personal space? "We all saw what you are capable of, Ferrian. And to be fair, frankly it scares the shit out of me. I don't fully understand how you are capable of doing what you do, but what you did for Remi ..." He let out a ripe curse, and the gravity of Cassiel's gratitude hit her hard. "To be honest, I feared, after seeing what you left behind in the alley, you had turned to a Daemon. But thank God you're not. I'd hate to have to face off with you when you're pissed."

She searched Remi's face for answers. Answers she had been deprived of earlier. His pinched expression as though he was silently flipping out on his friend was excruciatingly clear. "What's he talking about, Remi? What's a Daemon? Is it like a demon or something?"

"Yup, you guessed it," Roc barked out. "A Daemon is like you, only evil."

"I-I don't understand." Confusion and frustration

from all of the talking in circles pissed her off more than some dumb-ass remark. "Remi? Am I bad or something?"

"Oh, God, no. Ferrian, no you're not." His smiled beamed at her with as much pride as possible. "You're quite the opposite. You're what we call a Dark Angel. Before your transition tonight, you were considered a Darkling."

"Ah, you lost me again? To be clear, what's a Darkling?"

"It's a human born angel. Kind of like a hybrid. Half mortal, half angel," Cassiel explained, and stepped back when Remi nodded to him.

"When a Darkling transitions, they're put into a situation where they can either choose to rise above and help others or fall into permanent darkness. Your actions tonight, saving the female in the alleyway, saving me even though you were pissed off at me, sealed your fate as a Dark Angel. Don't you see? You were right all along. You are meant for something more. Dark Angels haven't walked the Earth in a thousand years and now, here you are."

There was so much to absorb, too much to comprehend in such a short time. Her chest tightened like it was going to explode from lack of oxygen as she swayed backward. Space, she needed space to process all this, and there wasn't enough space in the world at the moment. Biting her lip, she forced herself to stay right where she was and figure out what everything meant. "So what exactly is the purpose of a, what did you call it *Dark Angel*?"

He nodded solemnly to her as though she was revered as a holy being. "The purpose of Dark Angels is this, what you did tonight. Demons and Daemons walk this Earth.

You, as an Earthbound angel, are destined to protect the innocent, and in your case, help us locate other Darklings. You and you alone are the key to saving this world from Hell taking over. And, m'aingeal, one more thing," His smile grew wider still as he clasped her hands in his. His warmth radiated off him, soaking into her skin like the hot sun. "I'm not going anywhere, again."

Before another breath passed, she leapt into his arms, swathing her arms around him. Her heart swelled knowing those eyes she adored staring back at her, were hers to stare into for as long as she lived. It didn't take her half a second before she crashed her lips over his. It would eventually make sense, but now, all she wanted to understand was how long it would take to strip him down bare.

"Get a room, you two!" Roc howled out, clapping his hands.

It was then—feeling his hard body pressed against hers, and his supple lips caressing her with urgent need—the rightness of being with him like this melted away all of the fears she once had. "I was thinking the same thing as well," he murmured against her lips.

Scooping her up in to his waiting arms, he meant to launch skyward, until she pushed herself free. "Wait!"

"What? What's wrong?"

"Nothing's wrong," she giggled. "I want to stretch out my wings is all." Spreading out her wings, she finally allowed the sensation to filter through her as she glanced down to see the black feathers hinted with purples and blues shimmering in the pale moonlight. Her breath caught as she lifted her eyes to see Remi staring back at her. His smile was as wide as the ocean. She couldn't help but to laugh at the irony of it all. She was an angel after feeling like a monster her entire life.

"That's fucking awesome, she has silver tips!" Roc stalked over to check them out closer. Remi coolly swiveled her out of the way before Roc could get close enough.

"Not a chance in hell, Roc. She's mine." Glancing down at her wings, to see what Roc was talking, his eyes flared wildly at the sight. They trailed back up to meet hers as he set her down gently, and kissed her once more. "He's right. Can't say I've ever seen another Dark Angel with wings like yours. Like I said, you're one of kind, Ferrian."

"Wait, don't you have silver tips on your wings?"

"Yes. I guess you were meant for me after all." His finger traced the curve of her jaw, as she stroked his chest. His heartbeat raced beneath her palm, and she smiled impishly at him. "What do you say we get going then? I'll race you." He laughed, and the sound struck her with a renewed sense of happiness. Was it possible she had finally found her purpose and happiness in life? She wasn't completely convinced yet, but over time, she was sure Remi would do his best to make her realize it.

"Riiiiight. Good one." With a hard kick off the ground, she thrust skyward, soaring into the air as effortlessly as a bird. If she had imagined the way her life would've turned out, with her sprouting a set of wings, bounding into the air with the love of her life, she would've smacked herself back into reality. But this was her reality now. As Remi shot up to meet her, flying over the bay, the cool wind didn't have the same bite it normally would. Flying faster, she wasn't sure if she'd ever get used to the feeling of freedom she gained from her new wings. Hoping the excitement wouldn't dissolve quickly, she reached out to clasp his hand. Smiling wide like a fool when he interlaced their fingers. "This is … incredible!"

"Just wait, it gets even better with time." Her heart pounded in her chest thinking about it as she caught the subtle wink he flashed her way. "Follow the blue star, and you'll find home."

"Home? Oh crap!" She forgot about Beast. She couldn't abandon him. He had saved her in ways she couldn't fully understand. "I can't. I mean, Beast. I can't leave him behind."

His laughter cut across the air as he pulled her toward the direction of her apartment. "No worries, love. We'll grab the furface, then it's home."

A smile spread wide, and for the first time it reached her eyes. Home. A concept she never had before. Sure she had her apartment, but it was nothing more than a place to rest her head. Nothing of personal note decorated the walls. No pictures of adventures, nor magazines littering the coffee table. Home. The thought warmed her from the soul outward. Home.

CHAPTER
FIFTY-EIGHT

"**M**y liege! Sir, the Darkling ... she's transcended. She's one of them!"

Pitching forward in his throne made from the bones and skulls of the unlucky, pushing aside Lilith, Satan snarled at Lucifer's intrusion.

"And you're just now informing me of this?" His voice thundered around the Great Dark Hall, shaking the black marbled pillars down the length of football field sized room. "How long ago did she turn?" Flames flashed in his palms as he lifted one to Lucifer's line of sight. "How long?" He pressed, before hurling the ball of fire at his demon, searing the side of his face. Clasping his cheek, Lucifer shrank back. Satan wasn't one who waited for answers. Igniting another flaming ball, he watched the fear flare in his Prime General's beady blue eyes.

"It happened three weeks ago. Xaphan went to apprehend her, and bring her down here, but she killed him."

He snorted at the idea of a Dark Angel, a newling at that, killing a seasoned demon. In turn, it made his fury twist into a homicidal rage. "How does a Dark Angel best a demon? Please tell me before I toss your ass to the

Hellistics in the abyss. You're supposed to have this shit under control. Apparently I appointed the wrong asshole for the job."

"Sir, please forgive me. I put my trust in the wrong person, and it backfired. But I swear to you, I won't let you down again. I will kill the Darkling myself."

"You can't, you imbecile. She's untouchable now. But what you can do is track down the next Darkling and destroy it before those assholes upstairs gain another ally." Throwing the flaming ball at his Prime General, Lucifer swiftly dodged it, but not without feeling the effects of its slicing, searing sting across his shoulder.

"Sir, there's one more thing."

"What now!"

"There was another mortal held in the cells, where Xaphan had the Darkling hidden."

"And?"

"Vepar said the male was taken out of there. Maybe they have someone watching over him."

"You fool! Of course they do. Did you not listen to the prophecy the day I explained it? Unfuckingbelievable! I should rip off your balls and feed them to the barghest for your stupidity alone!"

"My liege, I'm sorry. I'll track down the mortal."

"You better. Find out who's guarding him and report back to me immediately. Or I will make good on my word. Go now, before I change my mind. Kill the Darkling, dammit. Find it and kill it now!"

Lucifer bowed hesitantly, lowering his eyes from Satan before spinning around to leave. The soles of his heels clanked frantically, echoing off the walls as he raced from the room. Satan sank back against his throne, realizing that the odds weren't in his favor.

Lilith leaned over his shoulder, tracing the black veined muscles. "Do you think he'll succeed, my liege?"

"If he has half a brain, maybe. I'm done with this truce bullshit. If God is going to let his little bitches step in, and guard the Darklings twenty-four-seven, then why shouldn't I do the same?" Tapping his clawed hands along the bone-covered arms of his throne, Satan considered what was to come. He needed to get his hands on the next one, and turn them quickly.

"You should do whatever you think is best."

"You're right." Glaring at his servant demon Calim, he pointed to the scrawny male, making the male tremble as he stepped forward.

"Yes, my lord."

"Call forth Mammon and Lassal. It's time to up the ante."

"Yes, my lord." The eyeless male slinked away as the crunching sound of his bones echoed of the marble and bone inlaid walls.

"Get your ass back up, Lilith. I'm not done with you, and summon Mersalis." Jerking her into his lap, her simpering smile curled up, as she licked the edge of her lips.

"Yes, my love. Whatever you desire.

CHAPTER
FIFTY-NINE

S lowly lowering the hood of her robe, her wet hair clung to the delicate flush of her skin. "Remi." She purred his name, the sound of it rolling off her tongue in erotic waves. Whipping his head up to meet her as she walked out of the bathroom, he thought Ferrian resembled every bit the angel she was. The steam escaping out of the door around her in billowy clouds, reminded him of an aura surrounding her, coming out of a fog laden dense forest.

Her eyes lit up like emerald flames burning hot for him with each sinuous step she took, closing the distance between them. In the weeks since she had transcended, each waking moment they spent together, he watched her open up like a delicate flower, blooming into her new life with ease. She was beautiful to the eye, with her soft milky white skin and long raven hair. And oh so deadly to the wrong people who dared to cross her. He reveled in her rich mixture of innocence and sinful decadence. It didn't matter whether it was the way she worked her body on him or her powerful ability to destroy anything in her path. She was everything he ever wanted. Ferrian was the perfect balance of beauty and deadly-intent, stirring his desires and searing through his blood.

Gulping past the lump lodged in his throat, he didn't need to peek down to see his sex had swollen in the seconds his eyes locked on to hers, staring at him from under a dark fringe of thick lashes. The scent of her arousal inflamed the liquid fire pulsing through his veins as he commanded himself to stay in his chair at his desk. Yet he couldn't turn away from her. She had once again stunned him stupid, rendering him utterly useless when it came to forming a coherent sentence.

"Remi," she purred again, ratcheting up his primal urge to strip her bare and spread her wide on his desk as he sated his lust. Sinking back into his seat, he drank in the sight of her, as the slash of creamy skin exposed from her robe splitting apart made his body jerk to move. Gripping the desk top to hold himself back was more than a feat in itself. His efforts were nothing short of Herculean, retaining himself there, the closer she came. The thundering of his heart beating to break free of its cage nearly deafened the sound of her sultry laugh.

"Resplendent," he mused as she sidled around the corner of the desk.

Stopping an arm's length away, she stood there for a moment as though she knew what she was doing to him. She was so vulnerable, and yet so sensual as she swung the robe's belt around in her hand. The flimsy satin cloth covering her body did nothing to hide her luscious curves, hidden for far too long. "Do you like it?" Oh how he loved this new uninhibited side to her, taunting him as she smoothed her hand down to her breast, down farther still until her hand came to rest on the delicious curve of her hip. "Bels picked it out for me."

His jaw dropped watching her sinful show as she leaned over enough to reveal two perfect mounds of supple flesh. Before he could muster up his voice, Ferrian slid across the desktop, pushing loose papers out of her way. Closing the distance between them, her fingers reached out for him, caressing the hard line of his jaw and slowly weaving her fingers through the tangles of his inky hair. The lower she leaned, the more the natural drape of her robe splayed open for his viewing pleasure. "You're so beautiful, m'aingeal," he said breathlessly. He had no idea what it was like to be drunk, but imagined it was something similar to the intoxication her presence brought on. Like an addict needing a fix, she was his drug of choice. One he would gladly drown in.

"You never did tell me what m'aingeal means?" Slipping him a sly smirk, she lifted a dark slash of brow at him. It hadn't dawned on him to tell her.

Pulling her legs to his chest and splitting them wide enough for his body to fit between them, he leaned down to kiss the soft skin, poorly hidden behind the ivory satin cloth. "It means," pecking another kiss along her ribs, he sensed her desires growing hotter, stronger with each touch of his lips to her flesh, "my angel, in Gaelic." He could feel her smiling without even beholding her glorious face. "My angel," he whispered it again against her skin as goose bumps abraded her flesh. "Aingeal is also your birth name."

"How do you know?"

"I was with you the day your mother died. She loved you so much."

"She died because of me, Remi."

"No," he lifted his eyes, and worried the past would strip away the building desires between them, "you're wrong. She lived because of you. She willingly sacrificed herself to protect you, because of love. She loved you, as much as I do, m'aingeal." Remi tenderly kissed the tops of her knees as he smoothed his hands down her thighs.

Her hands reached down to cradle his face, lifting his gaze to meet hers. A small tear wept from her eye as she brushed her lips over his forehead. "You brought me back to life and you made me feel what love is. How is it even possible you could be this wonderful?"

Sliding his arms around her waist, he pulled her slender body closer. "You deserve to be loved, and I'm the lucky male you chose to fall in love with. I didn't bring you back to life, Ferrian. You did. When you opened your heart to me, you opened a doorway to a fresh start. Don't ever forget that, m'aingeal, my love. I am yours, and always will be, as you are mine, I hope eternally."

Her trembling lips caressed his, as he waited for her to open up to him once again. Savoring the feel, and the taste of her wet tongue against his lips, Ferrian slowly licked the seam of his mouth, before finally slicing her way in.

"Ferrian." His whispering breath skated over her lips, and she leaned in farther. He couldn't breathe, could barely think as her lips melded to his. Her kiss, which began out soft as a feather, quickly built with heat and urgency, igniting the fire burning deep within his soul.

Guiding her down to the desk, his massive body covered hers as her thighs enfolded his waist. He knew trying to resist her was a battle he'd never win. Grazing his hand down the length of her body, she trembled from his touch, as her eyes stared back up at him, shining as brightly as the full moonlight. "How have I lived this long without you?"

Her hand smoothed down the hard planes of his chest, stopping at his heart, as she held her palm there long enough to feel the beating beneath it. Reaching for his hand, she placed it over her heart, holding it in place. With their hearts beating as one, they stayed entranced in each other's gazes. All life disappeared around them as they sank into a universe of their own creation. "I am yours always, as you are mine, eternally," she murmured softly against his lips. "I love you, Remiel, always and forever."

Crashing his lips down on to hers, he was ready to start the forever part right now. "Forever."

ACKNOWLEDGMENTS

First, I'd like to thank all my wonderful readers. Without you, all my crazy stories would still be pent up in my head, begging to be freed. Thank you for your continued love!

I'd like to thank my editor Melissa Ringstead for all your hard work. I do humbly apologize for being a huge pain in the ass! Thank you for working with me. Julie Titus, my fabulous formatter. My Betas, you guys are awesome.

Also, my phenomenal Cover artist, Stephanie White of Stephsbookcovers.com Brilliantly beautiful work, my dear. I can't thank you enough for producing such a stunning cover for this book. I am forever your fan-girl!

Thank you everyone who book this book and is ravenous for more in the upcoming sequel!

Facebook
www.facebook.com/Ava.Vixion.com

Twitter
www.twitter.com/@AvaVixion

Instragram
Ava Vixion

Pinterest
@AvaVixion

For more information on books, bio, excepts, check out
WWW.AVAVIXION.COM

www.ingramcontent.com/pod-product-compliance
Lightning Source LLC
Chambersburg PA
CBHW020500020726
47493CB00001B/113